FREEDOM

KATIE CROSS

To Kelsey Rae.
The untwin who sets me free.

PROLOGUE

Sanna Spence drew in a deep breath, feeling as if she were stirring a grave.

The ancient houses that stood in front of her paled in comparison to the soaring backdrop of Letum Wood. Mammoth trees grew out of sight, blocking canopy and sky, allowing only a muted sunlight to creep as far down as the forest floor. Directly behind Sanna stood a tree so large the roots towered over her head. Five houses stacked next to each other could easily fit across its girth. Eleven other such trees formed a circle around her.

"This is it," she murmured.

"Whoa," Jesse said, sliding all the way down his dragon's front leg. Elis snorted and stretched his wings. "This place is real."

"Real," Sanna said with a sigh. "And very, very old."

One hundred and fifty years separated them from this old Dragonmaster village, deserted after poachers from the Southern Network massacred the dragons and Dragonmasters almost to extinction.

The semicircle of dilapidated houses lay quiet, as if

sleeping. As if no one had abandoned them over a century before. Sanna stared with a sense of disbelief. After three months of slowly picking their way through the forest, teaching their dragons to fly, and mending wounds sustained in the battle against the mountain dragons, their rag-tag group of Dragonmasters had finally arrived.

This part of Letum Wood felt like sweet balm—she'd been here before, but no one else in the group had. The familiar, sprawling trees settled an agitation in her chest, as if something here recognized her. A bird twittered by, rustling a bush as it landed.

Jesse stepped closer to the houses. Behind them, the distant sounds of the other traveling Dragonmasters whistled through the trees. Only a few more minutes before all of them would spill in.

Sanna soaked up the quiet majesty while she could. It might not be this quiet ever again.

Everything seemed as safe as she'd imagined. The lowest branches on the soaring Ancients were so high up they were almost indistinguishable from each other, which ruled out a drop attack from a forest lion. Even the nasty, tree-infesting beluas could get lost in the grooves of the trunks here. Most beluas nested in the folds and crevices of the bark, but not here, in the circle.

No animals lived here.

"The houses don't look that different from Anguis," Jesse said, pointing to the half-dead structures. "They're the same, aren't they?"

"Talis couldn't erase everything," Sanna said. "The survivors of the massacre would have started Anguis shortly after they left here. This sort of building was all they knew."

She strode toward the closest house and stepped inside. Dust motes drifted from the half-open ceiling, which they'd have to repair. This house had been a lifesaver when she'd first come here with her dragon, Luteis, and had great need for a dry place. But they'd have to fix it up if they were to live here through the winter.

Dark stains of pooled blood on the floor briefly caught her attention as she exited the house again, moving onto the porch. Her shoulder brushed the doorframe, and she grunted.

"You all right?" Jesse asked.

"Fine," she mumbled, rubbing the sore spot.

She kept going—more carefully this time—thinking of Daid and the old dragon sire, Rubeis. She'd never seen either of them here, but she couldn't get them out of her head. Daid, killed by a mountain-dragon spy months ago, would never see this place.

Something cracked beneath her foot. She bit back a curse and withdrew with a wince. Jesse leaned down, then straightened back up.

"Old acorn. Are you sure you're—"

"I'm fine," she ground out. Her nostrils flared. The shooting pain up her leg began to fade.

Is it worsening? her dragon asked. Luteis peered at her from just outside, seething hot like a ball of fire. Burnt orange weaved through his all-black scales, as if a glittering jar of paint had been overturned on his back and dripped down his shoulders until he glimmered like a coal.

Shall I escort you elsewhere? Concern laced his tone. She swallowed hard, ignoring the silent question in his words, grateful that Jesse couldn't hear it.

No, thank you.

"Let's go in here," she said, gesturing to the next house. "This is the biggest one. I think it should go to your family."

Jesse opened his mouth to say something, then paused.

No doubt he was thinking of his mother. Babs had died in the battle three months before. The lack of life in his father's eyes was reflected in the despair of all the Dragonmasters— which was only part of the reason it had taken so long to find the Ancients.

"Yes," he finally said. "That would be appreciated."

He stepped inside after her. The room sprawled open, a gaping hole in the thatched roof allowing rays of blunted sunshine to stream in. Jumbled wood covered the floor. A dragon must have fallen on the structure to cause such enormous damage.

"They just . . . died here, I guess," Jesse murmured.

Sanna's nose wrinkled as she gazed around. Had time paused here?

"Left. With Talis," she murmured. "Those that could, I imagine. The rest would have died, yes."

Jesse ran his fingers along a table. "Do you think we'll ever know what really happened?"

"Perhaps."

Sanna dropped her bags onto the floor, then knelt down to pull them open. They had a few leafy greens and some bulbous mushrooms left over, but hardly enough to satisfy her ravenous stomach. The leto-nut crop had been poor this summer.

As if he'd read her mind, Luteis said, *I will hunt and scout out the area and return before evening. My old home is not far from here. I should like to visit it again.*

Sanna glanced outside. She'd forgotten that Luteis used to live close to here, alone. The ruins had been the first place he'd brought her after saving her from Talis's wrath, back when the old dragon sire still lived.

Thank you, she said.

Jesse began to walk through the house, looking at old objects, sorting through pinecones and damaged pieces of wood. Sanna made her way to the next house, a smaller one. Likely an old woman had lived here, if the dusty, heavy quilts and threadbare slippers meant anything. Had the forest goddess Deasylva kept all of this from moldering away? Some kind of magic, perhaps? The ghosts of those who had passed?

She scanned each room slowly and carefully. It would be perfect for her and Mam. And Isa.

Though Isa had her own life.

Her own new family.

Sanna swallowed, turning away. The approaching sounds of Elliot, Mam, and the others grew louder.

She stepped back out of the house, sobered by the weight of memories that lingered around her, just as several dragons lumbered into the circle. Here amongst the Ancients, with no bracken clogging the floor, the dragons seemed smaller than ever.

Do you enjoy having more undergrowth to hide in? Sanna asked Elis, whose eyes darted this way and that. Elis looked up, finding her immediately.

It feels safer than this, he said. *This is open. It feels . . . different. Not unsafe, just . . . different.*

Perhaps we can maintain some ground cover for the dragons to hide in but still keep the forest healthy.

There is balance in all things.

At one point, the dragons must have had some sort of system for living here. As servants of Deasylva, the dragons had historically helped the forest goddess care for the forest. They must have known how much bracken to keep and how much to get rid of. Now, they'd have to figure everything out all over again.

Despite having reached the Ancients, the overwhelming feeling of being lost sank deep in Sanna's chest.

"Sanna?"

Sanna blinked, looking up. She turned all the way to the left before she saw Mam standing only a few paces in front of her. Elliot and his remaining children limped into the clearing. Behind them stood Trey, Greata, and Hans, Finn's only surviving children. Elliot appeared gaunt, with deep lines on his face and a haunted expression.

"This is it?" he asked, his voice raspy.

They were all grieving, and had been for the last three months. But now they could start over. Release all they'd lost—which was everything—and find new freedom. No more Talis. No more threats from mountain dragons or dissenting witches. Sanna could truly serve them here. Help them recreate stability, grow new roots.

Now they had to survive, for if what the trees whispered to her was true, worse was coming.

"Welcome," Sanna said, arms spread, "to our new home."

1

THREE MONTHS LATER

The ruins of Berry lay in charred waste, silhouetted against Letum Wood.

Although over a year had passed since the Western Network's attack on the sleepy town, the wound felt fresh. Only a few witches had attempted to rebuild their pillaged homes. Most of the lots remained empty, littered by the fallen boards of what had been.

In some cases, nothing remained.

The village slept underneath a constant gray cloud that beckoned winter with foggy fingers, wrapping the barren landscape and choking the life out of it.

A cold wind whipped by, whisking Isadora Spence's thoughts with it. She shivered, tightened her cloak, and slipped back inside a broad tent.

Dirty canvas structures formed a city in the main meadow. Charles, High Priest of the Central Network, had set up a refugee camp here only a few months before. Those not brave enough to take their chances living in Letum Wood came here.

Battle-injured witches streamed in from attacks on the

borders, or worse. Most of those who came for healing died. The ones who stayed here to live were mere shells. Lost in their memories, fear, pain.

Eight larger apothecary tents, with witches bustling frantically in and out, formed a protective circle around the makeshift city.

Isadora headed for the apothecary tents again, intent on finding her friend, Lucey. Defender attacks against normal Watchers had all but stopped since Cecelia's death months ago in the East, leaving Lucey with nothing to do for the Advocacy. She volunteered most of her time here, helping however she could. Isadora often joined her, desperate to help in the war effort.

An upswing in inter-Network confrontations, with escalating violence along the border now that the East had completely isolated themselves, meant that Advocacy volunteers couldn't do much, anyway. They were either dying or too busy trying to stay alive.

The sharp smell of a cleaning potion assaulted Isadora's nose when she pushed aside the flap of the surgical tent. Light leaked through the thin canvas, which spanned as wide as a house and tapered at the ends. Witches lay on the dirt floor, moaning. Blood stained their shirts. These were the wounded who had been able to transport to relative safety. The most severe cases were tended on the battlefield.

Isadora, used to the coppery smell of blood after her eight-hour shift, gently stepped inside.

"Is Lucey here?" she asked a passing apothecary.

He shook his head and strode away without a word. Isadora frowned, then moved to the next tent. Not there, either. Two tents later, she'd still only found the stench of death, blood, and putrefaction.

"Where are you?" she murmured.

"I shouldn't be surprised ta see ya here. Although, maybe with some blood on ya. Formidable, eh?"

A familiar voice caused Isadora to whirl around, her heart leaping into her throat. Behind her stood a familiar witch with shocking red hair and lips like a butterfly. Her heart-shaped face and suspicious eyes betrayed her almost as quickly as her hair.

"Baylee?"

Baylee smirked. "It's only been a year," she said. "Not like I'd change that much. What are ya doing here?"

Isadora closed the space between them, clasping Baylee to her chest. Baylee stiffened until Isadora pulled away and inspected her at arm's length.

Something loosened in Isadora's heart. She hadn't seen Baylee since the attack on Berry. The school they'd both attended had all but disintegrated afterward.

"Baylee! Tell me you aren't here because you're hurt."

"Nah." Baylee waved a hand, stumbling back. "I'm fine. Just takin' care of some business."

She held a scroll in her other hand, her fingers curled protectively around it without crushing the fragile paper. Her hair, wild around her shoulders, nonetheless looked full and healthy. The rest of her—pinched, too thin, and clad in threadbare clothes—appeared unchanged.

"Business? What kind of—"

"Did ya go back to the forest after the fire?" Baylee asked. "Or have ya been here the whole time?"

"Both."

"Ya don't seem so good yaself. What happened?"

"My father. He was . . . murdered in Letum Wood."

"Demmet," Baylee said without wavering, something like experience in her gaze. "That's nasty. Ya angry yet?"

Angry that a dragon had murdered her daid and

plunged her already-weary family into an even deeper chasm? Angry that his death had carved a gulf between her and her sister? Angry that nothing ever seemed to go right?

"Filled with it."

Baylee stared at her, seeming troubled. "I was . . . I was worried about ya."

A hint of a smile softened Isadora's expression. "I've thought of you often too. While I was in Chatham City, I looked for you a few times."

Baylee's teeth flashed a light yellow when she smiled. "I'm impossible ta find, and for good reason. Chatham is where I belong. Lots of work there ta keep an orphan busy and food in her stomach."

"The other girls?"

Miss Sophia's School for Girls, where she'd first met Baylee, had been home to a motley group of girls sent away by parents only too willing to be rid of one more mouth to feed. The laughably pathetic school system in the Network had dwindled even further after the wars cut most funding.

Now, education was all but extinct.

"Don't know about most," Baylee said, a pained expression crossing her face. "Some of them went home or ran away somewhere else. A few found benefactors."

Isadora's brow furrowed. *Benefactors.* Witches in higher society would occasionally take on a younger girl to satisfy their baser interests. A different kind of whorehouse, almost impossible to track down.

But a valid option for a girl on the street only a breath away from starvation. Baylee had said it with the ease of someone who had lived on the streets her whole life, as if the inevitable end surprised only Isadora.

"You?" Isadora whispered. "Did you have to find a benefactor?"

Baylee recoiled. "No, ya daft idiot! Think I'd lay with a man for any amount of currency? Lots of work in the alleys for that, if ya can handle it. No, I found me a boss." Her fingers tightened ever so slightly around the scroll. "Good one. He's sworn me ta secrecy, or I'd tell ya more. I'm here doing his business. I can't stay long, but saw ya and wanted ta say hi."

A thousand questions rushed to the tip of Isadora's tongue, but she quelled them all. Baylee's shadier dealings came as no surprise. She'd been a scrapper her whole life.

"It's good to see you," Isadora said with a rush of conviction. "Really."

Baylee grinned. "Same. But what are ya doing in a hellhole like this?"

"Looking for a friend," Isadora replied, remembering Lucey again. "I come and volunteer with her when I can. She's an apothecary here."

Baylee's gaze snagged on something behind Isadora. Her face scrunched into a scowl.

"Oh no," she muttered. "Not him. I'm out of here."

Without another word, Baylee disappeared. An unexpected, imperious male voice sent Isadora's spine rigid.

"I half-expected you to be hiding with your sister in your beloved forest."

Maximillion.

She tried to breathe through a bolt of revulsion, hidden beneath a sudden thrill, that consumed her. She didn't turn around. Why gratify him? He was standing right behind her —she could feel it.

"I manage to tear myself away," she muttered.

Unable to bear it another second, she whirled around, stopping a hair's breadth from a very familiar chest. The smell of vetiver nearly overwhelmed her as she stepped back and stared into a pair of frosty eyes. Her heart skipped a beat, then resumed, racing.

Maximillion glared with all the power of a thousand suns, looking haughty, irritated, and magnificently attractive.

He lifted an eyebrow.

"Max." She forced the words through her rage-thickened throat. "Always a pleasure to see you."

His nostrils flared. "Maximillion," he snapped. "I've come to have a word with you, if you have a minute to spare."

A flurry of emotions rushed over her all at once, but she shoved them aside. For months she'd daydreamed—no, plotted—what she would say when she saw him again. The blistering words of hate and regret that would finally spill out of her, letting him know *exactly* what effect his cold indifference had on the world.

Not that he would care.

She set her jaw, tilting her head back to meet his gaze. In the folds of ice, she thought she saw a flicker of something. It disappeared, easing back into his glacial depths.

They hadn't spoken a word since she found out the truth about Daid's death over six months ago. Aside from a few messages with assignments from the Advocacy that she'd ignored, he hadn't even sought her out. Perhaps he'd forgotten the heat behind their unexpected kiss. She certainly had.

Or, at least, she'd tried to.

"I don't want to speak with you," she said.

"The feeling is mutual; I assure you. I come on business that is not my own."

Suddenly, Isadora's strength flagged. Hating him required too much effort.

The day had been a long one, passing slowly as she worked amongst the wounded streaming in from a battle near the Western border. All the more slowly because she feared each young male would be him, caught in the madness as he went to check on the Guardians there.

Her jolting stomach filled her with something hot and cold at the same time. "What do you want?"

His gaze met hers, pinning her. Under the power of his colossal indifference, she'd always felt pegged. Strangely seen and understood and naked and thrilled at the same time. There was no challenge in this world quite like him. She stopped breathing, arrested in silence. Just when she thought he wouldn't answer, he broke the spell.

"I have an update from La Torra."

"Oh?"

Six months ago, she'd battled the Eastern Network Ambassador, Cecelia Bianchi, on top of Carcere. Cecelia had been the first witch Isadora had pulled into the paths, something she hadn't known was possible. Afterward, the power had doubled.

Then tripled.

She thought of Fiona and Lorenzo and the rest of the band of misfits that had somehow formed a strange friendship on that island in the East. After the months she'd spent there, she found herself missing the sandy beach. The vast sky. The briny smell of the ocean breeze. She rubbed her arms. The warmth. Although it was only the end of summer, the first chill had already intruded on Berry.

Maximillion's gaze narrowed on something in the distance. "Carcere has been officially closed by Dante as of yesterday. The workers were forced to evacuate, and the castle was closed up. Even the Guardians have been removed for now."

"Oh."

"It's not likely to be real," he muttered. "Nothing with Dante ever is. The man is all smoke and mirrors. No doubt he's scheming something."

"What does that have to do with me?"

"I thought you cared."

"About Fiona and Lorenzo, yes. Because witches are important."

"No one said otherwise," he muttered. "Forgive me for wanting to keep you informed about your friends."

Her gaze narrowed. "That cannot be why you're here. Months have passed without a single word from you. What do you want, Max?"

He hesitated for half a second. A sudden wrinkle in his impenetrable armor softened her thoughts. Images of Cecelia and the filthy, dank stench of all those Watchers, locked in the magical prison for decades, whispered through her mind.

She looked away. He *had* gone to almost impossible lengths to save all of the Watchers, and he had succeeded.

"If I never saw La Torra again," she said, "it would be too soon."

A hollow silence rang in the air.

"I had no choice, Isadora."

She sucked in a sharp breath. She wanted to scoff.

No choice? He'd had *no choice* but to lie to her about Daid's death? To withhold information, denying her right to mourn until the moment that best served *his* interests? Daid had been dead for weeks before she found out. Maximillion had flatly lied to her several times, and he'd hid letters from and to her family.

Seemingly without remorse.

"You were held at knifepoint, were you?" she asked icily.

"It happened after you'd fled to the East and taken over the position—something I never asked of you."

"You had ample opportunity to tell me," she snapped. Heat ignited in her chest. She let the fire build, enjoying the way it wrapped through her bones and darted through her body. So much easier to feel than the heavy weight. The guilt. The questions. The feeling of utter and total betrayal.

He grabbed her arm, slamming her chest to his. His breath hit her cheek in a hot caress. Isadora paused, momentarily stunned.

"I kept you safe," he whispered. "I did what I had to in order to protect you."

At the tingling provoked by his touch, she wrenched her arm free.

"Don't touch me."

"You were living under Cecelia's nose, insisting you were an adult," he said, eyes burning. "What was I supposed to do? Distract your attention by telling you about your daid so you got yourself killed, along with everyone who was relying on you?"

"No! I-I mean . . . you . . . you should . . . that was *my* decision to make."

"It wasn't."

"You should have . . ." All the words that had spun through her head all those nights failed her. It had been so clear to her before, but now the waters seemed muddied. Suddenly, she didn't know what to say. "You should have—"

Nothing more came from her lips. She stood there, paralyzed by his closeness.

"What?" he insisted impatiently. "What should I have done?"

"Told me!"

"I did!" he growled. "The moment I felt it was right. The

moment I felt it was *safe*. When I gave you those stupid letters, that was the safest you had been. You slept for days after your confrontation with Cecelia. Could you have saved Lucey if you had known your daid was dead? If the anguish you feel now was distracting you on La Torra, could you have faced Cecelia and won?"

Her rage sputtered as she recalled that awful, strange night. Lucey, half-dead. Maximillion strapped to a star next to her, both of them slated for death by fire within moments. The way Cecelia's eyes had smoldered with hatred, and the darkness she brought with her.

Could she have saved them that night if she'd known about Daid?

No.

Her mouth snapped closed, then opened again. Ages seemed to pass before she summoned her response.

"That wasn't your call to make."

"Forgive me, but I disagree," he hissed. "You worked for the Advocacy, over which I have considerable responsibility. If I hadn't withheld that information until it was safe for everyone, your death—and all the others that would have resulted—would have been on my hands. You're a selfish beast if you think this is all about you."

"It's not just that, though, is it?" she snapped. "It's . . . it's everything I'm dealing with now because I wasn't home. Because you didn't tell me, Sanna hates me. We hardly speak, except to argue. So many Dragonmasters died while I was gone. And I wasn't there to help. Maybe I could have prevented Babs's death or . . . or Daid's! I lost my *family*, with no chance to say goodbye. Now, I . . . cannot atone for being gone." Tears brimmed in her eyes. "I lost my home, Maximillion. Because of you, I lost everything."

She met his gaze. Beneath all she'd said lay something

deeper, something laced with infinitely more pain than she dared touch, like a consuming, white-hot light. The real pain stemmed from this truth: he had been frightened of her that night on Carcere. She'd seen it in his eyes.

After, he'd left without a word. Not a single word. He, who had never feared anything, had shied away from her.

Her lips tingled, recalling his heated, passionate kiss earlier that fateful night. The fire in his eyes. Even a longing in his scant, avoidant touch.

"I . . . I'm not sure I ever can forgive you," she whispered, looking away, leaving the most important part unsaid.

Maximillion straightened. "Well," he said, his chest lifting in a deep breath. His expression, steady as glass, betrayed nothing. "I believe that says more about you than me, doesn't it?"

He disappeared, taking her heart with him.

2

Something is in the trees.

The hair on the back of Sanna's neck stood up as Luteis's serpentine voice whispered through her mind. She stopped moving and opened her mouth to breathe more softly.

Below her, Luteis burned like a blackened star. His long, graceful neck slowly swung to the right. Just ahead, Junis, a hatchling, had frozen mid-step. He stood still as a tree, not a muscle twitching except his nostrils.

Do you know what it is? Sanna asked.

No.

Is it on the ground?

Bruised shadows covered the forest floor in alternating hues of emerald and umber—nothing she hadn't seen before. None of the dried branches, now devoid of leaves, quivered with movement. Everything felt uncannily still. She took another silent step along the mossy branch. Nothing changed.

Yes, I believe it's on the ground, Luteis said. His voice

sounded larger in her head, which meant Junis could hear them now.

Not a belua, then. The massive, hulking creatures lived only in the trees.

His nostrils flared in silent appraisal as he sniffed. *Nor a lion.*

Silence thickened the air. Letum Wood was without noise only when something lurked in the deep shadows.

Sanna's shoulders tightened. Last time this had happened, Daid had died. She shirked the thought. Fatigue from hunting unsuccessfully for so long had made her paranoid. As if on cue, her belly grumbled. Luteis sent her a wry look.

She ignored him.

Only dim light peeked through the skyless canopy. Not too far away, the distant call of another witch rang through the trees.

Whatever it is, she said to Luteis, *we deal with it now before anyone knows it's here. The last thing we need is to frighten everyone into thinking we're not safe.*

Is it safe here? Luteis asked, voice musing.

Not the time to wax philosophical. Just figure out what it is. Junis, what do you smell?

A belua, High Dragonmaster.

Luteis paused. Sanna glanced his way in amusement. *A belua?* she repeated.

It can't be, Luteis said.

Confidence rang in Junis's young voice. *I smell a belua, High Dragonmaster.*

Luteis?

Annoyance fairly rolled off him. *I am not wrong,* he muttered. *Whatever it is, it's on the ground.*

Beluas don't touch the ground, Sanna pointed out. *The soil burns their skin.*

I'm forming a plan, he snapped.

She reached for her knife. *Something* was wrong here. A simmer built in her fingertips, hot as a coal.

The Dragonian magic.

Thankfully, learning to use Dragonian magic as a Dragonmaster had proven very straightforward: the magic acted to protect the Dragonmasters and the dragons.

It threaded through her wrists and into her arms like a wild, living thing. The usually dormant magic awakened only when danger approached any dragon or Dragonmaster. After six months traversing Letum Wood, she'd had plenty of opportunities to learn how to use it. She welcomed the heat, as familiar as an old friend now.

We need to figure out what *it is,* she said to both of them. *Before we play a game of magical fire. The trees wouldn't like that.*

Luteis grunted.

Perhaps we can eat it, Junis said. *Whatever it is.*

Let's just hope it's not a troll, she replied.

Junis's gaze snapped to hers, then away. An unspoken question lingered in his eyes. Would a troll really come this far south? She hoped not. They were mostly legend, anyway.

A twig snapped not far away.

Trolls aside, Sanna doubted anything nearby was as large as the forest dragons.

This situation was under control.

I know that smell, Junis said. *There's certainly a belua nearby.*

Luteis would have undoubtedly snorted his disapproval

of such a thought if another sound hadn't come from the left. An odd snuffle, like a distressed grunt. The ground trembled. Sanna slipped onto another branch using a vine.

It is on the forest floor, Luteis said, *and has moved.*

She scowled and glanced up. An hour left of light at most. The retreating summer sun grew cooler with every passing day, sending them into the clutches of chilly nights. But it was far too early for such weather. Barely the first month of fall.

Weeks of repair work still awaited them back at the circle of the Ancients, where they had arrived in early summer. Having to constantly scour the forest for food meant fixing the houses had been slow work. The waiting, hungry bellies at the circle wouldn't be pleased with her empty hands.

Despite the silence around them, a constant, steady chatter of dragon voices moved through the back of her mind in a quiet ebb and flow—loud when a dragon called to her in their mind, quiet when she wasn't needed. But always there.

A piercing scream rent the air. Dragon voices tripled in her head, filled with fear.

High Dragonmaster!

Sire!

It has taken Sellis.

A belua has entered the camp, came a calmer voice amidst the chaos. Cara, Junis's mam. *It is moving toward the houses with a hatchling. I believe it is heading for the witches.*

On the ground? Sanna asked, incredulous.

It is so.

Without another thought, Sanna leaped off the tree branch seconds before Luteis flew underneath it. She landed with a *thud* on the juncture between his broad shoulders. They dropped into a dive, heading for the ground. Luteis negotiated the complicated canopy with ease, Junis close behind. Seconds later, she caught a glimpse of mottled gray skin, moving across the ground with long arms and heavy knuckles.

"*Mori,*" she muttered. "A belua on the ground."

Luteis slammed into the dirt a few paces away from the belua, his wings spread wide in a wall. Openmouthed, he roared a plume of fire that forced the eyeless belua to skid to a stop, nostrils flaring.

A tiny dragon, recently hatched, dangled upside down from one of the belua's thick hands. Sellis. He wailed a pathetic mewling sound, tender wings flailing as the belua shook him. Too much of that and every bone in Sellis's body would be shattered.

Sanna clenched her teeth, hot with fury. Ancient magic flooded her, releasing in a practiced surge a heartbeat before Luteis roared again. The magic fed Luteis's fire. Flames raced from his mouth in billows, licking hungrily toward the belua.

Sanna plunged off Luteis's back, landing on the belua's shoulder before it could scramble away. It screamed as she drove her knife into the lean muscles of its neck. The hand holding the hatchling slackened but didn't let go.

Sellis screeched, wings flapping.

"Let him go!" Sanna yelled, yanking the knife free to stab the creature in the shoulder again. "You stinky, mottled beast!"

Another wave of flame cascaded from Luteis, thick as a tree and hot as the fires of Hatha. He just managed to divert his fire as Sanna dropped from the belua's back, knife abandoned in its muscle. Luteis had never hurt her before, but she'd been singed plenty this summer as they figured out the Dragonian magic together.

Steaming purple blood coated Sanna's feet. Sweat beaded across her body.

Junis! she called. *Be ready. I'll catch Sellis; you bite the belua. Luteis, fire.*

Yes, High Dragonmaster, Junis said.

Luteis threw another wave of fire, triggering a round of screams inside Sanna's head from the nearby trees. Behind their turbulent cries rang the panicked chatter of the forest dragons.

Mori, but she hated fighting. Everything panicked, even the trees, and she had to hear it all.

Junis's black shadow slipped through Luteis's flame as the belua screamed, face wrenched in pain. One massive arm, almost as long as its entire body, flew out, slamming into Luteis's chest.

He grunted but absorbed the blow. His fire stuttered.

Sanna darted away as Junis bit the belua on a blindly grasping hand. The belua threw back his head and roared, purple spittle flying in acidic flecks. Sellis fell. Sanna saw only a blur of dark movement. With one last shove, she leaped across the space and opened her arms. His hot little body landed on her chest.

Sanna stumbled over a root, righted herself, and slipped away seconds before the belua's flailing arms would have slammed into her back.

Be careful, Luteis said.

She supplied him with more of the heat as the belua roared. *I'm always careful when it comes to dragons.*

A vine dropped from the trees. She snatched it, wrapped

it around her forearm, ran, then lifted her feet to swing away from the fight. Luteis slammed the belua into the ground with his tail. It screamed, writhing in pain. The bluish-gray skin sizzled against the dirt.

Finish it, Sanna commanded. *Don't let it suffer.*

The belua screamed again when Luteis swiped out with a claw, cracking its thick neck. The meaty shoulders went limp. Silence followed, leaving the air hanging in a strange way.

Sellis cried out in a tinny, pitiful squawk of smoke. Not far away lurked the shadows of the other dragons. Sanna released the vine and placed her feet back on the ground, inspecting the hatchling.

Hints of ivory that would perhaps mature to a warm yellow lingered in the tiny scales. He was the length of her arm, so recently hatched that his eyes were still glazed and unfocused most of the time. He burned hot, though not as hot as some, and his cries quieted as soon as his mam's smell replaced the belua's stench.

He'd be a mild dragon, no doubt.

His mam emerged from the trees like smoke. She took Sellis gently with one wing, cushioning him. Streaks of burgundy ran through Gellis's scales in waterfalls. The design on her chest resembled bubbles on top of the creek.

Sanna stepped back as Sellis nuzzled his mam with a little sigh, seeming no worse for wear.

Safe, Sanna said to Gellis, feeling as much relief herself. She'd almost missed him. He could have fallen and broken a wing. Or been crushed under the belua's massive feet.

My gratitude, High Dragonmaster, Gellis said. Her calm, even cadence had always eased Sanna, though she rarely spoke. Sanna felt a swell of something. Hope. Warmth. A glimpse of the life she *could* lead with all the forest dragons.

All of them living in peace, safe in the forest, without other witches trying to hurt them.

It is my pleasure to help.

Gellis studied her with a careful, uncertain perusal, then turned her attention back to her saved hatchling.

Sanna, watching the two, slowly backed away. Her relationship with the brood had been tenuous. Fighting the mountain dragons and saving the entire forest-dragon race certainly had helped, but claiming the mountain dragons and becoming their leader hadn't. Being High Dragonmaster over both had proven ... difficult.

With a sigh, she turned, heading back to the meadow.

Witches had congregated in a circle near their old dwellings. Watching from a safe distance, no doubt. Jesse and Elis dropped into the scene from overhead.

"*Mori,*" Jesse muttered, one eyebrow raised as he studied the belua. His stocky body and broad shoulders were an oddly perfect fit for Elis, a thick dragon in his own right. The two of them had become fast friends. Elis wasn't as quick or nimble as Luteis, but he flew well, and led the others even better.

"This isn't a good sign." Sanna crouched next to the belua.

"Luteis." Jesse shook his head. "Your flame is so hot, and you throw it so far. I can't believe it when I see it."

He pleases me with his words, Luteis said, preening.

Sanna rolled her eyes. "Don't give him a big head."

"You have at least three times the power I do," Jesse said, without a hint of jealousy. He stared at his fingertips as he spoke. "Elis throws very hot fire, but nothing like Luteis's. I wish I could give him more when we're merged and fighting together."

Elliot ran out of the trees, panting. He stopped a few

paces away. Several pairs of dragon eyes appeared behind him from the trees.

"What happened?" he asked.

"Belua attack," Sanna said.

Elliot's brow creased. "On the ground?"

She nodded.

This one was desperately hungry to be hunting on the ground, Luteis said.

"Very desperate," Sanna murmured.

She strode around the body, grabbed her knife out of its shoulder, and pulled it free. When she threw the blade onto the forest floor next to Luteis, he gently charred it with his fire, burning off the sticky blood. Sanna left it there to cool, unable to take her eyes off the hideous beast.

Instead of terrifyingly stout and thick like all the other beluas she'd seen, this one was gaunt, at best. Ribs jutted from its sides.

"Solo," Jesse said. "I don't think I've ever seen one outside a family before."

"Or this thin," Elliot added.

"They've never bothered dragons before," Sanna said, "which means he wasn't just hungry. He was starving."

This is evidence of our much-greater problem, Elis said. His voice rumbled through the back of Sanna's mind. *One we've been battling for years now.*

"I know."

Elis closed his eyes and lowered his head in agreement. Elliot peered at her with a quizzical expression.

"Sorry." She rubbed a hand over her face. Speaking directly with the dragons through her mind made it so easy to forget to give context to other witches. As High Dragonmaster, only she could talk to all of the dragons. Jesse could only speak to Elis. Though, the dragons spoke freely with each other and understood witches.

"Elis and I agree that there's not enough food," she said, "even for the beluas. Likely, that motivated this attack. To make matters worse, Luteis, Junis, and I had no luck hunting today."

Thanks to Talis, the beluas have had one hundred and fifty years to populate to these numbers without restriction, Luteis said. *They are running out of prey. Hunger is not a problem isolated to witches and dragons.*

Sanna's troubled thoughts grew heavy. Moving back to the Ancients had been her only plan to provide more safety and more food. Neither were materializing the way she'd hoped. Feeding the horde of mountain dragons hadn't proven any easier. They'd been rapidly diminishing Letum Wood's reserves as well.

"Well," she said, "witches can't eat belua meat, but dragons can. That's something. And at least it wasn't a troll. No one was injured, and Sellis is with his mam. Everything came out all right."

Elis snorted. *Belua is stringy and tastes like slugs.*

Better than starving, Sanna retorted.

He didn't disagree.

"Let's get it moved." Her nose wrinkled. "Before the smell draws more of them to camp. In the meantime, search for leto nuts and bitter greens. I doubt there's any left this late in the year, but we can try. Luteis and I have to go north. We'll return after checking on the mountain dragons. Expect us back in the morning."

"Will you stay for dinner?" Elliot asked.

"I'm not that hungry. Give my portion to your children." Her stomach rumbled again, but Luteis wisely acted like he hadn't heard. "Junis, keep an eye on my mam and her house, please?"

Yes, High Dragonmaster.

Sanna slipped up Luteis's spine and settled on his shoulders. Jesse waved farewell, already backing away. Sanna could feel the earth shifting beneath them as Luteis crouched, sprang, and rose into the forest, wings unfurled.

A BURST of mountain wind hit Sanna's cheek with a cold prickle. She closed her eyes, relishing the cool air, but tucked her arms against Luteis's scales to draw in heat. Luteis skimmed the tops of the trees with his underbelly, snorting every now and then as he scented out potential prey.

So far, nothing.

You saved Sellis, Luteis said. *Well done.*

Sanna had been replaying the fight with the belua over and over until she'd started to doze into an uneasy half-sleep. Scrambling to save the hatchling. Nearly missing him. Watching the belua move closer.

She shuddered.

Her eyesight had been temperamental since a mountain dragon sprayed her in the face with acid. Blurry one day, dim the next. Over time, her vision had settled into a fuzzy halo around the edges, limiting her sight to a circle of what was directly in front of her. Her far peripheral vision didn't exist anymore, although the eyesight she did have was clear and normal.

Two recent applications of Luteis's healing blood to her eyes hadn't yielded anything, nor had the herbs Lucey had given her in strictest confidence. Trust with the dragons was growing, but strained.

If they knew she was slowly losing sight . . .

They'd already tried every possible healing concoction. Smearing mud, chewing *trico* leaves and setting them on her skin, pouring water, all to no avail. She'd even asked Deasylva for help, but the insufferable goddess just cryptically said, *To fix it now would alter your future irreparably*, and then never mentioned it again.

My sight. She was unable to say the words aloud. *Because of them, I almost didn't catch Sellis. What if—*

No need to ask that question.

Sanna paused. *But I have to. What kind of High Dragonmaster can I be if I can't fully see? Luteis, how can I help anyone if my vision keeps changing? The rest of the forest dragons will accept you and me. I believe they'll embrace the old way of life, with a High Dragonmaster and a brood sire. With dragons caring for Letum Wood. To be . . . friendly, even. But I can't if—*

There are other witches in the world who can heal. Perhaps we could visit one of them.

An apothecary that isn't Lucey? she asked.

Yes.

I hadn't thought of it. But maybe . . .

The idea of venturing into the Network to meet other witches seemed almost as horrifying as losing her sight. Daid used to travel to small forest villages to trade every now and then, when Talis ordered it. Isadora seemed to love the Network. But talk to others?

She wouldn't even know how.

The world, Luteis murmured, *is so very different in the mountains.*

The mountains loomed ahead of them, their craggy heights piercing the clouds. Snow, rock, and an occasional hint of life littered the steep world. Grateful to change the subject, Sanna watched the land pass below, fading from forest to brush to rocky terrain. Barely a week into the first month of fall, and already snow capped the peaks.

I cannot imagine what it's like to live in the open, Luteis said.

"Not a bad thing, I think, when you are the scariest predator."

Assuming that the North doesn't hide worse enemies.

Point taken.

Sanna kept her eyes trained on the sky. Distant shapes appeared and disappeared here and there, whether flying through clouds or moving by magic, she couldn't tell. She stretched, tugging on a crick that tightened her back.

The Dragonian magic that hummed between her and Luteis kept her safe. She couldn't fall unless she threw herself off. Technically, she could pace around his back, stretch, even stand on one foot, and never have to worry. But moving that much so high in the air made her a bit queasy.

Luteis glanced back, angling his long head to meet her gaze.

Are you still firm in your plan?

"Yes. It's time."

Metok will not tell you what you desire.

"If I command it, he'll have to."

Luteis harrumphed, then flew through the cloud of smoke ahead. The comforting scent of char filled Sanna's lungs, although she still felt uneasy. Commanding any dragon to do something they didn't want to do never felt good, but leadership occasionally required it for the good of every other dragon.

Stubborn beasts.

A familiar grouping of rocks appeared below. Despite their weekly flight up here, the strange layout of the mountains remained unpredictable. The terrain changed constantly due to landslides and tumbling boulders—or sometimes when the dragons created inhabitable caves.

Metok is already awaiting us.

Luteis dove. The wind whistled past Sanna's ears as she leaned in, stomach thrilling with the fast descent.

Mountain dragons popped into sight as soon as Sanna and Luteis landed. Some of them likely had already been there—their vague gray blending into the rocks at great heights. Several appeared only after Sanna clambered off Luteis's back.

One mountain dragon, a great deal larger than the others, but still small compared to Luteis, appeared right in front of her. Metok, the mountain-dragon sire.

Smaller, thinner, and more compact than forest dragons, mountain dragons flew unusually fast and changed color to suit their environment. They breathed acid instead of fire, and could speak only to each other and Sanna. Mountain dragons were also the only dragons with the ability to transport with magic.

Despite their feral appearance, Sanna could watch them fly for hours, mesmerized by their grace.

"*Avay, Metok.*"

He bowed his lean, serpentine head toward her. The smooth amulet she wore against her chest warmed when his voice rumbled through her mind.

High Dragonmaster.

Only a few mountain dragons had come with him. Five, she counted—more than double last time. They had no reason to trust her except for her position as High Dragonmaster. After all, she'd orchestrated an attack against them and endangered a mountain-dragon egg while trying to escape the previous brood sire, Pemba.

Trust, in the dragons' world, took ages.

"Things are well?"

Yes.

"Have the dragons eaten enough the past week?"

She slipped past Metok, tufts of dying grass scratching her ankles. Other mountain dragons circled overhead, unwilling to get too close to a witch. Rarely would they come any closer.

Yes.

She worked her way up a steep embankment. It led to a ridgeline that gave her a bird's-eye view of the caves that housed these beautiful creatures. "I've already told you I'd prefer it if you called me Sanna."

Such informality cannot be tolerated.

"Even if your High Dragonmaster asks it?"

If you command.

His voice had taken on an unnatural hiss.

She frowned but kept walking. Metok sprang into the air, flying ahead of her. While he didn't loathe her or wish her dead like Pemba had, he had never enjoyed her presence. Sanna went about her duties as High Dragonmaster slowly and carefully, allowing the integration to take time.

Still, she felt strange to them.

Unwanted.

When she gained the ridgeline, Luteis flanked her on the right, Metok on the left. Her breath caught as she squinted at the great, unfolding expanse of rock and snow. Metok was always perplexed by her awe of the mountains, though far more confused by her love of the forest.

Trees, he had once said with disdain. *Who could possibly need greenery in a world such as this? It provides no sustenance or shelter.*

With a narrowed view, she studied the opposite ridge,

where smaller cave dwellings littered the sheer rock face. A chasm, cut by a churning river, separated them. She had to move her head farther to the left and right than before, but eventually, she got a good look at everything.

"I'm happy to see more dragons with shelter. Particularly before the rough winter ahead. It's coming early."

A task we begin every year at this time.

Hidden in his voice was lingering disdain. They didn't need her telling them what to do. But they *did* need food, and distance from the magic and their goddess. Sanna couldn't help their annoyance with her frequent check-ins, but she could help them find food.

The decades-long lack of a High Dragonmaster had left half of them mad from the magic. Sanna stepping into the role had somehow cured that, though she didn't understand why. Something about the way the magic was structured. Goddesses too close to their own force, she imagined. The dragons' madness had almost entirely healed now.

Luteis kept his gaze firmly out on the vista, away from Metok.

Will that be all, then? Metok asked. *As always, we have taken care of our own needs.*

She forced herself to meet his gaze.

"I want to talk to the mams."

He remained expressionless. *As you are aware, you are welcome to speak to Selsay at any time you like, but not the mams.*

"I am the High Dragonmaster."

Metok's nostrils flared as if she'd slapped him.

Yes.

"The mams are breeding too much."

You would like to control that, also?

She clenched her fists and pretended he hadn't said it.

"There's not enough food. I want to tell them to stop so we can keep all the dragons fed."

We are not starving.

"You're not far from it."

Kind of you to tell us so.

"You're unwilling to help?"

His expression darkened. *I am . . . here to serve.*

Metok stood in an unusually difficult position. His goddess loathed his Dragonmaster, but he was required, through the magic, to have allegiance to both. He straddled that line very carefully.

Sanna softened slightly, but not much. Weakness only made things worse. Which was why Metok also didn't know about her eyesight.

"You don't like me, do you, Metok?"

His gaze snapped to hers. Even Luteis stared at her as if she'd lost her mind.

I never said such a thing.

"It's fine if you don't." She worked to keep her expression neutral. "I don't expect us to be friends. You're not obligated to like me. But I need to know if I'm doing something wrong as a leader."

He hesitated. *A master is still a master. I have no issue with you personally.*

"Then why won't you tell me where the mams are?"

Selsay forbids it.

"If I command you to tell me, you'll have to show me where they live."

Metok's nostrils flared. *It is so, High Dragonmaster. I cannot fight the magic that compels me to obey you.*

Flashes of Talis, fire, and Anguis pulsed through her mind. Her words echoed, making her sick.

If I command you to tell me . . .

"I don't want to, Metok." She forced her shoulders to relax. "I only want to make sure you're well fed and taken care of. If the mams continue to breed, the rest of you will starve. I don't want that. Deasylva speaks of war with Prana soon. You are bred to fight. I need you strong if it happens."

Metok's head perked up. Appealing to their vanity as warriors was sometimes the only way to get their willing obedience. In this case, she meant it wholeheartedly.

If? he asked, voice lifting. *Not when?*

"Please pass my message to the mams. Ask them to cease. Or implore your goddess." Sanna cast a wry glance at the mountains around them. "I know she can hear us."

Something like relief swept over him.

Yes, High Dragonmaster.

A storm approaches, Luteis said. *It is too cold for rain. We must leave or be caught in it. I fear for your unprotected body without scales or fire to keep you warm.*

Her leather pants and fur-lined jacket, no matter how scraggly, would be enough with his heat. Clouds gathered in the western horizon, sweeping closer. Their dark bulk lent an uneasy feeling to the sky, as if night were closing in too soon.

Sanna climbed onto Luteis's back. Metok's wings relaxed. He was relieved to see her go, no doubt there.

"Send hunting parties farther southeast in Letum Wood. Get what food you can," she called to Metok. "I'll tell the forest dragons in the scouting parties to leave you alone. Avoid witches at all costs. War is raging in the Networks, and I don't want them trying to pull you into it. Or for you to get a taste for witches."

As you say, High Dragonmaster.

"Let me know if you need anything."

Shall we prepare for battle soon?

The hopeful tint to his voice wasn't lost on Sanna. Metok had been upset for months now that they weren't actively harassing Prana. The mountain dragons had been edgy. Selsay bred them to fight. Hints of war from the Western Network had only stirred their bloodlust.

"Not if I have anything to say about it," she muttered.

The mountain air was oddly still as Luteis winged away.

3

The Central Network's High Priest meandered through a winding path in Letum Wood behind Isadora.

Charles's red hair stood out like a fire in the fading green of the forest, highlighted by the strange orange shade of his blazer. When he stumbled over a small rock in the path, nearly cracking his head on a tree, Isadora sucked in a sharp breath.

If anything happens to him while he's here, she thought, her hands clenched into fists, *Maximillion will kill me.*

Charles clasped his hands behind his back, head tilted to the side as he studied the thick awning overhead. When a piece of moss dropped onto his nose, he frowned.

"It's . . . quite high, isn't it?"

"Yes, Your Highness. Let's keep moving, shall we?"

He paused. Isadora's teeth worried her bottom lip when a roar sounded in the distance. Charles's already-pale skin lightened a shade further, betraying lacy blue veins.

"D-dragon?"

"I assure you, we're quite safe here."

An answering roar followed, then a slight tremor shook the ground. Isadora ground her teeth, forcing an easy smile. Charles stared into the trees, frozen.

"Safe," he murmured, "indeed."

"Shall we continue?"

Charles made a sound deep in his throat. "Fascinating. I had no idea the dragons were so . . . active."

Another belligerent bellow came from nearby. Then more stamping. The dragons *were* unnaturally active today.

"They usually aren't," she said.

"I *would* love to do a deep study of the forest." He stumbled past a collection of mushrooms, catching himself from falling by grabbing a tree.

He tugged on a vine, surveying it with curiosity. Isadora flinched, grabbed his elbow, and spirited him away before the top of the molding vine dropped on his bright-red head. The vine collapsed into a pile behind him. He continued on his way, oblivious.

"Perhaps we could transplant some of this ivy to my garden." His amiable expression vanished, replaced by a frown. "Later. After the war."

"It's been many decades since a High Priest has come." She forced ease into her tone. "I've already told you about Talis, the dragon sire that isolated us for a hundred and fifty years to protect us. Now we've moved into a . . . ah . . . *better* situation. We welcome you to . . ."

She trailed off, not sure how to finish the sentence. Just ahead of them lingered signs of an old camp abandoned months ago. Sanna had refused to have Charles brought to the circle of Ancients.

Too risky, she'd said. *Can't be sure others won't follow. Take him to one of the old camps. Mam can go with you and act like we live there.*

They passed a fallen log smoldering with coals. Luteis insisted on cleaning up the forest wherever he visited. Charred remnants of long-dead trees littered the ground. Already, new tendrils of growth snaked upward from the forest floor.

A stirring in the trees caught Isadora's eye. Overhead, Sanna crouched on a branch, blade in hand, and peered at them with inquisitive, suspicious eyes. Isadora didn't think it possible for her sister to appear *more* like a heathen. With her laced knee boots, lion-leather pants, and faded jacket, she fit the mold. Wild tendrils of strawberry-blonde hair stuck out of her braid.

"Egads." Isadora rolled her eyes.

"Pardon?"

"Forgive me, Your Highness. I thought I saw something. Over here, if you please."

To their left slinked something sprawling and orange. Luteis. He and Sanna were a formidable pair. Even Charles seemed to notice something. His eyes darted to the left. A subtle change in temperature crept through the woods, belying the chill air.

"I invited Maximillion to come today," he said. "He said he was busy, but I can't imagine doing what."

She ignored his sidelong glance. The muscles along the back of her neck tensed. *Ruining lives, probably, with his indifference and selfishness.*

Sanna dropped in front of them, landing with smooth grace. Charles leaped back, nearly knocking his own spectacles off. "Gah!"

"Sanna!" Isadora hissed.

Sanna ignored her, her attention wholly focused on Charles. The air warmed. Her knife twirled in her hand as she straightened.

"Your Highness," Sanna said, her eyes crinkled in a half-glare. Soot marks decorated her forearms. A gleam of something—stubbornness, likely—shone from her eyes. The good gods, why did she have to be so . . . so *blatantly* strange?

Charles blinked. "*You* are the High Dragonmaster? You two are twins?"

"Yes."

"Fascinating. Never seen a pair so different in my life." The surprise bled out of his expression. He stuck out a hand. "It's a real pleasure to meet you."

Sanna did nothing, making the back of Isadora's neck burn. Charles smoothly returned his arm to his side and glanced beyond her, into the forest. "The, uh, dragons," he said quietly. "Do you see them much? Are they . . . quite safe?"

"Would you like to meet one?" Sanna asked, her tone stained with a hidden something.

Isadora stepped forward.

"Sanna, no."

"Over here," Sanna sang, ignoring her entirely.

A rustle from the trees off to the left, then the telltale hiss of leaves against scales. Fire issued from between the branches. A sound gurgled in Charles's throat as Luteis appeared.

The dragon's obsidian scales and bright orange marbling came into view first, followed by his angular face and massive body. A wave of heat preceded him, blasting Isadora in the face. Luteis curled protectively behind Sanna, tail wrapped around her ankle, leering at Charles with his usual expression of indifference.

Charles, wide-eyed, shrank back a step. Sanna reached out, touching Luteis's leg.

"This is Luteis. He's the brood sire."

An awkward silence stretched between the four of them. *Like the High Priest is going to fight you for him, Sanna!* Isadora wanted to say.

But Sanna didn't take her eyes off Charles, his sparkling cuff links, or the wild wave of his shocking red hair.

Isadora stepped forward, putting herself between them with a warm smile.

"You may not be aware, Your Highness, that Luteis, as the brood sire, communicates with the dragons. He has been teaching them how to fly, and he assists my sister in all her leadership endeavors. As High Dragonmaster, Sanna is able to communicate with all the dragons through the Dragonian magic. Mostly in her mind."

Charles stammered something indecipherable, regarding Luteis's massive, seething form. Luteis lowered his head and nudged Sanna, nearly knocking her off her feet. Sanna laughed at something.

"I had no idea," Charles said. "Beautiful creatures."

Luteis snorted.

"Can he understand me?" Charles exclaimed.

"Indeed, Your Highness."

"Brilliant!"

Sanna scowled. "Of course you had no idea," she muttered. "Which is why —"

"—you are here now," Isadora cried, shooting daggers at her sister with her eyes. "We appreciate you coming to mend bridges that were lost many, many years ago. Long before you took power," she added through clenched teeth.

Sanna scowled and turned away.

"I brought this with me." Charles reached into a pocket. "This scroll is a list of the questions previous High Priests and High Priestesses used to ask the High Dragonmaster. That is, before the, ah, Great Massacre."

The paper appeared to be moldering at the edges and yellowed with time. He handled it with delicate fingers more suited to an office, or a musical instrument. Unwinding the scroll, he swallowed hard again.

"Ah . . . how many dragons?" he asked.

"Sixteen."

Charles frowned. "Is that all?"

"Yes," she snapped. "We've been fighting for our lives out here."

Sadness filled his bright-eyed expression. "Yes," he mused. "I can see that you have."

Isadora marveled at his compassion. Maximillion would never muster an expression like that. Just the thought of Max stiffened the hair on the back of her neck, and thoughts of Daid soon followed.

"Yes, very sorry about all you've endured," Charles said. "If I had known, surely . . ."

He trailed off, leaving the words hanging there. His brow grew heavy, and he stared past Luteis, into the forest, seemingly deep in thought.

What would you have done? Isadora wanted to ask. There was no help he could have given the Dragonmasters.

"We appreciate your compassion, Your Highness," Isadora said. "We are all doing the best we can right now."

"Er, yes. Is the loyalty of the dragons still strong for the Network?"

"No," said Sanna evenly.

Charles flinched.

"Their loyalty is to each other. For some dragons"— Sanna paused for half a beat—"to me."

Isadora let out a relieved breath. At least Sanna hadn't brought Deasylva into this.

"Is *your* loyalty to the Network strong?" Charles asked.

"No."

"But she will do everything in her power to protect the dragons and the forest," Isadora said quickly. "Sanna would never betray the Central Network because that would put Letum Wood in danger."

Sanna frowned.

Charles's gaze darkened, but the shadow passed as he regarded Sanna with unmasked curiosity. Sanna stood up to the silent inquisition without blinking, her expression as hard as marble.

"Do the dragons have any inkling of danger to the castle?"

Sanna glanced at Luteis, who had narrowed his glittering gaze. Finally, Sanna said, "In regards to the unfair, binding, and heavy weight of the ancient dark-magic agreement, no threats that Luteis is aware of."

Isadora fought not to roll her eyes.

Charles cleared his throat and straightened, tucking the scroll in his pocket. "Lovely. I'm happy to hear that. The last thing this Network needs is another threat. Is there anything I can do for you, High Dragonmaster?"

"No."

"I'm grateful for your service to the Network."

Without a word, Luteis slipped into the forest. Sanna gripped the nearest tree and climbed, disappearing into the branches. Charles watched in open surprise, and Isadora sighed. She doubted anyone had ever left his presence in such an absurd manner.

"Thank you again, Your Highness," Isadora said. "My sister is a bit . . . untraditional. She means well. She truly cares for the dragons and for Letum Wood."

"I can see that." He smiled warmly, clasped his hands behind his back, and started to walk. Isadora guided him in a circle back the other direction. He turned at her bidding, lost in thought as he stepped over a root.

"Thank you for seeing me through here today," he said. "I know it can't be easy to merge two worlds."

"Oh. Ah, thank you, Your Highness. Your astute observations mean . . . a lot. It's always my pleasure to assist any effort I can."

He picked his way through the forest with surprising ease now. Confidence filled his voice. "As Ambassador, Maximillion always attends when I have meetings with other leaders, such as this. Any idea why he adamantly refused to come today?"

Every muscle along her spine tensed.

"Maximillion and I are not close. I am not the witch best suited to answer that inquiry."

"I'm aware. He's been a beast since seeing you again, if you can imagine him even worse than his usual state." He glanced up toward the canopy. "I'd rather encounter a starving forest lion, to be honest."

"Such a witch is a puzzle to everyone, Your Highness."

Charles laughed. "Yes. Yes, he is that, indeed. But a blessing to the Network."

Isadora shifted, an uncomfortable itch between her shoulder blades. The memory of the horrific days that followed her return home haunted her. The days she'd spent scouring Letum Wood and the paths, alone, trying to find her family in her lost, grieving state.

Knowing Daid was dead, but nothing else.

Then she found them. Broken, nearly defeated. Scattered. Over half of them dead and most of the survivors glassy-eyed with shock and starvation. No one but Mam had even cared that she'd returned. Sanna had seemed . . . confused. Distant. Focused on keeping everyone alive in the aftermath of the battle and controlling the flow of food to their hungry bodies.

Weeks of silence and mourning had followed while Isadora struggled to cope with her new reality and her guilt.

She shivered, shaking off the painful memories.

"Dante Aldana," Charles continued, "the High Priest of the Eastern Network, has spoken of organizing a sort of . . . summit, if you will. A great negotiation. He has a plan for peace *rooted in historical precedent*, or so he said. He wants to present it. Should he see this through, and were I to follow suit, then Vasily of the Southern Network would agree to a cease-fire as well."

Isadora nearly stopped breathing.

"Truly, Your Highness? That's . . . wonderful news."

"One would hope, anyway, that such an offer can be trusted. I just received official word of it myself, right before I came here. Such . . . openness surely has roots in something. I wonder if Dostar might also agree to a cease-fire if the three of us have? Or if such a summit would really work with so many strong personalities . . ."

The words hung in the air. He shook his head.

"Never mind! Just the musings of a very tired man. Thank you, Isadora, for bringing me here. I look forward to my return next year."

Embedded in the words was a firm optimism that there would *be* a next year. Isadora nodded, forcing a smile. The war had long-lasting effects, and every day, they worsened. Poverty. Decay. Horrible conditions in the city, and poor farming in the country.

Not to mention the bloody battles.

There was no quick recovery from such deep scars. These wounds would fester for years, and Isadora saw some of that realization in Charles's eyes.

"Yes, Your Highness," she whispered.

He gave her a wry smile. "Have a good day, Isadora. I hope to see you again soon."

With that, he disappeared in the whisper of a transportation spell, leaving Isadora wondering.

～

Your sister is furious.

Indeed, Sanna replied as Isadora stalked toward them, a burning light in her eyes.

Next time, Luteis said, *we go to him.*

Sanna knew almost nothing about life in the Network, or what it would mean if she showed up at Chatham Castle on the back of a dragon, asking to see the stammering, spineless High Priest. She couldn't imagine it would go well.

Isadora stopped only a pace away, bright with fury.

"Seriously, Sanna?"

Sanna braced herself. "What?"

"Could you have been *less* inviting to the High Priest?"

"I wasn't rude."

"He might as well have been a belua!"

Probably would taste better, Luteis quipped.

Sanna fought back a snort. Her arms relaxed and hung at her sides. "Listen, Isa, I don't like him knowing too much about us. I can't keep everyone safe or control who knows about the dragons that way."

"Oh really, Talis?"

"Not fair!"

Fuming, Isadora folded her arms and glared.

Sanna lifted both hands. "What do you want me to do? I'm not part of your world. I don't care about their rules and regulations. You're lucky I agreed to this at all. If witches in the Network found out about the dragons, they'd try to poach them or recruit them into their wars."

"You *should* care. Just because you want to ignore the outside world doesn't mean it will go away."

Isadora hesitated for only a second before continuing.

"It won't go away, Sanna. In fact, it's only getting worse. Anguis is gone. It was a bubble that burst. We can't try to recreate it. You can't control the dragons' safety all the time. You just . . . you have to deal with that. You have to let it go and accept that this is life now."

Sanna opened her mouth, then closed it, too furious to speak. Control their safety? She was preparing to go to war with them!

Isadora sighed, the tension slowly bleeding out of her. "It was just the High Priest. He's as harmless as a sleeping gnome."

"Maybe the next won't be."

Isadora ignored her. "He's . . . he's just trying to do the right thing, and you didn't make it any easier. No other leader alive today would have come out here in the midst of all these dragons to meet you and try to support you. To forge a good relationship with the dragons. You couldn't even give him that."

Something cold solidified in Sanna's chest. Isadora had decided to live her own life. Sanna had reconciled herself to losing her already. But now, Isadora had *chosen* to put those other witches before their family. If she hadn't been so worried about the Network, she might have been here when Daid died.

She might have stopped it.

Sanna swallowed the thought back, the way she always did, because it prickled in her throat like a wild thing.

Instead, her resolve hardened. She wouldn't give way.

Everyone let Isadora just forget her family, her inheritance, but Sanna couldn't. This way of life still meant something, and she'd hold on to it with every breath she had.

"I'm trying my best." Isadora passed a weary hand over her eyes. "Please, just help me? Help me do the right thing for the Dragonmasters? The outside world *will* encroach, Sanna. And it may be with death and blood and fire. Maybe you and I can prevent that . . . somehow."

Sanna's mouth felt as dry as a desert, thick with all the things she didn't dare say. *Why are you so concerned about them when so many of* us *have died?*

In the end, something pleading in Isadora's expression caught Sanna's attention—the spark of something that used to be there before the death, destruction, and chaos.

"Fine," Sanna muttered. "Charles can ask his questions again, but Luteis and I will go to him next year."

Isadora's gaze clouded over. She opened her mouth, then closed it and looked away. "Fine."

Something lingered unsaid in her tone, but Sanna didn't want to know what it was. She straightened. "Are we done?"

Her voice came out colder than she intended. Luteis stirred in the trees behind her, rustling the drying leaves. A pang of hurt crossed Isadora's face. They stared at each other, at an impasse.

Say it, Sanna willed her sister, heart clenched. *Say that we are more important to you.*

"Yes," Isa said weakly. "Yes, Sanna. We're done here."

Sanna turned on her heel, grabbed a tree trunk, and started to climb again. Within minutes, her arms burned, and her palms ached. She moved fast, her fingers groping the branches by instinct. It seemed as if the tree itself lifted her, that the wind pushed her gently upward.

Luteis's wings lay against his back as he navigated the sprawling branches with his talons, slinking like a shadow.

Who was that witch? he asked as they moved.

"The leader of the Network," she said in between pants. She pushed off a bough with her legs, propelling herself higher. "His name is Charles. They call him the High Priest."

Is it the same role as High Dragonmaster?

"I don't think so."

He seemed quite uncomfortable. I am not surprised he should be a leader. I could sense his magical power. If I had to work with witches, I would want a great deal of magic to do so.

"All witches outside of Dragonmasters probably feel powerful to you," she said, "since none of us do magic. At any rate, it's no wonder things are falling apart out there, with such a timid witch leading everyone."

An interesting point. How many witches live in the world?

"Too many, I would imagine." She grunted as she grabbed a vine to climb up a blank patch in the tree bark. "As long as they aren't invading my forest, I don't really care."

He gave her a sidelong glance. *But you know how many mountain dragons populate the North and how many forest dragons remain here.*

"That's because I track the most important things."

At least I feel no stirring in my blood to indicate the old magic has returned. With great enemies on the horizon, we don't want to worry about that.

The thought of the thousands-years-old agreement that bound the forest dragons to Chatham Castle sent a little shiver through Sanna. What a weighty decision to make on their behalf. Then again, had her ancestor, Gregor, *not* made that choice, would Luteis be here today?

Would she?

Leadership seemed a world ripe with hard decisions and worse decisions.

"Well," she said, "we don't have to worry about it."

You are upset. When you make that face, I believe it comes from a place of pain in your squishy, defenseless body. What is hurting?

Sanna pushed harder, enjoying that pain. The thrum of blood, pounding of heart. It felt like years since she and Isadora had lain giggling in the attic in Anguis. Or snuck past Mam in the night to find food. Were they even the same witches? Did they truly know each other?

Still, behind it all lurked one encompassing—devastating—thought.

She could have saved him, Luteis.

It was the first time she'd said it, and her heart ached. Until the words left her mind, she hadn't known how heavily they'd been sitting there. Luteis landed on a nearby branch and extended his wing, preventing her from passing. His yellow-moon eyes stared hard at her.

What does this mean?

Sanna pressed her hands against her thighs and took gulping breaths.

"Isa," she finally said, looking up. Sweat trickled down her cheek, raising goosebumps on her skin when a chilly breeze whistled past. "She sees possibilities, right? She . . . she should have seen Daid dying. If she wasn't so focused on everyone *but* the Dragonmasters, maybe she would have been able to prevent it."

He paused, blinking. *I had not considered this, but I see what you are saying.*

"I'm so angry with her, Luteis." She pressed a fist into her chest. "There's a hard, heavy spot here. It's been there since Isadora returned. It hurts every time I see her. I see her and think of Daid. Of all he's missing."

The day Isadora unexpectedly returned flashed fitfully through Sanna's mind. Isa's wild panic. The fear in her eyes. The desperate way she asked for Daid, as if she knew but didn't believe it. Her clothes were torn, dress muddy, hair wild. She'd been searching for them for days. Mam collapsed in Isa's arms and didn't speak anything but Isadora's name for hours. Sanna shook out of the memory.

You haven't told her about your eyes yet.

"No."

A swollen silence.

Why?

"I don't know."

Sanna rested the flat of her palm on her chest, where the black spot weighed on her with the force of a thousand dragons. Then she let it drop to her side and pushed the anger away to deal with another day.

They had bigger enemies to face now.

4

I sadora glanced at the small note in her hand and worried her bottom lip as she waited outside the High Priest's office.

I WOULD BE MOST HONORED by your presence this evening at 6:30.

—*Charles*

SHE STARED AT IT, brow furrowed. Could this be about his meeting with the Dragonmasters a week ago? No, there was no residual business there. The High Priest, notoriously single and shy, surely wouldn't be asking for any romantic reason. She imagined his cheeks flaring crimson at the mere thought of courting a woman. Besides, that couldn't be it. Tradition dictated the High Priest never handfast.

Maximillion?

A breathless sensation caught her by surprise, but she stuffed it down. Not likely. Something else entirely, no doubt. Isadora slipped the note back into the pocket of her dress and smoothed her skirt for the tenth time.

The door to the office burst open.

"Isadora!" Charles called, hair spiraling around his head in a cinnamon halo like a lion's mane. "So good to see you again."

Isadora stood with a smile. "Always a pleasure, Your Highness."

He stepped out, warmly clasped her hand, and drew her inside. "Please come in. I can't offer much in the way of hospitality, but we do have some warm chamomile tea."

"That sounds lovely."

Warmth enveloped her as she followed him. Morning sunlight streamed through the windows. A cheery fire crackled in the hearth, and a thick rug softened the stone floor beneath her as they crossed to a threadbare velvet divan and two high-backed chairs with clawed feet.

She narrowly avoided a collision with his back when he stopped in the middle of the room.

"Max?" he called. "Where'd you go? Ah, there you are. Of course."

Ice snaked through her blood.

She turned to see several witches near the window, Maximillion amongst them. It had been more than a week since she'd seen him. Empty days filled with entirely too much effort to forget the smell of vetiver.

Now she wished for all of those days back.

Maximillion continued to consult with one of the three witches that flocked him. Isadora hadn't met any of them, but based on the way several quills wrote frantically on nearby scrolls in response to his orders, they had to be his

Assistants. Thanks to Maximillion's paranoia about the Advocacy, not even his staff knew the extent of Isadora's work with him.

Charles waved a dismissive hand. "Let him settle all that first. He'll come over when he's done. And how are you?"

"Well, Your Highness."

"Tea?"

"Yes. Thank you."

He poured her a drink and sent one to her with a spell, then motioned her toward one of the high-backed chairs closest to the fire. She sank into it, canting her body away from Maximillion.

"Is there something I can help you with?" she asked.

Charles fiddled with the end of his sleeve as he studied her. "Ah, yes." He cleared his throat. "Something."

When he fell into thought and said nothing further, several awkward moments passed.

Finally, Isadora asked, "How are things with Dante in the East? You had mentioned something about possible peace talks."

He startled. His bloodshot eyes caught her attention as he straightened, blinking rapidly. Somewhere behind her, a door shut.

"Right—sorry." He rubbed his face. "Didn't sleep last night. If you can believe it, that is precisely why I called you here to talk."

"The East?"

A cold voice cut in just as a shadow fell over her.

"No," Maximillion said, "about the manipulative way the High Priest of the Eastern Network wants to play us like fools in the name of peace."

Maximillion stood a few steps behind her, a dark, looming specter. She ignored him, gaze intent on Charles.

"Er . . . possibly, yes. Haven't entirely discounted that," Charles said in a conciliatory way. "But in circumstances like these, any talk of peace . . ."

Maximillion strode around the chair, coming face-to-face with Isadora. His glare burned all the way to her bones. Beneath his haughty exterior lay a hidden weariness, but she could read nothing in his expression. When he turned to Charles, his voice warmed by a degree.

"All orders have been executed as you wished, Your Highness."

Charles scoffed. "Such formality, Max. Stop! You originated every single one of those orders. There's no reason to act as if the ideas came from me. We may fool the Council, but I don't think we need to fool Isadora. Sit down! Relax a moment. We have much to discuss with this lovely young lady."

Maximillion's jaw clenched. He remained standing. Isadora silently toasted the High Priest as she sipped her tea, delighted to see Maximillion so unnerved by an order to be less than supremely uptight.

"We've discussed the importance of a bold front, Your Highness," Maximillion said, nostrils flared.

"Maximillion is trying to get me to be a greater leader and own my role as High Priest in a bolder way," Charles said to Isadora, leaning forward, eyes sparkling. "I'm not sure it will work. The good gods love him for it. Isadora, Dante Aldana has just reached out to me again. Transported here personally, if you can believe that. Didn't think he'd ever leave that Mission Castle."

"Magnolia," Maximillion murmured.

"The summit is on," Charles said, brightening. "Vasily has agreed. Dostar has yet to weigh in, but I accepted immediately on receipt of Vasily's assent."

Isadora's eyes widened. "Really?"

"Delightful, isn't it?"

"But—"

"It's a fool's errand," Maximillion said. "A ploy for control, not a bid for peace."

Something flickered across Charles's countenance. He sobered. "Do you have any other plausible alternatives, Max? Shall we say *no* to the proffered branch of peace and be the reason the world crumbles?"

Maximillion gritted his teeth. The implications of such a massive meeting between Networks whirled through Isadora's mind. All of these leaders were headstrong and determined, Charles excepted. Getting any of them to agree would be almost impossible.

"Forgive me, Your Highness, but what does any of this have to do with me?"

"Wonderful question, Isadora! I will not be attending. Such a negotiation could last for months, and with no High Priestess here, I fear the repercussions of such an extended absence. There's a certain power in being visible to the witches I serve."

An oddly on-target thought for a witch so inclined to flightiness.

"Do you have no High Priestess you want to appoint?"

"At the moment, no. Maximillion will go in my stead. He understands the delicacy of political campaigning on levels I never shall. I am not the strongest candidate. There are social intricacies I've never learned, and never hope to."

"Maximillion is well suited to navigating difficult conversations. Particularly those that can change the course of one's life."

Maximillion didn't even flinch, but his glower darkened. She lifted her teacup to him with a smile.

"Yes, well, that brings us full circle," Charles said, "to why I asked you to come here."

If possible, Maximillion's already-taut shoulders tightened. He'd snap at any moment.

"I, ah, wanted to ask if you'd accompany Max to the Southern Network as part of the Central Network's delegation."

Her heart dropped into her stomach like a cold stone.

"I'm sorry?"

"It's an odd request, I grant you that," Charles said, "but one I feel is quite necessary."

Another pregnant pause filled the room while Isadora scrambled to catch up.

Go to the Southern Network with Maximillion? A peace summit of this magnitude required . . . *finesse.* Training. Extensive knowledge of political history and current events. Modern dresses, at the very least! She had no idea how to interact with high-society witches. The bizarre customs of Network life still caught her by surprise.

"Your Highness, I'm flattered," she said, stammering. "But I fail to see how I could be qualified for such a position. I know nothing of peace talks."

"You know more than most, as you demonstrated when I came to see your sister. You have a proud, powerful bearing, Miss Spence. That matters more than nearly anything."

"What I know comes from the *Chatterer.*"

"More than most of my Council Members know, unfortunately."

Isadora stared at him, at a complete loss. No wonder their Network was on the brink of utter destruction.

Charles continued, "We could certainly send Max on his own, the way he prefers, and they would accept that. But I fear much would be missed."

"Such as?"

Maximillion watched her closely, with eyes like a hawk.

"Each Network is allowed to present a peace plan," Charles said. "Due to . . . special circumstances around the plan we wish to present, we desire a female in attendance. To be present with the High Priestesses in ways Maximillion cannot."

"As I already told you," Maximillion said, ice in his tone, "I refuse."

Charles ignored him, staring hard at Isadora. "On the point of you going," he said, voice low, "I am adamant. Max should not bear it all, nor can he be everywhere the way he likes to think he can. I desire eyes on all witches and influence in *all* spheres. Right now, we have no one who can be present with the High Priestesses. And who else exerts greater influence on their High Priest?"

To that, Isadora had nothing to say. She looked down at her lap, then back to Charles. A prickling sensation rose on the back of her neck.

"What would I do there?"

"Assistant to the Ambassador, perhaps," Charles said quickly. "Unless you feel like handfasting your High Priest?"

Isadora sucked in a sharp breath, but Charles only laughed.

"I jest, I jest. If I were to suddenly show up with a spouse without even having a High Priestess, it would be suspicious. Not to mention the trouble of bucking centuries of tradition that dictate I never have a spouse. Besides, not even you, with all your kindhearted ways and penchant for the right words at the right time, can deny that I am the wrong witch for this job."

Isadora lacked a response. Charles smiled at her, as if he hadn't expected one.

Thankfully, a letter appeared underneath the door, sliding between the cracks. It floated over to Maximillion, who read it without a change in his expression.

He turned to Charles. "Forgive me, Your Highness. This is an urgent matter."

A look passed between them before Maximillion strode out of the office, closing the door behind him. Charles's gaze landed on Isadora.

"He said he refused," she murmured, relieved he had gone. "How could I accept when—"

"He refuses on the grounds that he cannot guarantee your safety as an Assistant. He feels it's not an effective plan. And with you being a witch with . . . advanced . . . abilities . . . . ."

Isadora's eyes widened. He knew of her power?

His gentle grin settled her rush of fear. "Your secret is quite safe with me."

She frowned. "That's the reason he refuses to take me with him? Because I'm a Watcher?"

Charles hesitated. "Ah . . . other plans were proposed."

"And?"

Charles waved her off. "We're working out the details. Don't worry about Max. He's softer than he appears."

Isadora said nothing.

"Trust me when I say that I feel the situation necessitates the danger, and that we will take every precaution for your safety. The Central Network cannot withstand another year of these wars."

Isadora's heart felt like a fist in her chest. Her thoughts roamed to her family. To the cold expression on Maximillion's face. If she left now, she'd likely never repair the gulf between her and Sanna. Overwhelmed at the mere thought, Isadora shot to her feet and began to pace.

But if she didn't do it?

The summit could fail from a triviality she might have prevented. War would overtake the Central Network. Her family would suffer then, too.

Charles watched her for several moments, silent. The urge to slip into the paths tickled the back of her mind, but she pushed it aside. Too emotional. Too many possibilities. It would simply overwhelm her now.

If I don't go . . .

Her mind trailed to Berry. To the apothecary tents. Elliot's weary gaze when he went out trapping. Lucey's agitation since her return. The fear in every Watcher.

Her throat thickened.

I must.

Being home was difficult enough. Having nothing substantial to do was worse. Charles had given her a gift. Action. Something to *do* that could really help.

Isadora whirled around before she lost her courage. Her heart raced.

"I'll do it."

Charles's astonished green eyes peered at her through his thin spectacles. Maximillion had returned in the midst of her reverie. He stood only a few paces away now, face pale. His cold expression sent a chill through her.

Charles slowly stood, not taking his eyes from Maximillion. "That is . . . wonderful news!"

Maximillion's jaw tightened as he met her gaze. "Charles, a moment in private with Isadora, if you please."

"Now?" Charles leaned toward Maximillion. "You want to—"

"Only a moment."

Isadora's gaze darted between them. Charles hesitated for only a second, drew in a deep breath, and stood.

"Of course, old friend. I . . . I shall be just outside."

Charles buttoned his vest, nodded to Isadora, and strode out. The next moment, Maximillion grabbed her arm with panther-like grace.

"Are you mad?" he demanded.

She wrenched her arm away. "Don't touch me."

He advanced, forcing her to step back or be crushed. "You cannot go to a negotiation of this size with your powers. Dante Aldana and his wife will be in residence for the duration, likely with their new Ambassador. You're a fool if you think the Ambassador isn't a Defender, one that knows you from La Torra. What if he is your match?"

The backs of her knees collided with a chair. She stopped, standing her ground. "I'm an adult, thank you. I can make my own decisions. I've seen the Ambassador in the *Chatterer*. He wasn't on La Torra."

"You know all the witches that saw you, did you?"

"Well . . . no, but—"

"People die because of *buts* in a plan."

Isadora tilted her head back, meeting his steely gaze. Warming to the argument, she stepped toward him and jabbed a finger at his chest. "Charles asked this of me, not of you. It's not up to you to decide for me, the way you have in the past."

"Do not," he whispered, "touch me."

She backed up again, startled by the deep, angry growl. His eyes met hers, dangerous in their intensity.

"It is not on you to shoulder fate," he said. "Watchers have died, or worse, for it. War will always be inevitable, Isadora. If it stops now, it will come back later. You can't prevent all of it."

"I may be able to help prevent it right now."

"You'll risk your life on a *maybe*?"

"Don't you every day in the Advocacy?"

He scowled. "Not if I can help it."

The smell of vetiver trailed behind him when he turned away, arresting her senses. He stood at the fire, his profile silhouetted. She looked away, unable to bear the stark beauty of his broad shoulders.

"It's not just a potential Defender in residence," he said without looking at her.

"Then what?" she asked warily.

He let out a long breath, then turned to face her again. "Whomever I take needs to be secretive. Willing to be subtle, underhanded, sneaky."

"What?"

"Serafina, High Priestess of the Eastern Network, has approached me with a plan she believes will work. After some modifications to it, I agree. Unfortunately, as their High Priestess, she cannot present it. Dante has dismissed it. I plan to champion Serafina's plan at the summit."

"You?"

His nostrils flared. "Yes."

"But why?"

He paused, then let out a long breath. "She has made promises to protect Watchers as part of the agreement. Not just in the East, but all of Antebellum."

"Oh."

"It's the only guarantee we have to keep all Watchers safe. And her plan stands on it's own merits. With changes, it has become strong enough to win. To champion her plan, I'll need access to Serafina."

For the High Priestess of the Eastern Network to be seen consorting with an Ambassador in times like this? Serafina could be killed for such a thing.

"Oh."

"I need a woman to be friends with her. To pass correspondence without anyone else knowing. It could be dangerous."

Isadora met his gaze. "That doesn't frighten me."

"It should," he snapped.

"Carcere should have too."

He opened his mouth to say something, then closed it again.

"The risk is worth it, Maximillion."

"You're playing with fire." His voice, low and gravelly, made her stomach catch. Lines of light illuminated the strands of his hair. "You don't know what awaits you there. Your match could be among them."

Her mind touched briefly on her puzzling memories of Cecelia. *Some would say that the match augments the power,* she had said. *Although it also allows a weakness. Rumor has it that your match may join your paths. See what you see. May betray you. Murder you. Use your own power against you, even.*

"Don't you think they would have found me already, if they were going to seek me out? I use my powers often."

He paused, studied her.

"A fool's errand," he muttered. "This is more dangerous than any mission the Advocacy could send you on, and far more intricate than pretending to be a *lavanda* maid on a remote island. Dante Aldana will be breathing down our necks, ready to kill you the moment he learns your secret. We'll be living in one of the strongest castles in all of Antebellum, in a cold world that leads to death if you're lost in it. The tribes there are protective and unpredictable, and Vasily is no idiot. This is a game of Networks on a level you've never heard of."

He turned to face her, expression glacial. "Not the least

of which is that I cannot protect you while I'm in meetings all day."

"I never asked you to."

His expression was thick with disbelief. "Just like that, you decide to do something idiotic, and *this* is how it happens."

"How what happens?"

He turned, strode to the door without another word, and yanked it open.

Charles, in a startled tone, said, "Have you already—"

"No," Maximillion snapped. He disappeared down the hallway, Charles calling after him in vain.

Isadora stood there, alone in the High Priest's office, with a surreal feeling of disbelief.

So that was it, then? She was going to the Southern Network with Maximillion for the hope of stopping this war. She'd always thought being an Assistant had a certain appeal—though how an Assistant would get in with the High Priestess, she had no idea.

An exciting challenge.

Charles stepped into the room with an awkward, foppish laugh. "Well," he said, "that was . . . ah . . . what did he . . . ah, what did he ask you just now?"

"He merely tried to talk me out of it."

"That's all?"

"Yes, Your Highness."

"There was nothing else?"

"No."

Charles nodded, letting out a relieved breath, then held out his hands. He took Isadora's in his own warm, surprisingly calloused grip. "Isadora, you have my personal gratitude, and I shall consider myself deeply in your debt. You cannot know what it means."

"I have an idea, Your Highness."

He smiled knowingly. "Ah, yes. I imagine you do. Well, anything you need at any time, you let me know. There are other details to work out, but I think Maximillion will be in touch with you."

"Of course, Your Highness. Thank you. I must be going." She bowed and headed for the door.

Once she reached it, he called out. "Isadora?"

She looked back. "Yes?"

"He's a good man. Cold as a glacier, but the best I've ever known. Just . . . keep that in mind."

The door closed on him standing there, regarding her with an odd expression on his face.

5

A dead mortega hung from Luteis's talon as he soared back to the Ancients.

The antlers would be good for weapons. Elliot had a way of whittling them into knives for the witches to use in a skirmish. Singed marmots dead from fire and tied by a rope hung from the other talon.

Not much, but something.

The dragon cut through the night in near silence. Leaves half-clung to the rickety, bare branches below, giving the world a barren feeling. Pockets of strickenine moss that had overtaken the forest grew wild in this area.

Luteis, as the strongest hunter in the brood, used every spare minute to search for food. Sanna went with him only occasionally, using most of her time to help the Dragonmasters secure their houses or to work with Jesse and the other dragons.

Only two houses were habitable. All the tenacious ivy had been cleared, flooring fixed, and holes in the walls patched. Elliot and his family lived in one. Mam, Sanna, and Finn's children shared the other while they continued to fix one up just for Trey, Greata, and Hans. Adopting Finn's three children gave Mam someone to take care of, and Sanna was glad for it.

High Dragonmaster, Elis said in her head. *I report great success with Gellis and Magentis in flight today. They have achieved your goal of staying aloft for more than two hours. Their coordination at night also improves.*

Wonderful news. Thank you. Give them a day to rest, then challenge them to three hours of flight.

Only one day?

Yes. How are the hatchlings with fire control?

No signs of secundum yet, but that is to be expected.

Tomorrow, have them practice ascending and descending again. They can scoop rocks off the forest floor, then throw them at a target.

Yes, High Dragonmaster.

And Sellis?

Recovered fine from the belua attack.

Thank you for the report, Elis.

Sanna's thoughts uncurled in the deep night. The forest dragons had dramatically improved their flying skills. Some hunted well enough but still needed more stealth. She frowned.

Was there something she was missing? A potential weak spot, more preparation they could invest in? Two dragon races made the number of variables heady. As leader, how could she possibly control them all, provide certainty in such a frightening time without building physical walls around them, like Talis?

She never expected to feel sympathy toward that old dragon.

Elliot trapped for small animals constantly, seeming relieved to have something familiar to do after Babs's death.

He kept the Dragonmasters mostly fed, but nothing remained to store. The leto nuts they did gather were almost inedible due to the unusual weather.

Cara will eat this mortega, Luteis said, a hint of challenge in his voice. As if Sanna would say no. Luteis had an unabashed fondness for Cara.

"That's fine. The hatchlings can have the marmots. Mam will want the hides for shoes, though."

Sanna's mind rolled out over the carpet of darkness, wandering to paths away from the Dragonmasters. In her tunnel of vision, stars burned bright overhead. A small comfort when the full panorama wasn't visible.

"Luteis, do you feel trapped?"

Please explain.

She fidgeted off an itch between her shoulder blades. Dim light left her in an unnaturally dark world these days.

"A week ago, Metok said, *A good master is still a master.*"

Yes.

"The magic compels you to obey me, doesn't it?"

I believe so. I have always listened, and therefore, I have never been compelled. Except, of course, to meet you. The night of your Selectis.

Sanna blinked, startled. "You were compelled?"

He leaned to the left, lifting his right wing farther into the sky.

My goddess commanded, and I obeyed. I did not see it as an obligation, but I can see why other dragons might.

"You were wild once."

Yes.

The question nearly stuck in her throat, but she forced herself to ask, "Do you miss it?"

While I enjoy moments of solitude and quiet, I wouldn't wish to return to the months of solitary time. Nor my life without you. I find great power and freedom in my merging with you.

A breath of relief rushed out of her. "So you don't feel obligated?"

I didn't say that.

She scowled.

Such a thing cannot be simplified. Yes, the magic compels us to obey the High Dragonmaster, but obedience is in accordance with my desires. With a good master, it feels easy. Did you appreciate Talis?

"I'm not sure."

Talis, the now-dead dragon sire that had ruled Anguis before it burned to the ground, was . . . a complicated figure. While he had provided safety in a very unstable world, he'd done it at the cost of many things.

Though he offered security, he was still a master. He took away decisions. History. Mistakes you could have learned from. But without Talis, you might never have been born. Eventually, however, his power turned dark. Metok likely sees this much the same way. Perhaps necessary for now, but what later? And where, or when, does it stop?

Her stomach roiled. Was she just another Talis? No, a far cry from Talis. But the situation wasn't so different, was it? Hadn't she said as much to Isadora? Charles was a good leader now, but those that followed?

Sanna sat with that for a minute, supremely uncomfortable.

"What alternative is there?"

Inasmuch as I understand it, Dragonian magic is the bond between goddess, dragon, and Dragonmaster. One could argue that you are also slave to the magic. Are you not? Does it not exist within you without your asking for it? Does it not make things happen, force you to action?

His explanation only opened up more questions. Ones she knew he couldn't answer. Why have a Dragonmaster at all?

Where did all this start, and why?

Her mind spun back to the Western Network, where the desert dragons lived in the sandy cliffs, wild but not truly free. Some of them were tamed by witches and lived in families, where they served as protection or transportation. Others lived in the rocks, flying and defending and breeding, but never truly connecting with witches.

What was freedom, then?

Sanna's head hurt trying to keep it all straight. In the end, what mattered most was getting the dragons fed and avoiding war with Prana. As High Dragonmaster, she could never serve every dragon the way they wanted, but they didn't have to be *slaves*, either.

Did freedom exist in structure or in wild spaces?

Deasylva awaits. Luteis dropped into the trees.

Sanna sighed.

This time, she wanted to speak to the goddess.

I HAVE A GIFT FOR YOU.

Sanna stared at the bright writing on the dark tree trunk, Deasylva's only way of communicating with her.

"A gift?" she repeated.

Had she read Deasylva's words wrong? Squinting, Sanna leaned forward. The words remained the same.

I have a gift for you.

Despite the cold air, a stirring of warm wind brushed through Sanna's hair, tinged with the scent of honeysuckle.

Luteis's ears perked up. He adored gifts. The words on the tree trunk faded. Another one took their place.

Yes.

A vine fell, wrapped around something black that gleamed with different colors. Sanna reached for it and felt cool, heavy scales against her fingertips.

"A vest?"

The vest of the High Dragonmaster. Created from the scales of Luteis's ancestors. It is my totem. It is not unbreakable. If it becomes necessary, you have my permission to destroy it and all it stands for by force and fire.

A wash of sudden reverence rushed over Sanna. The ebony scales held together in a cascading pattern. They had subtle differences amongst their shapes—triangular, oblong, rounded, diamond. All of the scales were small, like those found on a dragon's face and those that surrounded the tender, weak heart scales. Together, they created a garment that felt unbreakable.

Sanna moved it, startled to find it flowed almost like water. She tugged, but it didn't give way. Her hand floated to her necklace. Selsay's totem. A representation of the goddess's power.

"For me to wear?"

As you wish. It would provide greater protection.

"Against?"

The upcoming battle.

Sanna froze, ice chilling her veins. "Battle?" she whispered.

Luteis stirred behind her. Deasylva's words faded, this time fresh ones appearing more quickly than usual.

Prana has called for war on the first day of winter.

Sanna swallowed past a lump in her throat. In the months since they'd come to the circle of the Ancients,

Deasylva had spoken of Prana now and then. Vague warnings. Odd mutters from the trees.

But nothing so concrete. They had focused on surviving and preparing for winter in a world nearly depleted of food. The first day of winter was less than three months away.

"The dragons will fight this battle, you mean."

As you say.

Luteis sidled closer.

The war of the goddesses is beginning, he said. *Deasylva whispers of a winter battle.*

"Where will the battle be?" Sanna asked.

In the West, came Deasylva's written words. *If we win there, she will not invade here.*

"Why does Prana want to fight?"

Prana desires revenge.

"Against?"

Her sisters, Sarena and me.

"What did you do?" Sanna couldn't help the accusation in her tone.

We saved lives.

Sanna bit her tongue. Something lay behind this. "What will happen if she gets her revenge?"

Witches will die in the floods that consume the lands. Dragons will be swept away, along with all the creatures we hold fondness for.

Sanna nearly choked. "We're supposed to handle all this in one battle?"

If we are wise.

"You have to be kidding! The forest dragons won't survive a battle that soon. We can barely feed the hatchlings. Cara has gone hungry most nights the past few weeks. I—" Sanna broke off, completely at a loss. "Deasylva, we can't! The world is in chaos. Isadora says that . . ."

She trailed off when more words appeared.

The world is in chaos because of this long-standing battle between sister goddesses. The witches feel the shift in magical boundaries, though they aren't aware of it. If you don't fight, you lose all *chance of life.*

The word *all* brightened more than the others. Sanna turned away. Luteis peered at her, yellow-moon eyes wide with uncertainty. He couldn't read, but Deasylva often spoke to him separately.

Sanna turned back around, glaring at the tree. "Is your life in danger?"

No.

"Let me get this correct," she muttered. "You want us to fight for our lives against another race of dragons because your sister wants revenge, but your life is not in danger? We die, you don't?"

A long pause, then, *Yes.*

"There has to be another way."

There are always other paths. I do not desire the destruction of my forest, witches, or creatures. You do not fight alone. Others are waiting.

"Like?"

There is no wisdom in knowing this future. Do you trust me, Sanna of Gregor?

"Mostly."

Deasylva had been far less distant the past six months, appearing on her own to tell Sanna how to do something unknown, or to direct them to food. But she would disappear for long stretches without explanation, or remain strangely cryptic whenever it suited her. There was nothing convenient about the goddess.

That slipperiness wasn't welcome.

I ask for your trust now. All will reveal itself appropriately. I will retreat from my forest for a time but will return for the battle.

"You're leaving?"

My power is pulled in many ways. I go to rest and prepare.

The goddess would do whatever she wanted, that much Sanna had learned to accept. Her thoughts skipped like a bug on top of water. She tried to force them to settle.

"How should I prepare the Dragonmasters?"

If a path to prevent the war presents itself, I trust it will find you. Gather supplies. Weapons. Strengthen the forest dragons and the Dragonmasters. Prepare in every way possible. I see much, Sanna. You will be there. You will be ready.

That meant many things. Inevitability, for one. The battle would happen. And she'd lead it. Somehow. Even with her broken eyes. But it also meant a grueling three months trying to prepare for an enemy they knew almost nothing about.

"Of course I'll be there. But it doesn't mean I'll like it."

Luteis wrapped his tail around her ankle, soothing her. Deasylva's parting words stirred up a brush of wind.

I trust you, Sanna of Gregor. There is a thin path to victory. It exists now. In acceptance, you'll find what you seek.

The cloying scent of honeysuckle faded. The writing on the tree ebbed like a sigh.

"In acceptance, you'll find what you seek," Sanna murmured. She turned to Luteis, hands held out in question. "Acceptance of *what*?"

Perhaps your place as lesser being to me.

Sanna scoffed. "Hardly."

At least you have this, Luteis said, using his tail to lift the vest. It spun slowly in front of Sanna. Reluctantly, she accepted it, running her fingers over the smooth scales. It was a bright, beautiful gift.

She slid it on, gratified when it fit snugly, not at all bulky, as if it were a normal extension of her body.

A gift from a goddess should not be taken lightly. Her totem means she trusts you. Taking Selsay's totem from Pemba was the only way you were able to save the mountain dragons and become High Dragonmaster.

"*Mori.* I forgot to tell her about food."

The *thump* of something slamming into the tree branch made Sanna jump. She reached over, startled to find a thick, tangled mess of vines and small, round objects.

Leto nuts, Luteis said, sounding as surprised as Sanna. *Many, many of them.*

The thick nuts, each as large as her fist, were plentiful and healthy. More than they'd gathered all summer. These would last for a few weeks, at least. Could be stored as well. Leto nuts filled the belly for longer than the bitter greens they scrounged for, at any rate, and they could use their shells to drink from.

Sanna fingered the rumpled vines with a sigh. "It's something. Let's go, Luteis. We need to talk to the rest of the dragons and take the nuts to Mam. It'll give her something to do. After that, we need to start preparing."

What is your plan?

"First? Fixing my eyes."

6

Isadora wandered Berry for hours, her mind awash with Charles's words and Maximillion's frosty expression. She'd make her way to Pearl's house eventually. But for now, she satisfied her caged energy and wild thoughts by simply walking.

A figure caught her eye not far down a gently sloping stone road. A slender female with mousy-blonde hair and dull eyes stared toward Berry as if she didn't really see it. Isadora sucked in a sharp breath.

Lucey.

The refugee camp wasn't far from here, about ten minutes on foot. Lucey's appearance against the bleak, gaunt landscape seemed all the stranger because not another soul was in sight.

Eager for the distraction, Isadora rushed across the road. "Lucey?" she called.

Lucey turned, gazing with unseeing eyes. She blinked, then seemed to return to herself. "*Avay*," Lucey murmured with a wan smile.

"Are you all right?" Isadora asked, reaching out for her.

Lucey smiled wearily, touching Isadora's cheek with the back of her hand, then letting it drop. "Tired."

"Just finish your shift?" Isadora asked.

Lucey shook her head, pulling her shawl more closely around her with a little shudder. "No, not tonight. I've been . . . out."

Lucey's small-boned hands, pale and weak, were clenched into fists. Since her capture and torture at the hands of Cecelia only a few months ago, she'd remained distant. Quiet. Often wandering through the forest when she wasn't busy at the surgical tent. Even her work there was erratic. She showed up unexpectedly and at odd intervals.

"Think of anything splendid on your walk?" Isadora asked softly, looping her arm through Lucey's. She tugged her gently, guiding her toward Pearl's. Lucey went without resistance.

"No. Have you seen Maximillion lately? I'm concerned for him. With so little Advocacy business, I hardly ever see him anymore. Yet he's still busier than ever."

"Ah . . . yes. Just a little while ago."

Lucey's eyebrow quirked. "Everything okay?"

"Fine."

They passed ramshackle houses, darkened with smoke. Lucey stopped in the middle of the road and stared at Isadora. Her pale face was drawn. She touched Isadora's hand, then winced and pulled away. "Out with it," she said.

The words burst from Isadora as if driven by pressure from deep within her chest. She recounted the entire conversation, including Maximillion's refusal to bring her. Lucey listened without saying a word, grooves deepening in her forehead.

"Maximillion hates me," Isadora finished, meeting Lucey's even gaze. "Or he fears me. I'm not sure which."

"An odd situation," Lucey murmured, "but Charles is right, you know. I don't know politics as well as Maximillion, but I do understand witches fairly well. The Network can't afford blind spots, and having a woman on the delegation would eliminate one."

"You think I was right to go?"

Lucey pressed her lips together, gaze narrowed, face peaked. She tired quickly these days. "Maximillion may be irascible and irritable and high-minded, but he's also a man of deep conviction. When Charles says Maximillion refuses because he cannot protect you, I believe him."

The slight edge of chastisement in Lucey's voice made Isadora curl into herself a little.

How could that even be true? Her lips burned as she recalled their sudden, passionate kiss.

"Maximillion is . . . not an *easy* witch to understand or love," Lucey said with affection in her voice, "but he is someone who deserves the benefit of the doubt." She put a finger under Isadora's chin and lifted it. Her nostrils flared as if the touch pained her. "You're doubting yourself, aren't you?"

"Yes," Isadora breathed. "I may have made a terrible mistake."

"Do you want to keep your family safe?"

"More than anything."

"Do you want to stop this war?"

"Who doesn't?"

"Do you trust Charles to make the right decision?"

"Ah . . . yes. I-I actually do."

"Would it be exciting for you to see the Southern Network?"

"Of course."

Lucey smiled, stepping back. Some of the color came

back to her face. "Consider those things when you doubt yourself. Besides, this may be the only way for you to truly protect your family."

"What about Sanna? The Dragonmasters?"

Lucey swallowed and leaned against a wooden fence. Her legs trembled. "Give Sanna time and space. She'll come around once things settle down. Now that they're at the circle of the Ancients, I hope more peaceful days may come."

"You think so?"

An expression of amusement crossed her face. "Should *you* be asking me?"

Isadora managed a short chuckle. The paths had showed nothing encouraging. She'd certainly looked.

Even after all this time, even with her newfound power, the wisps still didn't always make sense to her. They shifted, ever changing, prone to the strange whims of choice. As if they weren't *really* meant for this kind of thing. As if there was more to the magic. And so Isadora had avoided the paths, opting instead to explore her other ability—to see witches, discern their strengths and, by extension, their weaknesses.

Lucey's eyes drooped as she battled a yawn.

"Thank you, Lucey. You should go home, get some sleep."

"My pleasure. Tell Maximillion to answer my letters if you get a chance. I've missed going on missions with him."

A TEACUP, cracked down the middle and chipped at the lip, sat in Isadora's hand. She stared at the swirling purple petal design around the edges, thinking of Mam.

Her paints and beloved dragon-eggshell teacups were long since destroyed in the fire that had consumed Anguis. But the dragons still had hatchlings. They could always make more.

"Isa?"

Pearl's kind voice drew her out of her reverie. She glanced up, startled to see Pearl standing only a pace away, a concerned expression on her face. Isadora smiled and set the half-full teacup back down on the table.

"I'm sorry, Pearl. I'm just . . . preoccupied."

Late sunlight slanted through the windows at Pearl's house, warming Isadora's hair. The rain had cleared, leaving a damp chill in its wake. The last of the leaves drifted off the tree branches, fluttering to the ground, despite the time of year. Summer had only just ended.

Isadora sank into the chair across from Pearl, who peered at her over the rim of an empty coffee cup.

Pearl had only two chairs. The other three had been sold, along with her best tea set and dresses. Today, she wore a threadbare, long-sleeved dress with stains down the front. Soft gray curls framed her concerned face.

"Something happen?" Pearl asked.

"Just . . . thinking."

"Oh well." Pearl sat back, eyes shining. "Do share. A hot bit of gossip, perhaps? A quarrel with a lover? Do you have a crush on someone?"

Isadora chewed on her bottom lip. "Pearl, have you heard of Taiza?"

"The city of Watchers in the South?"

"Yes."

"Only in rumors."

"Do you know anything about it?"

Pearl shook her head slowly. "Not that I can think of.

Max has a copy of excerpts from *The Ronan Scrolls* that mention it. Believe that's where I first read about it."

"Me too."

"Why do you ask?"

"Don't know," Isadora murmured, purposefully leaving out the mission to the South. "Just can't stop thinking about it. Do you think it might still exist?"

If she were going to the Southern Network anyway, it seemed a waste to not search for the lost village of Watchers. To see if anyone still lived there, or if ruins existed, remnants of information.

"Ronan lived so long ago. Centuries. I doubt it, but . . ." Pearl trailed off for a second, gaze narrowed. "There's a chance I could find out. I've been transporting to the Great Library of Burke for more romance scrolls—the good gods know they have thousands of them. There's a librarian there." Her cheeks flamed a bright red. "He tends to help me out every now and then."

Isadora reached across the table. "A romance, Pearl?"

"No!" she said, squeezing Isadora's hand. Her own was warm and soft. Then she stood up. "Not yet, anyway. Oh! I almost forgot. I must get ready. Are you coming to the BLAUS meeting tonight?"

Pearl bustled into her almost-empty pantry without waiting for a response.

BLAUS. The Berry Literary and Upholstery Society. A monthly meeting that acted as a front for local Watchers. Isadora had been an active participant for the last six months in her desperate bid to learn as much as she could about her power. BLAUS members were Pearl's most devoted friends, but possessed little power themselves.

"Not likely able to come tonight," Isadora said. In fact, she didn't know *what* she was supposed to do next. Would

Maximillion send word? Come fetch her? When would they leave? She shouldn't have departed so quickly after agreeing. "I need to go home for a bit and . . . talk to Sanna."

"Not even enough for a cup of tea," Pearl said, frowning into an empty ceramic crock. Herbs she'd scrounged from the forest hung in dried parcels around her house, but tea only came from the Western Network. And the West had shut its borders to trade long before, effectively shutting tea out of Antebellum. Not even the bustling black market that had thrived during the wars could get tea this far north.

"It's getting harder and harder to meet, at least safely," Pearl said. "Any news from Max? Haven't heard from him in almost two weeks."

"I saw him this morning." Isadora sipped her tepid tea, her throat suddenly dry. "He seemed fine."

Pearl let out a long breath, shaking her head. "He's stubborn, the idiot man. Not a single word for me the last little while. Don't know why I put up with it. About drives me mad. Considering what he's been through though, I can't say I blame him."

"What *exactly* is in his elusive past?"

"It's not my story to tell. Suffice it to say that, when I found him on the street at thirteen years old, beaten to a bloody pulp and half-starved, he'd had a rather tempestuous history."

Picturing a scowling boy with Maximillion's chiseled features wasn't difficult. She'd seen something of his younger self in the magic before. Still, she struggled to imagine someone of his severity having been young. He seemed born a jaded, surly man. Pearl set several tins on her table.

"Wish I had something to feed them with, but herbs will have to do for tea. What are you—"

The gentle sigh of a transportation spell interrupted Pearl's question. Isadora glanced toward the front door.

Maximillion. His usual ice had gathered in his eyes during their short time apart. Ice . . . and something else.

"Maximillion?" Pearl asked. "Everything all right?"

Maximillion's gaze collided with Isadora's, but then he looked away. Isadora struggled to regain her breath. What was that raw intensity in his expression? He seemed . . . terrified.

"I apologize for my delay in responding to your messages, Pearl," he said. He glanced between Pearl and Isadora. "I've been busy."

"I know you have," Pearl said with a sigh, peering back at her herbs. "You always are. Anyway, how are you?"

Maximillion turned to Isadora, ignoring Pearl's question. An arc of fire stretched between them, setting her heart aflame. Her breath stalled so long she wondered if she would ever breathe again. In that time, his demeanor shifted. From uncertainty to something like fear, then back to the solid, steel wall he always had in place.

Pearl glanced up, seeming to sense the tension. She set her herbs aside. "Everything all right, Max?" she asked again.

"I came to speak with you, Isadora."

Isadora stood and put her hands on the back of her chair. The magic whirled in her chest, fluttering with bright intensity.

"Yes?"

Maximillion sucked in a deep breath, shoulders rising, and reached into his pocket. He pulled something out. A bracelet, braided with leather and glittering gemstones, dangled from his fingertips.

A shadow fell across his eyes, hiding the storm there.

"Isadora Spence," he said, "would you do me the honor of handfasting me?"

Isadora stared at Maximillion, dumbstruck.

An eternity seemed to pass between them. Surely she'd imagined those words forming on his lips. She blinked, dazed.

"What?" she finally whispered.

His nostrils flared. "I didn't stutter," he said, each syllable crisp with agitation. "I asked if you would handfast me."

"You must be mad."

"I agree."

She stared at the cord of engagement he held extended toward her. White diamonds sparkled along one edge, flanked by soft pink-and-yellow diamonds in the middle. An intricate metal filigree wreathed the space in between. The entire thing would have cost as much as a new home in Berry.

He'd lost his mind.

"Then . . . why?" she asked.

"It's the only way I will allow this ridiculous plan to proceed. There is no way to guarantee your safety unless I take you under my protection. Since you seem determined to be a nuisance, this is the next logical step."

She looked from him to the bracelet and then back again in horror. Handfast Maximillion? Tie herself to him for life to help her Network?

"This is insane."

"Don't tell me you've already planned your entire hand-fasting ceremony," he drawled with dark irony.

"No," she snapped.

"What, then? You want to handfast for love?"

She scrutinized him for any sign of amusement but found none. Handfasting for love, while romantic, wasn't something she'd thought much about. All Servants had married out of necessity. Her parents had been lucky with their deep affection and love. But she didn't wish to handfast out of political desperation. Certainly not to a witch that, on most accounts, seemed like he couldn't stand the sight of her.

"I-I didn't say that, either."

His gaze narrowed. Before he could attempt another guess, she stepped back. "It's impossible."

He withdrew the bracelet and tucked it into his pocket. "Fine. You may leave. I need to speak with Pearl."

Stunned, she stared at him. "Wait. That's it?"

His glacial eyes drove right through hers. "I have no desire to persuade you to handfast me. Still, you have been given the option. Without a handfasting, you cannot join the delegation."

"Charles will—"

"Not let you," he said coldly, speaking over her. "He and I swore an agreement this night. Without the protection of my name, you shall not attend."

Isadora's nostrils flared with rage. Of all the sneaky plans! He *would* go behind her back and make the arrangement with Charles that best suited him.

"You want to control me? Is that what this is about?"

"I assure you I have no desire to foolishly attempt to control a witch like yourself. I do not enjoy failing."

Pearl glanced between them, mouth slack, eyes blinking rapidly. Not a single word had escaped her lips.

Frantic, Isadora turned to her. "Pearl? This is madness! Surely you don't think that—"

"I'm not part of this, love," she said, training a long gaze on Maximillion. "This has nothing to do with me."

"You may have been Charles's first choice," Maximillion said, "but you are by no means the only witch I can take with me to the Southern Network. Your refusal is accepted. I have another witch to speak with now."

Something else flared in her chest at the thought. If handfasted, they would surely share a room . . . if not *other* things. Her throat swelled at the thought, and she gasped for air. But should Maximillion work so intimately with someone else?

Well, she didn't like that one bit, either.

"Pearl." Maximillion turned toward her. "Good to see you. I swear on my honor I shall return tonight to speak with you again."

"What would it mean?" Isadora blurted. "If we were to handfast, what would it mean?"

His glare met hers, sending a pulse of fire through her. How could her wits be so addled and yet so eager?

Maximillion drew in a deep breath, his shoulders lifting. "You and I would share a room. You'd attend functions with me as my wife, conduct meetings with the High Priestesses, and enjoy unparalleled access to all the comforts one could wish for. You'd be protected and taken care of during the mission."

Her cheeks bloomed with heat. She fidgeted with the end of her sleeve, unable to meet his gaze.

"Would we . . . that is . . ."

"Upon our return," he continued, ignoring her reluctant stammering, "we would obliterate the handfasting, as if it never existed. Charles has already agreed to sign to that as well. The only witches who need to know we were ever handfasted are those in the negotiation. And Pearl."

A relieved breath relaxed her entire body. Obliterating a handfasting was often a complicated affair, requiring the approval of a Council Member or a witch of even higher rank. Most handfastings remained intact. It was rare for witches to part, except on grounds of abuse. Even then, some wives were unwilling to lose the security of a home and food, even with their physical safety in jeopardy.

Isadora swallowed hard. The idea of going to the Southern Network had been daunting enough, but it was nothing in comparison to the greater challenge Maximillion had just given her. Being handfasted to him, with other witches scrutinizing their every move. They'd have to make it convincing.

"Do you really think you and I can make other witches believe we're handfasted?" she asked. "That we . . ."

Love each other enough to swear by it? The words caught in her throat. No one had mentioned love here, not even her.

She continued, "That we would have sworn that sort of commitment to one another? That would assume *some* affection between us."

Maximillion paused. "Not if you continue to blame me for the death of your father, no. This would require some work on your part." His gaze glimmered like a fire. "Perhaps some trust and forgiveness."

Isadora sucked in a sharp breath.

Another silence. Maximillion looked at his pocket watch. The *click* of it closing sounded like a crashing tree in the quiet.

Isadora looked away. Her thoughts moved slowly, as if greatly burdened. If the handfasting would be obliterated, this was simply another step in the whole plan. She didn't have to make it much more than that.

Besides, he had a point. Not only would being his wife give her certain liberties in society, sharing a room with him would feel safer. Her eyes traced his broad shoulders, and she gulped.

Or so she imagined.

She glanced at his face, rigid as ever, and wondered why he cared so much. Was his fear of failing strong enough to justify a handfasting? After all, he sought refuge from intimacy through his political machinations. Or did he simply take his role in the Advocacy so seriously that he protected her through his obligation to Watchers?

He looked at his watch again.

"I must—"

"I'll do it."

He froze, shoulders tense. Isadora drew in a deep breath and closed her eyes. The words felt strange in her mouth and sounded strangled as they came out.

"I'll handfast you."

His expression didn't shift. "Very well. Then I have only one request."

"What?"

His eyes held her in an intense, intimate way that she had no power over. "I ask only that you never lie to me. Guarantee me the truth in all things."

She held her breath, arrested by something desperate flittering over him.

"I promise."

Whatever vulnerability that had lingered in him disappeared.

"As do I. I shall make the arrangements. I can guarantee your safety as my wife, but only if you listen to me. If you act like a fool, you imperil yourself and the Network. In one week, be at my office in the morning, six o'clock sharp, for the official ceremony. We'll leave for the South thereafter, shortly after a debriefing session where I answer your questions regarding Serafina's plan. You shall receive a copy of it within the hour. Please, discuss it with no one. Pearl, you are welcome to attend as our second witness. Charles will be our first."

He transported away without another word. Pearl, staring at Isadora, fainted dead away on the floor.

7

S anna peered through prickly bushes coated with a sticky yellow sap that smelled like copper. Next to her, Luteis purred, his warmth especially tangible in the surprisingly cold air. The leaves had already fallen to the forest floor here. Her breath puffed out in clouds.

It appears to be a quiet witch village, Luteis said. *Though I have never observed so many buildings together before.*

Her stomach twisted in a thick knot. Anguis hadn't even been a village. The Servants had all lived far enough apart for privacy but close enough to respond to an emergency. When Talis had reigned, Daid had traded with one of five villages once a year, rotating so he only saw each village every five years. *Easier to be invisible if you're never known,* Talis had always said.

"Wish that had helped," she muttered.

What?

"Nothing, just talking out loud."

You remain. Are you afraid to leave the forest?

"Maybe." Sanna fidgeted. "I've never left it before."

This isn't really leaving the forest, just my presence. I under-

stand your hesitation to leave my indisputably greater strength, but you are still in Letum Wood. Also, your sister does it frequently.

"Don't remind me."

The sleepy village appeared indistinct in the early morning light, mostly blurry shadows. She had to study it for several minutes to see it all, craning her head back and forth to account for her narrowing vision.

Letum Wood surrounded the village on all sides, and they hadn't flown far enough to take them out of the forest and into the heart of the Network. Still, walking into a new place with unknown witches felt ... *wrong*, all the same.

"I wish I knew the name," she said, trying to plan out what, exactly, she would say. "Do you think there's even an apothecary here?"

I do not know such things.

"Well," she muttered, "let's hope there is. I can't lead the dragons into battle without better eyesight. Finding another apothecary is our only option."

Are you certain you can proceed without me?

"I'll be fine."

Be wary of your small, inefficient claws.

Sanna glanced down at her toes with a wry smile. She'd stubbed one yesterday on a root so badly it had cracked in the middle and started to bleed. Luteis had talked to her about it for hours afterward, unable to figure out the purpose of her toenails and why she *lacked talons*.

How do you know any witch will be more knowledgeable about eyesight than you? Or Lucey?

"I don't. But Lucey is gone all the time. I hardly ever see her."

Is the risk worth the reward?

"I'll be fine," she said. "Wait here."

He growled as she strode out of the woods, stumbling over a rock she hadn't seen. Her cheeks burned when he snorted. She slowed her pace, looking down with intention as she took deliberate steps. Walking seemed to take so long these days.

Without Luteis at her side, she felt naked in the open air. For his sake, she attempted to move with confidence, so he wouldn't worry.

Slowly, the darkness of the forest faded. The dry grass rustled as she waded onto a two-track road that led into the village, running between two rows of buildings—at least ten structures in total. The houses lay quiet, spitting columns of smoke into the chilly morning.

A female witch with jet-black hair stepped out of a building to Sanna's right.

Sanna stopped. The woman wore a bell-like, billowing skirt of variegated colors—made of all different pieces of cloth, like a quilt. Sanna kept her jaw from dropping. *Mori,* but did she wear ten skirts all piled together? There was enough material there to clothe all of the remaining Dragonmasters.

"Excuse me?" Sanna called.

The woman paused, glancing at her. Sanna remained too far back to read her expression.

"Yes?"

"Do you have an apothecary here?"

She paused, seeming to study her, then cocked her head. "Can't understand your accent. Say it again."

"Apothecary," she said, enunciating each syllable. "Do you have one here?"

The witch pointed to the end of the row of houses as if strange witches stumbled out of the forest every day. Then she disappeared behind the house. Sanna followed her direction, then frowned. *Which* building?

The red brick one, perhaps, Luteis said in her mind. *On the left.*

Sanna scowled, glancing back toward the foggy forest. *You're supposed to be hiding.*

I can't help it if your loud voice carries.

She felt eyes on her as she ventured forward, scanning carefully to watch who came and went. There weren't many —the village was very small. When she located the apothecary building, she almost ran into a wooden post sticking out of the ground, but caught herself in time.

Are you sure you can do this?

It was just a post, she snapped. *I'm fine. Why do they have that there, anyway?*

Witches are odd creatures.

Sanna walked up four rickety wooden steps, then paused, facing a brightly painted wooden door.

What now?

Did she walk inside? Rap on the door? She hesitated. Several candles burned in the shop window, warming it with buttery light.

You are well? Luteis asked. *You have stopped.*

Not sure what to do.

Enter?

I think so?

The door sprang open, causing a little bell to tinkle. A witch stood before her. He had warm eyes. A long mustache drooped all the way to his chin, despite his shiny, bald head. Sanna stepped back, nearly stumbling down the stairs. He reached out, catching her.

"Need an apothecary?"

"Y-yes."

Standing this close, his curiosity was apparent as he studied her, her hair, and her pants.

"Right. Come in."

THE APOTHECARY FOLDED his lean arms over his chest. Hints of body odor lingered in the air, amid stronger smells of marmalade and tincture of poppy. He wore a white shirt, which helped him stand out amongst the flickering shadows. Deep grooves lined his forehead as he studied her.

"Merry meet," he said.

"I . . . I'm not supposed to be here," she said, immediately regretting it.

Talis does not exist to prevent you anymore, Luteis muttered. *It is your right to go wherever you want.*

Sanna brushed that aside. Still. Too many things she couldn't control here. What if he started asking questions? What if someone saw Luteis? She had enough on her plate with Prana.

"Then why are you here?" the apothecary asked.

"Because I need help. I ate some kind of plant in the forest. And now I can't see very well."

A horrible lie.

"You ate something, and now you can't see very well?" He straightened. "That's a new one."

"It's true!"

His gaze narrowed. "Where are you from again?"

"The forest."

He rolled his eyes. "We all are. Your accent is different."

She clamped her mouth shut.

After a long moment, he sighed. "Fine. Follow me. I'll do an eye exam and see if I can figure this out. The eyes are a

separate system from the stomach. Doesn't make sense.
Now, if something had *fallen* into your eyes, that would
make sense."

He waved. Sanna followed him out of the room, through
an arched doorway. They passed through a hall, then
stepped into another room, this one more dimly lit. She
scanned it left and right to clearly see everything inside,
then ventured in.

"Have a seat just there on your right. Tell me more about
this poison you . . . ate."

"Ah . . ."

She couldn't very well tell him that she'd been riding on
the back of a forest dragon when hit with the acid of a
mountain dragon. That would stir up questions. Specula-
tion, too.

He tilted his head. "It *was* a poison, correct?"

"Maybe an acid."

"You ate an acid?"

"No."

"So the acid . . .?"

"Hit my face."

"Of course. Is there any reason you're being taciturn?"

"What's that mean?"

He sighed. "Never mind. You have scarring over your
eyes, which tells me you were probably hit there."

Sanna fidgeted. "Maybe."

"Let's just have a look at your eyes, then."

Without warning, he grabbed her face with his cold
fingers, put his thumbs on her cheeks, and pulled the skin
down. She jerked back, throwing a fist. Her knuckles
connected with his shoulder.

He let out a cry and seized her wrist. "Calm down!"

"You can't just grab me like that!" she said, curling away.

Do you require me? Luteis asked, his voice pitched with concern. *I can have the building on fire in five seconds.*

No! I'm fine. Stay.

"You're twitchy, aren't you?" the apothecary said, hands held up. "I said I was going to look at your eyes!"

"I didn't know you'd grab my face!"

"What did you think I'd do? Now, calm down and let me try again."

Sanna folded her arms tightly across her chest and only slightly flinched when he took her face again. His eyes came close to hers, staring deep into them as if he wanted to find something at the back of her brain.

"No redness," he murmured. "Equal dilation. Can you see my hand?"

He leaned back, poked, prodded, held a candle near her face, and asked how many fingers he was holding up in various positions. By the time he finished, her head throbbed.

"Can you fix it?"

"No."

She reared back. "No?"

"We can try a poultice," he said as he turned on his heel to rummage through a cupboard behind them. The clink of glasses followed.

"I've tried herbal poultices. They don't work."

"Might you didn't try the *right* ones," he muttered tetchily. "The eyes are very delicate. We could do drops of some kind."

"I've tried those too. What about magic?"

Asking for someone to use a different magic to heal her was surely a testament to her desperation. Isadora spoke so highly of common magic and the healing magic she saw at the camp where she and Lucey worked. Surely, there was something he could do. Some spell to reverse this damage. A healing incantation or . . . what did Isadora call them? Blessings?

He grunted as he pulled a book off the shelf behind him.

Her breath caught. How hadn't she noticed an entire *shelf* of books? Isadora had mentioned something like it before, but it had seemed too incredible to believe. The entire village of Anguis collectively only had a few books in the school before it all burned to the ground. Nothing like this.

"Magic . . ." he said. "Maybe for degenerative healing issues, but not acid. If I do the wrong spell, it could react badly. Worsen it."

Lucey had said something vaguely similar, if she remembered correctly. Her hope that he had new information had been in vain.

"So you won't?" she asked.

He shook his head. "Not for this. The risk is too great. We could accelerate your vision loss."

Lucey *hadn't* mentioned that. Sanna frowned. "What about a healing blessing?"

"Too late for that."

"Then what?"

He blinked, staring at her. She scowled. "I'm just supposed to . . . do nothing?"

"Well, yes."

"I don't like that."

"I'm sure you don't."

"There has to be something we can do."

The apothecary drew in a deep breath, glancing at his herb counter again. "I'm sorry, but there's nothing to be done. I've seen something like this before. The eyes are special."

"Has anyone ever stopped it?"

"You can't control this process. The eyes will do whatever they do. You could wake up one day and the vision may just . . . be gone. Or it may take time. You could have years, or days. More than likely you'll see a slow deterioration. Like a tunnel closing in on your main vision. Darkness may be more difficult."

Sanna's nostrils flared as she let out a long breath. Everything he said was already happening. Several awkward moments stretched between them.

"Right," she murmured, attempting to keep the tremor out of her voice. "Then thank you for your help. I . . . I had to know. How can I pay you? I don't have currency."

He paused. "Free," he said, waving a hand. "Don't worry about it."

"Thanks."

Grateful she couldn't see his expression, Sanna stumbled out of the close little shop and back into the sharp air. It roused her, and she stopped to pull in a deep lungful. Shaking her head, she slipped into the alley between his shop and the next. Only a few paces from the back door, Letum Wood began again. Gratefully, she vanished into the trees.

Luteis was waiting anxiously for her in the same spot she'd left him. She settled onto his back, pressing her face into his scales. His heat zipped all the way to her bones.

She'd just have to figure it out.

Promise me one thing, she said, *and we'll leave this matter closed.*

His ears perked up. He paused as if comprehending that she never wanted to speak about losing her eyesight again.

Anything.

If I can't see when we fight Prana—

I will be your eyes. Forever.

Sanna closed her eyes, let out a long breath, and whispered, "Thank you."

EXCEPT FOR LUTEIS AND ELIS, Sanna felt as if she spoke only to the trees.

"The battle of the goddesses occurs on the first day of winter, in less than three months. Until that time, we prepare to fight."

The words *for our goddess* stuck in her throat. She couldn't bring herself to say them.

The forest dragons lingered back, barely out of sight but intently listening. Their chatter ran quietly through her mind in fits and snatches, mostly indecipherable.

Why should we fight?

The goddess can fight her own battles.

We cannot lose any more dragons.

We are not ready.

Elis admitted to Sanna that Deasylva had spoken to almost all of them individually. A relief that she didn't have to break the news entirely. Especially after Talis, she didn't want to be Deasylva's only source of communication.

Still, the dragons didn't like it.

Sanna allowed them to vent their shock and annoyance while she listened. Most of the forest dragons still felt ambivalent toward Deasylva, though all had stopped denying she existed. Memories of Talis had started to fade, but not far. His legacy always lingered just out of sight.

"The sea goddess, Prana, has declared her intention to invade the land," Sanna continued when the surge of agitation began to wear off. "She wants power over land as

well as sea. The first day of winter is the height of her
power."

And if we don't fight? Elis asked.

"Then Prana will take over all of Antebellum. If you
aren't killed in the battle, you'll be drowned or forced into
subjection. If Prana floods the land, Antebellum as we know
it will be gone."

Silence followed.

Too dramatic? she asked only Luteis.

He sighed. *The truth often is.*

How is this possible? Elis asked.

The same question lingered, unanswered, in the back of
Sanna's mind. Why *would* Prana do this? "I . . . don't know.
Not exactly."

Grunts rippled through the forest before another burst
of outrage.

A sea goddess on land? It cannot be.

*It must be the dragons that fight? Leave the goddesses to their
own battles.*

She would rule us, *and therefore the land,* said Gellis. *The
High Dragonmaster is correct. We must fight for our lives and the
lives of our hatchlings.*

A dark shadow moved when Cara and Junis shifted out
of the trees. Sweet Cara, with her gentle eyes and missing
wings. Nothing but two stumps rested on her back now, the
wings extracted and burned off after Talis broke them.
Luteis moved closer to her but said nothing Sanna could
hear.

Cara's sad eyes lingered on him, then darted to
Sanna.

Grief had haunted Cara since she'd lost Rosy, her
youngest hatchling, in the battle against the mountain dragons. Sanna becoming High Dragonmaster over the moun-

tain dragons had carved an inexorable chasm between her and Cara.

One Sanna desperately wished didn't exist.

The rest of the dragons quieted. Cara commanded undeniable respect amongst the brood. Once an outcast, she was now lauded as the most trustworthy in the fickle way forest dragons had of throwing around loyalty. Cara paused, testing the silence. Her forked tongue flickered between her scaly lips, as if she were tasting the air.

Is it true? Cara asked Luteis. *Has it come to this?*

Luteis kept his gaze level.

Yes.

Then there is no choice.

Cara's sides heaved. Her gaze lingered toward the east, where Rosy had fallen.

I will fight. Cara's voice rang with resonance. *In honor of my hatchling in Halla, and for my hatchling that remains. But not for any goddess.*

Cara couldn't fight. She had no wings to take her to the West, but Sanna choked off the words. Luteis could tell her later. They needed her support now. A chorus of excited murmurs followed Cara's declaration, pulling Sanna's attention back.

Perhaps unwittingly, Cara had done her a great service. At least some dragons would make the decision on their own now, easing her job. The tone of the exchanges in her mind shifted entirely, and Sanna frowned.

All of them must fight, but they'd need time to get used to it. This would be the best moment to back away and let them ruminate.

High Dragonmaster, Luteis said, his voice reverberating in the strange echo that meant he was speaking to all. *Have you any further need of us now?*

Sanna cleared her throat. "Preparations begin tomorrow. Elis and I will make a plan for all forest dragons to strengthen their flight endurance. We'll have to fly a long way to the West, over the space of four days. More distance flying, work with the Dragonian magic between dragon and rider, and . . . more. Thank you for—"

Something large dropped in front of Sanna. She shouted, unsheathed her knife, and leapt back.

Tenzin, a desert-dragon messenger that often worked for the nomad Tashi, stared at her from less than a pace away. She should have been used to this by now. Metok popped in and out constantly.

Still, the strange ferocity in Tenzin's eyes sent a little shiver through her. She hadn't seen him since right after Daid died.

Several forest dragons hissed, advancing from the shadows. "I know him," she called, lowering her knife. "It's safe."

The forest dragons ceased their rampage. Sanna let out a long breath. "Tenzin, always good to see you."

The desert dragon narrowed his eyes but said nothing. He stood stock-still, nostrils flared. The forest dragons slowly shuffled away. A round contraption on Tenzin's neck shifted in a breeze. Sanna paused. Last time she'd seen Tenzin, Tashi had been with him.

She approached confidently. Tenzin eyed her but issued no growl or warning snap, so she continued.

"Good dragon," she murmured.

As she approached, he lifted his head higher, allowing access to his throat. She reached up and grabbed the circular contraption. A small latch at the bottom, wrapped in twine, protected it. She undid the knot and pulled the twine free. The bottom fell out, releasing a piece of parchment so thin she could see the silhouette of her fingers through it.

Tenzin immediately slipped back.

She held up a hand. "Hold there, my friend. I may need to send a reply."

Tenzin paused.

Sanna unfurled the parchment.

HIGH DRAGONMASTER OF THE FOREST,

YOUR PRESENCE HAS BEEN REQUESTED *by the sea-dragon sire, Yushi. He wishes to discuss recent developments between land, ocean, and sky.*

YOURS IN SERVICE,

Aki

SHOCK RENDERED HER MOMENTARILY STUNNED. Yushi, messenger of Prana. She'd met him once last year, while visiting the West. He'd tried to convince her that Selsay was the problem.

Sanna read it twice, once to herself, once to Luteis. "Land, ocean, and sky?" she murmured. "What does that mean?"

Your somewhat-recent acquisition of the mountain dragons, no doubt, Luteis said. *Or something to do with Prana.*

She flapped the paper back and forth. "Should I go?

This doesn't exactly seem like the best time to leave, considering . . ."

You'd be a fool not to.

Sanna reached down, grabbed some mud on her fingertips, and scrawled *YES* across the back of the paper.

Tenzin twitched when she gently shoved the letter back into the canister and secured it. The second she stepped back, Tenzin dashed off running before he rose into the air and disappeared amongst the branches. Sanna watched him go with a sigh, then turned around.

Elis? she called.

Yes, High Dragonmaster?

Let's get started on training. Luteis and I need to go to the West. You and Jesse are in charge while we're gone. Notify me immediately if you need something. Metok can send reinforcements from the North.

Yes, High Dragonmaster.

I sadora stood on the porch at Mam's, her heart a swirl of emotion.

Darkness enveloped the forest, cloaking her in shadows. A cool breeze trickled by, shifting the leaves far overhead in a rustling song with the promise of winter. Yellow, coin-like leaves already covered the dirt.

Isadora stepped back inside, quenching her terror for the day ahead with a hearty dose of guilt. She hadn't told Mam the details. Only said she had an *errand of mercy* to run on behalf of the Network that would take several weeks. She'd send more details later. Food too, hopefully.

Sanna had been busy with preparations for the battle against Prana, discreetly slinking around with Luteis and not saying much. Mam and Elliot had been inventorying their traps as winter approached.

All had proved distracted.

Mam's gentle sighs didn't waver as Isadora walked past her room, into the back where she and Sanna had been sleeping. The bare, rickety skeleton of this old house felt strange to her, even now.

Isadora stopped in the doorway, wishing Sanna were there. But she'd left unexpectedly. Something about the West. Sea dragons.

Battles to fight.

Isadora let her fingertips rest on Sanna's blankets, hating herself for feeling a sense of relief. If Sanna weren't here, she couldn't say *alay*. Couldn't part with angry words. Instead, they'd just separate quietly until their lives could come back together again.

If they were to ever repair their fractured bond, it could only happen once the Dragonmasters—and the world— found peace. Isadora couldn't aid that safety or peace here. She had to go where she was of use. She couldn't even merge with a dragon and fight alongside the Dragonmasters. None of the dragons would tolerate her, though they watched her, drawn to her power.

Dragon memory ran long, even with fickle loyalty.

"I'm sorry," she whispered to the air. "I must go. This is the only way I can help protect you."

She hesitated, torn between duty and desire, until the shuffle of boughs outside caught her attention. She couldn't stay any longer. Maximillion wouldn't take tardiness in stride on their handfasting day.

She gulped at the thought.

With trembling hands, she scrawled out a message with the last of Mam's mulberry ink.

I'LL SEND *word as I can. All my love.*

—ISA

. . .

With nothing more than a shawl on her shoulders, she stepped back outside. The cool air settled around her. New resolve filled her chest. Sanna might not understand now, but one day she would.

As she stepped off the porch, a rustle came from nearby. Darkness in a long, lithe shape glided out of the trees, accompanied by a rush of heat. Isadora stared into Elis's wide eyes. Jesse stood at his side.

Her breath caught in her throat. For a long heartbeat, the two of them stared at each other.

"Please," she whispered, "take care of them for me."

Elis closed his eyes and bowed. Jesse opened his mouth to ask a question, but Isadora transported away before he could get it out.

Despite the early hour, servants were already bustling through Chatham Castle.

The old stone bulwark seemed to never sleep, always humming with energy. The scrambling hubbub of the castle comforted Isadora. Something, even when all else seemed in chaos, remained steady.

Outside, a bruised darkness lingered over Letum Wood, interrupted by fingers of fog that stretched into the trees. Light trickled slowly from the distant sky, dimmed by the thick, overcast smudges. Nearly the second month of fall already, and constant cloud cover had overtaken the world.

Isadora stared at her reflection in Pearl's hand mirror, hardly recognizing the pale witch it reflected. Gilded ivory edges carved with vines, flowers, and chubby forest sprites encircled the looking glass. Isadora swallowed hard, noticing the faint, bluish skin under her eyes that made her look tired.

"You're a lovely bride, you know." Pearl patted Isadora's shoulder. "So lovely. I'm honored to be here with two of my favorite witches on this . . . *historic* day."

Isadora smiled, then set aside the mirror, a heavy pit in her stomach. Maximillion had provided a handfasting dress. Simple but elegant, with a layer of *linea* over several layers of silk. The gentle robin's-egg blue drew out Isadora's eyes, highlighting their color differences.

"Are you all right?" Pearl asked, studying her in concern. She stood an arm's length away, brow knotted.

"Yes, of course."

Pearl patted her arm again. "It's going to be all right, Isadora. Surrender to what will be. Oh! Oh dear. No one put lavender in the doorway. Excuse me, but I'll be right back. Can't be handfasted without lavender over the door."

Pearl disappeared, giving Isadora a moment alone in Maximillion's office. *Surrender to what will be.* A heavy ask for a Watcher that could, technically, see it all.

The quiet place, filled with books and not a speck of dust, seemed to buzz around her. Subtle hints of Maximillion lived everywhere—vetiver in the air, stuffy leather-bound books, piles of paperwork.

"I'm a poor substitute for a mam," a familiar voice said, "but I would love to be with you today."

Isadora spun around to find Lucey standing in the doorway. Her face was pale, her expression drawn as if she had a headache, but a hint of a smile lingered on her face. Isadora's heart pattered a little faster, and she threw herself into Lucey's arms with a cry.

Lucey winced but caught her, clasping her tight. "Goodness," she murmured. "Are you so frightened of him?"

Isadora bit her bottom lip to keep from crying, but the tears burned anyway. "Not of him," she whispered. "I just . . . I wish Sanna were here. My mam. Daid too. It's so silly— our handfasting won't last beyond this journey. But still . . ."

Lucey pulled away to tuck a stray piece of hair behind her ear. Her eyes, bloodshot with fatigue, held warmth. She cupped Isadora's face in cold, shaky hands.

"You're making a big step today, into a courageous unknown with a witch who is, let's say . . . *lacking* in typical social etiquette. He certainly can't be described as warm, which is a terrifying prospect in a husband. Even if it's only for a few months. Once this is over with, both of you will find your right match. This is, my dear, a mere formality. That's all."

Despite herself, a breathy laugh escaped Isadora. Lucey took Isadora's hand in hers, sucking in a breath through her teeth, then letting it out.

"Besides, who says your daid isn't here?"

Legends in Dragonmaster lore—what was left of it after Talis took over, anyway—spoke to a gauzy veil between this world and Halla, the place of rest where all Dragonmasters returned. On certain days, or during harrowing events, witches had reported their deceased loved ones appearing to them, to impart strength.

Isadora managed a trembling smile.

"You're right."

"You know, look at it this way. If things don't work out with Maximillion, you'll have a High Priest motivated to pay you a favor. And it could be worse. You could be handfasting Council Member Bray."

Isadora's nose wrinkled at the thought of the oily male witch with long, spindly fingers and creaking teeth. "Maximillion *is* handsome at least," she muttered. "I'll give him that."

"A fine concession," Lucey said, one eyebrow lifted. "The witch would be downright godly if he learned how to smile every now and then."

"Am I making a mistake?"

Lucey paused, studying Isadora's expression, then softly shook her head.

"Serving your Network is an honorable choice."

"Thank you," Isadora whispered. Her tears faded. "I'm grateful you're here. But . . . how did you know?"

"Maximillion. He asked me to come be with you this morning. I know," she added when Isadora's brow furrowed in surprise. "The man has a thoughtful bone in his body, if you can believe it."

A witch appeared in the doorway, flanked by several others. Charles, two Protectors, the High Witch of the Ashleigh Covens, and Maximillion, who stood as rigid as ever.

Maximillion wore a brown vest beneath a black blazer. A pristine white shirt, ironed to perfection, stretched across his broad shoulders beneath the jacket. The sweet scent of vetiver trailed into the room.

Downright godly was right. With his thick ebony hair, slightly curled, and those piercing eyes, she could hardly catch her breath.

The powers beckoned with a quiet swirl, but she ignored them. No seeing into the possibilities today. Today was just the present.

Charles hastened to her side, hands outstretched. "Merry meet, Isadora."

"Charles," she said warmly.

He took her hands. "Good to see you. You're lovely, you know. A perfect representation of our Network."

"Thank you."

"Shall we commence with business?" Maximillion asked.

Charles ignored him. "Do you have any last questions or needs? I believe Max has prepared everything, but I wanted to make sure *you* felt prepared."

Even though a thousand questions whirled through her mind, she shook her head. Revealing any of them would show just how in over her head she felt.

"No, Your Highness. I have no further questions. Thank you."

"The plan is straightforward," Maximillion said, stepping between them. Charles's grip released, and Isadora shifted back, nearly colliding with Lucey. "The trunks have already been sent and await us. You will need for no provisions."

"Thank you."

"As we discussed, Your Highness," Maximillion said, turning back to face Charles. "I will transport to update you as needed."

"Do what feels best, Max."

A scroll rose from Maximillion's desk and sped over to Isadora. "Your new history," he said before she could ask. "It's imperative that we have the same story. No doubt you shall be grilled about this kind of thing more than me. I stuck to the truth as best as I could."

His businesslike manner comforted her. A transaction— that's all this was. Isadora unfurled the scroll, relieved to fall into something solid.

· · ·

Isadora Spence

   Met: over a year ago, while on a walk in the woods.

   Handfasted: recently.

   Aspirations: to have children and support her husband on his career path.

She gritted her teeth and glared at him. A flash of what appeared to be amusement briefly flickered across his gaze, as if he knew exactly what she'd just read. Then it vanished. Isadora rolled the scroll back up.

"Well, then. On to business?" Charles asked, clapping Maximillion on the shoulder. Maximillion's nostrils flared, but he said nothing. He turned toward the High Witch of the Ashleigh Covens, a witch known for her discretion.

"We are ready to proceed."

Isadora's voice sliced through the air. "No, we aren't."

Maximillion turned to her, eyes narrowed. She met his hot gaze with one of her own. The fire building inside her made her tremble—she could hold it in no longer.

"A word alone, please?" she asked.

He hesitated a second too long.

Charles stepped back. "Lucey?" he asked, extending an arm. "I have some rather grumpy-looking plants I was wondering if you could help me with. I've found apothecaries to be a wealth of knowledge on proper care of plants, what with them composing most of your medicinals. These have absolutely stumped me."

Lucey shuffled forward, seeming relieved to step away. "My pleasure, Your Highness."

Everyone else bustled out. Isadora didn't tear her eyes from Maximillion.

"What is the meaning of this?" he asked coldly the second the door shut. "Second thoughts?"

"Can we actually do this?"

"Not if you're interrupting the proceedings every second."

Isadora threw the scroll at his feet. "You stuck to the truth? My aspirations are to have children and help my husband on his career path? Is that what you know of me? Is that what you *think* of me? If so, we're in for a very troubling journey. I cannot and will not pretend to be a witch I am not. To that, you must agree."

His reply stalled for half a second.

With a growl, Isadora began to pace, arms folded. "I'm exhausted and a bit traumatized by the rapid events of the past few weeks, but I can still convince myself to do this for the sake of the Network."

She sent him a sharp, sidelong glance. "I can convince myself that it will help keep my family safe. That it doesn't mean anything that you and I haven't spoken in months. Part of me can even believe you don't truly hate me." She stopped to stare at him, chest heaving. "But I cannot convince myself that we can pretend an affection that would convince anyone else we care about each other."

The muscles in his throat worked as he swallowed. "You think I hate you?"

"Why wouldn't I?"

His nostrils flared. "I see. Well, I am open to suggestions."

Her powers surged, refusing to settle. She winced as they careened through her chest, beckoning with an urgent whisper.

Be at peace, she said, pressing her fingers to her temple. *I am well.*

They settled with a sigh. Isadora drew in a deep breath. Meeting his hooded gaze cost most of her courage, but she forced herself to do it.

"I promised you the truth in all things, so I give it now. I absolve you of any guilt I placed on you for Daid's death. I was angry. Angry that he had been dead for weeks without me knowing it. Angry for what my family endured that I could have, perhaps, prevented had I been at home. The timing was a regrettable accident, and it was wrong of me to take that anger out on you. I apologize."

Some of the ire bled out of his shoulders. He nodded once, though she saw no softening of his expression.

"Forgiven."

Isadora refused to wait for an apology—he wouldn't give one. In fact, he didn't need to. He may have saved her life, and all those Watchers they'd liberated, by withholding that information. Still, his tone stung.

Dredging up the rest of her courage, she tilted her head back.

"Thank you. Now, if we are to proceed, I need some reassurance, however small, that you believe we can do this. That this isn't a doomed plan that will only drive us farther into our own entrenched opinions of each other."

Her heart slammed in her chest when something flickered through his gaze. Was reassurance what she really wanted? Was that what made her stomach tie itself in knots as she waited? Or was it something else entirely? Some other sign she desired from him. A hope of . . . something greater.

Something different.

Something . . . warm.

Maximillion paused before he stepped into her space. She didn't back away, holding her ground with the last of her resolve. When he stood only a breath away, his broad shoulders blocking the light of the windows behind them, he said, "If a handfasting must happen like this, you are the only witch I would choose."

Silence swelled between them. Isadora waited and, realizing nothing more would come, grasped his words with all the tenuous hope she had left. He didn't despise her, at least. It was a start.

"Thank you," she whispered.

He studied her, then stepped back. His cool facade slid into place, and he was again all business as he tugged at his jacket sleeves.

"Are you ready now?"

"Yes. You may call them back in."

Weighty reality descended on her when the rest of the party shuffled back inside. Lucey gave her a bolstering smile.

Isadora could scarcely believe she was about to be handfasted.

To *Maximillion* of all witches.

Conjuring an image of Sanna in her mind, she pulled back her shoulders. She had lived on La Torra by herself. Had been in danger of death many times and had patiently learned how to control magic far beyond her skill level. She would be called on for even greater acts of courage in the South and felt little fear over it.

Surely she could handfast a surly witch like Maximillion.

Isadora let her thoughts roll with undignified honesty, thinking over what he'd said. Over the compliment he'd given her. Perhaps the only thing moving her forward, beyond helping stop the wars, was sheer curiosity.

Who was he *really*? In close quarters, would he peel back the mask and allow her to see him as he truly was?

And why did she want to know so badly?

Charles reached out. "If you're ready, Isadora," he said gently, "we can proceed."

Maximillion lifted one eyebrow in sardonic question. His expression churned like a storm. Was there a hint of a challenge there?

"Yes. I'm ready."

Maximillion held out a bent arm. Isadora pulled in a deep breath and stepped forward, slipping her arm through his. The feel of his suit coat burned beneath her fingertips, as if she were holding a piece of coal.

The High Witch of Ashleigh turned to each of them, received nods of assent, and began the handfasting ceremony.

9

I n the Western Network, waves rushed up over the sandy beach, then folded back with a boiling hiss. The ocean threatened to reach her toes, but Sanna stood out of its reach.

She drew in a deep breath. Over half a year had passed since she'd stood on this spot of shore and first met Yushi. So much time had passed. She felt like a different witch entirely now.

Foamy gray clouds lingered overhead, covering the Western Network sky. The waves crashed with renewed frenzy. The peaceful calm of the beach she'd seen before was all but gone. A tempestuous shore greeted her now. Waves as tall as a witch pounded the sand.

Behind Sanna and Luteis stood the cliffs, sporting a thin trail from the beach to the top. The desert dragons lived in those cliffs, on the other side, facing away from the water.

Moisture lay thick in the chilly air. Even the desert had been cooler than usual when they flew across it. A distant storm filled the horizon with broiling clouds from the south to the north. It seemed to sweep in with occasional spurts of wind.

Aki, informal High Dragonmaster of the desert dragons, had motioned wordlessly to the ocean once Sanna had arrived. He stood far back now, blue eyes and rippling shoulders tense.

Are you ready? Luteis asked, looming just behind her. His sharp gaze remained on the water.

Not quite. Why do you think Yushi called me here?

I cannot begin to fathom why.

Hundreds of ideas came to mind, but none of them made sense. Last time, Yushi had tried to convince her that Selsay was the issue so that she'd make an alliance with Prana. Thankfully, she hadn't trusted *any* goddess.

Sanna abandoned the madness of her thoughts to focus on the task ahead.

When we go down there, she said. *I'll have to focus solely on Yushi in order to see his facial expressions. I may not be able to see much else. Will you make sure the water doesn't touch me?*

Why?

Just a hunch.

Of course. Unnerving element.

Then I'm ready.

I am with you, Luteis murmured.

Yushi awaited them, coiled in the pounding water. He straightened up as they started down a low hill. His red scales, adorned by a transparent emerald webbing that ran all the way up his spine, glowed in bright contrast to the waves. He didn't reveal his true size—his snake-like body extended into the water and disappeared in darkness. Those liquid ebony eyes stared right into Sanna's soul.

This was one dragon she *hadn't* missed.

Luteis growled deep in his chest as they approached. Sanna reached out, putting a hand on his leg.

It will be fine, she said.

I do not enjoy his presence.

I doubt even his mother would.

"Daughter of the forest," Yushi said, an unmistakable note of amusement in his voice. "You have returned."

"You called me here."

His eyes gleamed, sending shivers through her blood. "I did," he hissed. "Do you like riddles?"

"No."

"I have an easy one just for you."

"I don't care."

He paused to study her. "Then why did you come? To satisfy your own curiosity, perhaps?"

"For the dragons."

"The dragons." His gaze narrowed. "Most antagonizing to Herself. I find it delightful that you hate goddesses."

Sanna stared at him. He stared back.

"Aren't you High Dragonmaster over two races now?" he asked.

"Months ago, you tried to convince me that Selsay was the problem. I don't see any reason to trust you now, so forgive me if I ignore your questions."

"Regardless of where your loyalties lie, Selsay *is* a problem."

Sanna couldn't fault him for that.

She waited, hoping he wouldn't turn the conversation back to the mountain and forest dragons. The less she admitted to here, the better.

"Are you fond of Selsay now that you serve her?" he asked.

"No."

"And yet," he drawled, "you lead her most prized possession. How . . . interesting."

"Prana is the bigger issue."

He hissed, his eyes never leaving hers. "I agree. Herself has always been . . . tricky. Cunning. She is so even more now that her sisters meddle in her magic. It's her way, you understand, to wipe all life off of Antebellum to punish her sisters. They're tied to their land, so they are safe. We, however, are not."

Sanna's thoughts whirled back to her conversation with Deasylva. It sat heavy on her heart.

"You do not fear me the way others do, do you?" he asked. His gaze flickered over her shoulder, toward Aki. She wondered if his quick change in subject was purposeful.

"I don't know what others think about you."

He hissed again—a sound she assumed meant he was laughing. He slipped sideways in the sand, moving closer. Sanna resisted the urge to step back. He paused, something lingering in his expression. Curiosity, perhaps? A forked tongue slid out from between his scaly lips.

Unable to bear another moment near the water, Sanna said, "Tell me whatever message Prana has for me so we can leave."

"Why do you think there's a message from Herself?"

"Why else would we be here?"

"There is no message from Herself today, but I shall answer your question. You are here for *me*."

His clipped words betrayed him. His eyes darted to the side, then back. If possible, the waves seemed more violent than ever. Luteis shifted behind her, moving closer.

"What do *you* want?" Sanna asked.

"Much, of course," he said in an offhand way. "The same as any respectable sea dragon. Kelp. Pearls. To understand the true purpose behind the cycle of dragon deaths in the way of Dragonian magic. Massive, hulking sharks and their rubbery fins. Delightful. And, of course, freedom."

"Freedom?"

"How do you free a sea dragon?"

Sanna rolled her eyes. "I'm not answering your riddle."

"You didn't lie," he murmured, rising again. Did he ever stop moving? "You *don't* like riddles. Odd. Fine, I shall not reveal the answer. Freedom, foolish witch, is the yearning of every dragon." Yushi lifted his head, regarding Luteis. "Is it not?"

Luteis remained silent.

Yushi's inky eyes returned to Sanna. "And Dragonmaster? Isn't that your wish as well? You are as trapped as the rest of us in this . . . commanding magic. Magic created by a wayward goddess who loves to be a nuisance."

Sanna froze.

Did you know that? she asked Luteis.

No.

Yushi let out a gusty breath that parted the water in front of him. "Oh, you're surprised. You didn't know Prana made Dragonian magic."

The darkness in his gaze seemed to expand. Since he hadn't asked her a question, she gave no reply.

He blinked, the silence growing leaden. "And you have nothing to say?"

"No."

Another silence.

Sanna's mind raced. She *should* have something to say, but she couldn't form a thought to counter him. Her thoughts whirled too quickly, dizzy with what he'd said. Could he come here and speak against Prana like this? Was this true? Meddling sisters. Prana creating the magic.

"I sense something in you that's familiar." Yushi lowered his face, pushing closer to her. "You and I have something in common."

"I'd rather not know."

He hissed with his slippery forked tongue. His body moved sideways, backing slightly into the water. "You are a twin, are you not?"

Sanna frowned. "How did you know that?"

"I am one myself."

"So?"

He rose slightly, head tilted back as if affronted. "Do you not know the great honor it is to have a twin? Sea dragons aren't born alone. We share our egg with another dragon. A second half. A female to the male. Sea dragons are, together, complete."

Thoughts of Isadora flitted through Sanna's mind. She banished them. Doubtful the same applied to witches.

"Then where is yours?"

The scales of his forehead tilted down. He turned, looking out over the water to the west.

"Mushi is not here. I am left to roam free and serve our goddess's wild whims while she is captive. Held in the sea at Prana's desire, like so many of us."

Sadness colored his tone. Sanna bit back a sharp retort, startled by the shadows in his eyes. Did he actually mourn? Could a dragon like him feel love or affection? A fresh surge of water crawled toward her. Luteis reached for her, his tail around her arm, able to quickly tighten if needed.

"What is freedom to you?" she asked.

"Isn't it the same for everyone?"

"No."

His voice hardened. "Mushi is taken. Held captive in her

circular prison by dear Prana Herself until Prana gets what Prana wants. In the usual way of any goddess, of course."

"What does Prana want?"

"Revenge. They want, and they take. Does Selsay not prove this? Deasylva? Or did you volunteer for this position?"

Sanna hesitated. Selsay *did* prove it. Even her own goddess proved it, having given her the title of High Dragonmaster without asking.

A master is still a master, whispered Metok's voice.

Yushi grinned, almost maniacally. "You know I'm right, daughter of the forest. I can see the uncertainty in your . . . troubled . . . eyes. All witches strike me as dull thinkers. Worse, if you consider that they never ask the right questions."

"You didn't answer *my* question," she said. "What is freedom to you?"

"A lack of magic."

Sanna pulled in a deep breath. Like the desert dragons? She paused, allowing her thoughts to calm.

"You want me to free your twin, don't you?"

Water rushed over his scales. "Finally, the right question. I long for Mushi back."

"How?"

"It's a simple matter, really." He turned to face the waves, then glanced back at her. "For a witch like you? A little swim."

His fathomless eyes were nearly impossible to read. Sanna forced herself to stare into them, her mind whirling.

You cannot be considering this, Luteis said.

What if he's right?

What if he's playing a game?

"I would take you to Mushi so you can set her free.

There's not much work on your part, except for a few little . . . details that aren't incredibly important."

Sanna's jaw tightened. Yushi slithered closer until she had no trouble distinguishing the individual scales on his face. Her eyes ached from concentrating so hard.

"Give my twin her freedom, daughter of the forest, and the sea shall give you what *you* most desire."

"What's that?"

"Your eyes."

Sanna felt the breath pulsing in and out of her lungs, her heart beating, but for a moment she felt as if she lived separate from it all. How did he know?

Luteis tugged her back as the water rushed higher.

A sly smile slipped across Yushi's face. "I have startled you."

"She doesn't have that power," Sanna whispered.

"I didn't say Prana would."

All is not right, Luteis said as he pulled her away from the water again. It gushed closer, faster, with more power. She swallowed hard, thinking back to Anguis. To Talis. The high border around her childhood home that blocked out . . . all of this.

I know . . . but what if what he's saying is true? she asked. *Trapped dragons, held captive. I can't bear the thought.*

He knows your affection for dragons. He's playing it against you.

A pregnant silence swelled.

Luteis was right. Yushi stared at her with eyes a bit *too* intent. Studious. As if he were memorizing every movement of her face.

The ocean rushed higher.

But she was smarter.

"Goddesses are always surprising me," she said. "Particularly yours."

"Prana has been a trickster her whole life."

"Deasylva inhabits the forests—any of them. Where one or more trees are gathered, you can find her, if you look hard enough. Selsay has a similar rule with rocks, apparently. One little tree, one small rock, and the goddess can be there if she wishes."

"What is this unnecessary lesson for?" he snapped.

Sanna nodded to the foamy spray. "You expect me to believe you'd try to sabotage your goddess while she can hear every word you say?"

She leaned closer, so near his face she could smell the salt on his breath.

"Unlike other dragons," she murmured during a lull in the waves, "you are at a great disadvantage. You cannot leave your goddess. You must live in the water. She has total control over you, so what you ask is utterly impossible. I think you answer to Prana, and Prana wants you to kill me so the forest and mountain dragons are left vulnerable in the battle without a leader. How do you free a sea dragon, you ask? You don't. Because you *can't* free a sea dragon. You are chained to the very element your goddess controls."

Yushi studied her, oddly aloof. Her heart thrummed in her chest. Luteis's presence and tight hold on her were the only things keeping her alive, she imagined, when she saw the rage in Yushi's face.

"Then you can imagine," Yushi whispered, voice as hard as rock, "how frustrating our lives must be."

He backed away. When he spoke again, a current of something unreadable ran through his tone. "You have more intelligence than I expected, little forest witch. I assure you that murdering you was no intent of mine. Prana, on the other hand . . . let's just say she likes to test those she fights."

Another wave broke behind him.

"The war of the goddesses is two months away," he said. "You will never win, not even with two dragon races behind you. Dragons don't win wars; they win battles, and thereby deepen their own servitude. Rally your forces, little witch, and prepare for a massacre if you must. This is the cycle of history."

The waves retreated with him, the timbre of his serpentine voice making a horrible caterwauling sound. It took several refrains before she realized he was singing. He cut a vague figure against the flickering ocean as he disappeared.

Glints of color surged with the rolling waters. In them, Sanna thought she saw an army of sea dragons extending all the way out of sight.

AKI STOOD NEXT TO SANNA, peering toward the ocean with a troubled gaze. His eyes never left the water. They lingered at the mouth of a cave hidden in the high rocks. Sanna felt as if she were still at the edge of the surf, breathless.

"Sea dragons don't really all have twins, do they?" she asked.

"Not likely," Aki said, his thunderous voice low. "A story, I would imagine, to test if they could get you into the water and under Prana's power so she could drown you."

"You don't know much about sea dragons?"

"Almost nothing."

As she'd suspected.

A shudder skimmed her back, light as a feather, prickling her whole body with goosebumps.

"Do you think he's lying?" Sanna asked. "Do we stand a chance if the mountain, forest, and desert dragons fight against Prana?"

He frowned. "The desert dragons cannot be counted on in the battle. They cannot be compelled, like the forest and mountain dragons. The Dragonian magic is gone from them. Broken by Sarena herself, according to Avia. The desert dragons are nothing more than animals."

Sanna said nothing.

"What could she do to your Network?" she finally asked. The wind whipped her braid behind her. Desert dragons flew restlessly overhead.

"Consume it."

Sanna sucked in a sharp breath.

He didn't look at her. "It has already begun. The high tide is too high. The low tide too low for too long. Witches are cut off from the food that sustains them. Armies that defend us on land cannot get the sustenance they need. Storms blow constantly over Custos, our capital city. We are a desert people—our world is not made for moisture. Houses erode. Lives are lost. Eventually, the water will breach these high cliffs. When it does, it will follow the lower land and flood our cities. Destroy the desert dragons' homes."

His body seemed coiled, as if it took all his power *not* to move. He leaned farther into the wind, pushing against it.

"Yushi and I meet weekly." Aki dragged his bottom teeth over his lips. "Prana is a trickster and enjoys games. Every week, Yushi gives me a riddle from the goddess. If I return with it solved, I have bought time for my Network until the next week."

"If you lose?"

He gestured to the not-so-distant horizon, which

bubbled in clouds of tempestuous fury now. A distant crack of thunder rolled through the air. Despite Luteis's discomfort when he was wet, she fervently hoped for a storm.

"If Prana unleashes her fury, witches will die by the thousands. The ocean will surge upon us and never retreat."

"The storm?" she whispered.

"And it continues to grow, even beyond here. Others see it too. It is a sign of Prana's building impatience and power."

Or the end of the world, she muttered, thinking of all that water consuming the land. Luteis snorted.

Sanna's mind flittered to Isadora. Did her sister know about this?

Movement drew her attention. Two desert dragons wrestled each other in the air, snapping but not drawing blood. Without magic or deeper intelligence, they were wild creatures. Aki's position as High Dragonmaster was more tradition than anything. Without magical communication, he couldn't control his dragons.

Without magic, the desert dragons lacked advantage. Every race of dragon except the loosened desert dragons had some magical ablity. Mountain dragons could transport. Forest dragons had their secundum, a second fire that burned through almost anything.

Without magic, the desert dragons had nothing. They'd fall before the sea dragons or their magic, whatever it could do, in an instant.

I know almost nothing of the sea dragons, she said to Luteis. *And I hate that we have to fight them. They didn't ask for this.*

Neither did we.

Do we have a choice?

Doubtful.

Sanna frowned, turning her thoughts away from the

dragons. "Flooding the land is *one* way to control it, but surely Prana couldn't drown all the Networks."

"Can't she?"

Sanna sighed. She didn't know. The ocean certainly seemed vast enough for a watery baptism of the land. What good was the land if it was all dead? Why was Prana so angry with her sisters?

Aki's expression darkened. "I cannot maintain this forever. The riddles grow in difficulty, and I believe Prana grows impatient."

"You don't have to maintain it forever. Just until I harness an army and we defeat her."

He turned to her, incredulous. "An army?" he cried. "You can barely keep your own dragons from the brink of destruction."

"I'm going to stop this from happening."

"You can't stop a goddess! *They* stop *us*."

"I'll find a way," she said, her voice steel. "I'll build an army. I have two months. I can do it. I can find witches who will fight for us. Maybe creatures. The mountain dragons are ready for a fight yesterday. Maybe if we show up with enough force, she'll back down to save her dragons. Maybe it means *something* that I'm Dragonmaster over two races. That she was hoping to trick me into the ocean to kill me."

Aki, speechless, just stared at her. Eventually, he turned away, blinking.

How will you do this? Luteis asked.

By gathering every last dragon and witch that we can. Anyone willing to fight, even if we have to scour each Network.

The wars your sister speaks of have been extensive. Will there be anyone?

I don't know.

Remember that we will fight the sea dragons, not Prana. Like us, they bear the burden of their goddess.

We're not going to fight them unless we have to, I promise. But we have to plan for everything.

A plan, he said, *I regrettably agree with.*

She turned to Aki.

"Are you with me or against me?" she asked.

His sky-blue eyes studied her for several moments, easy to see against the darkness of his skin. "With you."

"Then I'll return before the first day of winter with an army," she said. "Prepare whatever witches or desert dragons you can. Send for me if you need anything. We'll come as soon as we can."

Aki nodded once and turned to leave. Sanna watched his retreating form, the powerful expanse of his back.

Where will we go to find your army? Luteis asked.

Where it will be easy to get our first addition.

A puzzled expression crossed his face.

Sanna risked one last look back at the water. Between gusts of wind and the hiss of waves, she heard a whisper.

Sanna.

In the distance, she imagined she saw Yushi staring at her, his eyes barely visible above the surface.

10

The moment the arduous transportation spell ended, the sharp scent of moldering leaves and snow welcomed Isadora to the Southern Network.

She opened her eyes to a muted garden of low, thick bushes. Understated flowers, a soft mauve in color, dotted the brush. Beyond, pine trees, clustered around a high stone wall, pierced a bright sky. A gentle wind sent a shiver down her spine. Hints of winter lived everywhere amid the faded colors and leafless tress.

A barren but lovely place.

The sheer number of South Guards in every open area left no doubt where she'd landed.

The sharp monolith of the castle sparkled like an ice sculpture. Thin turrets pierced the sky. Each facade glimmered with silver-and-blue crystals. She tried not to stare at the elegant towers, some interrupted by balconies, soaring at least fifteen stories high.

Long-distance transportation magic still muddled her thoughts. Several cleansing breaths later, she turned to find

Maximillion. He stood a few paces away, sharp eyes surveying the garden, entirely unruffled.

Maximillion looked at her. "Are you well?"

"Fine."

"First order of business is to get settled in our room." He glanced at her dress. "And have you change into something more appropriate. After that, you and I will talk logistics."

She suppressed the urge to smack him. Her dress was perfectly suitable. He held out a hand, his palm up. She stared at it for several seconds before understanding he meant for her to take it. Breath held, she slid her hand into his. As if on instinct, he interlocked their fingers, tucking her arm against his side.

Fire shot through her body.

"Don't forget," he murmured. "We're happily handfasted."

Unconvinced that Maximillion could be *happily* anything, she pasted a smile on nonetheless. "Of course."

"There you have it," Maximillion said, nodding. "The Southern Network. Doesn't look like much, does it?"

Isadora turned. The stone wall dropped away down a hill, leaving a view only partially obstructed by pine trees. From the bottom of the hill rolled an endless tundra of yellow grass. In the distance, she glimpsed a half-moon of forest, if the cluster of thick green trees could be called that.

Nothing hospitable here.

"It's quite . . . flat."

"And cold," Maximillion said. The wind whipped past them. "Let's find our way inside."

A fluid voice, like silk, called, "You have arrived."

Maximillion stiffened. A woman with dark eyes approached them. Her burgundy hair was swept into an elegant bun, and she wore an ostentatious dress, at least ten layers deep with different fabrics. Lace and jewels dotted her sleeves and neckline. Something in her manicured appearance reminded Isadora of Cecelia.

Isadora's own dress, that had seemed so elegant, felt absolutely understated in comparison. Perhaps Maximillion knew what he was talking about.

"Your Majesty," Maximillion said with a touch of frost in his tone. He bowed at the waist, straightening. Isadora curtsied.

The witch regarded them without any change in her curious expression.

Majesty was an Eastern Network title. This must be Serafina, High Priestess of the East and originator of their plan.

"It has been some time since we have seen you, Maximillion," she said. "I have missed your . . . lively discussions."

Isadora knew Serafina to be in her late fifties, but the witch appeared no older than thirty-five. Her presence commanded a quiet respect. The exact kind of trait one would expect in Dante Aldana's wife.

Not to mention her superb acting skills. If Maximillion hadn't informed Isadora that Serafina had snuck into the Central Network weeks ago to speak with him, she never would have suspected it.

"Lively," Maximillion drawled. "If one could call arguing for three hours over an open banquet lively."

"So long as it ends in drawn weapons," she said, eyes twinkling. "And a contingent of East Guards surrounding you, promising certain death."

"You have your husband to blame for that."

"Among many things."

With a demure smile, her gaze flickered to Isadora. Surprise registered in the depths of her umber eyes.

"I am delighted to introduce my wife," Maximillion said,

infusing a note of warmth that slid all the way to Isadora's belly. "Isadora Sinclair."

The merging of their names, like the collision of two worlds, nearly took Isadora's breath away. She hadn't thought of that yet.

Serafina's brows lifted. "Indeed? You are . . . handfasted?"

"I trust you to make her feel welcome. She's quite fond of long political discussions and tea."

Not entirely wrong.

Serafina blinked several times, her mouth open, before composing herself. Her dazed expression cleared. "Yes, of course. Well. I suppose I . . . I never expected you to marry, Maximillion. I am . . . it's my pleasure to make your acquaintance, Isadora."

She was puzzled by the High Priestess's shock. Was it his handfasting that surprised Serafina so deeply? Or something else? Perhaps Maximillion hadn't told Serafina the extent of his plans.

Isadora accepted Serafina's outstretched hands, allowing her to kiss both of her cheeks in a greeting meant to honor her as Maximillion's spouse. Maximillion watched, gaze sharp as a hawk, but Isadora ignored him. Even *she* knew not to touch the High Priestess unless invited.

"An honor to meet you, Your Majesty," Isadora murmured, curtsying.

"The honor is mine. Isadora, I will be happy to have you for tea."

"Tomorrow?" he asked.

"No," Serafina said. "Arayana has a tea then. We will find a time when the need arises." She turned to Maximillion, her voice quieter, sincere. "I wish you the best, Maximillion. You deserve all the happiness in the world."

"I'm not in the business of happiness. Are you the first to arrive?"

"Isn't Dante always?" she asked airily. "He's eager to get started and has been comparing historical proof for his one-ruler plan against Vasily's massive library. I came out here in search of Emilia, but she seems to have eluded me."

They strode toward the center of the garden, where a stone fountain bubbled with clear water. Leaves and decaying flower petals littered the ground beneath skeleton shrubs.

A cry came from the forest. "Mere!"

A young girl bounded to Serafina's side. Emilia, no doubt. Her youngest daughter, from what Maximillion had relayed before they'd left.

Emilia had the high cheekbones of her mother, softened with a girlish appearance, and bright eyes the color of chocolate. Her hair fell in lazy curls around her neck. She couldn't have been more than eleven.

Maximillion brightened. "Emilia," he said with a warm smile that nearly sent Isadora into shock. "Always a pleasure."

Emilia grinned. Instead of kissing his cheek, she held out an arm. Maximillion accepted it without hesitating, clasping Emilia's forearm in his own, the way they did in the Central Network.

A slow smile spread across her face. "I've missed you, Maximillion! Where have you been?"

"Busy saving the world. Emilia, this is my wife, Isadora."

Emilia accepted Isadora's hands and pressed a soft kiss against her right cheek. She pulled back, eyes shining. "You must be a special witch, indeed," she said, grinning, "to marry Maximillion."

"Who else has come?" Maximillion asked.

"Just us," Emilia said with the fluid confidence of her mother. Clearly, a girl born to this life. "Mere and I just arrived a few hours ago. But no more of that boring business. I have news."

"Already?" Serafina asked, appearing bemused. "What could have happened in the last ten minutes?"

"Pere has convinced Vasily to hold the welcoming ball tonight instead of tomorrow so that business will not be interrupted. The servants are in a mad rush. There's going to be dancing all night!"

"Of course he did," Maximillion muttered.

"He's quite eager," Serafina said with a pointed glance.

Emilia grabbed Maximillion's hand and twirled. He spun with her in a charming display of normal behavior that nearly made Isadora choke.

"I shall dance the night away," Emilia sang, releasing Maximillion to twirl, showing off the graceful pirouette of an accomplished dancer.

"You shall not," Serafina said firmly. "You have more protective-magic lessons to attend to with your tutor tonight."

"Mere!"

"She is determined to dance with you, Maximillion," Serafina said, brushing aside a lock of hair that had fallen into her daughter's eyes. "And you know she's my most determined child. Coming a week early, forcing me to stop and have her in the middle of a fairy circle in the forest. Couldn't be born on the water like the rest of my children."

"*Mere*," Emilia muttered, blushing. She followed it up with a rebuke in the lyrical Eastern Network language of *Ilese*. Serafina laughed under her breath.

"Forgive me, daughter."

"Emilia!" A high-pitched voice squealed from the trees to the left. "Emilia!"

Emilia wilted like a flower and groaned. "Not again!"

Serafina reached out, touching Emilia's face with an affectionate smile. "Just another hour or two, *mi amori*. Then I shall come and save you with another lesson."

With a long-suffering sigh, Emilia straightened, regaining her graceful composure. "Over here, Your Greatness," she called.

A chubby, red-faced child appeared from the trees, flanked by four frantic South Guards. Her thick cheeks nearly hid her eyes. She waddled over, flailing at her complicated dress, layers thick with lace and tulle.

"Emilia!" she shrieked. "Over here."

Emilia, shooting a hot glare at her mere, spun on her heels. "Hello, Zoya!" she sang. "I'm so glad you found me."

"Vasily's youngest child and only daughter," Maximillion said quietly to Isadora. "He has four sons that precede her."

Serafina watched her daughter disappear into the trees, pulled by Zoya's determined fist. The South Guards followed, awkwardly jogging to keep pace. With a chuckle, Serafina commenced walking.

"That must have been a long transportation," she said, casting a sidelong glance at Isadora. "I think we better let you rest in your room to prepare for the grand ball."

Maximillion nodded, placing a hand in the middle of Isadora's back. Her skin tingled where he touched her.

"It was good to see you again, Serafina. Give my regards to Dante."

Serafina's lips twitched, as if he'd told a joke. "Tonight, then," she said. "It was wonderful to see you again, Maximillion, and to meet you, Isadora. I am eager for our acquaintance to grow."

A SHORT, rotund maid escorted Isadora and Maximillion through a rear entrance, where the wall gleamed with fresh light. Had those been diamonds encrusted on the outer walls of the castle?

Isadora didn't know if she was more disoriented by the lavish decor or the feeling of Maximillion's arm across her back.

"Een here," the maid said. A bustling skirt billowed over her hips, bolstered by a rounded pillow beneath the material at her waist. She gestured toward a square wooden doorway. Maximillion guided Isadora ahead of him, and she ducked through.

"Eet ees very busy today." The maid clucked under her breath.

Servants bustled about in a mad scramble. Though short, the maid walked swiftly, forcing Isadora to hurry or be left behind. Maximillion strode behind her, greatcoat billowing. Silver statues of bare-chested women filled every nook and cranny of the halls.

"The High Priestess," the maid said, gesturing to a statue with a dismissive eye roll, "loves sculptures."

Rugs braided from something like coarse fur lay on the floor. The maid escorted them up a marble staircase just wide enough for one witch. Isadora rested her fingertips on the chilly balustrade as they climbed. The staircase spiraled into eternity.

"A good view," the maid panted, "for His Greatness's guests."

Red-cheeked and winded, the maid eventually stopped on the thirteenth floor. The top of this turret. No sounds carried from the madhouse below, casting an eerie silence in the space. Still catching her breath, the maid attempted a smile, half-hunched. One door awaited just off the stairway. She threw it open wide with a spell.

"Your room."

Maximillion advanced first, Isadora trailing behind. Her eyes widened.

Despite the thin staircase, the room was spacious. Sunlight poured in from windows five paces wide and slanted at an angle along the entire circular wall.

Across the room stood a sprawling four-poster bed with damask curtains hanging near each post. Opposite that, several armoires, a washbasin, and two broad cushions, as wide as Isadora's bed at home, sat on the floor. There were no divans or couches, only a broad table near the fireplace and a hidden tub and basin behind a screen.

"It's lovely," she said, turning to the maid. "Thank you."

The maid, beaming, bowed her head, bobbing back up immediately. "Lunch will be served shortly. Coffee and snacks on ze table. Thick *Yazika* coffee," she said proudly. "Strong enough to chew. Tonight, ze ball begins at eight o'clock."

With that, she swept out, and the door shut behind her.

Maximillion stood at one of the windows, gazing out. The light silhouetted his features, highlighting his now disheveled hair. Isadora passed a statue of a naked woman presumably washing under a waterfall, and peered out a window.

South Guards stood at sharp attention below, dotting the sprawling gardens. In the distance, a charcoal storm lingered in the western sky.

"Think this is how the birds feel?" she asked, breathless from the height.

Maximillion gave no reply. Isadora turned, and seeing

him in a narrowed-eyed haze, left him to his magic. She cast one last glance outside, then moved away.

A familiar trunk rested at the foot of the bed. Maximillion's. The three trunks next to it were, presumably, the ones he'd had packed for her. She glanced up at the bed.

Should she offer him half?

It was large enough to accommodate them both without requiring them to touch. But watching him brood by the fire made her think twice. Better to maintain boundaries and have him sleep on the floor, as he'd volunteered before they left.

Ignoring the bed—and the fact that this was their first true moment alone as husband and wife—Isadora crouched in front of her first chest. The buckles slid free under her hands. Tousled dresses lay inside the trunk, and she began to sort them.

"They searched it," Maximillion said, coming out of his daze. He shook his head, brow furrowed as he stared over her shoulder.

Isadora paused, halfway through the dresses. "But why?"

"Because that is Vasily. Paranoid, but wisely so. I anticipated it. There's nothing for them to find in there."

He reached into his greatcoat, pulling out several hidden scrolls. Serafina's plan.

Isadora hesitated, then continued combing through her trunks. Dresses of lace, linea, tulle, and silk, some even glittering with gemstones. The assortment dizzied her. Where had he found all of these?

"Dante had Vasily rearrange the ball on purpose, I'm sure," Maximillion murmured, pacing to another window.

Isadora straightened, gently closing the chest. "What benefit does tonight have over tomorrow?"

"Makes him appear eager for a resolution, perhaps."

"Maybe he is eager."

He frowned. "Dante Aldana's mind is complicated. He's unfortunately intelligent, which makes it even more tragic that he's committed to the one-ruler idea. All he needs to do is convince Dostar, and he'll have the vote."

"Vasily?"

"He'll go along with it, but put up a show of disagreement at first."

"How do you know?"

"A hunch."

"Is Serafina like her husband?" Isadora ventured.

"No. Quite different. More grounded. She has a deep love of her Network and law that he doesn't. Justice seems to be a forte of hers."

"An ideal High Priestess."

"Wasted in the East. She has no power and never will. She has as much sway in the East as a Watcher."

Clearly, if Serafina needed Maximillion to present her idea.

"Something we may be able to start overturning for Watchers everywhere."

He didn't contradict her, but she noticed he didn't agree. Instead, he passed the tray of coffee and pastries, reaching for a scroll tied by a piece of leather. His lips moved as he read it silently, then passed it to her with a spell.

"A schedule of events for the week."

Isadora perused it as he crossed the room. Nothing for her until the ball this evening, though an informal meeting over cigars and ipsum was taking place in the High Priest's office in an hour. She doubted the wives were invited.

"And what is Vasily like?"

"Stubborn," Maximillion said. "Like all Southern Network witches. But . . . not unyielding in the face of good judgment. Loves history. His wife, Arayana, knows nothing of Serafina's plan. Be discreet and keep it that way."

She chuckled at the haphazardly scrawled line, "*the ball will be this night,*" atop the crossed-out ~~Dinner With His Greatness.~~

An envelope appeared in front of Maximillion. Isadora caught a glimpse of Charles's sloppy handwriting before Max snatched it from the air and tore it open.

"I'm not sorry to be staying here for potentially several months, even if it is so many stairs," she said.

He made a noise in the back of his throat. Isadora touched the top of a pastry, startled when it dissolved into a pile of crumbs and sugar on the plate.

"They're meant to be dropped into the coffee," Maximillion muttered without looking up from the letter. "Trust me, it needs it."

"Oh."

Isadora tipped the plate, causing a sugary landslide into the delicate mug. With a tiny silver spoon, she stirred the black liquid, surprised to find it thick. The maid *had* said that, but she hadn't taken it literally.

She sipped it, grimaced at the bitter taste, then turned, cup outstretched.

"Here, try—"

An empty room greeted her. Isadora sighed. Not even his wife would know his movements, apparently.

She set the cup down, startled by the zip of heat in her stomach from the coffee. Her powers stirred, beckoning her. She dropped back onto the bed, stared up at the complicated tapestry stretched out above her, and gratefully dropped into a welcome sleep.

11

—————

Sanna slept through most of their seven hours of hard flight north.

Luteis's speed was almost breakneck, as if they were flying away from something instead of toward it.

Sanna started from sleep at Luteis's quiet words, *Metok has arrived.*

She turned, looking all the way to the right, to see Metok flying next to them. She'd summoned him hours ago with Selsay's totem, but he wouldn't meet with them until they'd crossed into the Northern Network.

Metok stared at her, easily maintaining Luteis's pace despite his smaller wings.

Metok, she said, straightening. *We need your help.*

Yes, High Dragonmaster?

I came to talk to the mams.

Metok showed no change in expression—a sure sign that she'd caught him by surprise. While she envied his ability to be almost unreadable, it counterintuitively gave him away.

Why?

"Because we're going to scare Prana out of fighting with us. If we can combine all of the dragons and maybe some witches, I think we stand a chance against her."

A glimmer of hope flashed in his eyes. *We are going to fight?*

"Hopefully not, but it's likely. I'm just preparing for our confrontation. You can pretend like you don't know where the mams are, but both of us know that's a lie. You are the oldest of all the mountain dragons."

He blinked once, then seeming to think better of disagreeing with her, said, *You are correct, High Dragonmaster.*

"Will you show me the mams without my commanding you to do it?"

No.

Something curled inside Sanna. She drew in a deep breath.

You must command him, Luteis said. *This is for far greater purposes.*

I hate doing it.

Leadership requires discomfort.

But was that *all* this was? Leadership? Or was it power masquerading as something noble? Like Talis? Sanna shucked the question off for later.

"Take me to the mams, Metok," she said. "I command it."

A burning tang of acid filled the air as he breathed out. Sanna held her breath and narrowed her stinging eyes.

As you wish, High Dragonmaster.

With his powerful legs, Metok tilted slightly more to the east. Luteis followed, and the silence of the high skies followed them.

I hated asking that of him, she said, feeling a heavy weight in her gut. *What if I have to do that again? What if I have to force the mams to fight?*

For the sake of all life on Antebellum, you must.

Sanna swallowed hard.

You're right. We must try.

THEY FLEW FOR HOURS.

Three other mountain dragons followed behind them, keeping their distance as they usually did. The mountainous terrain fell into craggy, treacherous depths far below.

Finally, Metok plunged downward through some wispy clouds. Luteis followed.

I have been almost this far north before, he said, glancing around with a huff. The air had grown thin, and she could feel the extra exertion in his lungs as he breathed. *When you were held captive by Selsay and Pemba. I believe I know where we are.*

Metok navigated through two peaks with an easy grace of flapping wings. As they rounded a tall chasm, Sanna's breath caught in the frigid mountain air. They flew into a ring of mountains exceeding the size of Deasylva's most gargantuan trees in the circle of the Ancients.

Luteis followed Metok, whose tiny form was nearly lost against these giants. In the midst of the foggy gray circle, forms flittered here and there, larger than Metok, but just as fast.

Selsay's most prized possession, Metok said. He settled on an outcropping of rock halfway up the closest mountain.

Sanna slid off Luteis's back, scanning frantically to take it all in. The peaks sloped down to open meadows, verdant trees, and a sprawling emerald lake.

"May Luteis drink?" she asked.

Metok paused, then motioned down with a nod. *As you wish.*

"Go," she said, nudging his flank. "I'm fine."

The mams may not be kind.

I'm not worried.

Your safety is my utmost concern.

They may not be kind, but they can't hurt me. I need you to be able to fly us home.

He hesitated only a moment longer, then shoved off the rock and plummeted straight down the mountainside in a testament to his thirst. The flock of mams thickened the air. They seemed to be throwing themselves out of the caves and into the chasm. Sanna waited, breath held, to see if they would come to her. They swirled like a flock of wild birds overhead.

They will not come until you call them, if you wish to do so, Metok said. *These mams have never met a witch before.*

Are they willing?

Metok didn't answer. Sanna reached out in her mind, into that open space that communicated with all the dragons. She refused to hesitate and appear weak before Metok, so she didn't give herself a chance to fear.

I am Sanna of the forest, High Dragonmaster of the mountain dragons. I have come to restore peace and safety. She threw a sidelong glance toward Metok. *To do that, I require your help.*

The frenzy grew, then vanished, leaving only empty sky.

Luteis? What's happening?

His response came several seconds later. *They are settling back along the rocks, watching you. There is one headed your way.*

Sanna saw the form coalescing. It surged toward her at a reckless speed, grower bigger by the moment. Metok shuffled to the side, leaving more space between himself and Sanna.

She sucked in a sharp breath, standing firm in her spot, as the massive form of an unswerving mountain dragon barreled right for her.

12

A cacophony of dresses hung around Isadora's turret that evening.

They were suspended by spells along the wall, glittering in gold, sapphire, mauve, and a burgundy that looked like wine when it moved. Their embedded gemstones sent rays of candlelight dancing across the walls.

Outside, the sun slanted toward the ground, sinking into the distant tundra like a ball of fire. The flames in the hearth sent out a cheery warmth while Isadora bustled around, pinning back her hair with the nervous feeling of a porcupine lodged in her stomach.

"Wretched corsets."

The gown she had finally chosen, a muted gold, shimmered when she walked. Long, sheer sleeves hugged her arms to the wrists, emphasizing the scooped neckline. A complicated web of lace and sheer fabric spilled down the front in rope-like designs, while vines curled through the waist. A train trailed behind her in a wide bell shape.

Utter elegance.

"Well," came Maximillion's dry drawl. "You clean up well."

Isadora spun around, the heavy fabric moving with her. He stood in the doorway, wearing a crisp black jacket that hung to his knees and a collared white shirt in perfect lines. He was freshly shaven, his curls a gleaming raven black. Her heart leapt into her throat. She turned away, wondering where he'd changed.

"You're an atrocious compliment giver."

"Does it fit?" he asked, eyeing the dress.

"Does it?"

"Hmmm . . ."

He studied her, eyes glittering, but said nothing more. Isadora patted the final strand of hair into the complicated chignon of curls that had taken her all afternoon and several spells to perfect. Pleased with the results, she turned to face him.

"Am I too decorated?"

"In the South? Impossible." He held out a bent elbow. "You shall see. Are you ready?"

"No."

Exasperated, he let out a long breath through his nose. "What now?"

"A compliment, please. A sincere one." She pulled her shoulders back. "I have a feeling you may need to practice how to give them."

"You . . . look lovely."

"A *real* compliment," she insisted. "If you cannot show me affection behind closed doors, I hold no hope for our performance during this ball. Like it or not, you shall have to dance with me, and most newlyweds have some level of affection while waltzing. A compliment would help me feel somewhat more inclined to like you."

"Not all witches marry for love," he countered, his jaw set in a stubborn line. "The marriages in this sphere are almost entirely political. You may see affection, but rarely love."

"I never said anything about love. We promised each other the truth. You can manage that now."

His cheek twitched, but he managed to say, "You are disarmingly beautiful tonight."

Fire soared all the way through her body. She nodded once in what was surely a pathetic attempt at disguising her liquid knees.

"You as well, Maximillion. You're quite handsome."

He ignored her, offering his arm again with an annoyed grumble. "If you please?"

Isadora accepted it. Her stomach roiled beneath her at the daunting thought of a ball packed with unknown witches, precise etiquette, and foreign customs she knew nothing about. Even if she didn't know it all, however, she trusted Max did.

That was enough. He'd see her through, if only because he hated failing.

And because, really, they *couldn't* fail.

"Very well," she murmured, shoulders set. "I'm ready."

HARRIED servants scurried back and forth as Isadora and Maximillion descended the final stairs. Instantly, a dozen pairs of eyes fell on them. Isadora drew in a breath—as much as she could with the corset digging into her ribs—and pretended she didn't notice the curiosity.

"They're not as scary as they look," Maximillion said.

"I'm not afraid."

He glanced at her out of the corner of his eye. "You should be."

"Well, I'm not. The good gods, you weren't joking. Look at this place."

The hall sparkled, teeming with witches all wearing layers of rare gemstones, silver, and gold. A fire roared to their left in a hearth large enough to dance in. Just outside the ballroom, a sweeping staircase led up a pair of unlit steps.

"One can never decorate more than the South," Maximillion said.

Isadora trailed behind him, eyes fastened on the luxurious adornments. Gemstones of every variety glimmered in the ballroom. Rubies. Garnets. Sapphires. Emeralds. They lined the punch bowl and glinted in the frames on the walls. A line of paintings depicting previous High Priests faded into obscurity down the room. Overhead, silk banners boasting the likeness of a polar bear rippled in the candlelight.

A silver-and-blue tablecloth lined a table that stretched all the way down the middle of the room. Silk napkins, folded like swans, graced each plate.

The chairs were upholstered with sapphire silk and inlaid with pearls. A simple reminder—not only did the South boast a plethora of rare gems, but access to the sea allowed them even more. The piping scent of roasted duck and orange sauce drifted on the air, mingling with the distinct scent of plum glaze and wine.

Isadora's stomach growled. Ages had passed since lunch.

"A ball worthy of the South," Maximillion said quietly. "Vasily has a habit of going a little bit too far."

"Like erecting a wall to keep the other Networks out?"

His lips tightened in a grim line. "Precisely. Dante is

known for extravagant balls. This surpasses anything I've seen in the East, which is no small feat and was certainly done on purpose. War notwithstanding, Vasily has had an abundant mining year, it would seem."

Isadora silently congratulated Vasily—she'd never seen anything so grand.

At the top of the room sat two chairs. The first, an imposing thing of gold and rubies, glinted from within a ring of torches. Vasily Romov, the High Priest of the Southern Network, stood near the elegant throne, receiving a stream of guests that wound around the room in a line.

Most of those in line were quite short—it seemed he had invited many witches from his own Network.

Vasily was a thin-cheeked witch with an extravagant beard that curled out a full hand's width in four broad whips, two on either side of his face. Ensconced in each curl was a large opal like a forest-dragon egg. His ruddy complexion nearly hid the gentle slant of his thin eyes. Isadora could see a resemblance to the small girl from the gardens.

Next to him was a lesser chair made of wood and lined with sapphires. In front of it stood a witch with bronze skin, her blonde hair towering high on her head, gems adorning each of her curls. Diamonds, sewn into the fabric of her dress, reflected the light of the candles that surrounded the thrones. The jewels on her skirt formed a polar bear. She glimmered, so dazzling Isadora could hardly look straight at her.

"Who is she?" Isadora asked.

"Vasily's wife." Maximillion's breath was a warm caress on her cheek. "Her name is Arayana. They married years ago. She's Dostar's cousin, from the West. Their union was Vasily's idea. You remember I said he loves history? He negotiated the marriage to forge stronger ties between the South and the West because a former High Priest did something similar historically."

The West and the South had been, to Isadora's understanding, less antagonistic toward each other, but she hadn't known why.

"Did it work?" she asked.

His shoulders hovered a breath away, far too tempting to avoid. She reached out, putting a hand on his arm.

"It's worked, for the most part, as best it could. As an attempt at creating peace between the two countries, it probably spared some lives, when the tensions first started. Unfortunately, Vasily's stubbornness goes deeper than any contract. Dostar has a strong allegiance to familial ties. He treats his cousin as a sister. Vasily has kept her pregnant from the moment they handfasted. She's borne him five children in ten years."

"The good gods. A miracle in times like these."

Maximillion stepped back, greeting a witch as they passed. Isadora, able to breathe freely again, refused an appetizer cradled delicately in an oyster shell.

"Will we join the line?" she asked. Every guest that entered the room headed right for it.

"No need."

"But—"

"I have already spoken with Vasily."

She thought of him disappearing earlier, and wondered. Had he done that so she wouldn't be overwhelmed?

The gathering of powerful witches certainly seemed daunting enough in appearance alone, but she didn't appreciate the meddling or lack of confidence, if that were the case. Isadora's breath lightened as they neared the whirl of witches dancing in the middle of the tiled floor.

"Where is Dante?" she asked.

Maximillion put a hand on the small of her back and turned her to face him, pulling her close as if to dance. "Across the room, near the thrones. He's standing by Vasily. You can see him over my right shoulder if you look discreetly."

A striking witch with the olive-toned complexion of the Eastern Network stood not far from Vasily. Dante, no doubt. He had slender shoulders and piercing eyes. She'd seen him in the paths before.

Serafina stood at his side, speaking with Arayana. Emilia lingered just behind them, lovely in a simple green gown with capped sleeves, looking bored.

So she had gotten to come to the ball after all.

With all the rumors that swirled about Dante, Isadora had half-expected a demon. He seemed entirely normal, with graceful shoulders and a confident smile. He reminded her of a mountain. Immovable. Confident. Filled with the rifts and valleys one had to carefully navigate.

"He's . . . quite handsome."

"If one could call such a dark soul handsome. Come," he murmured, taking her hand.

They slipped quietly through the elegant room, past countless clusters of witches. Maximillion mentioned them all to her by name while doling out his own version of a smile—or at least less of a grimace—and saying, "Merry meet."

"There's one representative missing," Isadora said, reviewing the crowd.

Maximillion plucked a goblet of red currant wine from a tray.

"Dostar."

Memories, both cold and hot, assaulted Isadora. The

night when the West attacked Berry, ravaging the town, setting fire to the school. The fearless way Maximillion had challenged the thick, towering West Guard leader. The gleam of malevolence in Dostar's eyes.

What sort of battleground were they meeting on now?

Isadora's gaze drifted back to the whirling couples with a pang of longing. Mam had loved dancing before she married Daid and disappeared into Anguis. She taught Isadora during the long winter days in Letum Wood. The memory of Sanna wrinkling her nose, complaining of wasted time, flittered through Isadora's mind.

She suppressed a smile. "Let's dance, shall we?"

Maximillion recoiled. "Dance?"

Before she could cajole him, the hall stopped talking as one entity. Maximillion glanced over his shoulder.

"Ah. His Grace arrives."

A subtle shift rippled through the room. As if Dostar had such a strong presence that it reached out ahead of him, clearing the path. She spun, skirt trailing, and looked toward the ballroom entrance.

Dostar's sprawling shoulders seemed a Network wide themselves. Dark eyes in a chiseled face surveyed the room, one hand on the hilt of a curved, gleaming sword. His eyes were bright, alert. Isadora had a feeling that nothing escaped his wary gaze.

Several witches filled the entryway behind him. West Guards, if their thin linen pants and bare chests meant anything.

"Your Grace," Vasily called from the other end of the room, extending a hand. Dostar hesitated, then stepped over the threshold and toward the thrones.

"In the West, when one enters a room after invitation without a weapon drawn, it's a sign of compromise,"

Maximillion whispered. "West Guards' lives revolve around their weapons."

Arayana stepped away from the throne, greeting Dostar with a kiss on the lips and a warm smile. He returned it fleetingly, his massive hands on her shoulders. The two exchanged conversation for a full minute before he embraced her again and released her back to her throne. After a few murmured words to Vasily, Dostar strode to the other side of the table. His horde followed, wordless, swords clanking.

Taking advantage of the brief lull, Vasily called out in the common language, his accent not as thick as Isadora had expected, "All have now assembled! Gather for the meal vile the food is hot and the drink varm."

With a hand on the small of her back, Maximillion guided her to the table, choosing two seats in the middle, allowing them full view of the room. A shuffle of bodies followed until everyone settled in.

Servants flooded the room, bearing silver platters. Isadora sat back as food appeared on her plate. Roasted fish. Greens with a slight crisp. Onions sautéed in butter. The gentle lull of conversation filled her ears, easing her tension. Maximillion spoke with someone on his left while Isadora took it all in.

When a servant filled her glass with water, she glanced up and saw four slender young women slip along the edge of the ballroom, eventually stopping at the end of the table where Arayana sat. They grabbed Arayana's dress, helping her sink into an opulent chair. Two of them made her comfortable, offering her drink, a pillow, and a place to discard her elaborate rings, which were too big to allow her to eat.

Isadora squinted. No, not women—girls, none older than eighteen or so.

"Shieldmaidens," said a raspy voice next to her. "The High Priestess is a protected creature in the South, with her own harem of girls dedicated to serve her. They're slaves, taken from their families in the silk clans south of here at six years old."

The witch who'd spoken held a glass of wine in her hand. She lifted her thin eyebrows, tipped her glass to Isadora, and took a deep drink. She was middle-aged, with strikingly dark eyes. Beads on a single braid in her hair shone green, gold, and arctic blue.

"I had no idea they had slaves in the South," Isadora murmured, glancing back at the girls. More lingered in the shadows.

"The South is a wild place. The High Priest is often gone, dealing with the mines or silk traders. The shield-maidens are trained to keep the High Priestess and the children safe. They may appear beautiful and subdued, but one would never want to fight a Southern Network shieldmaiden."

Isadora surveyed them again. Their bulky, billowing skirts would easily hide a weapon. And they all had short hair that couldn't be used against them. She thought she saw a hint of fabric around their ankles—pants beneath the skirts. Skirts easily shed, if needed.

"This High Priestess appears to be all beauty and fluff," the woman said, "but she is a surprising witch. Like you."

Isadora blinked. "Me?"

"Married to Maximillion Sinclair." She looked beyond Isadora. "A witch who, by all accounts, loves nothing but debate and being proven right."

Isadora's lips twitched. "In that," she drawled, reaching for her water, "you are correct."

A ghost of a smile lingered on her lips. "My name is Tamara. I have come as the gypsy elder to represent my witches and find us a new home. You are recently handfasted?"

"Very recently."

"Congratulations."

"Thank you." Though she sensed more beneath the surface, she let it go. "You have been living in the South for a while now, haven't you?"

Tamara nodded. "My witches found refuge here decades ago. The remote clans are accepting of those that, like them, have little. We live apart from them. We don't venture to learn the secrets of their silk, and they don't refuse us space to live. The arrangement has worked for many years, but my witches tire of the snow and driving cold."

"Where will you go?"

Tamara smiled, but it lacked humor. "Who will have us in times such as these? I remember desert and heat from my child-hood. I long for it again, as many of my group do. But . . . the lower Western Network is hostile and unforgiving, and its north side is replete with sand and strange creatures. The roaming dragons make it unsafe for us to move around. Besides, the spirit that resides there is . . . not whole. We desire land."

The word *dragon* sent a shudder down Isadora's spine. Sanna had told her about the desert dragons, but she'd yet to see one. Isadora speared another bite of fish.

Land. A heavy ask in such a time, when borders were closely guarded, secured by the lives of guardians.

The gypsies had relatively few witches in their wandering band. They couldn't contribute enough to a

Network to sway any leader to give up much on their behalf. In a time when thousands of lives had been lost to war, none would be willing to take them unless the gypsies would fight.

They were a notoriously peaceful group of witches, so that seemed unlikely.

Isadora had underestimated the intricacy these negotiations would require. For a moment, she felt lost in a whirling snowstorm.

Pull it together, she chided herself.

Isadora lifted her glass of water. "To powerful, surprising women."

A slow grin slipped across Tamara's face. She clinked her glass against Isadora's.

"To us."

"I HAD no idea you were such a charming dancer," Isadora said with a wry smile.

Maximillion's loose hold on her didn't waver as they whirled over the black-and-white tiled floor, dinner long since abandoned for dancing and discussion. Hours had slipped away with surprising speed, leaving the time well past midnight now. His gaze studiously focused on the ballroom around them instead of her face, something she took no offense at.

"One gains many skills in the pursuit of professional excellence."

Isadora suppressed a smirk. He could write this off as a job requirement, but the loose way he moved, the easy rhythm of his steps, suggested he did it naturally. Only a witch who truly enjoyed dancing, begrudging though it be, could lead her this way.

Charmed by the dazzle of the ball around them, Isadora surrendered to the steps, allowing Max to sweep her along. Her heart beat a quick, elated staccato. His sharp gaze followed nearly every witch in the room. He muttered something under his breath, and she wondered if he missed his quill.

"Do you take notes while you dance?"

A hint of color suffused his cheeks. "No."

"Talk to yourself, then?"

He seemed stiff as a board, suddenly. She regretted her teasing tone.

"Sorting things out," he muttered. "Meetings begin tomorrow. I'm making sure I remember names and details, that's all. While the leaders begin, you shall meet the wives."

"Indeed."

He glanced at her, sharp-eyed, as if he'd expected resistance. When he received none, his shoulders relaxed a little. "Just . . . be wary around Arayana."

"Why?"

He made a noise in the back of his throat.

Isadora glanced across the room to find Serafina smiling at a giggling Emilia. Dante was nowhere nearby. Maximillion whisked her away before she could study them further.

"Have you ever thought of smiling?" she asked.

His scowl deepened. "To what end?"

"To act as if you're enjoying yourself."

"But why?"

"So others can see it."

"They need to know, do they?"

"Might make you seem more approachable."

"That's hardly motivational. I don't want to talk to anyone else."

"Yes." She laughed. "You certainly seem to."

His eyes flickered to her, then away. "No," he muttered. "No one expects me to smile."

"Well, I can't argue with that."

"Maximillion Sinclair," drawled a deep voice. "It's my deepest pleasure to see you again."

Maximillion pulled them to a stop near the edge of the dance floor. Isadora's breath caught when she turned and looked into the seemingly endless eyes of Dante Aldana. Before Maximillion could respond, Dante stepped forward and pulled Isadora toward him.

"Don't mind me," Dante said, "but I'd like to cut in with your lovely wife, and I hardly think you'd deprive your High Priest anything."

Breathless with surprise, Isadora caught a glimpse of Serafina sliding into Maximillion's arms before Dante expertly folded them into the whirl of witches. She caught her breath. Kidnapped by Dante Aldana.

A promising first ball.

"The wife of the infamous Maximillion Sinclair," Dante said. He held her in an easy grip, close but not too close. If dancing with Maximillion had been comfortable, dancing with Dante felt like flying. The heady smell of tobacco filled her nostrils as they moved.

"I have been eager to meet you since I heard the rumor of your handfasting. Forgive my unconventional way of asking. Maximillion has a habit of being . . . protective . . . of what he thinks belongs to him."

"You couldn't have heard such a rumor long ago," Isadora said, striving for an even, friendly tone. "We were only handfasted this week."

He met her gaze, surprising her with true warmth. "Indeed, so I heard. It's been a while since I've seen Max so wrapped up in anything but his work as Ambassador. You are a witch to be congratulated, or understood. I'm inclined to think the latter."

Something lingered in his tone, but she dismissed it.

"Thank you. It's good to meet you, Your Majesty." She choked out the lie without a ruffle in her voice, thinking of Carcere, Cecelia, and the young Watcher who died on the stones at La Torra. His easygoing demeanor made it easy to forget what history lay beneath.

"None of that," he said with a friendly scoff. "Call me Dante. With a mutual friend like Maximillion, you and I shall be on a first-name basis. I confess myself eager to know more about your time with our Max. Did you meet on Network business?"

"No, but I understand the basis of your guess. On a walk in the woods. Quite unexpectedly."

His eyes glimmered with amusement. "Maximillion walking in the woods? Unexpected indeed. Did you grow up in the Central Network?"

"In Letum Wood, yes."

"Ah," he tsked. "That sinister old forest."

"It's not so bad," she said lightly, ignoring a pang of longing for the shelter of the trees.

He shuddered. "Too unpredictable for me. Give me the steady tide and the pounding of the waves," he murmured with a quick grin. "I heard a rumor that you attended a Network school. Did you like the system? Serafina and I have long hoped to revamp our educational system once all these wars have abated."

Why would he ask about the school system now? Then again, dancing with a total stranger was bound to bring up odd topics, she imagined. He had honed skills in conversation, for it flowed easily.

"I couldn't say, Your Majesty. I wasn't there for long. It was an odd school, run by a witch named Sophie who didn't have much to teach. With all the wars, there isn't much education anywhere, I imagine."

"A shame," he said, his eyes lighting on something across the room. Emilia, dancing with the Southern Network Ambassador—who appeared to be just her height.

The corner of Dante's lip twitched into a half-smile. "It's Emilia who's pushing us to better the educational system," he said with a heavy sigh. "She's bound to equalize education and opportunity for all witches."

"A beautiful idea."

His gaze found hers again, surprisingly studious and intent.

"My daughter was equally impressed with you, from what I hear. She has been talking about you relentlessly."

Her cheeks warmed. "I have only met her once."

"And she is a good judge of character. I like that Serafina insists on bringing her to all our travels and events. Emilia reads people well and is glad to inform me of her opinion. She gets it from her mother, of course."

His light laugh set her slightly at ease. She didn't want to like him but couldn't help but feel drawn to him. With his handsome features and infectious, rolling voice, she could see what Cecelia had been attracted to.

Thousands of memories of La Torra spun through her mind, ending on the moment Cecelia lost her life. Cecelia's hidden love for Dante had seemed tragic. Had it been returned? Or had Cecelia mourned what she could never have?

The Aldana family name bore a long, heavy legacy. One he surely wouldn't want to mar with elevating a mistress.

"Emilia seems very bright," she said, opting for safer ground.

"Too bright." He grinned. "Much too bright. She's the youngest of the three but I suspect the smartest. Serafina doesn't like to part with her and brings her everywhere. I think she can't quite let go of her baby. I don't blame her. I'd never choose favorites, but if I could, Emilia would be mine."

Isadora returned his smile. Out of the corner of her eye, she thought she saw Max staring intently at them, though he was still dancing with Serafina.

"I am eager to hear the plans set forth by the Networks," Isadora said. "Rumors around the ballroom say you have been hard at work with a plan that would put all of Antebellum under a single ruler. How . . . fascinating."

"Indeed."

Not an ounce of hesitation lingered in his expression. If anything, a hungry look came into his eyes.

"Much peace can be gained by uniting Networks. Six months ago, an . . . unfortunate . . . accident occurred in my Network. I closed my borders. After such a horrendous setback, everything seemed too large. Too intertwined. The killing had become too much. The constant war." He shook his head. "I couldn't deal with it anymore. Diplomacy clearly wasn't working. In my naïveté, I thought I could fix the issue by ignoring everyone else."

A flurry of grief appeared in his eyes, then faded.

Isadora kept her lips pressed together. He spoke of Cecelia's death and the subsequent saving of over thirty Watchers. Following the breakdown of Carcere, Dante had sent messages to the other Network leaders saying he would allow no one in and no one out, spurring a flurry of black-market activity and panic.

Isadora wondered now if Serafina had something to do with his decision.

His forehead wrinkled. "It ended up being an interesting experiment. The more my Network isolated itself, the more we suffered. Witches grieved missing family members. The economy, already bad, suffered from the loss of trade. The number of Guardians required at the borders depleted my villages of laborers. I can't imagine how the Central Network has managed being cut off from the sea. Then I realized I was being a fool. We need less separation, more unity."

Drawing a deep breath and forcing herself to relax into the music was the only way Isadora kept from stiffening. He carried passion aplenty. But was it real? Any powerful witch vying to consolidate the Networks under one ruling entity surely had selfish purposes.

"Six months," Isadora couldn't help but say. "Is that a fair amount of time to give such a massive shift a trial? For an entire Network to pivot? I would imagine it would take years to stabilize an economy. Particularly after a war."

Dante slowly smiled. "You have foresight, do you?"

Her breath caught. Foresight? Did she imagine something underlying in his tone? *Clever,* Maximillion had said about Dante. *And passionate. A dangerous mix.*

No. She was reading into things. On guard a little too much, perhaps.

"Meeting Maximillion has opened my eyes to the political world," she said with full honesty. "I speak only from assumption."

"Don't be uneasy. You're not wrong. Perhaps the trial was too short, but regardless, I felt pulled in this direction. We need to support each other more, not less."

"An intoxicating path," Isadora murmured when she realized he was waiting for a reply.

"Historically, the strongest. There are many precedents that show it to work. How can you know you've chosen the right path if it's based on what others *haven't* chosen?"

For a moment, she felt a breathless panic. *Path. Chosen. Historical.* Did she imagine his nuance in these words? The easy way he used them sounded almost like . . . well, like *her.*

Isadora shook that thought from her head.

Madness.

Instead, she focused on what he'd said. Could isolationism drive them deeper into these problems? What if they had it all wrong?

No, she couldn't ask that now. Not while so close to Dante, who had ordered the deaths of hundreds of Watchers over the course of his life.

He was murderous brutality masked by a pair of handsome eyes.

"Your turn has ended," Maximillion said, breaking into her musings.

Isadora hid her relief as she stepped away from Dante. The scent of vetiver filled the air, and Maximillion's warm arm wrapped around her waist, securing her, tucking her into his side with a bit more force than seemed necessary. She relaxed against him, placing a hand on his back.

The two great men stared at each other, equal for height, for several moments. To her surprise, something like affection appeared in Dante's gaze before fading into uncertainty.

"Maximillion, thank you for sharing. Please, come and visit us anytime. It has been . . . far too long."

Maximillion said nothing, lips thin and grip surprisingly tight.

"Thank you for the honor of the dance," Isadora said with a half-curtsy, meeting Dante's gaze.

He smiled warmly at her, bowed at the waist, and turned to go. Serafina appeared at his side. Without looking back, the two faded into the crush of dancers without touching.

"I'm suddenly tired of being around witches," Max muttered. "Come back to the turret with me."

A COOL BRUSH of fresh air roused Isadora from her thoughts about Dante. She turned her cheek into the wind and closed her eyes, enjoying the wintry whisper.

She stood on the balcony of their tall tower, peering out into the darkness of the Southern Network. An occasional flash of light illuminated the velvety sky—the streak of a falling star. In the distance, fires flared, then faded. The turret cradled her in a quiet, welcome intimacy.

Behind her, Maximillion paced through their shared room, muttering to himself. She hadn't changed out of the dress yet, and the smell of cranberry sauce wafted from the fabric.

After retreating gracefully from the ball, largely unnoticed, they'd climbed all the way to their room without a word. Once Maximillion shut them inside and secured the door with a spell, she'd recounted every word of her conversation with Dante to him.

Her magic swirled as if upset by her recollections. *Soon,* she whispered to the stirring powers. *Soon.* But it wouldn't be soon. Not until they felt a little more secure here. The magic settled with a sigh, bright and hot inside her.

"I'm sorry."

Isadora startled.

Maximillion stood next to her, gripping the railing with white knuckles. His words were short, stony, his jaw clenched tight, as if saying it had caused him physical pain. A curl of black hair tumbled onto his forehead and shifted in the wind.

Those were two words she'd never expected from him.

"For what?"

"I shouldn't have let him come near you."

"He certainly didn't hurt me. In fact, he's more . . . charming than I expected."

His scowl deepened. He shoved away from the banister and reached into his pocket, handing her a small scroll tied with twine.

"From Arayana, through Serafina, for you. You're cordially invited to tea with the High Priestesses in the morning. Early. There's nothing the South loves more than waking before the sun."

Isadora accepted the parchment. "Thank you. Do you need me to take anything to—"

"I'll know better after tomorrow."

Isadora recalled Serafina's comment in the garden. *We will find a time when the need arises.* She hadn't seemed overly motivated to get to know Isadora.

The most monumental negotiation in recent history was about to alter the course of every living witch in Antebellum. If Maximillion didn't succeed in convincing these leaders that isolationism was the only path forward, Watchers wouldn't be the only ones endangered. The weight seemed to hang in the air.

"Are you ready?"

"Yes," he said simply, then turned and disappeared inside, leaving her alone on the quiet balcony.

13

I *am Renor.*

Sanna's clenched hands trembled as she stood before the mountain mam, an elegant dragon with broad, translucent wings, a graceful neck, and a soft-featured face that lacked the reptilian intensity of her male counterparts.

Renor's scales didn't seem to change color. Instead, she was a light shade of gray, nearly matching the rocks.

Unlike male mountain dragons with their sharp, harsh angles, the mams were all smooth, rounded edges. A ridge ran down the back of Renor's neck, but she had no horns. In a distinctly animalian way, she seemed feminine, like a doe *mortega* back in Letum Wood.

And she proved to be a powerful, intimidating presence. She towered over Metok, though she still wasn't as large as Luteis.

Daughter of the forest, Renor murmured in a silky voice.

Renor stood uncomfortably close, allowing Sanna to see her clearly. She studied Sanna with open curiosity, no malice in her gaze.

The amulet on Sanna's chest warmed, and her eyes prickled. She blinked the sensation away. "You are beautiful dragons. I can see why Selsay closely guards you."

For many reasons. Have you come to find these out?

"No."

Renor whipped around with a snarl the moment Sanna heard a familiar *thump* of wings. Acid thickened the air for half a breath, forcing Sanna to stumble back toward the rock face. A boulder twice her height stopped her. She reached back, pressing a hand to the chilly rock to steady herself.

Heat shot from the rock and into her hand, warming her fingers like fire. Magic swelled through her arms and into her chest, as strong here as it had been in Letum Wood. Instead of letters and light on a tree trunk, whispers swelled in her mind. Voices, slightly serpentine, with a fading *hiss* at the end of each word.

Sanna held her breath, able to discern only snatches here and there. A conglomeration of languages and voices rang from the rock behind her.

. . . and the desert sister mourned her great loss while the dragons fell from her thoughts . . .

The winds were sharp today.

Beloved visited with her presence, and the other mams were pleased . . .

Interesting.

Feeling as if she were separating parts of her heart, Sanna pulled her hand away. The heat faded, as did the swirling whispers. Like the trees when they spoke to her in Letum Wood. Removing herself left her strangely . . . empty.

Did being Dragonmaster make her more sensitive to the magic of the goddesses?

Renor stared at her, eyes tapered.

Shadow flickered near the edge of Sanna's compressed vision. The voices untangled themselves fully from her mind.

Luteis landed near her in a formidable crouch, his teeth bared, wings unfurled over her. His heat washed over Sanna, warming her against the harsh wind that whistled between the mountains. Sanna held out her arms and stepped between them.

"Renor, he's the forest-dragon sire, and he's not going to hurt anyone. Relax, Luteis. Renor isn't here to hurt me."

Renor's gaze darted to Metok, then back to Sanna.

We are not your only dragons? she hissed.

The back of Sanna's throat burned from the sharp air. "No."

Luteis lowered his wings slowly, not taking his eyes off Renor. She ignored him and looked from Metok to Sanna, then back again.

If they had an exchange, Sanna didn't hear it. Finally, Renor relaxed a little. The air cleared.

How can this be? In all of Selsay's history, there has never been a shared Dragonmaster.

"A lot of things are unusual right now. What do you know of the war between Selsay and Prana and Deasylva?"

More than you, I would imagine, Renor said.

"Selsay tells you?"

Renor glanced out over the mountains beyond the circle. *Selsay tells us much. We are her greatest confidants. To lose us would . . . she could not bear it.*

"And her greatest weakness."

Renor's sharp gaze flicked back. She hissed. *Perhaps. Perhaps not. She speaks of war with the winter snows. Water from the West. Another cycle of death for dragons.*

"That's a brief summary of it. Luteis and I are trying to

gather an army to stop the war. We need more dragons and witches to stand up to Prana. Will you fight with us so we aren't all murdered in Prana's floods?"

Us, fight? Impossible. Renor shuffled back. *Selsay would never approve.*

"She may not have a choice."

Renor snapped toward Metok, who must have said something.

For several beats, there was only the sound of the whipping wind. Metok didn't cower, but he didn't meet Renor's gaze, either. She'd said something blistering, by his reaction.

Sanna felt sorry for him.

Finally, Renor turned back to her. *Our beloved Selsay has long fought with her youngest sister, Prana. This battle is nothing new in the scope of history and is not worth our deaths.*

"Has a Dragonmaster over two races ever stood up to Prana with an army behind her?"

Renor hesitated, then said, *No.*

"Then maybe this will go differently."

Does that make it your responsibility to change the future and interrupt the past?

"Who said I'm changing the future? I'm creating it."

Renor growled, then settled on her back legs like a begging dog. Not a breath stirred behind her, but Sanna had the sense that all the mams could hear.

You would not be our High Dragonmaster if Selsay didn't require something of you, Renor said, appraising Sanna. *Metok has not been exaggerating the dire circumstances of the world if a witch such as you is standing before me. We are sheltered from it.*

"I know."

Selsay's reasons for so protecting us are pivotal. We ensure the race of mountain dragons continues. What food we cannot harvest ourselves, the males bring to us, and each mam breeds once a year, though at different times. Very simple, isn't it?

Sanna's fingertips tingled. "And yet it's not," she murmured. "Your purpose is more than breeding, isn't it?"

Renor's gaze grew sharp.

"You're as much Selsay's servants as the males," Sanna continued. "And not just in your role of ensuring the survival of the race. Something else." She leaned forward, capturing Renor's burnt-orange eyes. "Something even deeper than that."

Sanna crouched and put her palm on the dusty rocks again. Her pants flapped in the wind as it brushed past, stirring up the voices in her mind.

The goddess visited, and it was warm again.

Wind and fire and snow and light. The days spin in an endless whirl.

Ten new hatchlings this day. No sickness in this safety. We shall not lose so many again.

In our goddess, we are safe.

Fire burned in Renor's eyes. *You intervene in our most sacred work,* she hissed. *You sully our history, and the history of our beloved goddess, with your touch. Release our voices before you intertwine your own. Once the stories of all goddesses are heard, they cannot be heard again!*

Sanna looked up, saw desperation behind Renor's rage, and removed her hand. The whispers faded, leaving nothing but the bluster of the wind in their wake.

Fatigue swept over her.

"They can't be heard again?"

Renor glared at her, glanced once more at Metok, and lifted her head. *I do not have to answer your questions unless you command me to. Will you command me to tell you that which we do not want to impart?*

Ah. So *that's* what Metok had told her. He'd found a weakness in Sanna after all.

These mams are powerful, Luteis murmured. *I can feel it in them. They have their own sort of magic.*

They're recording history, it sounds like.

Yes, but that's not all. They are recorders of history and hatchling-bearers, but I believe they are also the seat of the magic. As you are to me. The males are able to transport, but I believe the females may have even greater magical abilities. Perhaps similar.

Which are?

I am not sure yet. It seems that each dragon race is inherently different. There are similarities, but nuances I cannot account for.

Sanna swallowed, the temptation to command Renor overwhelming. Surely these mams *did* possess powerful magic.

Would that give them the advantage in the fight against Prana? Something that could potentially tip the scales?

If Renor was telling the truth, if a battle between goddesses had happened before, someone must have recorded it. Them, most likely. The things Sanna could learn from mountain-dragon history alone could vastly inform her response in the battle, or at least help establish what to expect.

But would the knowledge of history turn the war? And would it be worth losing trust and rapport with the mams? No doubt the males would hold it against her. There was a risk of even greater alienation from the mountain dragons, and perhaps a lesser force against Prana.

Sanna chewed on her bottom lip.

If you want us to fight in the battle of the winter, Renor said, *you must command us to do so. Individually. The males may be hungry to uselessly kill themselves, but we are not.*

Command them individually? There were thousands of mams here. Sanna's nostrils flared. Trust a dragon to make things as difficult as possible.

"If Prana wins, everyone dies."

Not us. Not even Prana can reach these heights with anything but rain. It is why we are here.

A tense silence passed while Renor and Sanna stared at each other. Hadn't Yushi alluded to the cycle of dragon deaths in previous history? Even Deasylva. Selsay had moved the mams here against this very possibility.

Coming had been a useless errand.

A rush of disappointment—maybe fear—robbed Sanna of her power. She couldn't do it. She couldn't command the mams to follow them to a battle where she couldn't guarantee their survival. If she couldn't protect them, did she even deserve to command them?

Not yet, anyway.

Perhaps she'd underestimated the enormity of building an army. If she wouldn't be Talis, they all had to be willing. Where would they find a willing army?

Would you like to begin commanding us now? Renor asked, gesturing with a wing behind her.

Sanna started, realizing she'd been quiet too long. "No."

Luteis's head lifted. Metok snapped to face her.

"For now, I won't command you to do anything you don't wish to. I'm here to save the dragons, not separate us. If you wish to join me in that, I'll welcome your support. But there is a chance I may come back before the battle to command your help."

Renor studied her. *You are not trying to manipulate me into giving you our lives by making yourself seem trustworthy?*

Sanna shook her head.

Metok gazed out over the mountains in silence. Renor didn't take her eyes off Sanna.

Then so it shall be, Renor said, her voice decidedly less sharp, although still a long way from friendly. *I will provide none of my mams for your battle unless you command me to. You have not done so. Yet. We accept that we must lose some of our children to this battle—it is the way of Dragonian magic. But we shall not willingly go.*

She shot Metok a withering glare. *Some dragons do not appreciate the design of our lives or our very reason for existence.*

Sanna let Renor's declaration linger in the air a moment before saying, "Then I shall return."

Renor inclined her head. *May you fare well, Sanna of the forest, fighting against goddess and history. The odds do not favor you.*

With a mighty shove, Renor launched off the rock and returned to the air. The rest of the females and hatchlings did the same, flying in circles in the expansive valley. Sanna watched their blurry, fluttering forms with a sinking feeling in her chest.

There really were no words for this situation that didn't start and end with *Talis.*

She couldn't show up at the battle with only forest dragons and mountain dragons and intimidate Prana into backing down. Not even if she had the combined magic of two Dragonmasters.

She'd have to figure out another way to find fighters in a world already weary of war.

Maybe this wouldn't be so easy.

Come, Metok said. *You both need to rest. You may sleep in our caves before returning to your forest home.*

~

"I'VE RECEIVED a letter from your sister. She's in the Southern Network doing some political work, if you can believe that. Says they eat onions at every meal, and drink wine from cups made of pure gold."

Mam crouched next to Sanna at the stream, each of their buckets sluggishly filling with water. Sanna stared at the creek, frustrated by the blur around the edges of her vision. She had to turn her head all the way to the left to see Mam even though their arms brushed.

"Is she well?" Sanna asked absently.

"Certainly sounds like it. I'm not very clear on why she's there ..."

Mam prattled on about the gowns Isadora had described. Isa had used magic to send some sweets back, and almost a full meal, but the younger children had already eaten both up.

Sanna listened only half-heartedly. They'd returned from visiting Renor three days ago, and she couldn't stop thinking about the conversation.

In all of Selsay's history, there has never been a shared Dragonmaster.

We accept that we must lose some of our children to this battle—it is the way of Dragonian magic.

Yushi had said something similar that she hadn't truly caught at the time.

To understand the true purpose behind the cycle of dragon deaths in the way of Dragonian magic.

Dragonian magic. Deaths. Battle. Magic that had originated with Prana. Exactly how *was* magic born, then? Sanna's eyes flickered overhead. Within the goddess, perhaps? By the goddess, more likely. Isadora had said thousands of types of magic existed in the world.

What else would a goddess do with her time?

Her mind drifted to Prana's desire to drown all life on land. Deasylva and Selsay would survive, but few, if any, witches would live in Antebellum again. Exactly how expendable were witches to their goddesses? And had this happened before?

A master is still a master.

She trailed her fingers through the water, allowing it to pour from her hands back into the stream.

"So I told Elliot," Mam continued, clucking under her breath, "you have to plant early in order for those to start growing in the spring. But I'm not sure he believed me. Babs always did that, you know."

High Dragonmaster.

The call came from a middle-aged dragon named Hellis. Sanna straightened, looking behind her. Mam continued talking, oblivious to the silent conversation.

Yes?

There is something you should see. We are outside the circle of the Ancients, to the north, on the trail that runs—

I know it. Call Luteis.

We have already done so. He is returning from hunting now.

Sanna regretted leaving. She hadn't had much time with Mam since they'd arrived at the circle of the Ancients. But Elliot and Mam, both grieving, had grown unaccountably close as friends. It reassured Sanna now.

"Sorry, Mam. The dragons are calling me."

Mam, still crouched by the stream, opened her mouth to say something, then stopped. She pressed her lips together and nodded. "I understand. Go."

With a frown, Sanna obeyed.

∿

An hour later, Sanna stood before a fallen tree as thick as Mam's house.

Blood of some sort? Luteis asked so only she could hear. A strange, viscous liquid covered the ground. She drew closer to the fallen tree.

There. A faint shimmer near the trunk.

Beneath the prattle of the forest dragons in her mind, she thought she could hear a groan. The low, fading pulse of a heartbeat.

The tree seemed to have been pushed over, if such a thing were possible. Its roots stood up in the air as if yanked out of the soil.

Like it had just . . . fallen.

The trunk lay at a slant, held by the mighty branches of the surrounding trees. One terrible windstorm could bring it crashing to the ground, where it would destroy anything in its path. Beneath it, water burbled.

Sanna scanned the area for several minutes, attempting to take the details in. Map it in her mind because she couldn't see it all with her eyes.

"It's not blood." She touched the soil. "It's something else."

Like the liquid your sister writes with?

"Ink?" she asked.

It smells similar.

"A poison, perhaps?"

I have never seen it before, but it's possible. Letum Wood isn't as healthy as it used to be.

She reached out to touch the liquid. The magic jumped to life in her hand and flew out her fingertips with a *snap*. She gasped, rearing back. Light zipped up the trunk in a spiral, then disappeared.

"Did you see that?"

Your magic responded to the tree.

Slowly, she reached back out toward the bark. When her fingers brushed the rough wood again, magic flowed out of her, this time with less enthusiasm. Light gradually illuminated the trunk, crawling in a circle around its edge.

"Luteis, look."

Something similar has happened before, he said. Warmth stirred as he approached, his tail swinging. *Do you remember?*

"At the stump," she whispered, recalling her first foray into the circle of the Ancients. She'd climbed on a mounting stump in order to get on top of Luteis's back. When she'd touched it, lines of light had revealed the names of previous Dragonmasters. "The tree had the names of my ancestors in it."

Sarasam the Lovely, he murmured. *Loxly the Mighty. There were many.*

"Can you read—"

Witch writing means nothing to me. I remember only what you said.

Sanna set her other hand on the trunk, breathless all the way to her stomach. Luminescence flared under her fingertips again, expanding outward. The magic skimmed through her blood, sliding in and out of her and into the trunk, as if they shared a connection. As if the tree poured into her.

It appears to be writing. Can you read it?

"Maybe."

Each ring in the jagged trunk was about as wide as the nail on her pinky finger. The scrawling script was elegant, a radiant white-blue, just like Deasylva's. It was just bright enough to make out on the sections of bark that still lay flat.

. . . in the days of Loxly the Mighty. The forest was old. Warm

*and cold. The days passed in peace and calm. Even the dragons'
roar was rare, for they delighted in the quiet. The servants of our
mistress walked amongst us . . .*

Sanna read it aloud slowly, then looked up. Luteis's face
was shrouded in shadow.

"It's . . ."

The history of the forest.

Her heart pounded. "And by extension . . ."

Of Deasylva, he finished.

Sanna's thoughts spun in wild abandon. The history of
the forest was, of course, written *in* the forest. Just like
Selsay. She'd touched many stumps before, but this had
never happened.

The implications are far-reaching, Luteis said, *like in the
mountains.*

"Because Dragonmaster history is recorded? Because we
could find answers about our elusive goddess?"

His expression darkened. *I hadn't thought of that, but it
doesn't feel right. If we have questions about Deasylva, we should
take them to Deasylva.*

"Who left us to regain her energy, remember?"

Luteis stewed.

"They're sisters, right? That means there may be information about Prana in the trees. We couldn't access history
through Selsay, but we can here. Can you take Isadora out of
my history?"

He paused. *I concede. There is a possibility that we learn
something about Prana from all this. I believe that the greatest
likelihood is that we learn something about* you.

Sanna's forehead ruffled. "Me?"

One can hardly tell when you're involved.

The tip of his tail whacked her in the back. She batted it
away impatiently. Then she pressed her entire palm against

the stump, watching every grain of wood glow under her hand. The magic stirred deep in her like an awakening presence.

"But imagine what we can learn from the Ancients," she said. "They must have *all* of history written in them, don't you think? Maybe each tree has the same history. Just different tellings of it. But the Ancients ..."

It appears to be a broken system. Luteis snorted at a leaf as it scuttled by, dancing over a thin skein of snow. *The trees must die for us to learn what they have to say.*

Sanna leaned harder on the jagged trunk. The stirring in her mind had grown, and something distant, syrupy, and very, very old seemed to be humming back there.

Perhaps interacting with the forest didn't mean involving Deasylva at all.

Another magic, maybe.

You cannot be thinking of cutting any of the Ancients down, he said, eyeing her. *It cannot be possible. They are far too large. The danger—*

"No," she murmured. "We wouldn't do that. But I do think those trees know something, and there must be another way."

Something dropped behind them with a *thud.*

Sanna whirled around, extracting the knife she carried at her hip. Metok stood there, staring impassively at her. She relaxed, sheathing her knife again.

"Metok," she muttered. "You scared me. I didn't expect to hear from you for several more days."

High Dragonmaster, Selsay sent me.

A rock dropped into Sanna's stomach. Her eyebrows rose. *Selsay?* she repeated in disbelief.

Metok met her gaze straight on.

We have a problem.

14

_____

"Welcome to my home."

Arayana Romov stood in the middle of an elegant, oval room, wearing a simple silk dress and a friendly smile.

The bedecked, dazzling witch from the night before had disappeared. Today, her hair fell in sandy-blonde ribbons around her tanned face, though most of it was pulled into a gentle queue on one shoulder. She had blue eyes, a kind face rounded by years of childbearing, and a robust bosom.

The distant chatter of children seeped through closed doors. Though lavish, the room showed signs of life, with a child's shirt draped over the back of one couch and a stray shoe peeking out from under a bookshelf.

"An honor to meet you in person, Your Greatness," Isadora said.

"The pleasure is mine."

Arayana's words were crisp, different from the Southern Network's typical accent. Her Western heritage, Isadora supposed.

The High Priestess waved a hand toward a table on a

sprawling balcony, set with a far more subdued arrangement than the previous night.

"It will be a light breakfast after such a grand ball. More tea than food."

From the distance came a bloodcurdling scream. Isadora whirled around as Arayana muttered between clenched teeth, "Please excuse me while I deal with my children. Have a seat, Mrs. Sinclair."

Jarred by the name, Isadora moved toward the balcony while Arayana hastened for a circular door in the far wall. A chill dampened the morning air, but warm torches dotting the balcony exuded surprising warmth.

A place marker with Isadora's name scrawled in a flowing script waited on the table. Seven teacups sat in a circle, each in front of a padded chair.

Isadora strode to the banister, studying the forest. Sunrise announced its arrival, gentle and quiet. Pink lace suffused the clouds like a marmalade palette. The world seemed to be sleeping, suspended in time as the sun peeked over the distant horizon. Below, a gong sounded. South Guards marched across the gardens, relieving the night watch.

A clinking sound drew Isadora's thoughts back to the balcony. Shieldmaidens rustled around in subdued blue dresses and starched white aprons. Two of them wore leather necklaces from which small colored vials were suspended. They clinked softly every now and then, indicating more vials lay beneath the cloth.

The shieldmaidens' slender forms belied their strength —Isadora could see a flash of a well-muscled arm every now and then, noticed the quick reflex as one caught a tumbling glass. Like dancers, they moved with grace and precision, every step intentional, murmuring to each other in a gentle language. Flashes of Talis—of Anguis—flitted through Isadora's mind.

She turned away, a lump in her throat.

To the west, a dark cloud lingered, leaden and heavy. Isadora's brow furrowed. It was much like the storm she had seen constantly to the southwest of La Torra. It hovered in the distance here, black as night and broiling.

"Beautiful, isn't it?" Arayana asked, gliding to her side, her flowing dress trailing behind her. "A storm on one side, the sunlight on the other."

"An unlikely dichotomy."

"It's been there for so long." Arayana's brow furrowed as she frowned at the distant storm. "At least the last year. I've asked Vasily, but he disregards it. The snow came so early and so heavy this fall."

"The storm never goes away?"

"No. It seems to grow."

Isadora gestured toward the tundra. One particular spot caught her eye, filled with thick trees, taller than the rest, and skirting a particularly broad stretch of emptiness. "Do you ever walk out there?"

"In the forest?" Arayana asked, voice pitched high.

"Yes."

"Of course not! That's high timber. The natives call it *destarta*."

"What does that mean?"

"I'm not exactly sure—tribal dialects vary so much. But it amounts to a curse. Odd place. Its trees are strangely thick and tall and different than the rest here. Legends have it that witches disappear there all the time. Not to mention the timber wolves. Families of them."

"Wolves?"

"Nasty beasts. Some clans use the destarta as a proving

ground. Boys become men, you know, when they can kill the destarta timber wolves. Some think that there's ancient, sacred ground somewhere in there. No one will approach that part. They're funny about death that way here. Protective. If you tread on sacred ground, they kill you."

Timber wolves and sacred ground. Foes Isadora hadn't considered. She turned at a noise behind them.

Arayana brightened. "Ah! You have come."

Serafina and Emilia stepped onto the balcony, each wearing quieter gowns than last night, though still luxurious by any other breakfast standard. Arayana wrapped Emilia in a warm embrace first, then kissed each of Serafina's cheeks.

"Finally!" Arayana said, her face flushed with pleasure. "It's just the ladies. Those stuffy old men and their ridiculous balls are such a strain, aren't they? I'm grateful we are not called to the opening meeting. Come! A delicious tea awaits."

Emilia smiled, hiding a giggle as Arayana linked their fingers and dragged her to the table. Set at ease by the surprisingly cordial atmosphere, Isadora sank into her chair not far from Serafina, who sent her a brief, distant smile.

The shieldmaidens set several platters on the table. Cheese carved in the shape of a six-pointed star. Dried fish with a smoky aroma. A bowl of some kind of thick, clear liquid that threatened to slosh over the side. Wrinkled berries dotting a plate filled with cream. Seven pots of tea, with names written on each pot. *Carambola. Paiz. Tartara. Shallen. Partor.*

"Try all the teas!" Arayana declared. "They are Southern Network specialties, and all of them will cure any ills left over from last night."

While the shieldmaidens served the drinks, tipping a

small amount of each tea into every cup, Emilia and Arayana fell into chatter about boys, ballgowns, and dancing. Serafina glanced at Isadora from the corner of her eye but remained largely silent.

Once the shieldmaidens withdrew, Arayana grabbed her first teacup. Isadora, Serafina, and Emilia followed suit.

Isadora selected the *carambola* tea first. The cool zing of peppermint hit her tongue, then faded to a subdued spearmint.

Arayana lifted a teacup toward Serafina and Emilia.

"To old friends," she declared. "May we live forever in each other's wisdom, light, and trust." The three clinked glasses. Arayana held her cup out to Isadora. "To new friends. May the bonds of our sisterhood be yours."

Isadora tapped her cup gently against Arayana's.

A distant screech and a flurry of male voices rang from the other room. Seconds later, a half-naked child with a head of blonde hair streaked by.

"Zoya!" Arayana called. "Put your clothes back on! *Emu!*"

"Emilia," Serafina murmured. "Perhaps you could assist Zoya with her lessons today? No doubt she'd enjoy Eastern Network history far more hearing it from someone who lives in the East."

Emilia's smile seemed genuine, if a bit tight. "Of course, Mere. It would be a pleasure. I shall . . . take my tea in the other room with Zoya."

Zoya's expression brightened.

"Emilia!" she cried, throwing herself at her. Emilia, following a shieldmaiden who commanded all seven teacups with a spell, trailed Zoya into a back room with only one last longing glance over her shoulder.

"So, Isadora," Arayana said. "Tell us about yourself."

Serafina waited, silent but studious. Arayana peered at

Isadora in expectation. Isadora swallowed hard, wishing for Emilia's friendly face back.

This is where she truly had to prove herself. Arayana knew nothing of Serafina's request to Maximillion, and Isadora would be a fool to not assume them both spies for their husbands. Everything said here would go back to the men. Perhaps, with Serafina, she may color the truth or withhold, but the High Priestess had proven nearly impossible to read.

Keep to the truth, Maximillion had said, *whenever you can.*

"Ah . . . I suppose it's a fairly simple story. I grew up in Letum Wood, have a deep love for my Network and traveling, and was recently handfasted."

"To Maximillion Sinclair!" Arayana leaned forward conspiratorially. "I cannot believe anyone would marry him."

Serafina cleared her throat and stared into her cup. Her dress rustled as if she'd kicked Arayana under the table.

An expression of horror crossed Arayana's face. "Oh! I mean—"

"It's fine," Isadora said, laughing. "I understand. He's not the softest witch, but he's surprisingly . . . merciful."

Serafina glanced up through her eyelashes as if startled, then away.

"Handsome, too," Arayana said with a sigh. "I wish you luck with him. Was growing up in Letum Wood terrifying? The stories I hear." She shuddered.

"Not at all."

"What is Maximillion like behind closed doors? Is he as unyielding and rigid?"

Warmth dusted Isadora's cheeks. "Ah . . ."

"Oy!" Arayana cried, laughing again. "Not like that! Is he

the same around you as he is around us? Cold. Stubborn. A bit taciturn, though gentlemanly."

Serafina was watching Isadora now, her gaze almost hungry. Isadora smiled awkwardly, discomfited by her strange expression.

"He's much the same, albeit a little less formal," Isadora said.

"He has seemed affectionate," Arayana murmured. "Are you close, or was this a political match like ours?"

Isadora suppressed the urge to squirm. This inquisition felt more and more deliberate. What exactly did Arayana want to suss out? Or was she just being friendly? Isadora's sheer lack of experience worked against her here.

She preferred the *lavanda* on La Torra to this.

"Maximillion and I have known each other almost two years now. We didn't want to be parted for so long if the negotiations went on for months. It was advantageous and affectionate for both of us, if not exactly political."

Arayana studied her, making a noise deep in her throat.

Seeing an opportunity to change the subject, Isadora said, "I've heard nothing of what plan the South is presenting. Has Vasily something he's excited about?"

Arayana trilled a laugh that seemed a tad too tight. "No specific plan for Vasily. He's much too cautious and doesn't like extremes. That makes it difficult to establish a firm plan in this climate of necessary extremes."

Did she mean to suggest Vasily *couldn't* get behind something extreme, like isolationism? With only four rulers negotiating, Vasily could end up casting the deciding vote.

"It's a rare opportunity that all Networks have to present options," Serafina said. Her subdued demeanor had faded, and a new light illuminated her face. "This kind of summit is without historical equal. Dante is championing one ruler for all the Networks, Maximillion isolationism, and Dostar a council to act as a sort of unified Ambassador. Vasily is coming in as a swing vote with no particular proposal. In all the political work I've read, I've heard of nothing that compares to it."

Isadora studied her, startled by the sudden spark of life.

"Living history," Arayana murmured, eyes alight.

"Dante's plan," Isadora said. "Can you tell me more about it?"

"A merging of borders and interests," Serafina said. For her part, her voice remained more warm than neutral, but only barely, as if she approved. "Instead of fighting against each other, we'd love to see a world where all can work for the mutual benefit of the other. Where none need fear for their lives. The historical precedent for such a shift is undeniable."

The exact opposite of her plan, at least in words. The execution could be a different story.

"But such a government is not active now," Isadora said, "which calls into question its efficacy. If it worked then, why aren't we using it still?"

Serafina stiffened. Arayana's eyes grew wide over the top of her teacup.

"Perhaps culture and situation isn't taken into consideration," Serafina replied, a challenge in her tone. She met Isadora's gaze directly and without fear. "These are very different times."

"Well," Arayana said, straightening with a nervous laugh, "let's save the politics for the men to debate. Isadora, did you know that Serafina and I have been friends for nine years? I've been married to Vasily for ten years now. My survival in a new Network, with new customs, witches, and languages, I attribute solely to Serafina. There was a time when I didn't think I'd make it." Arayana looked at Serafina with undeniable warmth. "Thanks to Serafina, I didn't take my own life."

Serafina's expression softened. "Because of the Law of Vittoria," she said, answering Isadora's unasked question, "I was permanently removed from my family after being raised in the depths of poverty, and handfasted to Dante when I was eighteen."

Ironic. Isadora had an idea of how it felt to be shoved into a new world one didn't understand. At least her own handfasting was a ruse. Smoke and mirrors. Serafina had been shoved into a glass box for the rest of her life.

"Without your consent?" Isadora asked, eyebrows rising.

"No." Serafina's brow furrowed. "I agreed to Dante's proposal because of my deep love for politics and my desire to promote public safety. He seemed kind enough, with drive and passion to keep him occupied. Though truly, accepting life as High Priestess was more for my family, my sister, than anything. When the Aldana family finds a worthy candidate, they make it hard to refuse. My family suffered for nothing but their own self-imposed consequences after my decision."

Arayana reached across the table and squeezed Serafina's hand. "When I first became Vasily's wife, I struggled with all the strange customs and expectations here, much as Serafina had when she married Dante. Serafina noticed, pulled me under her wing, and became like a sister to me."

Serafina smiled. "Our only true similarity is our deep love for our Networks. We are quite different."

Arayana grinned. "Indeed. Fortunately, I have come to love the South as my own, though my heart remains in the West. I would do anything for both of my Networks."

"And I," Serafina said quietly.

The tension had subsided with the deft change of subject, a testament to Arayana's natural skill as a hostess. Isadora sipped her tea, hardly tasting the odd concoction, while Arayana steered the subject to Emilia's dress.

If the two were as close as they said, Serafina keeping her part in the isolationism plan from Arayana had deeper implications than Isadora had realized. And Arayana's natural skill with witches meant she'd have to be doubly careful around her. If Vasily was truly a swing vote with no plan of his own, he potentially wielded the most power.

Something everyone would know.

A suspicion that she had vastly underestimated both High Priestesses' roles in this negotiation crawled up her spine. She was thoroughly in over her head now.

There was no going back.

THE NEXT DAY, driven nearly mad by the air in the quiet room and the restless powers, Isadora transported from the turret. She landed right into a spiny bush that snagged her stockings. Maximillion had just eaten lunch and left early to stop at the library—something about a list of current inter-Network grievances they'd started to discuss that morning, which would need to be addressed before negotiations started.

Muttering, Isadora wrestled herself from the bush, untangled her thick shawl, and tied it beneath her bust. It hugged her shoulders, providing a thin layer of comfort and warmth.

Her magic swirled in anticipation. Ever since their breakfast the previous day, she couldn't stop thinking about seeing the High Priestess's in the paths, though she didn't dare enter them in the castle itself. What if? It seemed irresponsible.

The thought had occurred to her that Maximillion wouldn't like this one bit, but he didn't have to know.

Not learning more about the High Priestess's seemed equally irresponsible. Surely her powers had *some* bearing on being here with him.

"Soon," she murmured to the prickling anticipation. "Let me make sure it's safe."

The ice castle was a mere speck in the distance. She'd intently studied Vasily's map but had still transported farther than she'd intended. The barren tundra, spongy beneath her feet and composed of what appeared to be layers of ice, snow, and dried weeds, rippled toward the horizon. Behind her, smaller trees gave way to larger ones, though even the tallest were hardly a twentieth the height of those in Letum Wood.

She lifted her skirts and ventured a little farther into the forest. It wasn't easy to navigate. She kept a wary eye out for anything unusual, sometimes stopping for minutes at a time to study the forest and get a sense of it, for it all felt strange to her.

Certain she was alone, Isadora slipped into the magic.

It welcomed her like an old friend. She let it breathe, and it flew out of her and raced through the ground in visible paths. The pressure in her chest eased. She allowed herself to luxuriate in the sheer relief.

After reveling in it, her eyes closed, she came back to herself in the Southern forest. The foamy sky, gray trees, and lifeless wind still surrounded her. No one appeared. No match popped up out of nowhere, drawn by her power.

She returned to the paths, allowing another bright surge

of magic to flow from her. Ignoring the populating chaos, she said, "Remove any paths. Show me Serafina."

Serafina appeared in the usual pillar of light. Her unbound hair fell onto slender shoulders, and her usually distant eyes showed something else. Fear? Her arms circled in front of her as if she were holding something tightly.

Frightened, whispered the forest.

"Hardly surprising," Isadora murmured, recalling something similar in Cecelia's personality when she was alive. "Show me Arayana."

Arayana's larger-than-life form appeared next. She stood with her hands at her side, a gentle smile on her face.

Eager.

Eager to please her husband? To have friends? To be a High Priestess? Undeniably, Arayana had motivations, just like Serafina. *What* they pointed to, Isadora had no idea.

Isadora called up Dostar next, but finding nothing surprising there, she commanded, "Dante."

Something fluttered over her arm. Immediately, she closed the magic and returned to the Southern Network.

The lonely, whistling wind welcomed her back. Heart pounding, she looked around. *Something* had touched her. A familiar scent lingered in the air. Onions. A hint of cranberry. It smelled exactly like lunch mixed with a whiff of a very distinct tobacco.

"Hello?"

She stood, brushing her skirts off.

Crack.

Heart pounding, she whirled around, grabbed a thick branch from the ground, and lifted it. A transportation spell waited on the tip of her tongue.

A muted cry followed, then a small voice called, "It's just me!"

Stunned, Isadora lowered the branch. Familiar brown eyes peered around a half-dead tree.

"Emilia?"

Emilia sidestepped a tall stump, looking sheepish. A high flush colored her cheeks, and her breath came in fast little pants.

"I-I'm sorry," she said. "I just . . . I came to your room to see if you'd like to have tea with me so I didn't have to worry about another protective-magic lesson today. That's two in one day! When you didn't answer the door, I peeked inside and saw you transport away."

Isadora frowned. She hadn't heard a knock. Then, she *had* been distracted by the pull of the magic.

"You can follow magic so young?"

"Mere taught me to follow a transportation spell in our protective-magic lessons. Said it could help keep me safe." Emilia chewed on her bottom lip. "So I, ah, followed you."

"All this way?"

"Well, it seemed such a fun adventure!" She gazed around, arms lifted. "And I didn't want to miss it. The South is so different from the East, but mere makes me stay inside. I want to, you know . . . *see* it."

Isadora recalled the gentle flutter she'd felt while in the paths. "Did you come near me just now?"

"No, but I only just arrived the moment you picked up the branch."

Isadora glanced overhead. Something had touched her —she felt certain.

"Did you see anyone else?" Isadora asked.

"No."

The oddity of the situation puzzled her, but now wasn't the time to focus on it. "Well, I'm glad you came," Isadora said with a warm smile.

Emilia grinned. "Good! Can I stay?"

Isadora held out a hand with a laugh. "Come. Let's keep walking."

Emilia cast her a sidelong glance as they strolled forward. "So, what *are* you doing out here?"

"I grew up in Letum Wood," Isadora said easily, despite the sudden tightness in her chest. "I miss the forest and thought I'd do a little exploring. Isn't much else to do here, as I've already spent hours reading about history today."

Emilia glanced around. "There really isn't much here, is there?"

Trees aside, she was right. Apart from a few chattering rodents, she'd seen no signs of life. Skeletal bushes, having long since lost their leaves, clacked together in the wind like old bones.

Isadora was grateful the subject had turned a corner. "Why do I have a feeling you also came to avoid a certain little girl?"

A sheepish blush flared on her cheeks. "Perhaps."

At a meandering speed, they ventured deeper into the forest. Isadora's thoughts eventually ran back to the magic and what she'd seen. *Eager. Frightened.* If anything, she would have applied the labels to the other woman. Serafina seemed the most eager, and Arayana the most frightened, though both held their cards close.

She wondered what Max would think of all this. Regardless, venting her magic had left her muscles looser, her body not strung quite so tight. She could have stayed in the powers the rest of the day. The quiet peal of Emilia's voice brought her from her reverie.

"Mrs. Sinclair?"

"What? Oh, sorry. I seemed to have lost myself in my own thoughts."

Emilia smiled. "What is it like being married to Maximillion?" she asked, her eyes shining with curiosity. "Is he as terribly boring as he acts in meetings? He used to be fun when I'd see him on his Ambassador visits."

"He's terribly something," she murmured, studying the trees ahead of them. The trunks were broader here. Something in them felt vaguely familiar. And the scrub brush wasn't so high now. Trampled grasses, some cut into narrow paths, indicated that *something* inhabited these parts.

Emilia shivered, rubbing her arm.

"Do your parents know you're out here?" Isadora asked, eager to turn the subject.

"Mere . . . was taking a nap. She's probably done now, looking for me in the library or with Zoya. She'll be furious I'm not studying."

"Perhaps we should return," Isadora said, her uneasiness growing by the second. Something wasn't right. "Shall we take tea in my room? That may cover you, just in case. Just don't tell your mere."

Emilia's nervous expression bloomed into one of relief. "Yes, please!"

"You first," Isadora said, relieved to be leaving. There was something uneasy about this wood. "We can always order the tea on our way back up the turret, and tell your mere we went on a walk together."

15

A distant *thud* jerked Sanna from a deep sleep. She shot upright, still tangled in dreams of the ocean, her heart pounding like a mad thing.

High Dragonmaster, Metok said. *We approach.*

She straightened, eyes bleary.

Metok flew next to Luteis, their long, easy wing strokes carrying them northward. Cool air swept along her skin, rousing her. Purple-shadowed mountains stretched in all directions, thick with a hazy fog.

You are well? Luteis asked.

Yes. You?

I am well.

Are you tired? she asked.

Very, but I will make it.

Do you need to hunt?

I . . . will be fine.

She pressed a hand to his scales. *I'm sorry. I know you're hungry and have been through a lot lately, with little rest.*

He lifted his head around and nudged her affectionately. Several mountain dragons appeared in the air around them in a winged formation. Sanna glanced at them but said nothing. Metok must have called them.

Metok, she said, *is the situation so bad that you would require reinforcements?*

Yes, High Dragonmaster.

Did the other mountain dragons come of their own volition?

He hesitated for a second. *Yes. To protect me and . . .*

And?

Our interests in the upcoming battle.

You are still eager to fight Prana?

It is what we were bred for.

Sanna's brow furrowed. They shouldn't be *bred* for anything. They should exist because they existed, not to meet the needs of a goddess.

I understand, she said.

Do you? He peered at her.

She thought of Daid. Of Babs. Of Letum Wood and Rosy and all the forest dragons that were already lost. She didn't relish the idea of losing any dragons, but she hated the alternative—Antebellum dying. Everything could literally disappear, forever, under a shroud of water.

Yes, she said. *I do.*

Metok held her gaze, then looked away without another word. She clenched her hands into fists, reassured by the heat that gathered there. The magic had been growing as they flew farther north.

Luteis moved silently through the air, skimming past clouds as Metok led them deeper into the mountainous world. Farther than she had ever gone before.

Sanna scanned the scene, trying to view everything all at once even though her eyes prevented it. Another distant *thud* reverberated from the cliffs. Luteis swung to look at it as Sanna scrambled to her feet on his back, standing at the juncture of wings and spine.

Ahead of them, mountains formed a solid rock face, like a granite fence stretching forever into the unknown.

Behind the wall lies the forbidden lands, Metok said. *The northernmost point in all the world.*

An icy gust of wind blew past Sanna.

Are you ready? she asked Luteis.

Yes.

Can you see anything?

No, he murmured. *I can smell something unfamiliar, however. It seems to be everywhere, coming from all directions.*

Another distant *thud.*

What was that? she asked.

That, High Dragonmaster, Metok said, *is a mountain troll.*

Her heart iced over.

Troll?

Metok gestured with a jerk of his head. A plume of dust rose from behind the mountain wall, followed by a heady bellow.

You see and hear their attempts to breach the outer perimeter of the forbidden lands.

They want into the forbidden lands?

No, they want out. Mountain dragons have been here for days now, watching their progress. They seem to grow more determined as they get farther outside their usual home in the forbidden lands.

Mountain dragons spiraled over the rock wall, calling out with screeches every so often. Beyond the wall, snowy peaks tripled to an endless degree, farther than she could possibly see. A barren world of ice and rock. Nearly as life-less as the sterile desert.

Luteis angled left, following Metok toward the sound of

screaming. The wind caught Sanna's hair, streaming it behind her as they crossed into a new world.

More percussive thumps.

Heat sprang to her tingling fingertips the moment she noticed massive bodies crawling amongst the rock. She reached for her knife.

"Mountain trolls," she whispered.

A deep sense of awe overtook her. Never in her life could she have imagined such large creatures. Forest trolls were long since extinct even though rumors and legends abounded, or so Deasylva reported.

Creatures that were remnants of the gods, she'd once said, *that shall never return here again.*

But mountain trolls? Sanna hadn't even heard of them. How long had they been lost in this strange world?

The deep, throaty bellow of a troll rang through the air. Because of its size, Sanna saw the creature amongst the rocks quickly. The giant thing sprawled bigger than Luteis. Sharply pointed ears stuck out from a rounded, bald head. Its massive arms clung to the side of the sheer rock wall. Thick, meaty hands held it aloft, hundreds of paces in the air. Other trolls climbed below it—some directly beneath. Though it was at least two hundred paces from the top, it didn't seem tired.

Her heart skipped a beat.

I count twenty already, she said.

Forty, Luteis replied, his voice grim.

Our last scouts counted thirty more coming, Metok said. *In total, we've observed nearly seventy-five.*

Sanna's head whipped around to face him. "Seventy-five mountain trolls?"

Metok's nostrils flared. *Yes.*

"Why does Selsay even have these?" she cried.

They were not her creation, High Dragonmaster. They were of the frost god, Gelas. Snow, ice, and the mountain trolls are the only things that remain of him. Until now, they have always stayed in the forbidden lands.

Sanna whirled around. "Forget gods and goddesses," she muttered, turning her attention back to the troll that had climbed the highest. "Once those trolls are free?"

They will ravage the North, destroying all.

Metok plunged, taking them in a fast descent behind the mountain wall. Sanna dropped against Luteis's back, flattening her body against his warm scales. They plummeted so rapidly her stomach seemed to be left behind.

She peered over Luteis's shoulder. Beneath them lay a sprawling lake rimmed in white. A river ran from the lake, disappearing between two of the smaller mountains.

Sanna used every second to study what she could see, attempting to draw an accurate picture in her mind because she couldn't see it all at once. A massive wall of mountains to the right, in the furthest northern reach, currently being scaled by trolls. Letum Wood far to the south, over a day away. Beneath them, a wide lake and a hearty river.

Wind blew past her as they descended toward the lake. Luteis landed next to Metok on the shore. The lake spanned larger than anything she'd seen before except the ocean. It would take at least twenty minutes to fly from one end to another.

No wind stirred. Half-submerged trees stuck out of the water like needles. The pristine water rippled in the middle, as if it were moving. Even when quiet, Letum Wood still had a subtle kind of roar—the trees, the wind, the sheer amount of magic. Up here, there was . . . nothing.

"What happened?" she asked.

Her voice seemed like it belonged to a stranger—an

imposter in so pristine a world. Metok looked toward the water. Rings of white branched out from the edges as if trickles of powder had been dropped along the rim. Chunks of ice floated on the surface.

Salt water. It has been invading here for weeks now.

"Weeks?" she snapped.

Metok didn't meet her gaze. *Yes, High Dragonmaster.*

"Have you known?"

Yes, High Dragonmaster.

"And you didn't tell me?"

Luteis wrapped his tail around her ankle. *Calm yourself. Your anger will do nothing to solve our immediate concern. Not to mention, I believe the mams are not far south. Metok brought us in an unusually wide arc, despite having taken us there before.*

Sanna let out a long breath. Of course. "We'll address that later, Metok. Are the mams safe?"

He hesitated. *They . . . are safe.*

"You're lying."

I cannot lie to my master. They are safe now, but they will soon not be safe.

"So Selsay told you to bring me to fix this problem because the mams are in danger."

He inclined his head. If her guess was correct, the mams were in the trolls' path. The only reason Selsay called her up here was to protect her darlings.

"You don't have to wait until it's too late, you wretched goddess!" Sanna yelled, glaring at the peaks. She stood on Luteis's back again, and he flew slowly over the clear water. The wind stirred, carrying the scent of brine. A whisper of her name danced from the face of the water.

Sanna.

A splash of garish red entered her field of vision. She leaned forward as Luteis skimmed past a jutting boulder, and peered into the reflection of the water. Yushi stared up at her from beneath the glassy surface, a hint of darkness in his gaze.

He disappeared, flickering back into the depths just as another mountain dragon popped into sight next to Metok.

A troll, we believe their leader, has reached the top, Metok said, turning to Sanna. His wings flapped quickly. *Do you fight with us, High Dragonmaster?*

Sanna's knife burned hot in her hand.

"We fight together."

THE STENCH of something rotten thickened the air as they climbed higher. Sanna glanced to the right. Empty. To the left. Empty. Luteis's hastily—but happily—constructed plan involved only two steps.

First, Sanna and Luteis would meet this troll and make an attempt to communicate, or at least ascertain if it had any intelligence.

Then the mountain dragons would appear all at once. With any luck, they could throw the troll off the edge and back into the chasm below.

Another crash sounded. Sanna rubbed her aching eyes. Even with less-than-perfect sight, she could make out what lay ahead.

"*Mori,*" she muttered, "it's massive."

As I feared.

The leader stood atop the wall, bellowing. For all appearances, it seemed to be male, with broad shoulders and biceps the size of hills.

He thumped a boulder the size of a house against his sprawling chest and roared. Then he pitched it to the side and swung his arms like clubs, grunting a deep, rolling sound of victory.

"*Mori,*" she muttered.

One troll was enough to keep five or six adult forest dragons busy. Maybe ten fighting together could quickly bring one down. While the mountain dragons contributed sheer numbers and ferocity, coordinated flight was proving to be a difficulty. Too many mountain dragons cluttered the air, making it difficult to engage with the troll and get away if needed.

"He knows we're here," she said as they circled closer.

The troll caught sight of her. Sanna kept her eyes locked on it. Luteis would have to watch for other dangers as well as fight and navigate, which didn't feel fair. She should be both eyes and magic for him, to see what he could not.

Luteis swooped left, flying out of reach above the troll, who carefully tracked them.

We do not have the luxury of time to plan a different attack, so let us act together in the moment, Luteis said.

"Let's take this nasty troll down."

Precisely.

More trolls, as tall as trees, moved with stiff but certain movements up the rock wall. When one slipped, an entire rockslide swept below it. The trolls in the avalanche's path bellowed in response, some disappearing with the rocks, others flattening to the wall and gripping hard. Seconds later, a *thud* sounded as the falling troll landed, then screamed in rage.

So that explained the noise.

Do you feel the magic? Luteis asked.

Heat streaked down her arms and into her fingertips. "Like fire."

Then let us send this one back down.

"It may not kill it."

What other plan do you have?

Sanna hesitated, glancing at the rocks. Killing one troll wouldn't be enough. Now that one had gained the top, others would follow quickly. Then they'd flood the valley and kill everything in their wake.

"I don't know. Think we can tire them out?"

Luteis eyed them. *Doubtful.*

Sanna glanced over her shoulder, watching as one of the smaller trolls, likely an adolescent, climbed. Hints of jutting teeth showed whenever the trolls bellowed. They seemed . . . upset.

"How much can a troll eat?"

I would imagine there's not much limit, he replied grimly.

"But they live up here. It can't be much, right? There's no food in the forbidden lands. Just . . . ice. Rock. Snow."

I do not know these creations. They are of the gods.

Sanna's gaze skimmed the mountains, the trolls, and finally, the lake on the other side. Something wasn't quite adding up.

Get yourself in position, she said as he completed one last circle. *I have an idea.*

Mountain dragons, she added as Luteis headed straight for the troll. *Be ready.*

The troll stood on the ridge, banging his chest and screaming. He trekked right toward Sanna and Luteis, heavy brow furrowed. Luteis dove, dodging a thick hand, then weaved around the creature's back. Though slower, the troll was not without advantage.

Massive advantage.

The troll turned, fist like a club, just as the mountain dragons transported all at once, appearing in a disorienting wheel around him. Acid sprayed the troll from all directions.

The troll closed his eyes, a gut-wrenching sound bubbling from his cavernous chest. He smacked two mountain dragons with an arm, throwing them careening into a wide arc. One of the dragons slammed into the rock wall, then fell, lifeless. Another struggled to fly, wing broken.

Send a dragon to help the injured one, Sanna called to Metok.

Already done, High Dragonmaster.

The prickling sensation in Sanna's fingertips curled up her arm, lingering like burning flames as Luteis swept closer.

"Steady," she murmured, standing on his back. "Stay steady."

Two wing flaps away from the troll, she released the magic. Luteis threw out his wings, stopping their forward movement, and screamed. Fire spouted from his scaly lips, illuminating the acid lingering in the air with a fantastic *bang*.

Sanna dropped against his back, held in place by the magic. The troll screamed. Black smoke clogged the air.

Mountain dragons harassed the troll with acid and rage, clipping his shoulders with their sharp talons, then diving away. The troll swatted at them, as if annoyed by flies.

A second guttural sound came from the mountain wall. Sanna scanned frantically, unable to find the source. Finally, about fifty paces away, she saw it.

Another bald head appeared. She stopped, honing in on it. A second troll heaved himself over the edge of the ridge, flopping on top with a bellow. This one wasn't as tall, but he made up for it in shoulder width.

Mountain dragons, Sanna called. *We have another. Do you*

see it, Luteis?

I do.

A small horde of mountain dragons flocked to the new troll. Taking advantage of the open space, Luteis swooped back in toward the lead troll again.

May I suggest forming groups of dragons assigned to each one? Luteis said, chest heaving as he dodged a thrown boulder. *Prevent the trolls from making it this far.*

Sanna ducked as another boulder whistled overhead and clipped Luteis's tail, sending them into a momentary spin. She clung to his shoulders until they straightened.

"Good plan."

You flatter me.

While Sanna relayed the orders to Metok, Luteis flew a tight circle around the leader, trying to disorient him. The troll ducked into a seam of rocks when Luteis sprayed fire again. Sanna spun around on Luteis's back, surveying the battleground with little comprehension. Unless she could stop and focus, her lack of peripheral vision made it almost impossible to truly know.

Metok and the other mountain dragons flew to the right and left in groups now, flanking the other trolls who'd reached the top. More mountain dragons circled overhead.

The lead troll let out another shout. The second responded. A chorus of indistinguishable calls rippled down the mountain face.

A new voice spoke in her mind.

High Dragonmaster, it said. Another mountain dragon. *I count one hundred trolls on the wall alone now. There are too many for us to manage. We need more mountain dragons.*

The second troll lumbered toward the first, Metok in pursuit.

What is your name? Sanna asked the new voice.

Danten. I am Metok's third-in-command. His second is with the mams.

So they *could* all speak with her. *Mori*, but they made her life unnecessarily difficult.

Thank you, Danten. I will come investigate.

"Luteis, we must go."

Panting, Luteis peeled away. *They are large,* he said, *but not brutish. I believe the trolls employ several tactics in fighting. They communicate with each other as well. They are not as brainless as I have been led to believe. These are knowledgeable creatures.*

How do they communicate?

I cannot tell. It does not appear to be by vocal words.

Several mountain dragons replaced Luteis fighting the largest troll as he and Sanna darted away. Sanna's eyes watered from the occasional breath of acid that drifted toward her. The impatient pulse of fire in her fingertips burned again, ready to fight.

Fly me over the trolls on the rock wall here, she said. *We need to know how many are coming.*

Together, they soared down the sheer cliff face. Trolls in seemingly endless numbers scrambled up the rocks, even to Sanna's limited view. Danten's guess of a hundred had been an underestimation.

Now that some had gained the top, at least two hundred were swarming the wall, clawing toward the top. Bloody streaks ran down the rock face. A troll would fall, shouting, and slam into the ground. Sometimes they'd land on their feet, catching themselves to try again. Others fell on their arms, crushing them. Or their faces, which seemed to kill them.

Sanna and Luteis dove through the dust. Dead trolls lay in piles below them, pummeled to death.

"Barbaric," she muttered.

Or desperate. They are a worthy foe.

Something is driving them to do this.

Prana.

Fly a little farther that way, she said, pointing beyond the rock dust. *Go deeper into the forbidden lands.*

Luteis flew fast, cutting through the haze into cleaner air above an endless vista of snow. The mountain barrier grew higher. The trolls seemed to be climbing the shortest section of the wall. Massive glaciers, glowing a light blue, some tall as mountains themselves, rose from the earth here and there. Tracks in the snow betrayed the trolls' true homes. They had come from all over. Sanna searched for . . . something.

"There!" She pointed.

A ribbon cut through the white ice. Luteis dove toward it. Water bubbled along a crevasse, forming layers of ice that branched into wider fans. More water rippled over the top and froze in delicate patterns.

"Prana," she whispered. "Prana *is* invading the North."

Their water, he said. *The trolls clamor for water. She has been overtaking all the fresh water. Perhaps allowing the ocean to flow here through the rivers that empty into it.*

It's a genocide.

High Dragonmaster, Metok said, his voice strained. *We need reinforcements now. There are too many gaining ground.*

Luteis, go back. Metok, get out of there. Stop fighting.

High Dragonmaster, we cannot—

That's a command.

Her mind went silent as Luteis soared back toward the wall. His energy was flagging. She could feel it in his slack muscles. In the last week, he hadn't eaten more than a sickly goat.

What is your plan? he asked.

Sanna hesitated. *Something,* she said, *that may not work.*

It was a long shot, at best. But potentially their only hope of keeping the trolls contained and preventing genocide.

Luteis pumped hard and fast to fly past the trolls working their way up the steep rock face. His chest heaved with exertion by the time he made it to the thin air at the top.

Six more trolls had summited. The mountain dragons hovered overhead now. At least they'd obeyed her. The acid-rich air burned Sanna's lungs as they passed several dead mountain dragons, crushed on the rocks below the trolls. Her heart clenched.

"We are done fighting here," she muttered.

Fury blazed in Metok's gaze as he came even with them, but he only said, *As you say, High Dragonmaster.*

"Stay here," she said to all of them. "If you die now, you can't fight against Prana. As frightening as *this* is, she is still the bigger threat."

A moment of hesitation overcame Metok.

She didn't give him a chance to object. "Luteis, take me to the top of the ridge."

With the ginormous trolls that could break your squishy body with their hideous faces?

"That one. I need to touch the rocks."

With reluctance, Luteis spiraled down, landing on the opposite side of the ridge.

An odd stillness met Sanna's ears. The trolls stared at her as she slid off Luteis's back. Only the grunts and groans of those attempting to come up the wall rang through the air.

The moment they move, Luteis said, *I take you away.*

Give me a chance.

Sanna stepped away from Luteis. The lead troll strode forward, shoving another behind him.

I will keep an eye on the leader, she said. *But I won't see the others.*

I will watch the rest.

Sanna stood in the flapping wind, hands held out. Then she slowly lowered her palms to the rock.

"Selsay," she said, keeping her gaze on the troll leader, who was staring at her intently. "If you don't want to lose your mams or give Prana the satisfaction of winning, now is the time to listen. You told Metok you needed me. It's because you can't communicate directly with them, isn't it?"

The rock beneath her hummed. A quiet voice entered her mind. *Yes. I have tried.*

Sanna thought back to the piles of rock at the bottom of the ravine. Were all those rockslides the result of Selsay's attempts to communicate with the trolls?

She wasn't subtle.

Can I speak with them? Sanna asked.

Not as you and I speak. They don't have verbal language.

How do they speak with each other?

Through the rocks and ice. It was the way of their god, Gelas.

Fine. I know what they want. I can get them fresh water. That's all I want to tell them, and I think they'll back down. Can you help me do that?

A pause. Sanna risked a quick scan, looking away from the leader to see no fewer than ten trolls waiting on top now. Those ten alone could start their way down the other side, heading toward the witch villages. The destruction would be unpreventable without sacrificing the mountain dragons and weakening their force against Prana.

Prana's exact plan, no doubt.

My magic can connect you, Selsay said. *You must do the rest. They are not my creatures but remnants of my brother. I do not wish them dead, or I would have simply destroyed them in a landslide.*

Why not? Sanna asked.

Deasylva tells me of their greater purpose.

The amulet on Sanna's chest warmed.

Fine. Allow me to connect to the lead troll through your rocks. I want to talk to him.

SECONDS LATER, Sanna felt an odd weight in her mind.

Startled by the sudden shift, she sat. It pressed on her. Remote. Burdensome. Her thoughts grew heavy but not slow. They moved steadily instead of too fast, settling into an unusually inert pattern in comparison.

The troll's heavy brow pulled down even more as if he, too, noticed a change. A sprawling hand clutched his head. His irises were a subtle shade of magenta.

An image of herself sitting on the ground floated in Sanna's mind, then out again.

He glanced toward a nearby grunt, then reached down, grabbing another troll by the wrist and heaving it up. She saw it as if she were him through pictures in her mind. The leader looked out over the forbidden lands with a heavy brow.

An image of sprawling ice walls came next, then tracks in the snow. Glaciers. Trolls walking past them in long lines, fanned behind the leader. She felt rocks humming under her. Sanna closed her eyes, stunned.

What is it? Luteis asked.

I think I see his thoughts.

An image of snow-capped mountains and deep, dark caves followed. Something like longing filled her. Deep. Ancient. She felt . . . a primal sort of fear beneath it all. Then a picture of another falling troll slid through her mind, the image filled with anguish.

They had no words, but they *felt*.

Sanna opened her eyes when she saw an image of herself. The leader stared at her, nostrils flared. Whatever prevented him from attacking, she was glad.

More trolls arrived at the top. Sanna breathed heavily. The longer Selsay's magic connected them, the thicker she felt. She thought she'd sink into the stone. As if she were *becoming* the stone. Ice ran in her blood. She felt . . . so cold.

She thought of a stream. The leader shuffled, startled, then shook his head. He hit his temple with a hand, then looked back at her. Sanna tried again, this time picturing the icy river below. The way it flowed in clear, rippling ribbons. Tried to imagine him bent over, drinking it.

A responding image came to her mind. Water in a fathomlessly deep lake. Crystal clear. Then it changed. Seawater filled it. Unknown fish. Salt, everywhere. A briny taste filled her mouth. She grimaced.

The troll's pointed ears stood up.

Sanna forced herself to her feet, even though her body felt like a bag of rocks. Her knees shook from the weight. She met the troll's gaze, picturing water again. He lowered his head.

"Luteis," she murmured, "do you have enough energy to use your secundum?"

Yes.

"How long will it burn through ice once you throw it?"

An hour under these conditions.

His secundum, or second fire, was a magical, tenacious

flame that stuck to an object and burned all the way through. He'd thrown so much of it during the battle with the mountain dragons that Letum Wood had burned for a week afterward. Ever since merging with her, the strength of his secundum had steadily increased.

"Go to the bottom and throw your secundum. Create a lake, something to get them fresh water to drink. Keep it well away from the salt water but easy to access."

I will not leave you.

A fluttering came from behind her. Metok had landed there, which meant she had been speaking to both. *I will stay with you.*

Sanna didn't turn to face him, her body too heavy for movement. She hadn't taken her eyes off the troll leader. The world swayed.

More trolls claimed the ridge every moment, most of them growling, knuckles and toes bruised and bloody from the climb. Tension ran through the ridgetop. Three more mountain dragons circled around Sanna as Luteis reluctantly dropped, diving down and out of sight.

Sanna gave the leader an image of Luteis's fire against the ice below. Then water forming beneath it.

Another image filled her mind. This one with the leader, head plunged into the ice floe, as if drinking. The leader stared hard at her.

Not sure how to affirm it, she simply gave the picture again.

The troll leader watched Luteis go, then grunted several times in quick succession, each noise different. The grunt rippled down the granite cliff face, moving from troll to troll. Sanna locked eyes with him again. Her heart felt sluggish. Slow.

Too heavy.

Water, she said in her mind, trying to imagine a small lake in all that snow. The leader began to pace, looking down, communicating with a series of grunts. His movements turned frantic.

The trolls on the wall, Danten said, *are retreating.*

Sanna didn't dare look. Her eyes were too heavy. Her arms felt like leaded weights. A series of images whipped through her mind. Climbing down the rocks. Scrambling for the water. The leader was excited. Maybe . . . hopeful.

High Dragonmaster?

She waved Metok back and called another image forth. The mountain wall. She tried to picture the trolls at the bottom. The leader looked back at her, his head tilted slightly to one side. He gestured downward with a punctuated movement of his hand. Sanna recalled the lake. The moving water, the salt on the banks.

She envisioned him drinking. Thought of clear refreshment.

Luteis could throw enough secundum to burn a significant hole through the ice. It should be enough to give them water until Prana and her seawater retreated. Assuming she did. The leader grunted to the trolls clumped around him. One started back down, climbing over the edge.

If she looked away from the leader, her struggling eyes would fail. He kept her gaze. More pictures and feelings followed. Something indistinct. Gratitude?

High Dragonmaster?

Metok's voice came to her as if through a tunnel. She blinked, looking away. She tried to find him but saw only shadows. Finally, she fell into the waiting darkness with a sense of a great weight lifting off her.

Everything disappeared.

The halls of Vasily's castle rang with a cavernous silence early in the morning.

After tossing and turning through the early hours, Isadora set out while Maximillion slept, lightly snoring on his bed of pillows on the floor.

A lonely wind howled outside, rattling the windowpanes as it swept across the tundra. No snow, but heavy, churning clouds filled the sky, blocking her view of the distant storm. Only a hint of sunrise danced on the horizon, leaving the sky a deep onyx.

The smell of bacon hovered in the air. Her stomach grumbled as she hurried along the route Emilia had described over tea the day before.

Over a week had passed since their arrival, and Isadora feared she'd die of boredom.

Serafina and Arayana largely continued with the business of raising their children as if nothing in their lives had changed. While Serafina transported back to the East daily to check on her other children, Emilia would wander up to

Isadora's turret instead of attending to her rigorous magical lessons.

"The library here is loaded with books and utterly boring," Emilia had said, her cheeks full of a heavy pastry. "I wish they had more storybooks about war. Don't tell Mere, but I'm supposed to study there, and I go to the kitchen instead. The servants let me talk to them and give me treats. I like the noise."

Isadora turned a corner into another empty hall lit by flickering torches. Wooden planks lined the corridor, covering the stone, giving it a semblance of warmth.

There. On her left—a short hallway, ending in a series of long, slanted windows just like those in her room. Halfway down it, she found a set of double doors forming a half circle. With cold hands, she grasped the doorknobs and pushed. The doors gave way slowly, with steady groans that betrayed their weight.

Isadora grunted, shoving them all the way open, and stopped.

The two-story room was packed with shelves on every wall. Sturdy pillows and fur-lined blankets were scattered across the polished wooden floor. Slowly, she advanced, allowing the doors to close behind her. A fire flared in the grate. She paused, assessing every nook and cranny.

Seeing no signs of life, she advanced.

"The good gods," Isadora murmured, "*this* is a library."

On the second story, a walkway ringed the room, its banister encrusted with glittering gems. Overhead, painted murals on the ceiling depicted scenes of war. Blood. Cudgels. Armor. Bared teeth. Screaming men. She turned away from the gory images.

Slowly, she circled the first floor, running her fingers along the well-dusted shelves.

"Eastern Network History," she whispered, passing a hand-inscribed plaque on one bookcase. Leather tomes with gold script filled those shelves. The next was far sparser, packed with haphazard scrolls labeled *Western Network History*.

Two bookcases held histories of the Southern Network, lovingly organized by book, scroll, parchment, and scrap. Though chock-full, it had an organized feel.

Historical Accounts of Local Tribes. Clan Names Throughout History. Secrets of the Silk Trade.

She idly wondered if there would be any mention of Watchers or Taiza here. Twenty minutes later, she had scanned all the history titles, and perused a few scrolls. The fire had burned low in the grate, allowing a slight chill to settle in. She ignored it, advancing to the second floor.

"*Southern Recipes Volume One. Ten. Fifty-Four.* Goodness," she said, reviewing three shelves. The recipes appeared to end on *Volume Eighty-Six.* Turning away, she stopped at the next shelf.

Historical Biographies of Famous Southern Network Witches.

Intrigued, Isadora grabbed a ladder and climbed. The biographies filled three high shelves—she had to go further up. One book caught her eye. A tattered binding, with missing letters and a ripped leather facade. Well loved, or sought after.

Either way, worth the work. She continued upward.

The sound of a *rriiipp* came a moment before her dress jerked her to the side. She cried out as her foot slid off the rung, throwing the weight of her body to the right. The ladder rocked as she clung to it, hanging off one side. The floor was at least ten paces below her. Far enough to break an ankle. Gripping the rung with both hands, she flailed in her attempts to hook her legs back around the ladder.

"Blasted skirts," she muttered. Finally succeeding in getting one foot around the ladder, she hugged it, slipped around the side with a huff, and climbed back down. A voice from just behind her made her jump, and she whirled around with a scream in her throat.

"Vell done."

Vasily stood there, a look of amusement on his grizzled face.

Isadora dropped into a curtsy. "Your Greatness. I . . . I . . . apologize for that display."

He stared at her, expression blank, until a sudden smile wreathed his features. "Not at all. I vas impressed you untangled yourself."

Isadora's lips twitched. "Ah, thank you. I . . . couldn't sleep. I'd heard you had a robust library, so I came to investigate."

His gaze swept the room with undeniable warmth, his daunting stubbornness entirely gone. "Yes, I love my books." His face, lined with age, was relaxed. He had the same gruff appearance but none of the inflexibility.

"You are velcome to my library anytime you like. No doubt it is boring here, yes, vith not much to do?"

"Er, not boring. Just . . ."

His eyes twinkled. "You can say it is boring. Come. I show you my private collections. They are my favorite books."

He offered her his arm, and she accepted. He wore a velvety robe lined with sapphire cloth. Fur slippers clad his feet, giving a brief glimpse of a hairy ankle with every other step. She'd caught the High Priest at an undignified time as well. Her horror over the ladder faded.

"My library is my sanctuary," he said as they walked down the spiral staircase. "I love to read."

"Do you have a favorite topic?"

"History, of course." He waved to the shelves of the historical accounts she'd already passed. "The Southern Netvork has a rich and terrible past. Ve are not as organized as the East or the Central Netvorks. Our leaders do not come by time served or by lineage. Ve vin this role solely based on military merit, strength, and honor. Such a legacy is unstable, so I seek to learn from those who have gone before. Not that it matters much," he drawled, "for it seems that the vars abound regardless of my education."

Dante's eagerness to establish historical precedent for his one-ruler plan suddenly made a lot more sense.

Vasily reached out toward a smaller bookcase, rested a hand on top, and murmured something indecipherable. The case swung open, revealing a separate, hidden book-shelf. He waved to it wordlessly.

Titles in the common language abounded. Isadora's eye landed on *Great Generals of the South* and *Battles That Changed History*.

So he particularly liked military history.

After asking questions about several books, she asked, "Do you have maps of your Network here? I should love to understand the topography better."

Vasily's bushy brows rose. "Ov course," he said, rolling his *r's* to great effect. "Over here."

He yanked on a panel in the nearby wall. It opened, revealing several layers of thick, hanging parchment with maps drawn on them. A wooden rod ran across the bottom of each to keep it weighed down.

He lifted the first, delicately turning it so it looped behind the others.

"The South," he said proudly, gesturing to a hand-drawn illustration at least five paces tall and five paces wide. "You see? The ice castle is not far from the Central Network border."

He gestured to the six-pointed star that indicated the castle. Indeed, it wasn't far from the Southern Covens of the Central Network, likely only a few hours by carriage. Beneath it, slash marks filled much of the area. Small trees, drawn as evergreens, grew thick along the eastern and western borders. Below that, the forest seemed to disappear into more slash marks.

"Tundra?" she asked, gesturing to the slash marks.

He nodded once. "Timber volf land."

"I've heard they're ferocious."

He grunted. "Babies. Violent vhen hungry, and territorial, but start a fire and they leave you alone. Here? The clans. They scatter through Netvork, alvays moving until you reach the sea. A trade route from here to the ocean with many villages." He pointed to several spots on the map in a haphazard line. "Fjords in the south, overtaken by glaciers. Only the smallest clans survive there. And my castle all the way up here."

"A lovely Network, in its own right."

Vasily cast her a sidelong glance. "Some vould say."

"You have a rich history, with beautiful witches. I would call that lovely."

"Perhaps." He lifted one shoulder. "The clans create trouble vith their demands about the silk trade, and the vitches fear their fake gods to the point of violence. The search for precious metals and gems turns good vitches to evil here. The loveliness you speak of hides herself."

"Your wall," she asked, peering into his eyes, sensing an unusual relaxing of his guard. "Why have you built it?"

Vasily hesitated, then gestured toward the historical accounts. "Our history is built on blood, slavery, and power through killing. I have studied the vays of the vitches before me. Learned from their mistakes. The other leaders? They never protect their vitches. Themselves, yes. Their vitches? No." His hand sliced through the air. "I seek to protect my Netvork however I can."

"And thus protect your position."

His eyes glittered as he studied her. "Yes."

The precarious politics of the South meant Vasily *had* to be stubborn and paranoid. He appeared to be in his mid-sixties—no small feat for a Southern High Priest. Soon, however, his physical strength would wane, perhaps leading to a challenge. He could lose everything. His position. His castle. Had he been leading the South by sheer force of personality all this time?

That made his swing-vote position even more unique.

A span of silence stretched between them while Isadora processed his imperfect attempts to do the right thing. The shieldmaiden slaves flittered through her mind. To protect a way of life built on the sufferings of others. Did he see the hypocrisy in it?

Eager to change the subject, she said, "You mentioned the silk trade. Many speak of it, but I know very little about it."

"Most know little." He shifted, seeming relieved. "It is the lifeblood of our Netvork, along vith gems, minerals, and metals."

"The clans have their own magic, do they not?"

He nodded once.

"Do you know it well?"

He shook his head. "I have stayed avay from it out of necessity. It is an odd magic, rooted in tradition. They don't velcome outsiders. To try only stirs up problems."

"Isn't all magic like that?"

He seemed startled by her question. "Vy, no."

Isadora's heart thumped beneath her ribs as she consulted the map again. "There are rumors in the Central Network that Watchers congregate here in the South. A place called Taiza. Have you heard of it?"

His eyebrows drew together. "Taiza?"

"Mmm."

Several moments of contemplation, then, "No."

Isadora hid her disappointment behind a sigh. "Well, no matter. Rumors are rumors. There are also rumors that the Southern Network is a bloodthirsty land filled with witches who will eat your beating heart." She tacked on a slight smile to soften the words, then had the feeling it wasn't necessary. He likely didn't care. "I'm not so inclined to believe those anymore."

Vasily studied her, released the map, and grunted as it settled against the others. "I vouldn't be so quick if I vere you," he murmured. "Many rumors are rooted in truth."

Isadora tossed *Timber Wolf Legends in the South* onto the bed. Emilia had loaned it to her. "It's dazzling and brilliant!" she had said.

More like gory and brutal.

Isadora stood and stretched, setting aside the whirling magic as she loosened her muscles.

Dinner waited beneath a silver platter on the table in the middle of the room. Outside, sunset had enclosed the world in a black cloak. She sent another log onto the fire with a spell and walked past her balcony door, glimpsing the darkened tundra outside.

The door slammed shut, and she jumped. Maximillion strode into the room with bloodshot eyes and rumpled hair.

"The good gods," he declared.

"Tough day?"

His glare could have rivaled a dragon's. Hands held up in a gesture of peace, Isadora turned away, giving him her back. He strode to the fire, poured a glass of wine, and brooded in front of the flames while violently undoing his kerchief. After a moment, he slipped into the paths.

Like usual, Isadora ignored his seething. She'd learned his pattern well enough. Once he had food and several moments of venting, he'd calm.

Her thoughts wandered, first to Sanna, then to the paths, then to Dante, where they always landed these days. She recalled the dance. The melody of the music. His carefully phrased words. *You have foresight, do you?* he'd asked.

Had she imagined a double meaning in his tone?

"Are you listening to me?" Maximillion thundered.

Isadora's concentration broke. She turned to face Max. The grooves on his forehead had deepened like ravines. He glowered at her.

"I'm sorry, what?" she asked.

"What's wrong with you?"

Isadora lifted her chin. "You may be angry, Maximillion, but you may not speak to me like that. I have done nothing to provoke your ire. Calm yourself, or sleep somewhere else and have a good time explaining *that* to Dante."

Something ignited in his gaze, then faded. He set aside the wine glass and licked his lips. "You're right. I . . ." His nostrils flared. He smoothed the front of his jacket. "I apologize."

"Accepted." She nodded to the table. "Sit and eat. Then we'll talk."

"I—"

"Sit. Now."

His chair moved backward with a spell. He glowered at her but obeyed. She sank into the chair across from him as the plates slid toward their respective owners. Isadora placed her napkin on her lap, then turned her attention to him.

"Tell me what happened."

Maximillion forked a piece of meat into his mouth, chewed, swallowed, and reached for a roll. "I was to start presenting the full isolationism plan tomorrow."

"Yes," she drawled, already perfectly aware. For the last two evenings, they'd obsessed over every tenet of the plan and every possible situation that might arise in negotiations. If she hadn't been so bored during the day, she might not have looked forward to the discussions so much. He'd seemed downright eager to see what she thought. It had fostered an unexpected camaraderie between them.

Max glared at his wine. "Now I shall not. Dante, who has already been presenting for the last week, has requested two extra days in which to solely review historical precedent. Before a vote could be taken amongst all of us on whether that would be fair, Vasily agreed to it. It's his Network. I couldn't very well protest so early in negotiations. But I didn't like it."

Isadora blinked, searching for the implication.

"It's a sign of favor," he snapped. In an unusual lapse of decorum, he leaned back in his chair, practically slouching. "I suspect they have some sort of subterranean deal here. Some hidden agreement."

"It was a single instance, Maximillion."

His eyes flickered to hers, then back to his food. He stewed in silence.

Deciding to turn the conversation slightly, she asked, "And Dostar? Does he seem to be reacting to Dante's plan with approval?"

"No." Forgoing his roll, he muttered something under his breath, straightened, and picked up his fork. With a careless mien, he asked, "And what of your day?"

"Boring," she murmured, glancing around. "I might go mad here."

"Your magic?"

"Restless, but fine. I'll need to use it eventually, however."

"We'll figure something out. Transport back to the Central Network for a few minutes, maybe."

"Do you need to meet with Serafina?"

"Not yet. I want to hear Dante out fully first."

Something lingered in his tone. Isadora wanted to pry into it but held back. Now wasn't the time. Besides, she already felt herself getting lost in the threads of this political tapestry after all her teas with the High Priestess's, who largely seemed to avoid the topic of politics.

Dante, as charming as he managed to be while dancing, was a cold-blooded murderer. She couldn't imagine what life had been like for Serafina since marrying him.

"Anything else?" she asked.

"Lunch is provided tomorrow, and the women are expected to attend. Dante has invited a singer."

Maximillion stood, pushing his plate away. Full darkness had fallen outside, coating the turret in warm shadows from the fireplace. The candle flames on the table danced, influenced by a subtle shift of air whistling underneath the door.

"I must update Charles," he said.

"Will you transport?"

"No. Written letter. He is . . . otherwise engaged tonight."

Maximillion moved back toward the fire, leaving Isadora to wonder what Charles could possibly be doing on a night like this.

She glanced toward the bed. Maximillion had slept on the floor cushions without a word, keeping his back to her all night, every night. His sleep had been restless, at best, and he'd awakened with a surly scowl that clearly hadn't improved all day.

With a sigh, she set her dishes on the platter. The lid sprang to life and hovered above the tray for a moment before settling with a clattering noise. The door sprang open to allow the tray to float out, then closed with a gentle *swish*.

"Well," Isadora said quietly. "I believe I'll . . . go to bed."

He said nothing, and she realized he might be in the paths. While Max was powerful, he had nothing like the strength of her magic, a fact that allowed him greater flexibility. Or at least made him less likely to be found out.

They hadn't seen any East Guards here, in any case. Yet. Likely, no Defenders were in residence.

Isadora slipped behind the screen with her long-sleeved nightgown in hand, a simple affair with no lace or frilly designs, just sturdy ivory fabric that fitted to her wrists. When she reemerged, Maximillion was still facing the fire.

Quickly, Isadora slipped under the covers of the giant bed. The sheets felt chilly, and heavy from the fur blanket. She curled into a ball, covering herself to her shoulders, and watched his lean, graceful form in the shadows.

Blushing from an unexpected pool of heat in her belly, she closed her eyes. Maximillion would be unbearable if he knew how deeply affected she was by the way he carried himself. The way the firelight danced across his strong jawline.

The memory of his unexpected, crushing kiss.

THE DAY before Maximillion's long-awaited presentation, Serafina entered the turret with the grace of a robin landing on a branch.

She stood in the doorway at first, taking in the surroundings. Dressed in a simple mauve gown with a necklace of garnets, she looked like an older version of Emilia. Her hair fell in waves on her shoulders, half pulled back from her face. Gentle crow's-feet edged her eyes. She was beauty with a hint of shrewdness.

Isadora curtsied. "Your Majesty, thank you for coming."

Nodding, Serafina rustled inside.

Thank you for your invitation to tea, the message to Isadora, received early that morning, had said. *I shall be there promptly at ten.*

Isadora had issued no such invitation.

"Good timing," Maximillion had muttered, though his eyes darkened. "She must be tracking this more closely than I expected. A listening maid, perhaps. I doubt Dante is telling her much."

"One of the shieldmaidens?" she suggested. She suspected that Arayana actually knew more than she'd originally believed, but had no confirmation.

Maximillion had simply stewed after that.

The door closed behind Serafina, and Isadora murmured an incantation Maximillion had taught her that morning.

Serafina stopped, one ear cocked toward her. Seeming satisfied once Isadora finished, she continued into the room without turning around. Light zipped around the doorway, sealing it from anyone who might try to listen in from the outside.

A circular table sat in front of the windows, overlooking a snowy world. Teacups, plates, and an arrangement of airy pastries covered the table, and two chairs flanked it, dressed with sapphire cloth and silver ribbons speckled with diamonds.

"Please," Isadora said, gesturing to the chair. "Have a seat."

Serafina complied, glancing at the windows.

"They were sealed this morning by Maximillion before he left. The maid came last night, the tea brought itself up, and Maximillion found no other magic at work when he left this morning. I believe you're safe here."

The tension in Serafina's shoulders calmed a little.

"Thank you," she said, meeting Isadora's gaze.

Startled by the force behind the words, Isadora nodded.

"I am happy to pour your tea, if you like," Isadora said, gesturing to the porcelain kettle. "But I often tire of people serving me and being ceremonious about everything. If you'd like an opportunity to relax from formalities, you may do so." Isadora gave a brief, uncertain smile. "I can't stand all these rules. I don't know how you do it all the time."

The comment was a gamble. If Serafina enjoyed the ceremony, she could be offended. If she didn't, she might relax. Isadora held her breath, waiting.

Serafina blinked twice, studying her. After what felt like an eternity, all her muscles seemed to soften at once. She leaned back in the chair and let out a long breath, then used a spell to pour the tea for both of them.

"Thank you," Serafina said again. "It's a . . . rare opportunity."

They were by no means easy with each other, nor truly

friendly yet. At least, however, the first barriers seemed down. Still, Isadora felt Serafina's careful inspection as she reached for a round pastry graced with frosting. As usual for the typical ostentatious display of plenty from the South, there would be many leftovers. Isadora already planned to transport them home.

"I appreciate your willingness to do this," Serafina said, "and I realize it's not . . . convenient."

Isadora set a tea bag into her hot water, watching the leaves slowly sink into the steamy depths. "It's my pleasure to have the opportunity."

Like Serafina, her words remained measured. Despite all magical precautions to protect them from listening ears, Serafina's life lay on the line. She'd take no chances.

Isadora grabbed a slip of parchment bearing Maximillion's handwriting and slid it across the table. Without touching it, Serafina read the words, where Maximillion asked about his suspicion of an agreement between Dante and Vasily. Isadora waited until it was clear Serafina had finished reading it, then reached for her teacup.

"The basis for suspicion is perhaps somewhat weak," Isadora said, purposely avoiding names—just in case. "But he's trying to be exhaustive. And prepared."

Serafina's brow furrowed. She fell into silence for several minutes before saying, "I don't know, to be honest. I've wondered myself, but I have no definitive proof. If there *is* any proof, he'd hide it from me."

"He doesn't trust you?"

Serafina shook her head. "He trusts no one except Cec —" She took a sip of tea. "He doesn't trust anybody. He's a passionate, determined, unusual man. A dichotomy in many ways."

Isadora tucked that in the back of her mind to think on later.

A dichotomy in many ways.

"Is he truly that excited about history, perhaps?" Isadora asked, grateful to think through all the possibilities that had been weighing her mind down.

"Winning," Serafina said. "He'll do whatever it takes to get what he wants, even if it's making a show of impressing someone else with historical proof."

"What does he want so badly?"

"The glory of doing what no one else in his family has done. Uniting all the Networks into one power, then attaining the throne."

With a shiver rushing down her spine, Isadora lifted the parchment, set fire to it with a spell, and sent the ashes out the window. The door to the balcony opened, admitting a gust of wind that twisted the plume outside and into the tundra. The tension in the room seemed to fade with the evidence gone. A beam of light, cast by Serafina, raced around the balcony door once it closed.

"Do you think they'd truly align?" Isadora asked, thinking of Vasily's proud bearing and Dante's charming grin. Could two such powerful men ever *really* form an alliance? Particularly under a plan that only allowed for one ruler? Their egos would likely get in their way. Such had been the last decade of wars.

"No, one would kill the other," Serafina said. "Both of them would plan to murder each other, and both would be aware of it. Success in a plan like this comes down to cleverness." Her voice quieted. "If his plan *is* chosen, the true winner is the one who survives the other three. That's the real game here."

Isadora let that sink in. Surely, all the leaders knew that.

Perhaps even Charles had an inkling. The Networks had been fighting for so long that they couldn't really conquer each other by force alone anymore. Their armies were too tired. The supply lines too depleted. The land too vast.

But a Network takeover from the top down? That was clearly on the table.

"I shall remain steadfast in watching for signs," Serafina added.

"Thank you."

"Your handfasting occurred very spontaneously." Serafina's gaze rested on Isadora's abdomen. "Was it necessary?"

The quick turn of conversation left Isadora reeling, but the topic filled her with fire. She swallowed hard, not bothering to school her flash of indignation. "I'm not pregnant, if that's what you're asking."

"I was." Serafina set her tea down with a sigh. "I'm relieved to hear that's not the case. Do you love him? Your affection seems real. When I first heard, I thought it was for this purpose alone, but as I've seen you together more . . . "

Setting aside the inherent insult in Serafina's response, Isadora focused on the question. Her heart felt as if a string had been pulled through it. Did she *love* him? What kind of question was that to ask?

And how was that her business?

She stared at the High Priestess, at a loss. Serafina was too advanced in the world to expect a love match from a political figure like Maximillion. Not to mention the sheer force of his personality certainly didn't scream *happy lover*. Serafina, herself, hadn't married for love.

"Is love a requirement?" Isadora asked coolly.

"Of course not. I'm simply curious. Where you handfasted?"

"At the castle."

"Who was there?"

"Ah . . ."

"And what did Maximillion wear?" Serafina leaned forward slightly, but no apology appeared on her face. "I'm curious about exactly how he'd handle such a traditional ceremony. He's not comfortable following a crowd, and he'd never do something just because culture expected it. Your cord of engagement is lovely, by the way."

Was he forced into this? was the implied question.

Isadora resisted the urge to touch the bracelet on her arm. Even aside from the fact that Serafina seemed to have Max pegged and appeared hungry for odd details, Isadora paused.

Could there be an ulterior motive for such questions? Was she working for herself in this interrogation? The pressure to smooth Serafina's questions into something else without answering them made her palms sweat.

Deciding to firmly pivot the conversation, she said, "You don't like me for him."

Serafina gave a humorless smile, one eyebrow lifting. "You're very bold. And correct," she murmured, but Isadora heard no warmth in the tone. "It's certainly not personal. I don't like anyone for Max."

"Is that your place?"

"I admit a certain level of fondness or affection for him," she said slowly, as if choosing her words with precision. "While he may not return the same feelings, I've known him longer than anyone here. No one else will look out for him. He certainly won't look out for himself. He'll do whatever it takes to achieve his aims."

Just like Dante.

What was she missing here? Were they former lovers? No. Impossible . . . wasn't it?

Isadora held herself back from deeper questioning. She'd think it over later. Instead, she focused on reading the changing expressions in Serafina's eyes, as difficult to catch as shifting light.

"I see."

"You don't," Serafina said. "Not at all. But how could you? If he hasn't told the woman he's handfasted to, I certainly won't. Let it suffice that there is history here you know nothing about."

Stunned into silence, Isadora simply stared at her, blinking. An overwhelming desire to defend her marriage to Maximillion filled her throat. She wanted to prove herself worthy of him. Wanted to tell Serafina that she did deserve him—and for good reason. The urge caught her by surprise.

If he hasn't told the woman he's handfasted to . . .

This tea certainly hadn't gone as expected.

"If he doesn't return your affection," Isadora said, finding her voice again, startled to hear it was mellow and even. "Then why ask him to present? Why not Dostar? As a High Priest, he surely has more power and sway."

"It had to be Max. For my own selfish reasons, and because he deserves the opportunity to . . . get what's due to him. And," she added, "it seems the only way to truly protect all of my witches. I've been puzzling over this plan for years now, and it's the only hope of . . . well . . . *safety* for all. Besides, Dostar wouldn't consider it. Not for a second."

"An interesting hope," Isadora muttered, "considering the Aldana tradition of murdering witches based on inherited magical ability."

Though she never said the word *Watcher*, it hung between them. Isadora stopped breathing. Maximillion would have her throat for saying such a thing.

Serafina stood with a rustle of her dress and a flash of

her eyes. "Thank you for your time and the tea. I look forward to . . . future conversations."

The door shut behind Serafina with unusual force. Isadora held her breath and sank lower into her chair with a frenzied swirl of magic and a deep groan.

That didn't go well at *all*.

17

Sanna woke slowly.

When she forced her eyes open, they felt like hot sandpaper. Her entire body ached. In the distance, she thought she heard shuffling.

She blinked several times before the picture cleared in her circle of vision. She frowned. The darkness around the edges had encroached further. What had once been fuzzy was now dim, closing off the band of her sight even further. She saw little more than a fist held out in front of her now.

Luteis?

She pushed off a rock floor, feeling nothing overhead and cool slate below. The air smelled . . . cold. Dry. Wind twirled around her ankles, stirring her hair, and she shivered. No matter where she looked, she only saw gray. The cocoon of darkness, served only by a point of light ahead of her, likely meant she lay in a cave.

I am here.

Another shuffle and the warm wrap of a tail around her ankle. She turned, noticing a comforting glint in the murk.

Luteis's wide yellow eyes blinked. She focused on them, remembering the trolls. The weight pressing on her chest. Selsay allowing her to communicate in the strange way of images.

She leaned against a wall, feeling suddenly dizzy. Her mind whirled like the weather outside. Eventually, her thoughts settled into a mixture of relief and disbelief, punctuated with Luteis's concern.

You are well?

Yes.

They might not have recruited anyone to help them fight yet, but they'd won this one against Prana, at least.

Luteis stayed close to her, keeping her warm in the chilly winter air. Outside, blankets of snow fell in lazy drifts. A rare mountain dragon winged by here and there. Luteis wrapped his tail around her, and she leaned into him. In all the world, he was the only thing she could truly rely on.

You have been sleeping for days, he said, pressing his face against the ground next to her, watching her with his steady gaze. She reached out a hand, her fingertips grazing the delicate scales of his face. He let out a purr deep in his throat.

"I feel like I've been sleeping for days. How are you?"

Tired. Hungry. But better.

The expression on Yushi's face as he peered at her from the gathering seawater rippled back through Sanna's memory. A bolt of concern seized her. They'd prevented the mountain trolls from wreaking havoc for now, but an even bigger problem remained: the sources of fresh water were slowly being tainted.

Prana's takeover of Antebellum wouldn't require floods over the whole land. She only had to control the fresh water. Would the goddess move south, turning all the water brackish? Or had she simply been trying to push the mountain trolls over the wall?

She felt a deep thirst and an even stronger hunger. The mountain dragons wouldn't think to get her water or food. Food was scarce enough, and anything here wouldn't be cooked. No, she needed to return home.

But even home wouldn't have much food.

Elis, she said, reaching out with her thoughts to speak to him. Her mind wasn't as sluggish, but it still felt like moving underwater. Several seconds passed.

Yes, High Dragonmaster?

Luteis and I will be home before dark.

Yes, High Dragonmaster.

Is there any food?

Another long pause. *Not much. The witches eat once a day, and the dragons once a week. Without Luteis, we have struggled.*

Thank you. We'll see you soon.

A settling of air preceded the silhouette of a dragon at the front of the cave. *High Dragonmaster,* Metok said, *you are well?*

"Yes, thank you, Metok. But we must be going. Luteis and I must hunt and scout out new grounds."

The snows come, he said, dark eyes glittering in the low light. *It would be wise to get ahead of them.*

"Thank you."

Metok hesitated, then bowed his head in the usual mute way of mountain dragons. *We are grateful for your help and acknowledge that, without a Dragonmaster, the trolls would not have remained contained. Perhaps there is room for . . . partnership.*

Sanna stared at his vague form, startled. "Thank you, Metok."

As brood sire, I am eager for my dragons to fight Prana and fulfill our destiny as warriors for Selsay, but I will trust your wisdom as we approach the winter.

He bowed his head again, then sprang away. Luteis stood, stretching like a scaly cat, as Sanna related what Metok said. A wave of heat rushed over Sanna, mixing with the chilly wind. It would be a cold ride home.

An unexpected offer of trust, he said.

"Indeed."

But a hopeful sign.

"Yes. I'm starving, and so are you, and we have a lot to do."

What is your plan now? he asked, eyeing her.

"First, food. Second, talk to the forest dragons. Let's reassess what we know, what we have, and what we need. After that, we need to actually find fighters. We can't stand up to Prana like this."

She said nothing of her further diminished eyesight and the low pulse of panic in the back of her mind. Did it matter anymore? She'd fight this battle regardless. Telling Luteis would only cause him to worry.

Where will you find food if I cannot find any, either?

"We'll find something. We have to."

IN SHORT, Elis said, *attempting to recreate what a battle may look like has yielded some preparation. Our dragons have seen marked improvement with flying, fire, and communication together. I'm ... quite proud.*

Sanna stood at the base of one of the Ancients, watching three forest dragons wheel through the air with more dexterity than she'd expected. One threw fire at a round target made of rocks on the ground, hitting it directly in the middle. Another burned a thin, precise line of secundum through a long-dead tree trunk. It seared through, crumbling the tree to ash and continuing into the soil. Elis had started to pick up on Luteis's caretaker habits, which meant the forest surrounding the Ancients had never been so clean.

"It's impressive to say the least," Sanna said. "It will only help our war against Prana. It's five weeks away now."

Ten forest dragons stood in a tight circle around her. What used to be an uncertain formation marked by haphazard responses had grown in discipline. Elis's skill as a leader and Jesse's nurturing temperament had done wonders for the forest dragons' confidence. She didn't doubt that only they could have done it. She didn't have their capacity for patience.

She turned to Elis. "Thank you. You've exceeded all my expectations. I can hardly believe the progress you've made."

If a dragon could purr, Elis did so then.

Behind them came the *thud* of makeshift wooden hammers. Trey and Greata had been making new wooden shingles over the past month. Trey nailed them to the roof of his future house now, closing the dragon-sized hole that had once been there.

Sanna turned to look at them. "And progress on the houses is equally impressive."

"They'll be winter ready within a week," Jesse said from next to her, hands in his pockets.

"None too soon."

A pang of guilt struck her. Thankfully, the Dragonmasters had carried on in her absence, but she felt awful for leaving them with such a heavy load. Elliot never stopped trapping. All the walking had nearly run him ragged, the effort yielding only enough food to keep them from starving. The younger kids chopped wood, gathered kindling, and scrounged for any type of food.

Snowflakes twirled from the branches overhead, borne on a gentle breeze. She thought she felt a stirring in the back of her mind. Low, deep whispers. They soon quieted. The trees sometimes spoke that way.

Jesse glanced up, expression troubled. She nudged him.

"Scared of a little snow?"

Her attempt at levity failed. He swallowed, his throat bobbing. "Only of sea dragons."

Jesse had seen the ocean on their first trip to the West. The desert dragons. The broader world. He knew just how big this battle could get. Elliot, Trey, and Greata had no frame of reference yet, although they planned to fly and help. She wasn't sure if that was good or bad.

Sanna sobered, thinking of Yushi. Of their failed attempts to amass an army. She'd stayed up late with Luteis hunting, discussing ideas as they crept silently through the wood. While she prowled the high bracken for smaller creatures, he'd soared overhead, sniffing out mortegas and throwing out random ideas.

Beluas cannot fight.

There are no more forest trolls.

Would the desert witches go to war, perhaps?

No creature from Letum Wood could effectively fight with them. The journey was too far. No witch, either, that they knew of. There were no dragons in the South or East, and the mams would only fight if forced. Which, judging by their current numbers, seemed more and more likely to be necessary.

Yet, in the back of all this lurked something infinitely more uncertain. Sanna felt itchy, as if she couldn't quite reconcile everything.

Something wasn't right.

She untangled her thoughts and returned to the present, then reached out, touching Jesse's arm.

"We'll figure it out," she said. "I promise."

He stared hard at her before finally nodding. His shoulders relaxed. Behind them, Elis had released the dragons.

"Thanks, Sanna."

After Jesse left to help Trey, she remained alone in the circle except for Luteis.

Did you notice, he asked, breaking the awful silence in her mind, *that Selsay kept the mams within a circle of mountains?*

"Yes."

And Yushi mentioned his supposed twin being kept in a circle as well.

"Yes."

Do you think it means something?

Sanna slowly turned, unable to behold the behemoth trees with her limited sight.

"Yes," she said slowly, thinking of the fallen tree and the magic that had illuminated it on her touch.

Fly with me. He extended his tail. *I want to show you something. You will require a torch.*

~

HOURS LATER, Sanna sat on a branch that could have easily been a hill.

It stretched into the darkness, ending somewhere beyond sight. At her back stood a stalwart, venerable trunk.

Luteis hovered only a handspan from her, eyes darting here and there.

In all of my life, he said quietly, *I have only approached one of the Ancients so directly once, and it happened on accident. I fell from the canopy and landed here.*

"You fell?" she whispered.

He snorted. *I was injured in flight when first learning. I landed here. Days passed while I recovered, but I did recover. Vines came to me in a kind of cradle. Sometimes, in the depths of the pain, I thought I heard whispers. Reassuring voices. They were . . . friends.*

A dense feeling hung in the still air. To move quickly or speak loudly seemed wrong. Sanna reached out a hand, touching the trunk. Sheets of bark, some as large as the houses they lived in, protected the mountainous tree. She saw no tangled vines from persnickety fairies or cast-aside leto-nut shells from climbing gnomes. Aside from curtains of moss, the tree was pristine.

"The trees whispering, you think?"

As you say.

"So, why did you bring me here now?"

Luteis had flown her around the tree, inspecting it from top to bottom, and then landed here. Her narrow view had made it impossible to see more than a small section at a time, forcing them to loop the same spot several times.

I wanted to show you this.

He gestured with a nod to the trunk, where a clear opening between sheets of bark led into the tree like a tunnel.

I ventured in there while bored one day. I couldn't get to the ground without injuring myself, and it was weeks before I could fly again. Deasylva brought me food, but I was young. Seeing this tunnel, I followed it.

"In there?" She pointed to the opening.

He lowered his head, peering at it. *Yes. I didn't go far. I felt
. . . as if I shouldn't proceed. As if it weren't mine. Something
stopped me, though I saw nothing.*

"A creature?"

A feeling.

Sanna would have snorted, but in all this, something
seemed to be searching for *her*. Something vastly older. The
magic stirred in her fingertips.

This branch seemed to be in the exact middle of the
tree, if it was possible to measure such a thing. Each layer of
bark was anchored to the piece behind it, but some didn't
connect entirely, allowing a sort of . . . maze. She waited at
the juncture of branch and trunk, feeling magic hum into
her feet.

"I can't see in there, but I can feel that we're supposed to
go in."

He hesitated for only a heartbeat. *Where you go, I will go.
I was not welcome before, but . . . it feels different today.*

Sanna reached for the torch she'd brought at his insistence. Luteis set fire to the wood tied with a tacky moss that
would burn for hours. The flame illuminated Sanna's eyes
with a brief flare, and she felt a nudge of comfort at seeing
the light ahead.

"Thanks. Let's go."

Most trees balked in her head at the sight of flame, but
she felt no anxiety here. Just a slow-moving presence as she
advanced into the darkness between bark plates. Luteis
followed.

Sanna stepped cautiously, probing with a toe before
each step, and a carved path revealed itself. The uneven
layers of bark eventually gave way to a more solid wall.
The winding trail allowed them both passage if Luteis

kept his wings tucked. His broad, warm presence reassured her.

After several minutes of shuffling, Sanna paused. Not even a hint of light from the outside leaked in, and her torch revealed nothing but more darkness. But the space felt airy. She held her torch higher, finally seeing the light bounce off the wall to her right. Luteis opened his wings, able to brush them along the sides.

We are not the first to come here. Someone must have created this, Luteis said.

A hiding place, you think?

It could be many things.

Sanna couldn't imagine who had come before them—nor how long ago. It certainly seemed that something had created this passage. Time, perhaps, or the tree itself.

She reached out. Smooth, grainy wood, polished to the touch, met her fingertips. She pressed her hand against it. Luminescence sprouted from her fingers, rippling outward. The magic activated and vanished, as if the tree had absorbed it.

Then light sprang into life.

Lines of a familiar white-blue light illuminated the grains that ran in circles through the tree. It raced overhead, brightening the soaring, cave-like chamber. Luteis's burnt-orange scales glowed like a coal.

Something pulsed in the background, sluggish and warm. Her mind stirred. The magic flared in her hands as if recognizing an old friend. Another whisper came into her mind. Deep in voice, with a steady cadence, like Daid when he woke early in the morning.

You belong to us.

Luteis's eyes snapped to hers. Sanna's heart skipped a

beat. She pushed her hand back into the bark, feeling the magic flow from her. The tree accepted it, just like the rocks in the North. Sanna gave from what felt like an endless well inside her, as if the power were looping back into her body.

"I do," she whispered.

We have waited for you.

Other deeper, aged voices murmured. She couldn't make out their words, just the reverberating tones. Their expansiveness, their *ancientness,* filled her head. The depth of the magic seemed to know no bounds, and she feared she'd be lost in it.

"I am Sanna of the forest."

We know you and your dragon servant.

"He's not my servant. He's my friend."

You are . . . different than all the others. We sense a deep loyalty to your dragon friends but not to our goddess. Is this true?

"Yes."

Silence.

We have waited for you. This time it was amplified, as if many of the trees spoke all at once.

"We need help," she said.

Deasylva said you might come. You need the forgotten. That which witches have cast aside for eons now.

The voice came more easily now. The deep, rolling timbre filled her mind, surprisingly gentle despite its sheer size. Surely she stood somewhere in its pulsing heart.

"Who are the forgotten?"

We have never been asked.

Luteis watched her closely, keeping half his body in the passage that would lead them back out. She stood alone in the middle of the room.

The odd silence continued until she opened her mouth

to speak, but the tree continued, *In the beginning were four sisters, the goddesses. And four brothers, the gods. They formed this world.*

Lines of light coalesced into four figures on the wall of the tree, bright enough that Sanna could make out individual details in the sisters. One had extraordinarily long hair. Another's locks were cut short. Two of them stood at sharply varying heights. The four brothers had the same differing qualities but broader shoulders. The light faded.

But Antebellum *was special. This was the only land with magic.*

An uneven map appeared, a great blob of land. Antebellum. She'd seen faded maps of Antebellum in Babs's lessons as a young girl, although she hadn't cared much about them at the time.

From the goddesses flows magic. They create, give, take, hide, and reveal. But they must proceed with caution, for every magic they create demands balance, and what has been made cannot be unmade.

A chorus of hums joined in the background. The other Ancients seemed to sing with this tree. She could feel the souls of the trees around her.

They lived for millennia in peace. The four goddesses coexisting with their brothers. Forming magic. Witches. Mortals. To some they gave, and from some they took. It was . . . a peaceful time. We, mere saplings as our goddess grew into her power, remember little of the early days so long, long ago, when witches first lived.

The images on the wall faded.

The gods created the mortals, and the goddesses the witches. Eventually, witches and mortals destroyed each other. Jealousy. Pain. The gods of ice, wind, fire, and sky threatened the goddesses.

The gods would always protect their mortals, so they left for another land, abandoning the four sisters.

Prana, a trickster, bored and eager for something new, created Dragonian magic. The sea dragons hassled witches. Violently demanded loyalty to the goddess of the sea. Sarena, the eldest, tried to stop her youngest sister. Prana would not desist. Dragonian magic grew, and the other three sisters took part to protect their witches.

"They created their own dragon races," she murmured.

Prana took exception to the meddling in her magic and threatened to flood the land, destroying the witches and creatures her sisters loved.

Sanna glanced at Luteis. He stared at her with wide eyes. "Sounds familiar," she murmured.

Sarena attempted to break the magic and save the world, but one sister cannot destroy the magic of another. Sarena's land was flooded for her attempt, destroying many.

"Sarena only broke the magic of her own dragons instead of the magic overall, right?"

How greatly she mourned.

The other voices mumbled their assent. A stone rose in Sanna's throat. Her heart pounded as she recalled her conversation with Yushi.

What is freedom to you? she'd asked.

A lack of magic.

A vague understanding grew in her chest. A clarity she didn't want. She inhaled sharply, trying to breathe around her horror because it couldn't possibly be true.

Dragonian magic was created so that dragons will serve their goddess in whatever manner she prefers, the tree continued. *Dragons* exist *to serve their goddess. Is this not known amongst your kind?*

The voice sounded surprised.

Sanna hesitated. She understood it differently. Dragonian magic protected the dragons and the Dragonmasters. It allowed her to communicate directly with Deasylva and compelled dragons to act. It allowed connection between dragon and witch. But in the end . . .

Dragonian magic *was* the master.

A deep groaning rippled around them.

We know only the soil to which we're tethered. Our experience comes from years with Deasylva, since the beginning. We as saplings, she young in her newfound power. There is little of the wide world we truly understand.

Whatever Prana wants, another said. *It will not be for the betterment of the world. It never has been. May you fare well in your quest. This is the forgotten, that which no one has asked.*

Come back to us, said another, *for we know you.*

Their voices faded. Like the magic, they bled away, ending with a final sigh and a barely audible *you belong to us.*

Sanna removed her hand. "Thank you," she whispered.

She turned, walking up the path back to Letum Wood. Her eyes and head ached. Once in fresh air again, she blinked.

Vengeful goddesses. Gods and mortals. Created magic.

A master is still a master.

She felt as if she'd emerged from an earthy womb. Everything was different. Her world had shifted and would never be the same.

Luteis stood next to her. She put a hand on his flank and met his gaze.

"We've had it all wrong, Luteis," she whispered. "It's not Prana we have to defeat in order to save the world. Yushi said it before. *To understand the true purpose behind the cycle of dragon deaths in the way of Dragonian magic.* Prana killing because of her stupid whims? It's happened before, and it will happen again."

Luteis's brow grew heavy in silent question. She let out a long breath, her hand dropping to her side.

"It's the magic we must break."

18

Maximillion glared at the fire.

Isadora, just returning from a cordial walk around the gardens with Emilia and Arayana, stopped in her tracks. He didn't acknowledge her presence, so she set aside her warm gloves, shrugged off her cloak, and stood by the hearth.

"You're going to glare a hole in the fireplace," she said, rubbing her hands together. Gray clouds burgeoned on the horizon, threatening snow. Never in her life had she seen this much winter. The cold air flushed her cheeks, but she felt more alive after being out of the close turret.

"Your magic," he muttered. "I can feel it from here."

"I know."

It swirled within her, restless. She'd transported home last week, checked on Mam, wandered in the paths, visited Pearl, and returned within four hours. The reprieve had helped, but not truly satisfied. So little use of so much power made it feel like electricity jumping in her veins.

"You need to transport home and vent it again."

"Tomorrow," she promised.

He grunted.

"Is something on your mind?" she ventured, hands held to the warm flames. He glanced at her, back to the fire, then to her again. When he leaned forward, his left leg bounced a little.

"Dostar made an excellent point today. My plan to deal with the black-market witches will never work," he muttered. "I hate it when he does that."

She chuckled under her breath. The nuances required in planning the establishment of peace throughout four Networks boggled her. For the last week, Maximillion had been presenting of every tenet of the isolationism plan. After a one-day break, Dostar would present his.

"Glad you've realized it. Now what?"

"Sending witches to the dungeons if they've crossed the border will only burden us. We can't have borders so strict that prisoners can't be handed over. That would leave us to feed or kill whatever witches are desperate enough to cross. We have to send them back." He stood, throwing his coattails behind him, and began to pace. "But there are too many holes in that. I have to figure out an alternative."

"Would you like some special help?" she asked, infusing significance into the words. If he answered affirmatively, she'd know to offer another invitation to Serafina for tea.

He scowled. "Not yet. We can puzzle this out easily enough."

Her heart warmed at the thought of him wanting her help as a partner. A tap came on the door.

"Come in!" she called.

The door opened, admitting a tray loaded with platters and glasses. It settled onto the table, and the door closed. Isadora lifted one lid and breathed in the scent of hot soup filled with melted cheese, bread crumbs, and rubbery onions.

"A little food may help you feel better," she said. "Come. Eat. The brown bread is crusty and delicious with soup, no doubt."

"No."

Isadora rolled her eyes, grabbed him by the shoulders, tugged him to the table, and shoved him into the chair. "You're unbearable when you're hungry and stumped. Then we can talk this out together."

The lid over his plate whisked itself away to the sideboard while Isadora settled across from him. "Have you spoken with Charles?" she asked.

His brow grew heavy. "Yes."

A knock sounded at the door, louder than the tap that had announced the food's arrival.

Maximillion frowned and called, "Who is it?"

"Visitor for you, sir," came a maid's voice. Isadora started to rise, but Maximillion motioned her to stay. He reached into his jacket and, finding something in an inner pocket, moved toward the door.

"Coming," he called.

He glanced at Isadora again. She nodded. Who would come and visit them at this time of day?

The door opened. Maximillion's expression didn't waver. "Thank you," he said to the maid. "She's welcome."

A familiar head of mousy-blonde hair, now lined with subtle streaks of gray, slipped into the room. Isadora waited until the door had closed and the maid's footsteps had faded down the staircase to push away from the table.

"Lucey!" she cried. "Why are you—but, what's wrong? You look so pale."

Lucey rushed for her, embraced her with a wince, then

turned around to face Maximillion. She took a step back, putting space between the two of them. Her body was skin and bones under her baggy dress.

"I'm sorry for this," she said.

"Not at all," he replied, concern in his gaze. "What's happened?"

"I-I came as soon as I could." Her voice trembled.

Isadora stepped back, putting a hand on her shoulder. "Lucey, sit. You're shaking."

Lucey collapsed into Isadora's chair. Her pale face—so white that blue streaks ran under the skin—appeared hollow, her eyes bloodshot. Had she been crying? She twisted her hands over and over, chewing on her swollen bottom lip.

"Lucey?" Isadora asked, setting a warm hand on her shoulder.

Lucey startled, then grimaced and shied away from the touch.

"It's the Advocacy. I-I just came from the rendezvous point."

Lucey's breath seemed to stick in her throat, coming out in shuddering gasps. Something cold and hot moved through Isadora. Maximillion crouched next to Lucey and grabbed her arms, his hold gentle but firm.

"What happened?"

Lucey blinked several times. His touch seemed to restore some color. She nodded, swallowing hard. "Around the time you left, rumors of a resurgent group of roaming Defenders started to circulate. I sent out a notice to all Advocacy members, but nothing happened, so I didn't tell you. All the reports came back fine. Everything has been . . . so quiet since La Torra."

She closed her eyes, letting out a short, fast exhale. Then

she shook her head. "A note came from one of our Advocacy members in Berry just an hour or so ago."

"Sophie?" he asked, brow furrowed.

Lucey nodded.

Isadora's eyes nearly bugged out. "*Sophie?* As in Miss Sophia's School for Girls?"

Maximillion waved that away impatiently. "Yes. What did she say?"

"I don't know!" Lucey said. "You know Sophie. It was something vague and cryptic about *birds* and *flowerpots* or something inane like that. I went to check it out, and she . . . she was . . . she was already gone."

His entire body tensed.

Lucey's lips quivered as she nodded, answering his silent question. "Dead."

With little difficulty, Isadora recalled the last time she'd seen Sophie. The strange way she slipped from semi consciousness to her usual vapid self. She'd been vague as the wind and odd, desperately in love with Max and unusually self-serving, but certainly not deserving of death.

"Someone destroyed everything," Lucey said. "Not a board of the old school remains. Not even that horrible shack she lived in. Nothing."

Isadora's magic flared, desperate for use. She hesitated, looking to Max. As if he could sense her silent request to go into the paths, he shook his head.

"How long ago?" he asked Lucey.

"Not fifteen minutes. I-I came as soon as I—" She turned away and put a hand to her head. "Forgive me. My head . . . it aches."

"You don't feel well?"

"No," Lucey gasped. "Not at all. I'm sorry. I thought I could come. I thought . . ."

Maximillion put a hand on her shoulder, and she drew in a deep breath. He muttered something that sounded like a calming incantation, then met Isadora's gaze and motioned her to step away.

"Rest yourself for a moment, my friend," Maximillion murmured. "Let me talk to Isadora."

With another deep breath, Lucey obeyed. Her eyes fluttered closed as she slumped further into the chair. Maximillion put a hand on Isadora's arm and pulled her close as they backed away.

"I'm going to Sophie's," he whispered. "I'll send word. Stay with Lucey. She's . . . not well. I'm worried for her. I think she reentered the Advocacy too soon after Carcere. This is likely stirring up all kinds of memories."

"Of course. Please be careful."

He hesitated. "I may be gone all night. I need to warn the Advocate and—"

"I'll handle here," she said confidently.

He opened his mouth to say something, decided against it, and slowly nodded. "I . . . thank you."

Then he was gone. Feeling his absence keenly in the silence, she turned. Lucey, still pale and trembling, sat at the table, holding herself. Isadora returned to her side.

"Lucey, you—"

Lucey sucked in a sharp breath, eyes screwed shut. "I thought I was ready," she murmured. "I thought I could handle it, but I can't. I-I'm not. This is too much. It's . . . it's too much!" She doubled over with a keen.

Lucey had had a hard time returning to life after La Torra. Being locked up for ages in a dark cell, with no word from the outside world, had changed her. She'd never spoken about what had happened, if they'd tortured her, what she went through. But her emotions had been far wilder ever since. The littlest things, even an unexpected motion or sound, sent her into a fright.

"No one expects you to help run the Advocacy the same way, Lucey. No one even expects you to still help. You—"

"I'm sorry." Lucey stood, her eyes haunted. "I-I must go back to my home. My birds."

Seconds later, she vanished. Legs wobbly, Isadora sank into a chair and sat in the quiet, her mind wheeling.

THE WIND GUSTED NEARLY all night.

Isadora sat up just before dawn, startled to find the heavy storm had stopped, leaving behind only icy cold. Her breath crystallized in front of her, stealing into her heavy nightgown and thick blankets. Snow coated the balcony, as heavy as custard.

The shuffle of feet ascending the turret stairs came from the hall. Isadora slipped out of bed, wrapped a blanket around herself, and opened the door just as Maximillion reached for the knob.

He stalked inside, yanked his coat off, and threw it on the table. Wordlessly, he collapsed in the chair nearest the hearth. Firelight rimmed his gaunt features. The clock ticked overhead. Ten past four.

Isadora breathed a sigh of relief to see him safe again.

"I went to her place," he said as she pattered to his side and sat in a chair next to him, wrapped in a thick blanket. "It's exactly as Lucey reported it."

"Sophie's dead?"

His nostrils flared. "Dead. It doesn't appear that she suffered, but she seemed to put up a fight. Pearl agreed to oversee preparations for her funeral. I've spoken with the Advocate. They are personally investigating."

"Why Sophie?"

"Indeed."

How absurd that Sophie, of all witches, was part of the Advocacy. The thoughts churned like an eddy, giving an odd sense of surrealism to the night. Her mind butted up against something. She frowned. What was she not seeing?

Then a glimpse of clarity.

Hadn't she spoken of Sophie recently? Yes. While moving. No—while dancing. It was . . .

A cold chill washed over her body. Dante.

I heard a rumor that you attended a Network school. Did you like the system? Serafina and I have long hoped to revamp our educational system once all these wars have abated.

And how had she replied?

I couldn't say, Your Majesty. I wasn't there for long. It was an odd school, run by a witch named Sophie who didn't have much to teach. With all the wars, there isn't much education anywhere, I imagine.

No. That was pure happenstance. A moment of conversation that meant nothing.

Or was it?

Something heavy sank in her stomach. Racing now, her mind flipped back to the spot where she'd slipped into the paths here in the South. There had been a touch that had pulled her out. She'd been viewing witches in the paths, and the touch had come right when she'd commanded Dante . . .

She slouched, her head spinning.

"Isadora? You're pale. What in the good gods is wrong?"

Maximillion was crouching next to her now, a heavy hand on her shoulder. She reached out, grabbing his arm, feeling more stable once she had ahold of him.

"What is it?" he demanded.

"Tobacco," she whispered. "I smelled tobacco."

"What?"

"When I used my power," she said, shaking her head. Quickly, she relayed the day in the forest, when she'd looked for Serafina and Arayana, and Emilia had followed her. She'd been pulled from the paths by a touch, and she'd smelled a hint of tobacco on the air.

"Dante," she murmured. "I-I think it was . . . maybe it was Dante. The smell in the forest? It was the same I smelled while dancing with him. Maybe he felt my magic and followed me . . . oh, Max . . . Dante may have seen me while I was in the magic. He . . ."

May have been called to me by my use of power.

The idea that *Dante* could be her match and called by her power was . . . absurd. Still, panic surged through her veins. Everything seemed to stop.

Serafina had said *he was a dichotomy in many ways.*

And Isadora had puzzled over his oddly worded question at the ball. *You have foresight, do you?*

She wanted to vomit.

Maximillion stared so hard at her she thought he was trying to break her. But his gaze seemed distant. Then, blinking calmly, he came out of his magic, swallowed, and asked, "Did you tell him about Sophie?"

Tears welled up in her eyes. "When we danced. But only vaguely! He asked about the school system and whether I attended. Said he wanted to reform theirs in the East, for Emilia and—the good gods, Max. I had no idea."

"No, he would have gotten any clue out of you before you had a chance to learn political machinations," he said, clearing his throat. Regret lingered in his tone. "As I said. Cunning."

He straightened, moving away. Horror tripled through Isadora's body. If she hadn't engaged in that conversation, would Sophie still be alive?

A sob thickened her throat. "Max, I never thought—"

"It's not your fault. You didn't kill Sophie. He would have found out some other way. If there is, indeed, a connection. There may be no connection here at all. A rogue Defender, perhaps. An ex-lover of Sophie's. We don't have actual proof it was the Defenders."

The steadiness of his tone set her more at ease, although she still felt sick to her stomach. He stood at the fireplace. The idea of Sophie having an ex-lover would have made her laugh at any other time. Instead, she choked back a cry.

"Is it possible?" she whispered. "Could Dante be my match? I may have inadvertently called him there that day, and he left before Emilia could see him. I . . ."

Maximillion sucked in a sharp, weary breath. "Yes. The odds are . . . ridiculous that he, of all witches, is your magical opposite. But to say it's impossible . . ."

"Then Sophie's death is a message to me!" Isadora cried. "She was a former teacher of mine. He may have thought I felt some affection for her. If he truly loved Cecelia and mourns her, he'll want to make me suffer for what happened on La Torra. This could be just the beginning."

Maximillion's expression indicated he'd already thought of that.

"I need to visit the Advocate again," he said, rubbing a hand over his face. "Let them know. Have them do more . . . searching. They can see if it's possible Dante is the most powerful Defender in Antebellum."

"It would certainly explain his desire to destroy Watchers."

Annoyance flickered in his gaze. "Not all Defenders are

monsters, Isadora. We'll know more by tonight. Get some sleep."

After he transported away, Isadora stared at the fire, the memory of vapid Sophie heavy in her mind. The cresting guilt crashed like a wave, and she collapsed to the floor in sobs.

19

*H*ow *does one destroy magic?*

Sanna lay on Luteis's back, staring into the canopy. He crouched on a high branch, unmoving, waiting for a sign of life below. Above the canopy, storm clouds covered the night sky, leaving the forest in darkness. She closed her eyes, unable to see anything anyway.

Was this what it would be like when her sight was totally gone?

She shoved aside her panic. She'd have to think about it later, at a more convenient moment.

I believe magic destroys itself, Luteis said.

How?

I've never attempted, so I cannot speak with authority. Like the ancients, Deasylva always spoke of balance.

What facets of Dragonian magic had to be balanced? Had she thrown off the balance by being Dragonmaster over two races? If a goddess gave too much power, would the balance suffer?

There had to be rules.

In some ways, it felt like the ancient trees had only

stirred up more questions. After the last four days of thinking and strategizing, she almost wished for the simplicity of a battle again.

Now they had to win a battle *and* break a magic.

Luteis's heat kept her warm despite the chilly night. Hours of flight away, the Dragonmasters slept. But Sanna's hungry belly kept her motivated to stay with Luteis. She hadn't eaten since yesterday morning.

Think Aki would know? she asked.

Perhaps.

I wish Isadora were here. She knows magic better.

Luteis drew in quick breaths, likely scenting something out.

For a moment, Sanna allowed herself to think of her sister. Mam's updates from the South. The food Isadora sent that likely kept the children from near starvation.

I believe you made the correct decision, Luteis said, *when you had Metok send mountain dragons to find Tashi. She is wise. Not only will she help us find other witches to fight for us, but she may know more.*

Thanks.

She felt a pulse of relief. Being a leader felt disorienting, at best. She never knew if her decisions were the right ones. Like trying to shoot an arrow in the dark. She eventually had to loose the bowstring, but she never wanted to hurt anyone.

Three hours, four quail eggs, a few small critters, and an old mortega later, they landed in the circle. A familiar witch with white hair, dark skin, and a bright smile awaited them.

"Tashi," Sanna said quietly, sliding off Luteis's back.

Tashi grinned, her teeth gleaming. "Good to see you again, High Dragonmaster."

Metok was nowhere to be seen—only Tenzin, Tashi's loyal desert dragon, was with her.

"Did Metok find you?"

"Metok?"

"My mountain-dragon sire. He was supposed to send mountain dragons looking for you on my behalf."

Tashi tilted her head. "No."

"Then why are you here?"

"Because you are looking for me."

"But how did you know?"

Tashi clicked, and Tenzin shifted closer. "The desert told me. Deliver your food, and climb on your dragon. We have a long flight ahead of us into the heart of Sarena's land, where I have someone you need to meet."

20

Three days later, the trickling sound of water woke Sanna.

She groaned and rolled onto her back. Was this heat from Hatha? Had she died? If she had, Deasylva had better send her to Halla. She deserved a rest and reward for all the work she'd done. But only the fires of Hatha would be this hot.

Her eyes flew open.

She lay on her back on a sandy hill, under a lip of red rock. Outside, a fresh field of stars extended over a dark desert, brilliant as a handful of sunshine in water.

She blinked several times, then sat up. Sand slid off her. *Luteis?* she asked.

I am here. We are almost ready to leave.

Before Sanna's sluggish mind could piece that together, Tashi stood near her. No sand stuck to her powerful legs when she grabbed a water pouch and tapped it against Sanna's arm.

"Drink. We'll be flying through the night again before we arrive at first light. Avia will be waiting."

Three days of sleep and two full nights of flight already separated them from Letum Wood. Sanna didn't like being that far from her dragons with the battle a month away, but her desperation drove her to follow Tashi into the desert. They had to find someone to help fight.

"Thank you," she said.

Cool water dribbled out of the pouch, which never emptied. She couldn't imagine what kind of magic had created such a thing. In a world like this, it was the difference between life and death. Tashi had supplied her with food. Tough dried meat that tasted glorious, and a flat kind of wafer, thin as a fingernail, that she'd cooked on a hot rock.

Luteis waited outside. Thankfully, the heat rarely affected him.

The distant horizon was darkness on darkness—the vast sand only barely reflecting the stars in a more subdued ribbon of light. She stood, brushed the crusty sand off her leather pants, and deeply regretted not grabbing her skirt and sandals before they left.

Tashi shot her a sidelong glance, though her voice was carefully moderated. "Are you ready?"

Though clad only in a sleeveless linen shirt and a pair of pants, Tashi seemed indifferent to the diminishing heat.

"Yes."

Tashi gestured ahead, her palm glowing in the rising moonlight. "Then let us finish our course."

As the morning heat overtook them, Sanna stumbled after Tashi through an endless landscape of sand. Its lack of firmness left every step feeling like a sinkhole.

With no landmarks except hilltops, it felt like they were going nowhere. Sanna followed uneasily, unable to make out details in the vast vista.

She kicked her feet into the sand instead of placing them, finding greater traction that way. The fuzzy edges of her vision had dimmed to darkness, creating a perfect circle now. Her eyes ached from the unending brightness of sun on sand.

In the distance, a strange groaning rippled through the desert.

Did you hear that? Luteis asked from where he flew above her.

Tashi stopped walking.

Yes, Sanna replied. She cocked her head and cupped a hand around her ear to hear better, but the sound had fallen quiet.

Tashi didn't even pause. "It's the desert."

Tashi moved with surprising speed in the sand. Her muscular calves kept a steady pace. She was, no doubt, more accustomed to such work, but it seemed more like she just belonged there.

Though the sun had just risen, sweat beaded on the back of Sanna's neck and trickled down her spine, making her lion leather cling to her skin.

"Why do you love the desert?" Sanna asked.

"It is one of my homes."

"Were you born here?"

"Some would say, though no one really knows. I love the simplicity. The lack of clutter. It is minimalistic, and I thrill to the challenge of survival." Tashi stopped, arms spread. "We have arrived."

Sanna could make out nothing but a monstrous pile of

sand she prayed they wouldn't have to climb over. "Where?" she gasped.

A grin split Tashi's lips. "To Corvallis, the heart of the desert."

She gestured ahead at the endless layers of sand. Tenzin flew at a fast clip overhead, his shadow passing over the expanse. The sound of tinkling bells rang as if from the desert itself, drawing Sanna's attention back to the hill.

Had it just shifted? It seemed . . . bigger. And if Sanna's eyes weren't mistaken, there was more than one such slope.

Luteis dove closer, following Tenzin's quick movements. At first, Sanna saw nothing distinct through the heat waves, but then the mound definitely moved. Wind whipped past them, stirring dust into billowing tails.

"Come." Tashi beckoned with a wave. "We shall speak with Avia."

"Avia?"

Tashi walked straight at a second mountain of sand that *definitely* hadn't been that high before. Sanna followed, feeling more than seeing the shifting granules around them. The hills parted ahead of Tashi, clearing a path.

"Does it do this for everyone?" Sanna asked as they continued into the rapidly parting tunnel. It closed behind them, like a sandy tomb. She gulped. One good breath of wind, and she would never escape.

"Not everyone."

Luteis, what do you see?

You are walking toward an oasis. A fairly large one, surrounded by several high mounds of sand. The sand seems to be moving into these . . . mountains. There are many unfamiliar smells.

Sanna scanned frantically, attempting to discern what

was in front of her. Only murky snatches of sky were apparent before the view suddenly opened up.

Tashi stopped, spreading a hand. "Corvallis."

A valley dipped below them at the feet of giant sand mountains as large as any peak Sanna had seen in the North. Sounds from below ricocheted off the loose walls. Tenzin landed ahead of them, skidding down the embankment with childlike glee.

Tashi continued down, the sand cascading in front of her. Then she sat, laughing and sliding on a loose rug of granules down the enormous hill.

Other witches called to each other, notes of excitement in their voices. Sanna swallowed hard. *Mori*, but she hadn't expected an entire civilization. While she couldn't make out many details, she saw something like structures. Heard bells and children.

Life.

Did they come from the sand? Sanna asked.

No, Luteis replied, landing next to her. *The sand simply hid them. Or, perhaps, magic did.*

Tentatively, Sanna started down. The track Tashi had taken had already disappeared back into a smooth facade. She stepped into it, breath held. Descending required hardly any time at all. The sand seemed to pull her.

Witches in loose, flowing white shirts swarmed Tashi. Children hung from her arms as she teased them in a language that sounded more like clicks and whistles than words.

They do not appear to be afraid of me, Luteis said with some relief as they settled on firm ground. *At least, all who have seen me don't seem bothered.*

Tashi turned, two children hanging off her shoulders,

and called, "High Dragonmaster of the forests and mountains. You are welcome here."

Several pairs of eyes turned to face Sanna.

She drew in a deep breath and shuffled forward, viewing as much as she could without turning her head every direction.

Tashi called out in the other language to the congregating witches, a beaming smile on her face. Witches emerged out of solid structures built into the walls. Towering trees with green fronds sprouting like branches littered the circular ring at the bottom of the sand mountains. Smaller bushes with long, wiry leaves sprouted from the very middle of the circle.

Luteis's nostrils flared as he slipped behind her. *Water,* he said. *The most I've ever smelled in the West.*

This is the biggest oasis we've seen.

It is more than that.

Another circle?

Luteis snorted. *Precisely.*

Witches numbering in the hundreds appeared, rushing toward them with elated shouts. They clamored around Tashi, then Sanna, then Luteis—quickly recoiling from his heat, which made them laugh. Luteis kept his wings folded in, then raised his head and snorted fire. The children giggled until they fell over.

I have a feeling they don't receive many visitors, Luteis said wryly.

"Come," Tashi said, guiding Sanna through the close press of sweaty bodies. "We will meet Avia."

"Avia?"

"The grandfather of the desert. These witches and their ancestors have lived in the desert since it began. The stories are ancient, as ancient as you will find anywhere."

Sanna didn't have time to ask what that had to do with building up an army. The crowd surged forward, carrying her farther into the broad circle, which seemed to be peeling away into an even greater space. Witches separated her from Luteis now.

You are well? Luteis asked.

Yes. Sanna barely dodged a flying elbow. She kept her head ducked and her feet moving quickly. *I'm all right.*

Can you see?

Not much.

Say the word, he murmured, *and I shall remove you from the crowd.*

Sanna let it go, not wanting to give insult or raise suspicion. Besides, she was drawn forward by her own curiosity. They passed through rows of open structures, built by pillars made from hardened sand. Milky glass panes blunted the overhead sunshine, muting the intense light.

Still, snatches of color here and there reflected the sun. Turquoise. Butter yellow. Glittering green. Whatever they were, they hung from the sand structure and appeared to be made of glass.

Where am I now? she asked. *There is so much color.*

It appears to be . . . a place.

That's helpful.

I am not aware of the habits of these witches. Or any witches.

Sanna begrudgingly conceded. He really didn't know witches well. *A market?*

Is that where witches trade?

Yes.

Then I believe you are correct.

The ground became firmer, almost like stone, as the crowd swept her along, still chanting. She could just make out the word *Avia* between whistles. The mountains of sand ringing them sloped gently upward, and she realized there were holes and colored windows in the hills themselves.

Glass, Luteis said, *is everywhere.*

The bright colors, you mean?

All glass bottles. They are round and fat, or tall and thin. I never imagined so many. For what would witches use them?

Water, perhaps.

Something appeared in front of Sanna, but she couldn't stop in time. Her nose smashed into someone's shoulder, and a dozen hands pulled her back. She tried to shake them free, but a sudden silence descended on the crowd.

"*Mori,*" she muttered. "That hurt!"

"Avia," someone whispered behind her.

Everyone dropped to their knees with a sudden *thunk,* leaving Sanna grimacing, standing alone to stare into the wrinkled, wizened eyes of an old man.

Small, shriveled, and tanned to a deep bronze, he gave her a gummy smile that revealed only a few teeth. His vinegary breath hit her like a slap.

"Daughter of the forest," he whispered, "you have come."

21

I sadora woke up in her bed, blankets pulled around her shoulders, her head pounding. Bleary, she gazed at the clock. Ten thirty. Breakfast sat uneaten on the table. She ignored it. Had Max carried her to bed after he'd returned? She only remembered crying on the floor.

Messages from Arayana and Emilia sat unopened on the table. Without reading them, she used an incantation to reply.

Sick with a headache today. *Please forgive my absence. I'm sure I'll be well again tomorrow.*

Driven by thoughts of innocent Sophie, and unable to bear the snowy turret another moment, Isadora wrapped herself in warm furs and transported back to the spot in the forest that she'd visited before. She had to see the place again. Remember it exactly as it had been when she suspected Dante saw her.

And, if possible, see him in the paths.

She'd be quick. Controlled. Not so unrestrained in letting the magic loose. She'd demand, not channel.

The brisk air helped straighten her thoughts. Massive trees surrounded her. Their long, limber branches reached out like spiny arms in the blustery day. Snow was already melting into her stockings, cooling her shins.

This wasn't the same place.

But why hadn't she transported back to the right spot?

Sensing something strange in this wood yet again, like an unfamiliar magic, she called out in imitation of the Southern Network greeting. "*Elo?*"

The magic whipped in a frenzy inside her. Isadora swallowed, just about to open the paths, when an unfamiliar sound came from just behind her. She canted her head. A rustle of wind? No. Footsteps. It was . . . gentle. Low. Like . . .

A humming growl.

Isadora whirled around, gasping. A family of four timber wolves stood just behind her, fanning into a V formation. The closest bared its teeth, nose twitching, eyes yellow as the moon. Its front shoulder surpassed her hip in height, leaving its head somewhere near her elbow. Thankfully, it was the largest of the group—but the others weren't much smaller. They stood at least as tall as her waist.

Three of them snarled. Based on the indents in the snow, they'd been sleeping.

"The good gods," she whispered, sucking in a sharp breath. She held up both hands. "I-I'm not here to hurt you."

The front wolf growled, head lowering.

Isadora's eyes darted around. Ten paces behind her, the trees revealed an open space at odds with the rest of the forest. Most branches stacked together at the bottom of these trees, intertwining like they'd been woven on a loom.

But two of them were strangely blunted, preventing the cross of branches. The space between them was dark. Different. Like a doorway.

Isadora recited the transportation spell, but nothing happened. She held her breath and tried again. Nothing.

With a yip of fear as the wolves closed in, she attempted again.

A flash of movement shifted in the corner of her eye too late. A yowl, then hot, sharp stings in her shoulders as a wolf smashed her into the snow from behind. A fifth wolf she hadn't seen held her immobile, snarling in her left ear.

Isadora commanded a fire spell, and heat flared near her neck. The wolf screamed, rearing back. The snow collapsed beneath her as she tried to scramble free, her back searing with pain. Something sharp gouged her hand. She cried out, feeling a rush of warmth across her palm. When she looked down, her heart nearly stopped.

Blood dripped into the snow from her palm, near where a rusty knife lay atop a pile of sticks lashed together, like an altar. Feathers, nearly stripped from weather and wind, hung limp around a knife hilt strapped with leather.

Gasping, Isadora grabbed it, then swung it in a wide arc.

An oncoming timber wolf yipped as the knife connected with its shoulder. The aged blade glanced off the bone but pierced the thick fur near the wolf's shoulder. It fell to her side, then retreated as Isadora backed away, wielding the knife.

"Get back!"

Two others advanced, snarling. She loosed another fire spell, hitting them right in their noses, sending them reeling, tails tucked. She scrambled back, her heart in her throat. The strange gap between trees lay a breath away. In it, a door hung on two squeaky hinges, drifting gently in the wind.

Throwing herself through it, she landed on hard-packed dirt, rolled onto her back, and reached up a single foot—bootless, though she didn't know when that had happened—and slammed the mysterious door shut.

The door closed, disappearing into a perfectly lovely snow scene.

THE CLATTER of Isadora's own teeth woke her.

She didn't know how long she'd lain on the ground, shivering and soaked to the bone.

Prickles stabbed her body, and blood ran from her palm. She was shaking so hard she could barely see. Her dress had refrozen, forming into a sheet of crackling ice. Hot pain ripped through her shoulders with every breath.

"Th-the g-g-ood g-g-g-ods."

Struggling to her numb feet, Isadora stumbled through the snow, forcing her fuzzy mind to think. She'd landed *somewhere*.

Trees soared overhead, imposing and thick. An occasional glimpse of a cloudy sky peeked through the greenery. But when she reached out to touch a tree, it was nothing but air. Not far away, another tree was real, the bark flaky and cold. A firm magical boundary existed between the two trees, creating the image of a false forest. It also kept the timber wolves out.

But why?

Untroubled snow lay thick on the ground. Isadora padded through it until a building appeared on her right. A small house, two stories tall. The door hung open. Its windowpanes were etched with frost, and no life appeared within.

She stood in the doorway.

"H-h-hello?"

No answer. Shoving through the door, she nearly tripped over a chair in the middle of a rectangular room. There—a hearth at the far end. Desperate, Isadora slammed the door shut, grabbed the chair, and shoved it into the hearth. She cast another fire spell. Within moments, flames licked the chair. She grimaced as her blood rose toward the warmth. Soon, the table and another chair lay sacrificed.

Minutes later, a roaring, jolly fire began to thaw her frozen bones. She clenched her teeth through the pain. The cold had sapped her strength, and using magic to warm herself faster would only require more of it. Not to mention the exquisite agony of the incantations that could rewarm the body.

She'd have to go through a lot worse to use one of those.

Once the heat restored agility to her fingers, Isadora peeled off her socks and dress and lay them close to the fire, keeping on only her shift. She winced. The back of the dress had been reduced to tatters and was coated in blood.

Unable to move quickly, she rifled through the house. A few thin glass vials, like the ones the shieldmaidens wore, lay in the drawers. Behind a door was a moldy fur coat, half-eaten by moths and smelling of turpentine. She donned it anyway, wincing as it touched her open wounds.

Another bedroom and a linen closet both turned up empty. Up a narrow set of rickety stairs was an attic with a single bed, a window, and an empty bookshelf. No other signs of life. Steam rose from her clothes by the time she finished her exploration.

Without knowing much of Southern Network history,

she had an idea of what this place *could* be, if it wasn't just another abandoned village.

"Taiza," she murmured.

Why else would timber wolves guard it? Why else would there have been a knife, right where she needed it, resting on the bracken like an offering? A Watcher had put it there, had seen her choose to come here. The magical boundary must have prevented her from transporting away.

What felt like hours later, her shift finished drying. The sun sank into the far horizon, casting an early darkness. Thoughts of Maximillion spurred her on. Dinner would be soon. He'd return and she'd be—

She shut that thought off.

She left her dress there to molder, pulled her wrap more firmly around her, and fashioned a crude pair of snowshoes out of boards from the table. She'd look around for five more minutes, then transport back.

Outside, more abandoned houses appeared here and there until she stood in the midst of the small village. Had the inhabitants left in a hurry? Its size wasn't impressive. Likely, not more than a hundred witches had lived here at any given time.

Another whirl of the powers, as if they had just woken up, caught Isadora by surprise. If this *was* Taiza, protected by an ancient magic, this might be her only opportunity to see Dante in the paths safely.

With a sharp intake of breath, Isadora opened the magic.

It swirled around her, welcoming her gently into the paths of Letum Wood. Wisps of Sanna, Maximillion, and Isadora herself appeared, springing to life in the forest.

"Dante," she rasped. "Show me Dante."

The wisps disappeared. Her magic seemed to draw itself

out of her. Unrestrained, it flowed free of its own accord. Poured into the sacred-feeling space. Everything seemed bright, soaked with power.

Then shadows. Darkness. Dante appeared in front of her, expression heavy. The forest didn't stir. She thought she heard a gentle wind whisper, *Ruthless.*

Though she couldn't be sure it wasn't her own traumatized, terrified mind.

Still staring at his cold eyes, she shivered. "Remove him."

Isadora remained in the paths for several minutes, allowing the magic to run free. If it called her match, they wouldn't find her here. Couldn't, if the legends were true. Still, she couldn't have stopped the magic if she'd wanted to. As if it recognized its home and wanted to play here for a while.

Finally, when the energy ebbed, Isadora closed the paths.

Pain slammed her on her return to Taiza. The cold was colder. Her body trembled. Her shoulders throbbed with startling intensity. For the first time, tears rose in her eyes. She had stayed too long in the paths. Her body bore the consequences now.

Something flickered at the edge of her vision, drawing her thoughts back to the present. She turned carefully, seeing a square of white flapping in the wind. A piece of parchment tacked to a tree.

Isadora waded over and snatched the parchment. It was written in a hand she could hardly make out. But she could tell it wasn't in the common language. The symbols were a more ancient rune. Though only four symbols made up a single line, there were twenty lines, all right down the middle of the page. Each symbol altered only slightly.

Isadora folded the parchment and recalled the transportation spell, suspecting the magic would let her out, even though it wouldn't let her transport in. There would be questions when she arrived in this state. Transporting back would lead her right to the gardens, bloody and half-frozen. With any luck, she could avoid any South Guards and sneak through the servants' entrance.

Bracing herself for Maximillion's inevitable reaction, she tore off the furs and transported away, hoping to never see Taiza again.

"WHAT IN THE name of the good gods happened?"

Maximillion's fury nearly broke Isadora's tenuous hold on her control. She took three steps into the turret, body shaking. Thanks to the old coat she'd left behind, she still smelled like a dead thing. He recoiled, hand over his mouth.

"Please shut the door," Isadora said quietly. She'd waited twenty minutes in the gardens so the South Guards wouldn't see her, and another fifteen in a coat closet to avoid a gaggle of maids. A hasty spell had cleaned up the blood she'd left behind, but the extra effort had almost cost her consciousness.

"But—"

"Please, Max," she whispered.

Nostrils flared, Maximillion kicked the door with a foot. The moment it shut, Isadora collapsed. Maximillion caught her a second before she landed in a heap.

Until she smelled vetiver, she hadn't realized just how much she'd wanted to see him. A gentle hand landed between her shoulder blades. She cried out.

"Your back," he said, pulling his hand away. "There's blood everywhere."

"Please," she gasped, clutching his arms. Her knees knocked together. "Take me to the fire. I-I'm so cold."

He lifted her gently, cradling her against his chest. Seconds later, she sat on a chair in front of the flames, cocooned in warmth.

Finally, safe. Trembling consumed her. Her teeth rattled.

Maximillion crouched next to her, distress in his eyes. He wore a pair of black pants and a buttoned shirt parted from collarbone to navel. She'd returned halfway through him changing. His skin appeared bronze in the shifting fire-light, and entirely too warm. She wanted to curl up against him and fall asleep in his arms.

"How hurt are you?" he asked.

"V-very."

Seconds later, a warm, heavy coat dropped onto her shoulders. She bit back a muted cry of pain. He hesitated, hands hovering over her back.

"Isadora—"

"I'll t-t-tell you e-e-everything," she whispered. "O-once I'm warm a-and clean."

"Fine. You'll need to change," he said, all business now. "And bathe." A simple white gown appeared on her lap. "Put it on backward so I can access your back and . . . clean whatever happened there. Then you can bathe, eat dinner, and tell me exactly what idiotic thing you've done now."

She hesitated, glancing from the gown to him.

He rolled his eyes. "The good gods, Isadora. You are my wife."

Her eyes widened. "I-in name o-only!"

"You think I haven't—fine. I'll . . . turn around and . . . make you a cup of tea while you change."

Relieved to have him in charge, she numbly obeyed. Her awkward fingers made any deliberate movement difficult.

Taking the old shift off posed little problem, but the night-gown felt slippery as silk. By the time she finished, he was impatiently holding a cup in his hands and tapping his foot, his broad back still facing her.

"R-ready," she finally said, lowering herself into the chair.

He turned around and passed the cup to her. "It will warm you. I'll send for a vial of remoulade potion from Lucey. That should heal you quickly, but we'll still need to clean the wounds."

He parted the gown at her back, letting it fall to either side.

Gently warmed chamomile tea flooded her mouth, tinged with a slightly sweet taste. She downed the rest, savoring the purl of heat in her belly. He stood behind her and poured another cup. She eagerly drank half of it, then stopped, curling her hands more tightly around the warmth.

"Not too deep, it seems," he murmured. "Though not superficial. They're too wide for stitches. You're either very lucky or insanely stupid. I suspect both."

A soft touch probed around the worst of the pain. Isadora sucked in a sharp breath, pressed her forehead into the cup, and blinked tears back. A quiet cry escaped her like a hiccup. The tip of his finger ran down the side of one wound as gently as a silk thread.

"A claw?" he asked, his voice now suspiciously even.

One traitorous tear rolled down her cheek. "Timber wolf," she whispered. "It, ah, attacked from behind."

She braced herself for a retort, her shoulders clenching. The warmth of the tea spread, winding through her blood with unusual speed. The sharpness of her pain eased a little.

He crouched next to her, put a hand under her jaw, and

lifted her face. Another tear tracked down her cheek. For a long moment, she stared warily at his unreadable gaze.

His brow furrowed. "Are you all right?" he asked softly.

Isadora pressed her lips together and shook her head, defenses crumbling. He brushed a strand of hair away from her face, then pulled her close without a word.

Releasing a sob, she closed her eyes and let him pull her into the warm hollow at his neck, surrendering to the steady safety of his arms.

Isadora had fallen asleep in his arms. An hour later, he shook her awake with an ungracious, though gentle, hand. He forced her to drink something else horrible, having obtained several helpful vials from Lucey. A calm, fluid-like ease moved through her bloodstream now.

Recounting the events in Taiza to Maximillion was almost as painful as his cleaning of her wounds—which he hadn't seemed overly gentle with. He was less than impressed by her Taiza suspicions.

"To what end was this search conducted?" he muttered, finishing the wrap around her palm. The remoulade potion still sizzled in the cut, smoke curling out of it as she sucked in a sharp breath. The potion stung.

"You learned nothing from finding it," he continued, "even *if* it was Taiza. Except, perhaps, how not to fight timber wolves."

She'd kept the written note tucked in her bodice and didn't mention it at the end.

Leftovers of spiraled ham and crisp purple beans topped by a dollop of whipped butter and, of course, onions, sat luxuriously in her stomach. A lovely sort of drowsiness threatened her now.

With a stern glare, Maximillion handed her another glass vial from Lucey, filled with a second foul-smelling liquid. Reluctantly, she accepted it and tipped it into her mouth.

And regretted it.

The taste of damp mold filled her mouth. She quickly swallowed to keep from vomiting.

"Should help the pain," he muttered.

"What happened today for you?" she asked, reaching for another drink of tea.

"Dostar presented more of his plan. In all, he proposes a council be established between Networks, with two members per Network to act as a governing entity and various regulations and rules associated with it."

"Not bad."

"Sounds an awful lot like having an Ambassador, doesn't it?" he muttered. "Look where that got us."

He leaned against the fireplace and stared at her back for several moments before emitting a gusty sigh. "Tomorrow we debate the finer points of his plan."

"And then?"

He shoved away from the fireplace, eyebrows knitted together. "We take a short break to think, discuss, and revisit mediation for current grievances, then begin to narrow the options between the three. Vasily remains the swing vote."

Tension knotted her stomach at the thought, but then she slipped back into the looseness the potions had given her. She blinked several times, attempting to fight off the blur.

Maximillion's brow puckered. He stared harder at the fire, as if the flames held his answer. "This business with

Dante potentially being a Defender," he murmured, shaking his head. "It mucks a few things up."

"Everything," Isadora slurred. "If he is my match, he cannot rule Antebellum."

"Too much power."

"All Watchers would die or be forced into perpetual hiding. Maybe Serafina can help us."

"Right," he said scathingly. "We'll just trounce up and ask her if her husband is the most powerful Defender in Antebellum? She may trust me, but I don't extend the same."

Had she imagined the short, punctuated sentence to be riddled with something? She opened her mouth to ask, but nothing came out.

"I'll be discreet," she said, but it sounded more like, "Dishes me creed."

His gaze caught hers for a moment. Her lips burned, recalling their passionate kiss in the East that still haunted her dreams. Without trying, she could still feel the heady pressure of his lips against hers. The deep notes of vetiver that gave her an impossible amount of comfort. Maximillion was something like magic, but infinitely more powerful.

She longed for such a thing again. Desperately. Unequivocally. In a way she'd never wanted anything before.

"Max," she whispered. "I—"

She stood, but her knees gave way. For the second time, he caught her. She leaned against him, resting her head on his shoulder. When she closed her eyes, she thought she could feel him relax. Tighten his hold. Maybe draw in a deep breath near her hair.

Or maybe it was just the potion.

Her consciousness began to slip away again, taking the pain with it. He lifted her, allowing her to curl her body around him for the moments it took him to cross the room, then gently laid her in bed. Her eyes opened, blinking to clear the foggy picture.

"Get some rest, Isa," he said, voice tight. "I must return to speak with the Advocate and get their update. Charles has also requested a briefing."

With that, he disappeared.

Isadora blinked, wondering if she imagined regret in his eyes. Her thoughts skipped like a rock through water, idly pondering if the vial he'd given her had been a sleeping potion.

Seconds later, she dropped into a dreamless, thick sleep with the realization that tonight he had, for the first time, called her *Isa*.

anna sat in the middle of Avia's sand house.

Sunlight poured through multicolored window-panes. Emerald, fuchsia, and royal purple colored her skin. She wiggled her fingers, fascinated by the brightness.

Had her vision grown so dim? She pushed the thought back, her throat tightening. She couldn't think about that now.

Two male desert witches fussed around Avia as he settled onto cushions made of coarse animal hair. One of the witches wore a baby strapped to his chest. It snored quietly, tiny eyes squeezed shut.

Next to Avia floated a small rug that seemed to never leave his side. He'd sat on it while Sanna walked behind him, following him up a sandy slope and into this house, which loomed above all the others. At a sharp command from one of the attendants, she'd sunk onto a pile of circular braided rugs, sitting significantly lower than Avia.

While the witches circled Avia, bringing him a globular

glass of water and draping a gauzy cloth around his naked shoulders, Sanna peered at her surroundings.

A square window facing the middle of the oasis streamed a prism of colors into the room. On the wall hung more glasses in varying sizes. Up close, Sanna could just make out slight details. Changes in the curvature. Shards of colored glass embedded inside. Some had a hole in the middle, the glass cleverly crafted around the hollow.

The narrow room allowed only the two of them to sit, right across from each other. Avia raised a hand, dismissing the two men, then turned to Sanna.

"They are caretakers, our men," he said, clucking under his breath as they left. "While they raise our children, the women work the sand and glass and looms. But sometimes they annoy me. Why must they fuss like I'm one of their children? I may be old, but I am no child."

Given how old he must be, his voice remained strong and firm.

"You speak the common language."

He grinned. "We all do in the West. We have no need for other languages, except in Custos. And among the tribes, but they are almost a different Network." He waved a hand. "Occasionally we speak in an ancient language, but in the true desert, we have no time for making up our own. We are constantly in pursuit of water."

"I am—"

"The daughter of the forest, yes." He tapped an ear with a spindly finger. "I know. The desert told me you were coming. Do not give me your name. I know everything about you that I need to know just by seeing you."

He leaned forward. His spine curled slightly at his shoulders, giving him an eager look. Sanna's eyes were drawn to a half circle of broken glass tied around a rope on his neck.

"I hear you are High Dragonmaster of two races." His eyes brightened. "Lucky daughter, indeed."

"Lucky?"

"None other have had that honor."

Sanna clenched her teeth. *Honor* wasn't the word she had in mind.

He continued, almost dismissively. "Prana has long loved antagonizing her sisters. She must be getting anxious." His eyes glinted. He lowered his head, one hand near his mouth. "She does that, you know. Stirs things up when she gets bored."

"But why?"

"Because she can! She's a goddess. Besides making magical systems, what else are you going to do for eternity?"

Sanna opened her mouth to counter, but she didn't even know what to say.

Fortunately, he didn't seem to mind. "The desert told me what you need."

"Can you help us?"

"We do not have many fighters to spare. All of our work must go to finding water and making glass and finding the right sand. It is our life."

A bolt of anger pulsed through her, but she forced it back. The *right* sand? Did different types exist?

"Then why did Tashi bring me here?"

He straightened, legs folded in front of him, palms on his knees. "Because the desert is always whispering. I am the one the desert speaks to the most, now that the power of the High Dragonmaster is gone. When Sarena broke the magic between her and her dragons, the desert chose one witch to caretake it. It is now I who help care for all the land."

His wrinkled hand touched the broken piece of glass on his chest. The legend of Sarena whispered back through Sanna's mind.

"How did Sarena break the magic?"

He shrugged. "One would presume she created a powerful imbalance."

"So the magic destroyed itself."

"Aha. You *are* smart."

"But how did she do that?"

He shrugged. "I have never known Dragonian magic, and the sand has not recorded it."

Avia unwound a complicated story that Sanna struggled to follow, jabbering about a watery prison, clashing goddesses, and livid dragons bound to one eternal fate: servitude.

". . . and then Sarena released her dragons," he concluded with a cluck of his tongue. "Her attempt to break the magic succeeded for her part, but the rest of the dragons were still bound to their own goddesses. The only thing she achieved was alienating herself from the magic, an outcome she had not anticipated."

Sanna blinked, startled by the quick ending. "Why did she hide?" she managed to ask. "She has been presumed gone ever since."

He laughed so long and loud it grated on her nerves. Finally, wiping tears from his eyes with the back of his hand, he said, "She is no more gone than you!"

"But the desert is . . ."

"The desert. Sarena is a simple goddess with few needs. The land reflects the goddess. The turbulent, ever-shifting sea. The sterile, isolated mountains. The abundant, life-giving forest. Sarena's land is her mirror, and an appropriate one at that. The goddess can no more abandon her land than she can cease to exist. Witches will believe anything except the goddess paradigm these days."

Something caught Sanna's attention, though she didn't know what. The back of her neck prickled. "What happened after she freed her dragons?"

"It is not truly known. At least, the desert does not know it, and the desert only sees what the desert sees. Maybe that's why it brought you to the circle."

"Tashi brought me."

"Yes." He blinked. "To the circle."

"What circle?"

He whipped his finger in the air. "To Sarena's circle. The seat of her power. The heart of the desert." He tilted his head in an almost comical expression. "You do not know of the circles?"

"Not officially, but I've observed."

"And you are the witch to save us?" He laughed wheezily. "We shall all die!"

Sanna fought back the urge to snap at him. Instead, she let out a long breath. "Why don't you tell me what you think a goddess's circle is?"

His glee faded, folding into an intense expression that made him appear to be an entirely different witch.

"The concentration of a goddess's power, where she most often resides. All of them are different. Some legends say the circles are the seat of their power, but that isn't truly known. We live within the desert—with Sarena, if you will. It gives us longer life, deeper magic. It also requires our allegiance." He shrugged. "A fair trade."

But *was* it a fair trade?

"Prana is going to flood the land if we don't stop her," she said. "I was trying to find more witches or dragons to fight with us, but I've recently realized that may not work. Now, I think I need to destroy Dragonian magic."

He grinned slyly. "Prana is a problem but not *the* problem."

"I know."

He reached toward his neck again, touching the half circle of glass that hung there. Bright colors faded into each other. Emerald into sapphire into magenta. The edges had been worn smooth. A puzzled expression filled his face.

"But you cannot kill a goddess, and unless you kill her or break the magic, you will achieve nothing."

"We can't kill a goddess. I understand that. But if we break the magic that binds the dragons to her in obligation, we can stop these battles. Forever. Except . . . I understand very little about magic. I only know that it requires balance. I don't . . . I don't know how to fracture the balance and save the dragons."

"Interrupting the balance of any magic would require great power and even greater risk. A magic is made by a goddess! To break it would be beyond what a mere girl such as yourself could ever handle."

"And yet, I must."

He frowned. "Then fate will guide you. You must simply accept her."

"I don't believe in fate."

"But she believes in you," he said with a wily smile. "To the desert goddess, to be wild is to be free. You will one day respect that about her."

He gazed wistfully outside. "Still, I cannot help you break a magic. The desert whispers it is not mine to do. Now, a story. That I can do. The desert," he said with a happy cry, grabbing another glass bottle, "tells me of a time

when the volares were many, and the witches prosperous . .
."

She gave his next story a minute, hoping to hear more
about Dragonian magic, but seeing that it was discussing
flying rugs, she let her thoughts roam. She'd seen all the
goddesses' circles now, except Prana's. Knowing more about
the goddesses had certainly changed her path, but it had
yielded no further aid to their army, nor a clear direction.

Frustrated, she bit her bottom lip.

Yushi's voice rang through her mind. *Mushi is taken. Held
captive in her circular prison by dear Prana Herself until Prana
gets what Prana wants.*

Revenge.

WILD WINDS SWEPT through the desert that night.

Luteis's giant body blocked the mouth of the cave Tashi
had led them to after they left the circle. They'd only stayed
long enough to drink, eat, pack supplies, and head back
toward the forest.

Then a storm had descended.

Luteis's scales prevented sand from spilling inside and
choking them. Thunder and lightning cracked overhead,
but no rain fell. Tashi had given Sanna a long drink from
her leather water pouch, but thirst lingered in the back of
her throat.

Tashi sat with her back against the cave wall, one leg
bent. She wore a pair of pants sewn loosely up the side with
black thread, revealing hints of smooth skin. Her linen top
paled against the darkness. She held a sharp knife in one
hand and a piece of wood in another, slowly carving the

wood into something misshapen. The heat didn't seem to bother her.

No doubt she'd been subjected to worse.

Old bones and discarded animal carcasses, long since baked by the sun, burned with a strange pink flame. It cast thin, gauzy shadows, illuminating everything in a heatless rosy glow. Some kind of desert magic, no doubt.

Sanna rolled onto her back and stared at the top of the cave. *Elis,* she asked, reaching out with her mind. *Can you hear me?*

Yes, High Dragonmaster.

All is well?

Yes. With you?

How could she encompass everything in a short answer? Finally, she said, *Yes. All is well. Can you give me a report?*

Gladly.

His comforting flight reports gave her something to think about for the moment. Hatchlings throwing better fire. Trey showing increased confidence in commanding the Dragonian magic.

Above all, Elis said, *Jesse's sire, Elliot, shows great promise in flight. I am encouraged that we have strength in our ranks, if not numbers.*

Thank you, Elis.

After posing several questions about weapons for the witches, ways to work with the mountain dragons, and expectations for the shoreline when they arrived, Elis fell silent, leaving Sanna to her thoughts.

You are quiet tonight, Luteis said, peering at her from the other side of the cave.

I can't stop thinking about what Avia said about creating imbalance in the magic.

For a witch who hates goddesses and magic as much as you do, he said, snorting, *you are tangled in them often enough.*

I've noticed.

Tashi hummed quietly to herself as she worked, focusing on the wooden figure. Sanna straightened.

"How well do you know Aki?" she asked.

Tashi glanced up, then returned her attention to the stick. "He has paid me to be a messenger several times."

"Do you think he'll allow the desert dragons to fight with us?"

Her expression hardened. "It is not his place to refuse them whatever they want. They are free."

"Yes, but maybe he'll be upset if they do fight."

The corners of Tashi's mouth twitched. "Perhaps. Perhaps not. The dragons will do as they want either way."

A cry came from outside just as the thunderous sound of rain descended. Luteis curled his tail in toward his body, admitting a hulking figure. Tenzin. The rain steamed off Luteis's exposed scales, filling the air with vapor.

Tenzin lumbered in, a sheen of water wetting his scales. He shook, flinging the droplets onto the red-rock walls. A cold breeze brushed Sanna's face as Luteis blocked the cave entrance again. Rain pounded on the sand like thousands of drums.

"Rain is not unusual at this time of year," Tashi said. "But the colder wind is strange."

"Does the weather change at Prana's whims?" Sanna asked.

"Around here, yes."

"Elsewhere?"

"It can. A sign of her power and an attempt to reach farther inland. Her floods are not only from the ocean. She can influence the weather, send storms inland. It would rain for days. Weeks. Then months. Eventually, there would be no escaping the water. The storm on the western horizon, haven't you seen it? She desires to reach everywhere."

Tashi returned to her whittling. She didn't touch Tenzin, who hunkered against the far wall, his distrusting gaze on Luteis. He peered at Sanna next, shamelessly staring until the already-blurry edges of her vision faded into a halo. Finally, he snorted, sending a cloud of sand into the air, and burrowed deeper into the ground with his eyes closed.

"He's not as cuddly as yours," Tashi said with amusement as she gestured toward Luteis, who opened one eye a slit.

One can hardly call a dragon cuddly, Luteis murmured to Sanna.

"Yet he seems loyal to you," Sanna said to Tashi.

A fond twitch of Tashi's lips gave her away. "Tenzin is content as a messenger dragon. He stays with me because it pleases him to travel often, and he knows I'll provide food and shelter from the rain. He is under no obligation. If, one day, he tires of traveling with me, he could fly away and disappear. It would be his right."

A heavy feeling settled on Sanna's chest. "Unlike the mountain and forest dragons, you mean."

"Yes."

"It's odd," Sanna said.

"Why?"

"Because dragons have had masters all their lives. Why is this desire for freedom coming up now?"

"Maybe it came up in the past, but you weren't aware. You have been isolated for so long."

Sanna's thoughts spun out for several moments before she asked, "Do *you* think the desert dragons are truly free?"

Tenzin's eye popped open to stare right at her.

"What do you think?" Tashi asked.

Sanna tried to hold Tenzin's intense gaze. "I think they're smart," she said. "I think they're unbound, which is a disadvantage as much as it is an advantage. They haven't connected with witches the way forest and mountain dragons do, and whether they *can* remains to be seen. They may never experience the powerful relationship that can come from the magic. But they live without obligation."

There was a long, crackling silence until Tashi quietly asked, "Which is of greater value? Connection or freedom?"

Breathlessness filled Sanna's chest. "I think about that all the time. I *think* freedom, but I don't know. I could be wrong. I could be placing my trust in something that isn't right when there is so much I don't know. What if I do manage to break the magic? What would that mean? There would be a price to pay, and I would be forcing witches and dragons to pay it."

"Pay they might, but the next generation wouldn't. It is not only this generation we must think of."

The confidence in Tashi's tone did little to comfort Sanna. Luteis's tail wrapped around her ankle, and he nuzzled her leg with his snout.

I am no servant of yours, he murmured.

His body shifted as he settled deeper into the sand. A breath of cold air blew into the cave. Tashi tossed the wooden trinket into the fire, curled up in a ball on the floor, and closed her eyes.

If a path to prevent the war presents itself, I trust it will find you, Deasylva had said. With no further help from Avia presenting itself, she'd have to trust that.

If she could.

Sanna leaned back against Luteis and stared at the

pinkish flames, comforted by their vibrant color. Her eyes closed. Sleep whisked her away with the gentle shuffle of Luteis's wing pressing her close and sheltering her from the strange winds outside.

23

The quiet of Vasily's library calmed Isadora.

The tall, slanted windows, alternating white and blue glass, looked like icicles cutting through stone. She pulled her shawl more tightly around herself, tucking it into her wide belt to secure it and wincing slightly when it put pressure on her shoulders.

A week had passed with her locked in the turret, her wounds aching at every movement. Her palm had healed quickly thanks to remoulade, a rare and ancient healing potion that sped up the process, cutting off days. But it was extremely expensive and difficult to make, so Isadora had used it only on her visible cuts.

So far, no one in the castle seemed any wiser to her visit to the forest, to Taiza.

She moved through the library, determined to find translation materials for the Yazikan language, the parchment from Taiza tucked firmly in her dress. Fifteen minutes later, she used a spell to pull a thick, heavy book off a shelf near the back.

"The Yazikan Language," she murmured, running her

fingers over the common-language title. Below it was another line, presumably in Yazika.

She sat at a table and flipped through the book, studying the picture-like characters of the language. Each page was split into two halves, one with Yazika writings, the other with common-language equivalents.

The table was equipped with an inkpot, a quill, and small scrolls for taking notes. She unfolded the fabric-like parchment from Taiza on her lap. Most of its symbols were comprised of circles and lines, of varying thickness and placement. No two runes were the same.

She set to work, searching each page for the Taiza symbols. It seemed nearly impossible. Still, she persevered until a knot in her neck forced her to take a break. She stood, tucking the note back into her pocket, and stretched by the fire.

"A deceptively cold morning, isn't it?"

The purring voice made Isadora's spine clench. She drew in a deep breath and turned, coming face-to-face with Dante. He stood so close his breath hit her face. She took a step back. He smiled, though it didn't reach his eyes. Whatever warmth he'd pretended at the ball had utterly faded.

Isadora returned his cold glance. His lips twitched.

Behind him, Emilia beamed. "Merry meet, Isadora!" she cried. "Isn't that how you say it in the Central Network?"

"Yes! Merry meet."

"Do you always amuse yourself in quiet libraries?" Dante asked, eyes flickering around. He stood with his hands clasped behind his back. Emilia held several tattered tomes with scratched-out spines and jagged edges.

"I see you've found several books of interest," Isadora said, ignoring his question.

Emilia brightened. "I love to read."

Dante snorted. "A bald-faced lie."

Emilia blushed, then laughed. Some of her hair had come loose from her braid in a charming fall of locks around her face. "He's correct. I hate reading. Mere insists I read two hours a day. *For the benefit of my enlightenment.*"

"More protective magic?" Isadora asked in amusement.

Emilia rolled her eyes and groaned. "Yes! The war tales of the Southern Network are far more interesting. Pere has promised not to betray me, but I found the goriest tellings."

A glimmer of secret amusement passed between the two of them. Dante, the cipher, with his rare ability to be infuriating, deadly, and charming all in the same breath. Isadora wanted to scratch his eyes out.

Because now she knew *his* secret.

"Your secret is safe with me," she said to Emilia with a little smile.

"Researching the Yazikan language?" Dante asked, his voice a smooth ribbon. "How very . . . interesting."

"There's some fascinating history there. Currently, I'm most interested in the tale of a depraved High Priest who attempted to take over the Central Network but met with utter failure. He ended his life on the streets of his own Network, where he was starving to death after his defeat. That isn't the least of it." Her icy gaze met his. "Tales of murder, war, intrigue, revenge, loss, devastation, and . . . *unmatched* magical power in unexpected places seem to abound. The possibilities are endless."

Dante laughed, nostrils flaring. The sound wasn't unpleasant, but it was laced with something. Challenging. Sinister.

Eager.

Emilia lit up like a candle. "I'd love to read such stories!" she said. "Where are they?"

"I hear they're best read in their native language." Isadora gestured to the book behind her. "Hence the studying."

"Even a story so complicated and strange?" Dante asked, his eyes boring into hers. "So unknown and . . . *vastly* under-appreciated? One can never tell just what can happen to those we refuse to truly see."

"I do love a challenge," said Isadora evenly.

His teeth gleamed when he smiled. "Even when the stakes of the game are higher than you anticipated?"

"Not high enough to stop me."

Dante's smile grew.

She curled her fingers into her palms until her nails bit the skin. The pain anchored her to the moment and narrowly kept her from slapping him.

He grinned as if he could taste her pent-up emotion. "Well, a . . . *superb education* such as yours will surely never lead you astray."

"Indeed," she muttered, teeth clenched.

"No doubt the many dialects of the Yazikan language will work against you, though. That book, for example, is based on an old dialect, outdated for centuries, with only a mild reflection in the modern language. You won't likely find much to help you there. But you knew that already, didn't you?"

"A detail of which I was already aware, thank you," she said. "My choice was deliberate."

A fleck of curiosity lingered in his gaze. "Indeed. What *have* you found on your little adventure, Mrs. Sinclair?"

"Can we have tea again together, Isadora?" Emilia asked, breaking the tension. "I had such a lovely time."

Isadora smiled. "Of course. Perhaps tomorrow afternoon?"

"Yes, anytime!"

"Good evening, Isadora," Dante said, bowing with exaggerated energy. Emilia backed away, waving, then hastily curtsied when he scowled at her. They shuffled off together, and the door closed behind them.

Isadora gratefully returned to her table, but stared blankly at the book, turning the pages every now and then only to maintain the illusion of continuing.

Her heart still pounded in her chest. She *hadn't* known that about Yazika, and though she couldn't explain why, she sensed that Dante knew it.

With a growl, she closed the book, sent it back to the shelf with a wave, and stared into the fire, lost in thought.

MAXIMILLION'S FROWN marred his handsome features as they passed into the ballroom later that week, his arm around Isadora's waist.

His hair gleamed. A hint of stubble shadowed his face. She wanted to run the tips of her fingers over it, but kept her arms at her side instead. His affection after her experience haunted her nightly. She wanted nothing more than that warmth and concern back.

Dante, Serafina, Vasily, and Arayana stood on the far side of the room in a circle of other witches. The beginnings of yet another lavish dinner awaited. Isadora's stomach growled with reluctant anticipation. Every week, Vasily pulled out another elegant feast, filled with daring new recipes—and mouthwatering desserts. She felt guilty with each bite, thinking of Mam and Sanna at home.

"Rumors are," Maximillion murmured, "that Dostar had

to return home tonight. Flooding, apparently, in one of his cities."

The Western Network had been a hotbed of magic, violence, and instability for ages, as if the hot sands made witches prone to violence. Some of the oldest texts left in Antebellum blamed it on the withdrawal of the goddess of the desert, Sarena. The ancient magicks of the West had been nefarious, if the aged stories could be trusted. With what Sanna had told Isadora of goddesses, it seemed likely.

"Must be very bad."

"Or a ruse."

"I'm glad I don't have to worry about Sanna being tangled up in that," Isadora murmured. "At least Letum Wood can protect her."

They stood just inside the ballroom now, amid rich witches from the various Networks. Vasily had called for a special celebration now that all the plans had been presented. The vote to narrow it down to two plans would be in two days.

A historic movement forward, at any rate.

Yesterday at their luncheon, Serafina had reluctantly admitted she felt Dostar's plan had no legs to stand on. Arayana had responded only with a concerned frown.

Isadora readjusted a fur-lined shawl around her shoulders. She could move without much pain now, thanks to the potions given to her nightly by Maximillion, and his surprisingly gentle ministrations. She wore plenty to cover her back and shoulders, just in case, opting for an elegant black gown with a high neck and wrist-length sleeves.

Charles's red hair and flushed cheeks popped into view. He was grinning, as usual. "Delightful, isn't it?" he cried.

"Indeed, Your Highness," Maximillion said.

"You've held your own proudly, my friend," he said with

a shudder. "This is no easy crowd. Can't imagine seeing these faces every day and having to debate their plans. Not to mention tracking such long conversations. Egads, but the headache it would give me. I've just been dancing with the wife of the Western Network Ambassador. Charming woman. Didn't speak a lick of the common language, but we managed well enough."

Isadora eyed the witch he spoke of, a round woman with thin hair and large front teeth. The odd exchange of grunts and sign language that must have comprised their conversation almost made her giggle.

Charles's voice lowered. "Heard a bit of gossip I thought would interest the two of you. An increased number of Defenders have been reported among the Southern Network clans lately. The Defenders have been helping the Watcher residents. Intriguing?"

Maximillion studied him with tapered eyes. He'd deliberately refused to update Isadora on the Watcher situation, and had stolen her *Chatterer* scroll. She'd quickly transported to the Central Network and bought another one, only to find that Defender attacks were still on the rise, particularly around Chatham. She kept it stuffed under the mattress, which he seemed to have an allergy to.

"Where did you hear this news?" she asked.

"Overheard it from the Southern Network Ambassador while dancing with his wife."

"But he's never spoken a word of the common language."

"Charles is an accomplished linguist," Maximillion said.

"Really?" she cried. "I had no idea."

Charles reddened all the way to the tips of his ears. "Not much," he said, waving a hand. "Just a few here and there."

Max sent her a droll look. "Eleven languages, to date."

Before she could respond, Charles extended a hand.

"Isadora, would you care for a dance? If it's all right with your husband, of course."

Isadora kept her eyes fixed on Charles. "It's all right with me. That's the only permission you need seek."

Wisely, Charles swept her away before Maximillion could fit a word in edgewise. His dancing proved to be as erratic as his hair. One moment he flowed gracefully. The next, he stumbled over her toes, causing more than one pained wince and apology.

"Your Highness, I'm quite sorry if I offended you by my surprise over your linguistic education."

"Not at all."

"Do you know the Yazikan language well?"

He dodged another couple by an inch, nearly colliding with a carved wooden statue as he recovered.

"Not even accomplished historians or linguists know Yazika *well*. It's complicated, to be sure. But engaging. Some witches have calculated as many as 115 dialects, with various nuances that different clans have adopted. I'm accomplished in two dialects, conversant in three, and can read up to twelve. Current usage runs close to twenty dialects throughout the Southern Network. Did you know that the castle has its *own* dialect?"

"Impressive, Your Highness. If I were to give you a sample of Yazikan writing, would you likely be able to translate it? Or at least tell me which dialect it comes from?"

A crushing weight landed on her toes. He winced. "So sorry."

"No need, Your Highness," she said through her teeth.

"If it was written within the last ninety years, yes. I've mostly reviewed their current literature. The dialect spoken at the castle is one of the two I'm very comfortable with. What is it?" he asked conspiratorially. "A shopping list from the High Priestess, perhaps? Oh, an excerpt from a romance novel?"

His eyebrows waggled.

She fought a scowl and chewed on her bottom lip, hesitating. Did she dare tell Charles the truth? As if he sensed a shift in her energy, he pulled back slightly, nearly guiding them into another couple but dodging at the last second. The only casualty was her left little toe.

"No, Your Highness, nothing like that. You see . . . I've, ah, found a piece of parchment that I'd love to understand."

"A mystery!" he cried, then lowered his voice. "Tell me about this parchment. Is it tawdry?"

She leaned closer. He smelled like cotton and wine, an impressively intoxicating mixture.

"May I trust you?" she whispered.

"With anything."

"I believe I've found the remnants of what used to be a village called Taiza."

His grip on her tightened, nearly imperceptibly. "Taiza?" he whispered. The gleam of excitement turned into something else she couldn't read.

"You know it?"

"Indeed. The old Watcher village. I've heard much about it, though nothing formal."

Deciding to tell him everything, she briefly explained what had happened, barring the timber wolves.

He listened, half-stomping her toes, nearly sending them both flying across the floor twice, and finally exclaiming, "Extraordinary!"

"Would you mind helping me? I must know what it says."

"Not at all. I'd love to try, but I'd best have my books to make sure I'm accurate. May I get it back to you? Several things on my plate the next couple of days, you know. Plants have been dying in my arboretum, and there was a Council Member who had a question for me. The slightest variation in thickness on certain Yazikan characters can change the meaning entirely."

The sheer, boring mundanity of his life almost made her hair stand up. He was *dealing with a Council Member* while Maximillion bore the brunt of the Network on his shoulders. She glanced at Max, saw him scowling their way, and rolled her eyes.

Perhaps he deserved it.

The hum of the violins faded. Isadora stepped back as Charles snapped two fingers, looking triumphant. His distraction nearly steered them into a decorative tree, but she pulled him back in time.

"Seven days. I can return it to you in seven days. Will that suffice?"

"Of course, Your Highness."

Isadora withdrew the folded paper from an inner pocket in her dress and passed it to him. His deft fingers took it quickly. Before she realized it, he'd tucked it into his jacket pocket with a lopsided smile.

Maximillion appeared at her side just as Charles faded into the crowd, disappearing with strange grace, like sleight of hand.

"Deft escape artist," she murmured.

"Are you done?" Max asked, voice as cold as a glacier. Feeling a prickle of rebellion at the back of her neck, she ignored him, seeking someone else in the crowd to dance with. Such a lovely party didn't deserve his gloomy rain.

"I'm not done," she said. "Unless you're prepared to dance with me, the way a newlywed should."

"I don't dance twice with the same person."

"You can certainly make an exception for your wife."

"I shan't."

"Then I'll see you at the end of the party."

He grabbed her wrist.

Isadora stiffened all the way down her back. Her fingers curled into a fist.

"You would offer me that insult?" he hissed.

Isadora felt the storm in him without seeing it. A trapped rage, bubbling ferociously. Underneath it simmered something like fear.

"It's no more than you give to me every day I try to be your friend and you refuse to let me."

Isadora left him standing there, fuming like a teakettle.

It didn't take long for the Western Ambassador to ask her to dance, and then a rich landowner from the South— she eclipsed him in height by at least a pace, but he was surprisingly quick on his feet. When their dance ended, he twirled her so violently she spun twice, wobbled, and landed in the muscular arms of the closest witch she could grab.

Maximillion.

"Outside," he muttered with a glower, steering her toward a balcony. "Now."

Isadora stepped onto the small veranda with a little shiver.

Despite the languid snow, the night wasn't bitterly cold. Fat flakes melted as they landed on the stone balustrade. Carven gargoyles leered overhead, half in shadow, half in snow.

Maximillion moved up next to her and gripped the snowy banister, knuckles as white as the falling cotton.

Isadora composed herself with a deep breath, her head full of vetiver. "Can I ask you a question?"

Her tone had lost all vague annoyance. Determination, even anger, filled it now.

He made a motion with one hand.

"That night on Carcere . . . were you afraid of me?"

Several seconds of intense scrutiny answered before he whispered, "Yes, but not for the reason you're thinking."

Then why? The question stuck in her throat.

"Serafina is my aunt," he said before she could muster the courage. "My mother was her younger sister. The two of them were close, at one point. Reputedly, anyway. My mother died when I was young, so I rely solely on the recollections of other people."

To prevent him from scurrying away like a frightened rabbit, Isadora said nothing. She stared out at the snowy fields, seeing nothing but a young boy with a bruised face.

He continued, toneless.

"My mother's name was Maria. She lived in the slums, working as a flower girl—even lower in status than a *lavanda* maid. She would find flowers in the fields, then try to sell them. A difficult enough job in the summer, it left her starving in the winter. When the call issued from Magnolia Castle that the High Priest was searching for his son's future wife under the Law of Vittoria, my mother and Serafina both tried to get his attention. Serafina, with interest in politics and an extensive education pushed by her father, Mansfeld, despite their poverty, succeeded. My mother had never been able to hold onto a thought for more than a few seconds. Flighty, they called her, but passionate."

He leaned back slightly, resting his weight on his palms. A lock of hair had escaped near his forehead. Isadora suppressed the urge to push it back with the rest of the curls. In the torchlight, she thought she saw Serafina in the curve of his nose. In the thick eyelashes that hid uncertain eyes.

"Desperate with jealousy, my mother married a hotheaded man named Antonio. She became pregnant with me and missed the Network-wide handfasting of Serafina and Dante. The two sisters rarely spoke afterward. My mother died not long after my seventh birthday."

His knuckles shifted, tightening. She feared the stone would be crushed beneath such a grip. The image of the boy in the paths sprang back to her mind.

"After her death," he continued, "Antonio, already a difficult, belligerent, *angry* witch, became nearly unmanageable. I attended Mere's funeral, prepared to ask Serafina to save my life by taking me away."

He paused, throat working. Nothing except steely-eyed pain showed in the sharp angles of his jaw. "She never came. She sent a letter saying that Dante wouldn't allow it and that she was sorry. I lived with Antonio until my twelfth birthday, when I finally hit him back. The blow broke his nose, shoving the bone into his brain, and killed him. After that, I ran away."

Isadora's heart clenched like a fist. "And eventually found Pearl in Berry."

He nodded.

Pieces of the puzzle flew together. The joy in Emilia's happy squeal when they had arrived—the warmth of his greeting. The hesitant, longing reserve in Serafina's face. The odd way she seemed hungry for the sound of his name, her prying questions.

I admit a certain level of fondness or affection for Max, she'd said. *While he may not return the same feelings, I've known him longer than anyone here.*

"Emilia is your cousin, then," Isadora said.

"Yes."

"It makes sense now, seeing you. Seeing them. But I never would have guessed it otherwise. Do you miss your parents?"

"I only wish I'd killed my father sooner. To my memory, my mother was a jealous woman who wanted more than life had given her. Antonio had a knack for beating me when he was angry at her, so she distanced herself from me. But . . . she did care for me."

A thousand thoughts ran through Isadora's mind, coalescing into a single strand that, like the magic, hummed.

Abandoned. Left on his own. Thoroughly alone in a world of pain from the beginning. It seemed a miracle Maximillion should be as functional and merciful as all this.

He shifted, clearly uneasy.

She had the feeling he'd never told anyone this much in his life.

"Thank you for telling me."

He stared at her, gaze as dark as ever. Pain lingered behind it.

Isadora reached out, putting a hand on his chest, near his beating heart. Her own raced, thrilling to the touch. He swallowed but didn't push her away. Instead, his gaze bored into her as if daring her to hurt him as well.

"When I first started to learn the magic," she murmured, "it showed me something about you. I can ask to see a witch, and they appear before me. The magic then gives them a word. My sister, for example. Her word is *courageous.* Hardly surprising. Pearl's? *Goodness.*"

A slight tilt of his head seemed to indicate his agreement.

"You were the first witch I saw. I'm not sure why it was

you. It showed you as a broken, beaten little boy, then a furious teenager, then now. As a man."

"And?" he asked, voice raspy.

Troubled by the shadows stirring in him, she said, "Merciful."

He blinked, then looked away. Isadora closed the distance, pressed her face into his chest, and wrapped her arms around him. He sucked in a sharp breath but didn't move, seemingly frozen.

"You're not your father, or your mother," she whispered. "And, for what it's worth, the magic hasn't been wrong yet. I, for one, find you infuriating, impossible, and the most lovable man I've ever met. I don't know how you accomplished it, but you've done the impossible and risen above the ashes of your past. I think you're wonderful, Max, and I'm honored to be here with you."

For several moments, nothing happened. Then, slowly, gently, one arm came down to rest on her shoulders. It lay there like a burning weight that took her breath away. He tightened his grip as if holding on to life itself.

A minute later, the door opened, admitting a giggling pair of witches attempting to sneak into a private corner. They caught sight of Isadora and Maximillion and disappeared back inside.

As if caught, Maximillion pulled away and pushed her back. His eyes rotated through several emotions until he seemed to make a decision. His distant facade returned. He looked like an ice sculpture, all frozen planes and bitter frost.

"Your loyalty to your Network is appreciated," he said, "but you should know I'm not interested in love or happy endings."

Any progress they'd made shattered. Her stomach sank

into bitter depths, all the more because of the truth she'd said to him. She'd opened herself, and he'd turned his back.

She couldn't even speak as she watched him become, again, a glacial stone figure with a beating heart.

"When this is over," he said, "we'll return to our lives as acquaintances. Our professional relationship can go back to the way it was, and you will be free to find a man who truly deserves you."

Her voice trembled when she said, "If you think we can go back to what we were before, you're a bigger fool than I thought."

His jaw tightened. He spun on his heel, leaving the veranda without another word.

24

W *ater.*
    Like fire. It burns.
    Like fiiiire.

An ear-splitting keen broke through Sanna's sleep.

She jumped to her feet, startled awake, to find herself in utter blackness. The warm burn of Luteis's heat behind her was the only reassurance that she hadn't dropped into a nightmare.

She blinked, rubbing her sleepy eyes, and looked around again. Still nothing.

Four days ago, they'd returned from the desert, rejoining the ongoing preparations. Elis and Jesse had orchestrated things beautifully, far better than she could have done. Still, tension and the chronic lack of food loomed heavy, not to mention an impending battle and their utter lack of fighters.

Her reappearance with no further help hadn't improved the mood.

Her mind slowly recalled hunting with Luteis, finding a meager forest lion he ate while they sat by a brackish-tasting stream.

She closed her eyes to better focus. Why had she woken up? Oh, right. Screams.

The panicked wails that had awakened her grew sharper, resonating into her chest.

Luteis. She reached back for him. His yellow eyes popped open, glowing like lanterns. The only thing she could see.

I am awake.

Do you hear it?

No.

It's Letum Wood. The trees are upset.

He uncoiled. Sanna stood in the chilly sweep of a low breeze.

What is wrong with them?

They're ... burning?

She focused in on it again, beyond the rustle of dried leaves. The high voices tripped over each other in panic.

The water.

It burns.

I shall wither.

Save us! Goddess!

I think something is wrong, Sanna said. *They're ... scared. They keep saying the water burns.*

Burning? He huffed, air moving in and out of his nostrils. *I smell no fire.*

The water is burning them? Sanna cocked her head, but the frantic wailing was too difficult to decipher.

Water? he asked.

Sanna started toward the trees, then stopped. She could see nothing. For a moment, she felt as if her world had tipped sideways. Darkness surrounded her on all fronts. Not even starlight guided her. The tightness in her chest dispelled when a warm touch came on her ankle.

Luteis's tail.

Come with me, little one.

As if he knew, Luteis's wing swept her off her feet. She slid onto his back, settling immediately into her spot on his shoulders.

The tightness in her chest eased. She let out a long breath of relief, stuffing her panic away again to focus on the immediate problem.

Where do I go? he asked.

To the nearest tree.

Luteis complied. From the distance came a strange tinkling of water that sounded out of place. Too loud. She reached out, pressing her fingertips to the bark. An explosion of noise erupted in her mind, fraught with terror. Voices, old, high, and in between, louder than the whispers.

Where is the goddess to protect us?

The water burns.

I cannot survive.

Like fire. Fire. Fire. Fire.

Sanna yanked away, gasping.

You are well? Luteis asked, his neck craned, one eye peering at her anxiously. She reached out, feeling his snout.

Fine. The trees are not. Go to the stream.

Her circle of vision faded into a strange, heavy blue, the depth of a bruise. Sunrise was coming. Luteis slinked through the forest and stopped at the stream.

Sanna sniffed.

It . . . smells wrong, she said. *What is that?*

Salt. Brine.

Her heart seized. "Salt?" she whispered.

The cacophony of trees rang through her mind, more frantic here. Some faded, keening into a lower pitch, as if they were . . . dying. Sanna groped along the trees, ignoring the bursts of sound, and finally broke a mossy branch free.

Luteis, light it, please?

Luteis blew a gentle fire on the branch. The moss flared, curling into itself until the bark caught fire. It wouldn't last long, but it momentarily illuminated the stream.

Sanna held it down, casting flickering light on her feet. Water streamed by, swollen past the bank she'd drank from earlier. When she crouched, the smell intensified. Yushi came to mind almost immediately. This water smelled like the ocean.

Sanna touched the water, then her tongue, and recoiled. "Salt."

The trees began wailing anew. She looked up at Luteis, holding the torch between them to see his face. Her throat thickened when she saw the same fear in his eyes.

"Prana has made it into Letum Wood," she whispered.

He paused. *Can we stop this?*

"The water must be backflowing from the ocean like in the North."

Prana is trying to destroy Letum Wood.

"If this river is flooded, so are the others. The rivers give life to Letum Wood. We . . ."

She opened her mouth, but the *thud* of something falling right next to her stopped her. She leapt back, swinging the torch around.

Luteis snarled, stepping forward. *Tashi,* he said.

Sanna searched frantically until she recognized Tashi's cool expression in the flickering light of her torch.

"Tashi?"

"Aki sent me," she said, her voice flat. "Prana has consumed three small cities on the coast. The ocean continues to rise, heading toward the capital, Custos."

"Did he fail the latest riddle?"

"No. Prana's enjoyment of the game waned, so she stopped playing. She has started enacting her revenge early. Yushi is in the waves, calling for you. He says the time has come and demands you fight now."

"It's too early!"

Tashi's expression didn't waver. "Prana doesn't care."

Sanna sputtered, stuck between shock and disbelief. It couldn't be happening *this* soon. Not after she'd seen the West and Aki. All the months of preparation, and now it started too early on the whim of a goddess. She had no army!

"But I don't have fighters."

Luteis nudged her from behind. *We go.*

But we aren't ready. We haven't planned flight patterns or trained the dragons for the sand or—

They are ready.

But the mams! We can't even ask them for help now. There's no time to go up there, and I'd have to command them all individually and . . .

We can do this, little one.

Luteis, I don't know how to break the magic.

You will figure it out.

Sanna's retorts died on her lips. She hadn't planned for this, amongst all the preparations. *Why* hadn't she planned for this? Hadn't several witches warned her that Prana was tricky?

High Dragonmaster? Luteis asked. A gentle reminder. She'd been quiet for a while without meaning to.

"Gather the forest dragons, Luteis," she whispered. "We leave immediately. Tell Elis first, then the others."

Mam flashed through her mind, then Isadora.

"I'll tell the Dragonmasters when I finish here with

Tashi," she continued. "Have Elis tell Jesse not to mention it yet. It needs to come from me."

With great reluctance, Luteis shuffled into the forest and left Sanna and Tashi to speak. A long silence passed between them. Finally, Tashi reached out, clasping Sanna's arm. Her eyes burned with a ferocious light. Sanna didn't need perfect vision to understand her desperation.

"Be who you truly are, and you'll know what to do. Many creatures owe you their lives, and they will give it. Trust in fate."

Tashi disappeared into the darkness.

A brush of warm wind and the smell of honeysuckle drifted by. Sanna whipped around to touch the closest tree. The bark illuminated under her hand.

"Deasylva?"

White-blue writing appeared on the bark, clear as day. *I will be with you and my dragons.*

Sanna let her hand fall away, a knot of fear heavy in her throat.

"Don't forget this."

Mam's voice came from just behind Sanna. Sanna glanced up from where she was sharpening her knife at the table, her mind errantly tracking the forest dragons' conversations. The mountain dragons had been as silent as ever—Metok oddly so. He'd acknowledged her command to prepare, then nothing.

Movement bustled outside. Jesse, the forest dragons, Luteis, Trey, Elliot, Greata. They had twelve forest dragons and five riders. The mountain dragons would transport on Sanna's command, meeting them above the Ancients to fly

West together. United, they would all approach the battle as one, taking the travel time to learn the others' flight patterns and habits in advance of the fight.

Firelight illuminated the table where Sanna sat. She could feel its warmth but saw nothing except vague blurs when Mam moved. Rising panic threatened to overwhelm her again. She managed to crush it by sheer willpower.

"Don't forget what?" Sanna reached a hand out.

Mam pressed something against her palm. "Your vest. The one you brought back from the forest a few months ago."

Sanna ran her fingers over it. She'd forgotten. The gift from Deasylva. Winks of color glinted in the low light. Although it made no sense, she felt a rush of confidence all the same, as if it imparted something to her.

"The Dragonmaster vest," she murmured.

"Put it on."

The strange garment had been sewn together with a thick string that felt as if it had skeins of metal running through it. She slid into it, startled to find it hugged her like a glove all the way to the waist, where it peaked in a V around her hips. Instead of weighing her down, the extra weight soothed her.

She breathed deeper, felt lighter.

"It will protect you more than any spell you could do, I would imagine," Mam said. Her voice caught.

"Mam, I—"

"You can't see, can you?" The words rushed out of her mouth, as if she couldn't stop them.

Sanna froze. "What?"

"The acid from the mountain dragon. It's affected your eyes."

She sucked in a long breath, then released it. "Yes."

"Why didn't you tell me?"

She leaned back against the chair, relieved to finally be able to talk about it.

"I . . . I didn't know how. You've been dealing with so much. Daid's death. Babs's. Relocating again. Losing so many dragons . . . and Isa. Isa leaving all the time. Isa being different. I . . . I didn't want to give you even more to worry about."

Mam's hand settled on her shoulder. Sanna jumped, not expecting the touch.

"A kind thought," Mam said, "but I don't need you to protect me, Sanna. I may not have been very . . . *here* . . . lately, but I am still your mam. I can still read you like a book. How bad is it?"

Tears again. She blinked them back. "Almost entirely gone now. It's narrowed even more in the last week. I can see through a small circle."

She tried to close her thumb and forefinger into a comparable size, settling on an approximation of a large marble. She tilted her head all the way back to search out Mam's gaze. "That's all."

Fear lived in Mam's countenance. She didn't even try to hide it. She brushed a hand over Sanna's hair, pushing a strand off her forehead.

"How?" she asked. The simple word encompassed so many questions.

Sanna's nostrils flared. "I don't know. But I must go. If I don't, who will? Besides, the dragons don't know."

"You may not see the path now," Mam murmured, cradling Sanna's face in her warm, soft palms, "but eventually you will. It always comes, and you have always seen it."

Tears filled Sanna's eyes. The pressure she'd been ignoring for weeks broke open. The truth of her diminishing eyesight crashed over her in long, lonely waves. She had just enough to see *some* things, but not enough to truly lead.

"I don't know if I can do this, Mam," she whispered, her voice stark. "This is too much for me. I'm scared. I don't want to mess up, to cost lives. To lead us down the wrong path."

Mam wrapped her thin arms around Sanna and played with her hair. "Think of your daid. Could he have done it?"

"Yes."

"Then so can you."

Mam pulled away with a teary smile, filled with anguish and love and a deep well of something Sanna had never seen before.

"Oh, *amo*," Mam whispered. "You are so much like him. Don't you think he'll be at your side? Don't you think he's cheering you on? You can't control everything, Sanna, and you were never meant to. Let go, and fight with what you have. The path will appear."

Sanna's breath quavered. "Yes, Mam."

"Will you come back?" Mam asked, her voice cracking.

"I promise."

Mam brushed back another strand of Sanna's hair. "I'm sorry this happened to you. I know what pressure you're under right now. I love you. I'm sorry we lost your daid and that, for a while, you lost me. But please . . ." She gripped Sanna with both hands. "Know that I love you and your sister more than anything."

Tears thickened her voice.

Sanna, feeling a flow of love as profound as Prana's depths, fell into Mam's arms with a cry. They clung to each other, Mam silently crying into Sanna's shoulder, until a voice called from outside.

"Sanna? The dragons are ready."

She pulled away. "I love you, Mam. Tell . . . tell Isa I love her too."

"Tell her yourself when you return."

Sanna moved toward the table. She found her knife after only two attempts and slid it into the sheath at her hip. Her fingers prickled as her mind spun out to the battle ahead. Mountain-dragon formations. The length of forest dragons' secundum.

She suspected—or hoped—she would still be able to communicate with and control the movements of the dragons after she broke the magic. The magic was inherent to them. It would survive in this generation, likely, but not be passed to the next.

If she broke the magic, of course.

Somehow.

Finally ready, she turned around. Mam walked with her to the porch, subtly guiding her through the house she still felt like a stranger in.

Sanna felt Luteis's heat just ahead of them as they strode outside.

All are ready, High Dragonmaster, he said.

Sanna stood there, drawing in another lungful of Letum Wood, and squeezed Mam's hand.

"*Alay,* Mam," she whispered. "I'll see you soon."

"Come back."

Mam released Sanna.

The other riders ringed the house, waiting. Elliot. Trey. Greata. Jesse. Dragon scales flickered here and there, gleaming off the torches. The very air felt charged, poised. Waiting.

She moved toward Luteis with confident steps. Four stairs down. Five strides to his wing. He extended it for her with a gentle rustle, just as she expected. She climbed up under the sheer power of familiarity, then settled on his shoulders.

Metok, she said, reaching out with her mind. Only a second passed before she heard his response.

Yes, High Dragonmaster?

Are you and your fighters ready?

We await you above.

The mountain dragons would easily endure the long flight. Now, thanks to Elis and Jesse's continued patience and work, so would the forest dragons. No forest dragons remained behind except for two females, a young male, and the hatchlings. Cara waited back there, Sanna could feel her gaze.

"We need you back here, *amo,*" Mam called. "I love you."

Luteis shoved off from the ground and into the sky, the swoosh of wings and bellow of dragons following behind.

25

Glittering piles of snow so deep they could bury a witch alive filled the gardens.

Isadora's breath billowed in front of her as she studied the empty scenery from far above. The tips of her fingers and nose ached, but she stood on the balcony anyway. The fur in her coat felt soft against her cheek. She burrowed deeper into it, hands stuffed into the pockets on the side.

The warmth of the turret called to her, but she ignored it, her thoughts on Maximillion. Since the ball two days ago, they'd cordially ignored each other. No eye contact. Not a word. This morning, he'd left before breakfast and hadn't sent a note.

She didn't want to return to the emptiness of her turret prison. Even the magic whirled uneasily inside her, as if it responded to her heartache.

A square of parchment popped in front of Isadora. Startled, she plucked it from the air. The hasty handwriting was immediately recognizable, even in the fading light of sunset.

Lucey.

· · ·

ADVOCACY INFILTRATED *after a Watcher was tortured and gave some names. Defenders attacking in all Networks. It happened quickly. We're trying to locate and warn our members, as well as Watchers. Both are targeted. Will update you soon.*

ISADORA'S POUNDING heart threatened to beat out of her chest as she imagined the fear ripping through witches across the world. She squinted at the scrawl at the very bottom of the parchment.

DO NOT COME. *I repeat, Isadora, do NOT come. I send this only to warn you—be on guard. Don't tell Max unless you have to. I will take care of this. The Advocate has written several letters to me already—they are aware.*

ISADORA CRUNCHED the parchment in her fist and strode inside. She focused on the next step: find Max. Immediately. Of course they wouldn't just stay *here* while Watchers lost their lives in the Central Network.

She reached for the doorknob to the stairway, but a cold flash of understanding stopped her. Dante would be behind this, surely. He'd be waiting for her to storm into the meeting and make accusations. Her gut tightened.

Maybe this was his plan.

He wanted to see Isadora and Maximillion scrambling to participate in the summit *and* handle the Watchers. Such a distraction meant Max would make a mistake, and Dante could pounce.

Subterfuge. How could Max negotiate for the Central Network if he were busy saving Watchers? And if he didn't save the Watchers, all the better for Dante. There was no way for Dante to lose here.

She paused, sucking in a sharp breath.

What could be done from here? Nothing, likely. She could scramble around with Lucey, but her presence might create more issues than it solved.

Frustrated, Isadora backed away from the door with a growl, then plopped into a chair and immediately entered the magic without regard for the consequences. The paths unfurled with unusual chaos. Her own paths crowded out Sanna's completely.

As usual, the changing nature of the wisps did little but muddle her, giving so many possibilities that she banished them all, leaving an empty forest.

She sat in the magic, stunned by the sheer number of possibilities that had presented themselves. Was the magic more sensitive, betraying more details than before, or were there simply so many potential futures?

A stirring came from behind her. Recognizing it, she left the magic and opened her eyes.

Maximillion stood above her. His usual scowl had been replaced with something far more neutral. Even hesitant.

"You were in the magic," he said, his tone distant.

"Briefly."

He made a noise in his throat and put space between them. "The vote was unanimous against Dostar's plan, which advances us to the next round tomorrow. Hardly surprising," he added, "considering that Dostar isn't even here."

She expected to feel a flood of relief that they'd at least made it to the next vote, but emptiness gnawed at her chest.

Before she could reply, a rap came at the door. "Message for Ambassador Sinclair from His Royal Greatness, Dante Aldana. A last-minute dinner has been announced to celebrate today's good work. It will begin sharply at six o'clock. Your wife is invited."

"Demmet," Maximillion grouched. "We need to leave now to make it on time. Blasted stairs. You'd think they'd come up with a room placed a bit more conveniently."

Isadora clutched her hands in her lap to keep them from shaking. The dinner and socializing would last at least until midnight. If she skipped it, that would give her time to check on Pearl without Max knowing.

He rubbed a hand over his face. His eyes had grown blearier than ever. "Are you all right?" he asked, studying her. "You've gone suddenly pale."

"Fine. Thanks. Would you mind if I stayed in tonight?" She put a hand to her head, grateful she didn't have to lie. "I'm not feeling well."

"You've always jumped at any chance to get out of this gods-forsaken turret."

"A headache."

He stared at her. "Has nothing to do with our conversation at the ball and your sudden abhorrence of my presence?"

She coolly met his gaze. "No."

He frowned, then nodded once. "Very well. Can I get you anything?"

"No, thank you. Good luck at dinner. I'll . . . await an update."

He cast her a suspicious glance, then left without a word, his shoes echoing on the stone floor.

Isadora waited one minute, twirled her cape on, and transported away.

D<small>IZZY FROM TRANSPORTING</small>, Isadora stumbled onto Pearl's doorstep.

Thin leaves scuttled across a patch of snow on the stones. The tendrils of pressure and darkness from the transportation spell disappeared as she lifted a hand to knock.

The door hung ajar.

Isadora sucked in a sharp breath.

The remnants of broken plates lay scattered on the floor, sparkling in the moonlight. Overturned chairs drew her attention to the table, which had been broken in half. Scratch marks raked across the plaster in one wall. Isadora whispered a spell to illuminate the room. She advanced, glass crunching beneath her feet.

A ball of light moved several paces ahead of her. Scrolls, books, and feathers were strewn on the floor, torn and damaged. All the cupboards hung open. She stepped over a broken crate.

"Pearl?" she called. "Pearl, are you in here?"

No answer. Frantic, she searched the house. Nothing. No letter. No sign of life. Had they ransacked this place after she left? If they had killed her, she wasn't here.

Isadora stepped over a pile of sheets ripped to shreds on her path to the back door, which also stood ajar. Her heart lurched into her throat.

There was only one place to go from here.

I<small>SADORA STOOD</small> outside Charles's office with a weak feeling in her stomach. She'd transported to Chatham Castle and come directly here, pleading for a chance to speak with him.

A Guardian had slipped inside, growling, leaving her alone in the hall. The castle lay in quiet repose during the dinner hour.

Charles appeared in a halo of cinnamon, concern evident on his face. "By the good gods, what are you doing here?"

"Your Highness, I apologize for the unexpected visit. If I may speak with you alone?"

He studied her, unease in his eyes. With a decisive nod, he stepped back, allowing her room to walk past. A discreet glance passed between him and the Guardian, who disappeared into the corridor.

Charles motioned to a chair with clawed feet and hideous fabric. "What can I do for you? Is Maximillion all right?"

"Fine. I came on . . . well, Advocacy business."

"I assumed so."

"Why is that?"

"What can be done? Twenty deaths reported already."

His usual foppish manner had subsided into something a great deal wearier. Had the effects of the war gone so far that even the High Priest, with his unflappable energy, showed signs of it?

Isadora cleared her throat. "I received the news. My contact said Defenders were on the rampage, killing Watchers. So I went to check on Pearl and . . . found her house ransacked."

He straightened. "She's practically Max's mother!"

"Yes. There was no sign of her. I-I can't be sure whether she's been taken or—" She choked, unable to finish the thought.

His brow had grown heavy over his tired eyes. "Frightening."

If anything had happened to Pearl, there would be no stopping Max. Any ground gained in the South would be cast aside as he sought to find or avenge her. Suddenly, she appreciated the irony of her position. Hadn't Max faced this same conundrum when Daid had died?

"And you came here after?" he asked gently.

"Yes. I . . . I don't want to tell Max until we know more. I fear Dante has done this in an attempt to distract him from his work there. The first vote was just cast, and Max's plan is up against Dante's. It makes sense that he'd be more desperate."

"Agreed," he said immediately. "Max cares deeply for her. He would be distracted, at best. More likely livid. He's a man of impressive control until he's sufficiently goaded, and then he isn't."

And then he isn't. She thought of Max's story of his father and wondered if she should fear him more. She didn't. At least, not until he broke her heart.

"I would search for Pearl myself," Isadora said, "but I can't, and I don't dare bother L—my contact, who has enough on her plate now. I thought since you are the High Priest . . ."

She let the thought die out on her lips.

Charles frowned at the fire. "I can take care of that."

"Really?"

"I may not be so efficient and useful as Max at these kinds of things, but I am kept apprised of the things happening in my Network. I shall seek out the Advocate and let them know."

Isadora's eyes widened. "What?"

Startled, he stared back at her. "Max hasn't told you who the Advocate is?"

"No."

Charles grinned with his whole face this time, regaining his usual expression that seemed leagues above the darkness hovering over the world. Seeing his boyish side gave her a little comfort. Even if he wasn't much for business, he did offer something like hope.

"It's hardly my place to tell you, as I'm only a small cog in the vast Advocacy machine. I'm sure Max will betray them. One day."

Questions spun through her mind. She set them aside and reluctantly returned to her purpose.

"Then will you let me know what the Advocate finds out about Pearl as soon as you can? In the meantime, I'll try to keep Maximillion focused. He doesn't know about any of this." Isadora swallowed hard. "I . . . I hate lying to him."

Even if he is frosty.

"Immediately. As soon as I receive word myself. In the meantime, I'll see that someone goes to her house and watches for further movement. You've done the right thing, Isadora, allowing Max to concentrate."

Relieved, Isadora relaxed slightly. "Thank you, Your Highness. I can't tell you what it means."

She stood to go, but Charles stopped her. "Wait." He conjured a folded piece of parchment and held it out to her. "Just finished your translation yesterday. I meant to send it but was distracted by an emergency in the gardens. Rare, noxious weed, is all. No need to be concerned."

She accepted the parchment. "Thank you, Your Highness."

His brow ruffled. "It's odd. I've never seen anything like it before. It's the same two words, repeated in nearly every contemporary Yazikan dialect. That's the reason it's a list, you see."

"Every dialect?"

He nodded, seeming bemused. "Yes."

"What two words?"

"*Don't look.*"

Isadora tensed. *Don't look.* Unease rippled through her. What was that supposed to mean?

"Whoever the message was written for, it was clearly meant to discourage them from some kind of search."

"Indeed."

"Are you looking for something?"

"No." She stood to go, thoroughly flummoxed. He followed, tucking his hands into his pockets.

"Thank you again, Your Highness."

The door creaked open as she moved toward it. Isadora glanced back, saw Charles silhouetted against the flames, and stepped into the hall. Seconds later, she disappeared into a transportation spell, relieved to be going back.

A breath of air whispered across her face when she returned to Vasily's gardens. The dark clouds covered the sky entirely now, as if the storm had finally reached its desired destination. The charged air momentarily reminded her of La Torra and the night of Cecelia's death. She pulled in a deep breath, feeling it happen all over again.

"We can feel your magic," Cecelia had snarled. *"We can feel the connection, perhaps before you can, because you didn't even know it existed. Every time you use your magic, you bring us closer and closer."*

Her whirling mind slowed, peeling away the layers of fear for Pearl. For all the Watchers and Advocacy members —some killed, some hiding, some hopefully safe.

But that meant the stakes were too high for games now.

The only option left was to call her match by using the magic. To force Dante's hand. She could, at the very least, confront him *in* the magic—if that was how it worked. She'd done something like that with Cecelia.

She'd stop him before this went too far for both the Watchers and the entire Network, and she'd do it tonight.

SNOW FELL SOFTLY OUTSIDE, collecting on the balcony. Isadora sat in a chair near the fire, closed her eyes, and slipped into the magic.

The paths unfurled around her in a latticework of trees and shadow. Seeing Luteis flying with Sanna in every wisp on her paths, she relaxed. Sanna was fine.

She sent away all the paths and drew in a deep breath.

Then she let the magic go.

The power soared free, cutting through the air in a spiral and then winging around like a whip made of strands of light. The forest brightened. Leaves tripled on the trees. A string of flowers descended from the canopy overhead and elongated in front of her. The scent of honeysuckle drifted by.

She sent any control she had over the magic into the forest.

Paths sprang up in vivid detail, leaving wisps so pristine and delicate she felt as if she could step into them. The possibilities crowded for space, showing moment-by-moment movement.

"Show no wisps," she commanded.

The wisps disappeared in gauzy towers of smoke.

"Show me Maximillion."

The pillar of light bloomed, forming a perfect replica of

Max—even of the lines of concern on his forehead. He glowed so brightly she recoiled, holding up a hand to shield her eyes.

"Show me Max in ten years."

She'd been testing the magic ever since she first stumbled into it, but hadn't pushed it this far yet.

Maximillion changed, but not by much. Silver streaked through his thicker, longer curls. His expression sharpened, his face more lined, aging with unsurprising grace. She paused, struck by his features. Were those smile lines around his eyes?

The magic shifted, growing. It flooded past her.

Unbidden, wisps reappeared.

"No wisps!"

They remained, populating in every direction as far as she could see. The boundless magic carried an almost-sinister refrain now. It flowed unrestrained *through* her instead of *from* her.

Was there no limit to what it could do? She scrambled for control again, but the magic flooded past her like an angry river.

"No!" she called. "Wait. Stop!"

The wisps continued forming. Maximillion at the dinner. Facing Dante. Vasily. The glint of a swinging weapon. Blood on white-and-black tile.

Isadora's heart nearly stopped.

The sheer enormity of the power threatened to consume her. The magic held her fast, pinning her into the paths by sheer force. Its friendly warmth had disappeared. Her body radiated a blinding light. With such boundless power came equal danger.

Could *any* Defender avoid finding her now?

The magic was too alive. Too restless and ancient. All

consuming. Even . . . *agitated*, as if it sought to protect something. But what? And what did it have to do with her?

More wisps of Maximillion appeared. Blood. Weapons. Fire. Rage. Maximillion with blood on his face, fear in his eyes. Then kneeling, bound. Lying on the ground, pools of blood surrounding him. Violence awaited him in every wisp. All but one.

"No!" Isadora whispered.

With the last of her reserves, she let out a guttural cry. Groping for release, she attempted to close the magic again. A sliver of hesitance, like a flailing thread, emerged from the stream of power. She grabbed it.

The pulse of the magic slowed. Isadora seized the strands in her mind, wrenching it back under her power one thread at a time. When she finished, darkness seeped in at the edges of her vision.

She closed the magic, returning to the room with a frantic gasp. Heart pounding, head filled with images of Maximillion's imminent demise, she rushed from the turret, slamming the door behind her.

26

W
e have arrived, little one.

Luteis's voice nudged Sanna awake. She straightened, blinking. Cool air swept across her back, and she shivered. Luteis's burning warmth left her front sweaty, and her back cold. Her blurry vision cleared only slightly.

What do you see? she asked.

The ocean. I am flying over it now, not far from land. There are thousands of sea dragons of all different colors in the water. They look much like Yushi, from what I can see.

His voice remained impassive as they banked to the left. Humidity swept over Sanna's cheeks, brushing against her eyes with a gentle caress.

Beneath them, waves roared. Not too far away, a crack of thunder growled as if chasing them away.

Her stomach turned to stone as the flickering colors of sea dragons filled her vision. Like flashes of ribbon, they moved in the water. Mauve. Burgundy. Garish yellow.

Fly farther out. I want to see how far they go.

Luteis complied. Minutes later, she still could make out

their forms in the water. Thousands on thousands of them. Far beyond their own numbers.

That's enough, she said quietly. *We must head back to land. I need to speak with Aki.* Her head tilted back as she studied the sky. The leaden clouds threatened rain. *Do you see any desert dragons?*

Flying over the beach, some in their caves. Hundreds of them. They won't get close to the water, but they appear curious.

And the rest of our brood?

His body shifted as his head turned. *They are on the beach, resting. They did admirably and have not lost all their energy, thanks to the last oasis. Though the rest was brief.*

Metok and the mountain dragons?

A surprising note of pride infused his tone. *Pose a formidable force. To see them all flying behind us . . . I am honored they are here. Their numbers thicken the sky like a storm.*

Sanna turned on instinct to look behind them. She saw hints of dragons in the air but was unable to tell how many. The thought of Metok and his battle-hungry dragons gave her a measure of peace. The sea dragons, confined to the water, would have specific disadvantages—even as they held the upper hand in sheer numbers. They couldn't fly, she reminded herself.

However, the forest and mountain dragons would be comparatively easy to drown. To wrestle a sea dragon from the water and haul them into the air until they died would be almost impossible. They'd have to be killed in the water, which would also guard them.

The odds didn't favor her dragons.

Her stomach sickened at the thought of harming the sea dragons. Killing mountain dragons in self-defense had been bad enough, but knowing what she knew now about goddesses and the sick cycle of Dragonian magic, she couldn't imagine bringing death to any dragon.

Any witches? she asked, forcing her thoughts elsewhere.

I see Aki and Tashi in a camp on the beach.

"Take me there."

As they soared over the snapping sea dragons, her chest stirred. The weight of what they had to do sank deep into her chest, leaving her breathless.

The storm comes, Luteis said.

"Yes," she murmured. "It does."

High Dragonmaster, came Metok's voice. *You are required at the top of the beach, near the rocks.*

SANNA STUDIED A GROWING mass in the distant sky. Dragons flying toward them, but these were too big to be her mountain dragon males. In the fading light, she could just make out what appeared to be broad wings. Her heart caught in her throat.

Metok stood next to her, staring at the sky.

Did you bring the mams? she asked.

Ten different mountain mams flew gracefully toward them, skimming low over the desert sand. She wondered what Renor thought of the desert and ocean, a world so vastly different from their mountain heights.

It is not the mams that are here to fight, he said.

A hulking figure appeared out of thin air, crashing onto a sandy bank with a livid bellow. Every creature at her back let out a terrified shout, scrambling backward, leaving only Sanna and Luteis standing there.

A troll.

The troll leader shoved a fist into the sand, grunted, and

looked up. From his hands and knees, he met Sanna's gaze. Her heart hammered in her chest. She crouched, pressing her hand to the slab of rock at her feet.

Despite a sudden heaviness, an image swam into her mind. Trolls. Lining the shore, shoulder to shoulder, and scowling at the sea.

Sanna straightened before the leaden feeling robbed her mind again, feeling its stirring weight in her chest. Two more trolls appeared from beneath mountain mams that appeared. Renor circled Sanna overhead, eventually settling on the rock by the troll, and stared hard at Sanna as more mountain mams appeared with trolls.

Sanna approached, letting the whispers of the forest dragons fade in her mind. Ten trolls stood behind their leader.

"You have come after all."

To deliver aid, Renor said, *on command of our goddess.*

Do the trolls come willingly?

Renor's nostril flared. *I have communicated with the leader. In payment for your service, he and ten others have come to fight. If they survive, I will return here with my mams, and we will use our magic to transport them back home.*

Sanna studied the growing number of trolls gathering behind Renor, unable to get a count with her limited sight. From what she could see, they gazed around, grunting, humming, thumping to each other. Their nostrils widened and narrowed. The leader kept his gaze on her. She met it, but only barely.

A thousand questions filled Sanna's mind. How did they transport the trolls here? Was their great power transportation? Such is what she and Luteis had suspected all along. But why were the trolls so willing to fight? Was it really about the water?

She shoved those questions aside. It didn't matter. She had fighters—large ones—and fighters is what they needed. Sanna crouched back down, pressed her palm to the rock, and felt the weighty connection with the leader.

She sent him the only picture she could think of— kneeling on one knee, her hand over her heart, and then returned the image he gave. The troll lifted a hand to his head and drew it away. Warmth flooded her. Gratitude. Eagerness. Loyalty. She couldn't tell which came with more strength. She straightened.

"Then," she whispered, "we accept. Before you leave, Renor, please tell them to wait where they are. They'll take commands from me only."

"Aki, High Dragonmaster of the Desert, will gladly see you," Tashi said.

Tashi's hair spiraled around her head in blonde tendrils, dampened by the humidity of the sea behind them. The smooth slope of her forehead and strong, graceful shoulders spoke to a power Sanna hadn't noticed before.

If ever they'd needed it, they did now.

The ocean, at least a hundred paces away, seemed to slip closer with every breath. Two witches, a male and a female, stood near the waves. Both were strong but wiry, with skin browned by the relentless sun. Long braids ran down their backs, brushing their thighs. They eyed the sea, murmuring to each other every now and then.

As the water moved closer, they stepped back, marking its progress with a stick. Slowly, it closed the space between the waves and the cliffs. Once the water breached the cliffs where the desert dragons lived, it would be an easy shot into the Western Network, which was a downs-lope away.

Hastily constructed tents filled the beach, and half-naked West Guards darted in and out of them. The wall of rock wasn't far from the water now. In only a few hours, these cliffs would likely be underwater. Only a thin trail led up the rock face into the desert beyond. A precarious climb.

What would happen to all these witches during the battle?

From the midst of the haphazard camp, Aki strode toward Sanna. He frowned as he moved, every step contracted and powerful, as if he expected an attack at any time. Sanna watched warily.

He stopped a few paces away, stared at her for a long moment, then swept an arm back toward a nearby tent. He put three fingers to his chin, then drew them away. She repeated the gesture.

"High Dragonmaster," he said in a deep voice. "You are welcome again. Please, come inside."

Luteis followed until she reached the tent flap and glanced back at him. "I'll be fine."

All the same, he replied, *I shall wait for you.*

"Your dragon is protective of you," Aki said.

"Yes."

"With a horde of trolls following you, I can understand why."

Sanna's lips twitched. "I have that effect on magical creatures."

Aki made a sound in the back of his throat. He moved ahead of her and pinned the tent flap open, allowing Luteis to see her. Quick scans revealed that the tent was empty except for a few swords and some bulbous, spiked weapons.

"My High Priest has come to assess the fight," he said.

"He has agreed to give us West Guards to face Prana. He is in his tent now, awaiting my assessment."

Sanna frowned. She hadn't expected this. "Your assessment?"

Aki's shrewd eyes met hers. "Of you."

She stood up to his silent perusal with a stifled sense of deep annoyance, perhaps rage. Now wasn't the time to test her.

Or was it?

"I'm not here to play games," she said quietly. "I'm here to stop this war. Should that fail, to fight the sea dragons until Prana relents. If she doesn't? Fight until we cannot anymore."

Something flickered through his eyes, then disappeared. "What is your plan?"

"Confront Yushi first," she said, relieved to have someone to review her strategy with. "I doubt I'll be able to talk Prana into peace, so then we'll fight. If you have any idea of how to create imbalance in a magic, I'm open to hearing it."

His brow furrowed. "Imbalance in magic? What for?"

"I'm going to win the battle, and I'm also going to break Dragonian magic."

He stared at her. She met his gaze, unwilling to break the silence.

Finally, he let out a long breath. "I can't advise you on the magic. But for the battle, we are here to support you. You have one hundred West Guards at your disposal. How would you like them to fight?"

Sanna drew in a breath. An unexpected boon, nearly as powerful as the trolls because witches could move faster and with greater cunning. But if they couldn't ride dragons, would they really be able to serve?

"On the ground," she said with confidence. "Dragons will fall and be injured. I want witches available to tend their wounds so the sea dragons don't kill them. Many could survive. Forest-dragon blood has healing properties, so your West Guards should collect any that falls and give it to any injured witches or dragons. But when I say retreat, you have to retreat. The space between the ocean and these cliffs is going to close, and I don't want anyone stuck here. The trolls will guard the edge of the water to prevent sea dragons from coming ashore, but there will still be fatalities."

"And the desert dragons?" he asked, eyes tapered. "What is your plan for my creatures?"

"They are free already, aren't they?"

A long pause swelled between them until he nodded once. "As you say."

"Will they follow me into the battle?"

He held out a slender object. "This," he said, "is a whistle that all the desert dragons have been exposed to since their hatching. We use it to call them to food if they're tamed. Even the wild ones know it. If you blow it during the battle, I believe some of the desert dragons will aid you. I cannot promise it—their allegiance is to themselves. But those who have been raised in our desert families will fight a threat if given the right call."

The whistle looked to be made from rock, whittled with long, smooth strokes, then sanded. It hung as long as her finger, a deep red like the rocks.

Aki proffered it. "Take it."

"But . . ."

He reached out, grabbed her hand, and closed her fingers around the whistle. Sanna swallowed, feeling the weight of the world on her shoulders.

"Don't you want to lead them?" she asked.

"That is not my calling. It is yours. You are the dragon leader, and all will follow."

"Will you be there?"

His lips twitched as if he was suppressing a smile. "I shall fight. I am with you as best as I can be from the land."

"Go on a forest dragon. Stellis would—"

"I will stay with my witches, but I appreciate your offer. We'll help the dragons that fall, and fight the sea dragons that come too far onto land. It may not be much, but little things often add up to something great."

Sanna tightened her grip on the whistle. Her throat thickened. "Thank you. I'll do my best for them, Aki."

"I know. You have my utmost gratitude and respect, High Dragonmaster. I will report this to my High Priest."

Sanna stood there, hesitating. A thousand questions whirled through her mind. But the words wouldn't come. Unable to articulate a single thought, she simply nodded.

The canvas flapped open wider in a gust of wind. She hadn't noticed the speed of the oncoming darkness until then, but already the storm covered the whole sky, stretching out of sight and into the West. Banks of black clouds crawled toward them in a thick, broiling mass.

Sanna stopped, studying the sky. Desert dragons paced nearby in agitation, letting out occasional nervous snorts as they eyed the approaching behemoth.

We must go, Luteis said. *Our dragons have drunk and eaten what little food we have left. They are amassing. Word is that Yushi is calling for you.*

"On my way."

But her leaden feet didn't move as she stared at the desert dragons. They made low, agitated bleating sounds.

They were free. But would freedom destroy them?

Was promising the dragons freedom the right thing to

do when she had no idea how to fulfill it? She dabbled in a world of goddesses and magic, far beyond her ability, her understanding, or her comfort.

Be who you truly are, and you'll know what to do.

Sanna headed for the beach, her thoughts spinning.

WAVES CRASHED LIKE WAR DRUMS.

The wild storm charged the air, whipping Sanna's braids into a frenzy. Wind pressed against her as if testing her resolve. The briny smell of the sea burned her nostrils. Luteis's tail never left her ankle.

Yushi had slithered out of the ocean thirty paces away to stare at her. A storm of his own brewed in his dark eyes.

"Daughter of the forest," Yushi called. "Are you ready for the next great massacre in a long history of Dragonian bloodshed?"

Sanna advanced four steps. The sand felt cool and firm beneath her. Water pooled at her toes, then slithered away.

"We don't have to fight," she said.

"Oh," he murmured, "but according to Prana, we do. And Prana compels us through the magic, just as your goddess compels you. So, yes. We *must*."

She tightened her hold on her knife, feeling desperation all the way into her bones. "I'm here to ask Prana to back down and spare our lives. Surely there's another way to work this out."

"If you want this to truly stop," he said, "you ask the impossible."

Luteis's tail tightened around her ankle. Another silence filled the salty air. The wind screeched, throwing sand against her skin.

Sanna's nostrils flared when she whispered, "I don't want to kill any sea dragons, Yushi. It's not your battle, either."

He stared hard at her. His gaze flickered to her chest, where the amulet hung, then back to her face.

Finally, he looked away, punctuating every word. "Still, there must be a fight. Prepare for the unleashing of power you've never imagined, High Dragonmaster. I will see you in the water."

Yushi slithered back into the waves. Sanna could hear the water roar as it closed in, reaching for her. Cool foam nibbled at her toes. This time, she didn't step away, not surprised to hear a distant whisper as the ocean touched her skin.

Luteis yanked her away.

"Oh, and High Dragonmaster?" Yushi called. "Don't fall in the water. She's waiting."

"You are a slave to your goddess."

Sanna's voice rang out over the gathered dragons, but to be sure they understood, she repeated herself in her mind.

They occasionally stirred, restless in the humid air. Behind them crashed the pounding tide. Loose sand tickled Sanna's bare feet. She'd long since shucked off her sandals, preferring the feeling of her skin against ground.

Forest, mountain, and desert dragons rippled in front of her in the oddest conglomeration of creatures she had ever seen. The forest dragons ringed her only a few paces away. She could feel the reassurance of their heat. Behind them lingered an uncountable horde of mountain dragons. West Guards and desert dragons were interspersed amongst the others, and a few desert dragons had taken wing overhead. Somewhere near the beach waited the trolls, stony with silence as they stared at the rippling, vast water.

Despite her tiny circle of vision, she could feel the weight of their stares. The quiet was all consuming against the crash of the sea. Sanna pulled in a slow, steady breath. Luteis's tail around her ankle bolstered her confidence.

"I also am a slave to Deasylva and Selsay," she continued. "Dragonmasters are slaves to the power, just like dragons. Let us not forget that the goddesses require *us* for their fights. We cannot defeat a goddess, but we can defeat her magic. Tonight, if you fight for me, I will promise you freedom. I will end this magic."

To her right, Jesse sucked in a sharp breath. Forest-dragon whispers stirred in her mind. She wished she could see Metok's expression amid the murmurs, but she wasn't sure where he was in the mass.

"But . . ." Elliot murmured. "The magic?"

"The magic binds us to the goddesses, and it's what compels you here tonight. I ask you to fight for your freedom. Not for your goddess. For yourself. Fight to save the world from Prana's tyranny and I will do the same.

"If we don't fight, she will flood the land. She will kill as many dragons as she wishes. Entire races will be destroyed, including witches. I vow to set you free tonight if you vow to fight."

She paused. She wanted to command them. To guarantee her force. To ensure every last dragon gave their all.

But she couldn't do that. It wouldn't be right.

"Do you promise?"

Their response exploded in her head. The magic reared up, fanning from the tips of her fingers all the way to her chest, meeting in the middle near her heart.

Freedom!

I will die for my freedom.

For the freedom of my hatchlings.

For the freedom of all dragons.

Luteis braced her with his foreleg when she stumbled back, thrown by the force of all the dragons speaking at once. Even mountain-dragon voices whispered through her mind. Most of them hadn't once spoken to her, but all of them frantically scrambled to be heard now. She drank in their eagerness, their power, confident she had chosen correctly.

Slowly, they fell quiet again.

We follow you, High Dragonmaster, Metok said, the final voice in a reverberating silence. *To our freedom.*

You have always been our leader, Elis said, shuffling forward. Behind him, all twelve of the forest dragons bowed to her. *We follow you willingly.*

Her heart swelled, heavy and light at the same time. Heat flooded her body, washing through her like a warm bath. The battle was about to begin. She'd promised them freedom, and she had no idea how she'd deliver it.

But she would.

"Then we fight," she called, shoving emotion aside. She clutched her knife. "Rank up. It's time."

Have you made a promise we may not be able to fulfill? Luteis asked quietly. *Are you trying to control something that you cannot?*

I don't know, she responded. *But I really hope not.*

27

When Isadora rushed through the double doors into the formal dining room, she expected screams. War cries. The bellow of battle.

Instead, a calm dinner scene glittered like a fresh snowbank.

Diamonds covered the surface of the dining table, sparkling atop a white tablecloth. Cream-colored plates, made of diamond dust, dazzled in the candlelight. Only eight chairs ringed the table—an unusually intimate dinner.

All eyes looked up when Isadora skidded to a stop, heart pounding. Maximillion rose, not a hair out of place. There wasn't a speck of blood or tension or hostility to be seen.

Across the table, Dante grinned. He stood, a wine glass held high, as if making a toast.

Dread sank all the way to her gut. Out of fear, she'd made the cardinal mistake—trusting the possibilities. The future relied too much on randomness and choice. But . . . why had she seen Max dying in every wisp but one?

And why did Dante look so smug?

Maximillion rose warily. He reached out a hand, his lips parting, but Dante cut him off.

"Just as expected! Please, Mrs. Sinclair. Sit down and join us. I was regaling the company with a story you may enjoy. You look like you need to recover your . . . power."

Isadora's nostrils flared. The hair on her arms stood up. She didn't say a word, feeling the edges of her magic stirring under his gaze. Maximillion shifted. A small, gauzy bird appeared at his ear, unnoticed by the others. Max tilted his head toward it almost imperceptibly, listening. Seconds later, it disappeared.

Isadora's knees felt weak.

"The story," Dante continued, recapturing Isadora's attention, "is about a witch named Cecelia. I believe you knew her."

His gaze hardened.

"Of course you did, for it was *you* who murdered her. Carcere. La Torra. And a Central Network mission that not only infiltrated my prison and freed almost forty guilty heathens, but resulted in the murder of my Ambassador."

"Your Ambassador killed herself." Maximillion shifted closer to Isadora but was still half a room away. Shadows moved along the edge of the room. Guardians, likely.

"Cecelia," Dante said, "was confronted by a Watcher far more powerful than she and pulled into the magic. Something that no one knew to be possible. Shouldn't be possible. Whatever the Watcher did to her there pushed her to take her own life. I have that on good authority."

"Not on the authority of the Watcher in question," Isadora said, "the only other witch who would know what actually happened."

An amused smile graced his lips. "Not until now." He swung toward Vasily. "Your Greatness, as promised, I brought the little usurper here. I present to you Isadora Spence, handfasted wife of Maximillion Sinclair, and the most powerful Watcher in Antebellum."

A leaden silence descended in the aftermath of his announcement. Arayana had a perplexed expression, as if she weren't sure what to make of the revelation. Serafina had turned away, her face pale. Maximillion appeared next to Isadora right then, shoving her behind him and training a murderous glare on Dante.

Vasily studied her with narrowed eyes.

"He speaks the truth, Your Greatness," Isadora said to Vasily, stepping out from behind Max. "I am a Watcher, and the most powerful in Antebellum now."

"As a Watcher, she can see the future," Dante said. "And as a Watcher of her demonstrated power, who knows the end of her sight? Is that why you handfasted Maximillion right before you came here?"

"My being a Watcher has nothing to do with my presence here. I . . . care deeply for Maximillion. I love him."

The words filled her throat, startling her. Fool that she was, they were no lie. She felt their full depth in that moment.

Maximillion's shoulders tightened.

"An insult," Dante called, "if you expect us to believe that you came to the most important meeting in modern history without the intent to manipulate the negotiations. A quick handfasting to Maximillion ensured her a place here. She walked amongst us and interacted with our wives. No doubt her husband told her of our discussions, allowing her to see the future and pivot everything to the benefit of the Central Network."

"I don't see the future, Your Greatness," Isadora said to Vasily. "I see possibilities for the future, and I don't need to be present to do it. I could have done such a thing in the Central Network. It's a moot point. Besides, the magic isn't certain. Most possibilities I see never come about."

Like tonight, she thought, feeling her regret more keenly.

This had been a trap. Dante must have been planning on harming Maximillion in order to generate those exact paths. When she didn't show up for dinner, he'd decided on several ways he could kill him.

Even something as simple as that could affect the paths.

Dante's gaze glittered with dark mirth. "It even explains why the Ambassador is here and not the High Priest," he said as if she hadn't spoken. "Perhaps this subterfuge goes even deeper than we can see here, as it so often does with Watchers. Did Maximillion and Isadora plan this out years ago? Perhaps *they* had Greta install Charles as High Priest so they could be here together today. They would have seen it with her powers."

"That's absurd," Isadora said. "I didn't have my powers then."

"Your Greatness," Dante said, turning to Vasily again. "I believe we have all been played by the Central Network. This violates the terms of the summit and immediately disqualifies them from any say in the future of Antebellum."

Maximillion snarled. Furrows lined Vasily's forehead. Even Arayana seemed frightened, glancing between Isadora and her husband with fear in her eyes.

No doubt seeing an opportunity, Dante lifted a sweeping arm toward Arayana. "Your Greatness, did Mrs. Sinclair declare herself a Watcher to you?"

Arayana hesitated, looking from Dante to Isadora.

Isadora nodded at her in silent permission.

Arayana swallowed hard. "No."

"Is it not true that, by law in the Southern Network, a

Watcher must declare themselves in advance of a political meeting?"

Arayana exhaled. "Yes," she whispered.

"I think it's very clear we have a spy in our midst, Your Greatness. Any plan she has been a part of cannot be considered fair. Our wives, I believe, have suffered the most. To protect them and our children, we must ask the Central Network to leave this summit."

"An act of war," Maximillion hissed. The tight angles of his body coiled like a lion ready to pounce. "And *fascinating* timing. With Dostar in the West and the Central Network so conveniently removed, you have open opportunity to enact your one-ruler plan without opposition."

"By majority vote," Dante said coldly. "Even if Dostar were here."

Vasily and Dante would constitute a majority as long as the Central Network was removed. How Dostar voted didn't matter. The bitter realization flashed through Isadora's entire body.

They had utterly failed.

Maximillion's fists clenched as if the thought occurred to him as well.

"I ask a personal favor of you now, Your Greatness," Dante said. "Mrs. Sinclair murdered my Ambassador, Cecelia Bianchi. It's only right that she meet justice in the Eastern Network, where she committed her heinous crime."

Serafina stood. "Your Greatness, may I—"

"Silence," Dante barked.

Serafina's lips bobbed like a fish. Her hand clutched at her throat, as if a silencing incantation had wrapped around it. She dropped back into her chair, stunned.

"Cecelia killed herself," Isadora said to Dante. "She

threw herself off the top of the castle in despair, not because I harmed her in the magic."

"Silence!" Dante roared, his eyes glinting and his voice uneven. "She would have never removed herself from this life or from m—"

He cut himself off and turned back to Vasily, trembling. "A personal favor." His pointed gaze was impossible to miss. "Your Greatness."

Vasily's lips tightened into a thin line.

Isadora braced herself. Whatever power Dante held over Vasily, she'd bear the brunt of it. Did she imagine hesitation in Vasily's beady gaze? The kind man from the library seemed so unlike the High Priest before her. And, in the end, such a witch owed her nothing.

She met his eyes in a poor attempt to quell her panic.

For a long time, he said nothing.

"If this alone will not convince you," Dante said, "then let us ask her about her violation of your sacred ground."

"What?" Isadora cried.

Vasily squinted. "Go on," he muttered.

"You see the future," Dante said, "yet you can't remember leaving the castle, finding a sacred burial ground, and desecrating it by stealing a scroll that marked the lives of the dead?"

Vasily's hard eyes met hers. "Is this true?"

"That's not . . . that's not what it was."

"No?"

"Your Greatness, I was on a walk one day. I . . . ran from timber wolves and found a place I now believe was once Taiza."

Something registered in his face, perhaps the memory of her question about the lost village.

"While there, I found a piece of parchment nailed to a tree. It certainly wasn't a burial ground."

"Had Southern Network witches died there?" Dante asked.

"I don't know!"

"Then you should have asked!" Dante shouted, slamming a fist onto the table and rattling the dishes.

Serafina jumped.

"But you didn't, did you?" Dante demanded. "No, you simply walked onto their sacred ground, burned several artifacts, and took the parchment. Do you even have it anymore, or have you destroyed it?"

"I have it in my room."

Maximillion's rage simmered off him in long waves. Isadora clenched her hands into fists. She hadn't told him about the parchment.

"Take her," Vasily muttered to the South Guards, flicking his stubby fingers toward Isadora. "Mrs. Sinclair, you vill go to the Cage vhile Dante arranges transport back to the East for your trial. You may do as you vish vith her."

Maximillion stepped between Isadora and the approaching South Guards with a snarl. "You will kill me first," he said calmly.

He produced a knife with a spell and grabbed Isadora's wrist, yanking her against his back. The South Guards paused. One of them spoke quietly in Yazika to another, then looked at Vasily in question.

The images from the paths rushed back to Isadora's mind. The magic whirled.

"Stop this," she whispered. "Don't fight them."

"Maximillion," Vasily called, "let her go. She has broken my laws."

"Your Greatness," Dante said, stepping forward, "my

Defenders are trained in handling witches with such extreme power. Allow them to detain her, for the security of your Guardians. Watchers are often trained in the elusive arts. I wouldn't want any of your witches harmed."

Isadora would have laughed if her throat hadn't felt like a desert. Elusive arts? Most of the Watchers she knew were far more concerned about their tomatoes.

At a brief nod from Vasily, East Guards marched into the room, flanked by two other witches she recognized, but only distantly. Defenders, if the desperate hunger in their faces meant anything.

Maximillion must have seen it, because he sent her a sidelong glance.

"Been busy in the paths?" he muttered.

She swallowed.

"Over my dead body, Dante," Maximillion said, holding her tighter.

"Your decision, Max."

Serafina let out a cry, but Dante silenced her again with another spell.

Maximillion's fingers twitched, but he didn't move. East Guards surrounded them in a half circle now, short swords drawn. Isadora eyed them, a pit opening up in her stomach as the Defenders carefully approached.

One good pulse of her power, and they'd be on the ground. They didn't scare her.

But Carcere did. The possibilities in the paths did.

"Max," she murmured, "let him take me. They can't hurt me."

"They can," he said through clenched teeth. "They will. He'll keep you locked up like a plaything, forcing you to tell him what you see or endure torture you can't imagine. Physical pain. Rape. You name it. There will be no breaking you out this time."

"But it will buy you time to negotiate something for the Network. This is spiraling into a disaster. You may have a hope of saving all of Antebellum if I'm not here. I trust you to break me free. Even if it's eventually."

His nostrils flared. "He cannot have you, too."

Lingering pain was laced through the steel in his tone. Her heart ached for him.

Isadora glanced back and briefly saw Serafina staring in horror. The room seemed to have paused, frozen in time. There was only one way to keep Max from death. To prevent this summit and, by extension, the rest of Antebellum from crumbling.

"Max," she whispered, putting a hand on his arm. "I've seen this in the paths. This *must* happen."

"You're lying."

"Will you take that risk?"

"Let us have her," Dante called, "and I will agree to discuss keeping the Central Network in the summit."

"If you don't," Isadora murmured, "the world will fall. My life isn't worth it."

"If you want my wife," Maximillion growled to the East Guards closing in, "you'll have to take her from my cold, dead hands."

Dante sighed. "Very well."

Movement flashed in Isadora's peripheral vision. She shoved Max, but she was too late.

A heavy *thud* and the glint of a short sword—an East Guard using an invisibility incantation.

Max crumpled to the floor.

A Defender snarled at Isadora, breath foul. Everything seemed to slow. A hand grabbed her shoulder, hauling her back. Her heartbeat pulsed in her ears, blocking out all other sounds as the Defenders tore her from the room.

She turned to see Max, blood pooling on the floor at his temple.

"To the Cage, gentlemen," Dante called jauntily. "Until we can take her to our beloved Carcere."

Isadora slammed into the wall, her head cracking against the stone. Her ears rang, and she fell into darkness.

Isadora awoke to the caterwaul of a blizzard.

A heavy door slammed, rattling her teeth. She climbed to her knees, her head aching so intensely the pain coiled down her neck. Two East Guards grumbled something about being cold and stepped back. One of the Defenders stood a few paces away, leering at her as if he were starving.

"Take one step toward me," she snarled, "and I'll unleash power that will have you begging for death."

She released a breath of magic—just for a moment— and the Defender paled. Gasping, he stumbled after the East Guards.

"This isn't imprisonment!" she shouted after him, gripping the bars. "This is death!"

Snow blinded her, the cold driving all the way into her bones. She glanced through the slatted bars. Only swirling snow lay between her and the hidden ground far below.

Shivering, she drew her arms more tightly around herself. In her elegant silk dress and pathetic slippers, she might as well be naked.

"Wonderful," she muttered.

The Cage was a large structure made out of a metal like dark opal. It swung in wind, completely open to the air, held aloft by an iron chain as wide as her waist. The floor extended far enough across that she could barely lie down, but the gaps between the bars at her feet would make for an uncomfortable—even treacherous—wait.

Her frosty breath billowed, her thoughts as frantic as the storm. She sucked in a sharp breath. Letting her mind get out of control would only make this worse.

First, she had to set aside fears for her life. Dante wouldn't kill her yet, at least not on purpose. They'd return for her soon.

Second, she had to trust Maximillion to make the impossible happen. To negotiate a path forward in an unprecedented situation. She couldn't worry about the world right now—she just had to get out. Then she'd find Dante and . . . something.

She shook the bars, and the Cage swayed in the wind. Her stomach lurched, head still pounding. She tried to transport, but a suppressive magic stopped her. Even her attempts to bend the metal with magic were unsuccessful.

Power zipped through her in earnest now—an annoying distraction. She couldn't form a proper thought.

"Help!" she called. "Help!"

The wind whisked her voice away, blending it with the shrieks of the blizzard.

Scowling, she crouched, her back to the worst of the wind, and slipped into the paths. Thankfully, they waited for her, immune to or stronger than the Cage's suppressive spell.

The magic rushed up to greet her, enveloping her all at once in warmth. She welcomed it, grateful to slide into Letum Wood. She'd have to be more attentive than usual. She might be in the magic, but her body was back in the Cage and could die at any moment.

Chaos reigned in the paths.

Her usual paths popped up in a complicated weave. Max's wisps crowded hers in thick bursts, but Sanna's were far denser. Isadora glanced longingly at them but resisted the urge to wander them. She commanded away Max's and Sanna's, viewing only her own.

As soon as she advanced into her paths, the wisps changed. Seconds later, they morphed again. All the immediate wisps showed her in the Cage, but they also showed her . . . here.

She paused.

In the past, the wisps had shown her body where it lay. Never in the magic. They'd never changed so quickly, either.

One particular wisp ended in blinding light, not darkness. Tens of paths sprouted off from it, so thick that no wisps even appeared, for there wasn't any room.

Confused, she summoned Max's paths again. His revealed a magical fight amongst other horrific possibilities, including darkness, Carcere, a seven-pointed star, and Vasily twirling a massive ax dripping with fresh blood.

The magic, shivering inside her, broke free. She let it go. She could, at least, sufficiently distract Dante with her magic. Or so she hoped, for he'd seemed no worse for wear at the dinner.

She released so much of the magic at once that everything changed. She went from holding the magic within her body to letting it hold her. The power poured around her in ribbons of light, illuminating the forest, filling her with an infinite power that would surely kill her.

The trees seemed to ignite. Radiance filled the air. She cupped her hands over her eyes, shielding herself from the stunning brilliance. Just when she thought she couldn't take another moment, the magic closed itself.

Isadora's body felt like a distant dream. Aching. Sore. Somehow attached to her, but she wasn't sure how.

The Cage swayed beneath her in the tempestuous wind. Summoning all her power, she opened her eyes. She must have been in the paths longer than she thought, because it wasn't so cold anymore.

She blinked, her sluggish mind slowly registering that she *wasn't* in the Cage. In fact, she wasn't even lying down.

She was moving.

"Come. On."

The struggling voice came from just behind her. Isadora tilted her head back, barely recognizing Emilia. Was that *blood* smeared under her nose?

Wind whipped Emilia's cloak around them, cracking it like whips.

"Emilia?"

Emilia nearly dropped the arm that was holding Isadora upright. "You're awake!" she cried. "Oh, wonderful! Please tell me you can walk."

Isadora tried to reach out, but her arms were slow to respond to her commands. Fatigue, heavy as bricks, weighed her down. Then she felt something move underneath her. Her feet.

Emilia let out a cry, half-relief, half-sob, and looped an arm around Isadora's back. The jangle of clanking keys came next.

"We're almost there."

"Where?" Isadora mumbled, but the wind whisked away her question.

Several fumbling steps later, a wooden door opened,

spilling torchlight into the night. Isadora looked back at the Cage just before they stepped inside.

"*Chesu,*" Emilia muttered, dropping Isadora like a sack of grain. They'd arrived on a circular landing in one of the narrower turrets—Isadora registered that much.

Emilia wrenched a torch off the wall and held it over Isadora, murmuring something. The torch flared. Heat flooded the space.

"Y-y-your face—" Isadora said.

"Let's talk about that later." Emilia waved her hand as if batting away Isadora's concern. The torch floated in the air. "I had some issues getting the keys, but not to worry. Figured it out."

"H-how—"

"How did I know? Because I saw it happen."

Isadora frowned.

Emilia bit her lip, then put a hand on her head. "In my paths. I'm . . . a Watcher too."

"What?"

Emilia grabbed Isadora's hands and started to rub them. The friction sent a prickling sensation tearing through her. Isadora winced.

"We can talk about that later. But now you're almost frozen," Emilia said. "Probably only a half hour from death. I know some spells that will warm you up, then we have to go back to the dining room. Things are getting very ugly in there."

"Wh-what's happening?"

"Vasily has locked everyone inside. They've already voted the Central Network out of the summit. They're just working on the final tenets of the one-ruler agreement. It's been almost an hour since you were in there. Please, I must get you warm. Can I use the magic on you? It's . . . uncomfortable."

"D-do it."

"It's going to hurt."

Isadora's mind skipped like a rock over a pond. "I-it's fine."

Emilia hesitated, then started to command magic in earnest, with the kind of confidence that comes only from deep knowledge. She'd been living as a Watcher in the East. Suddenly, the extent of her protective-magic training made sense.

Pain stabbed under Isadora's skin, flooding her from shoulder to toes. She clenched her teeth and braced herself. Within ten minutes, her eyes were screwed shut, and she was barely suppressing a scream. Heat flooded her sluggish limbs, whipping through her veins.

"It should fade soon," Emilia said, her voice strained as she rubbed Isadora's feet and calves.

Isadora pressed her lips together. A wave of relief followed minutes later, like a cool balm in the wake of fire.

She opened her eyes and held up a hand, flexing her stiff fingers, able to move them. Her toes and ankles responded promptly to her command. Her teeth, which had been chattering violently, were still.

Emilia scrambled to her feet. "Ready?"

Isadora nodded. "I must get back."

Emilia hooked an arm under hers and tugged. "I'll take you."

They navigated the turret stairs, slowly at first, then more quickly as her body continued to warm. Isadora kept one arm around Emilia, the other against the wall.

Emilia, daughter of the witch most known for his ruthlessness against Watchers, was a Watcher herself. The implications spiraled farther than Isadora had mental space for.

"I saw the paths just as dinner started," Emilia whispered as they turned out of the turret. "Sometimes, when I can't attend the functions, I-I go into the paths to see what I'm missing."

Isadora winced as they shuffled down a hallway. Her muscles were warmer, but they still hurt.

"Who do you see for?"

"Women. Any woman I've met if they're older than me. I haven't been able to see for girls younger than me, like Zoya. It started last year. Mere says that's early for a Watcher, but not unheard of."

"Why are you going against your father?"

"Because I want a better world for Watchers, and Pere is too caught up in traditions to see that we're not dangerous," she said quietly. "I want *everyone* to be safe. He's . . . he doesn't know about me. Maybe we should have told him, but Mere was too scared. Besides, if Pere's plan succeeds?" Emilia shuddered. "The paths are not friendly."

Emilia must be a powerful Watcher in her own right to see for so many women.

In all, Isadora wasn't very surprised. Emilia had always been different. She squeezed Emilia's shoulders. "Thank you. It was dangerous and foolish, but I'm grateful you saved my life."

And potentially the world.

Emilia slowed before they turned the corner into the dining-room hall. Isadora paused a few steps away from the double doors, gathering her breath. Suddenly, *not* looking at the future seemed like a terrible idea. She had no idea what she was about to face.

As if sensing her fear, Emilia grabbed her hand. "Whatever it is," she whispered, "you're strong enough."

"Have you seen?"

Emilia shook her head. "I didn't dare look that far."

Isadora nodded and pressed Emilia against the wall. "Stay behind," she murmured. "I don't want you in there."

"I'll stay with you for a few minutes if you want to go into the paths and see—"

"No. Sometimes not knowing is our saving grace."

28

Y our idea, Luteis said, *is to fight the sea dragons and hope we can pressure Prana into stopping the battle.*

Sanna swallowed hard. Their plan had no hope of working. None at all. But until she knew how to break the magic, it was all they had.

Yes, but only until we figure out how to break the magic. Then maybe it won't matter.

Thunder crackled overhead as Sanna and Luteis flew over the churning waves. Her gut coiled like a mass of snakes. The trolls stood as formidable sentries at the edge of the water. It crashed against them, but they were immobile. Sea dragons thrashed in the froth nearby, but no troll seemed cowed.

The familiar chatter of the forest dragons calmed her—even if they *were* terrified. They could fly now but still had no real experience outside Letum Wood. These forest dragons weren't warriors. Most of them wanted to curl up and sleep beneath a tree and not wake up for a week.

So many sea dragons.

The ocean is dark.

If we fly into that storm, shall we drown?

Fear vibrated in their words, but she ignored it. *This situation is under control, and so am I,* she told herself.

Still, her hands trembled.

The chanting of sea dragons rose like a death march. With every word came another pulsing wave or crack of thunder, as if their hideous song was magic, and the magic was angry. Salty air surrounded her on all sides. A fat raindrop trickled down her cold skin.

The mountain dragons flew overhead alongside a few curious desert dragons. With concentrated effort, she could set aside the forest dragons to hear only the mountain dragons. Metok orchestrated them with exactness and precision. The mams had disappeared, transporting away. No doubt someplace safe.

Everything was under control there.

The pressure of the whistle weighed on her chest. Sanna drew in a bolstering breath as she reached for it. Aki waited back on the beach with the West Guards. She pressed the whistle to her lips and blew it.

It gave off no audible sound, but every desert dragon nearby turned in midair, wheeling toward her. She scanned the black, seeing nothing but vague shadows.

Hundreds, Luteis said, *are coming toward us now.*

The flapping of hundreds of wings sounded around them within a minute. Desert dragons circled overhead, forming a rotating ceiling above her.

It isn't all of them, Metok said. *I can see some lingering in the rocks above the beach. But it is many.*

It will help, she replied.

Jesse and Elis approached on her right, flying into a gust of wind.

"What now?" Jesse called. "It's almost completely dark.

We've been circling for twenty minutes. The ocean grows angrier with every passing moment. Why are we just waiting here?"

Sanna's heart thumped. In truth, she didn't know what to do now. She'd heard tales of wars, but never of where and how they began. This impasse could last all night. She wouldn't be the first to draw blood.

"Prana may begin when she wishes," Sanna replied.

Something stirs in the sea, Luteis said. The sound of crashing waves drowned out the panicked cries of the dragons.

Jesse swore.

Luteis's shoulders twitched as he turned, flying back toward land.

A line of sea dragons appeared, rising out of the waves in vague pulses of color. She could see only a strange, bioluminescent contrast against the darkness. They *glowed*.

How many? Sanna asked. They seemed fathomless to her limited sight.

Numberless, was Luteis's thin, delayed reply.

Attempting to distinguish all of them rising from the water was fruitless. Sanna gave it up, disheartened.

Keep your courage, she said softly, stroking his neck. *We'll figure this out.*

Even if you do figure out how to break the magic, we don't know what it will mean, what consequences will follow. Did the desert dragons lose their magic slowly, or all at once? Will it truly be freedom to live without everything we have ever known?

Sanna listened, but dismissed the questions from her mind as soon as he asked them. There could be no wavering tonight. Tonight, she had to set them free.

Somehow.

Dragons, Sanna said, speaking to the forest and mountain dragons collectively, *prepare yourself. The sea dragons have arrived. I believe they mean to take the cliffs when the ocean surges, and head inland. We must stop their progress here.*

The hisses of all the dragons rippled behind her. Forest dragons might not be warriors, but they *were* angry. Were they, too, thinking of Talis and Daid and Rubeis?

Luteis dropped back down toward the beach, where the forest dragons waited.

Think the sea dragons will come out of the water to attack? she asked.

Not near the trolls—at least not alone. They'll have to have a concentrated attack on the trolls, and they may. But within the waves, their bodies are long enough that they can fight without entirely leaving the ocean. We know they cannot be out of the water for long. Yushi admitted that himself. They'll pose a significant threat if we're flying low.

We have to fly low to harm them.

Movement drew Sanna's gaze to the right. She turned to see a flash of white fangs and a splash of bright purple against the ocean.

Rage filled Luteis's voice. *I don't think that will be a problem.*

With a bellow, he leapt, tackling a looming sea dragon with fangs as long as Sanna's arm. Luteis's talons sliced through its face, and it fell with a screech. A second sea dragon rose from the water, heading for Sanna, but Luteis knocked it away with his tail. The chorus of bellows from the trolls arose in the background, followed by heavy thuds.

Go higher, she said. *I have to direct the dragons.*

To all her dragons, she said, *Mountain and forest dragons, attack.*

The magic crawled through her chest as Luteis returned

to the sky. Mountain and forest dragons dropped toward the ocean in full response.

Tell me what you see, she said.

Sea dragons are crawling onto the beach to fight the trolls, but not meeting with success yet. Some are twice the size of Yushi in circumference. One rivals Elis in girth. In length, I cannot see where they end. They are formidable, even against the trolls.

A West Guard wielded a curved sword, slicing the lower jaw off an attacking sea dragon. Blood gushed onto the sand, fading to pink as a cresting wave swept it back to the ocean.

Another loud bellow. The deep, guttural tone would be Aki and his West Guards advancing into the sea-foam with their machetes, sliding in between the trolls that protected the beach as the water crested.

Any visible weakness noticed yet? she asked.

The sea dragons have no limbs, which leaves them open to injury. I believe you were correct. They are trying to claim the beach.

Just behind the beach rose cliffs dotted with desert-dragon nests. Claiming the beach would cripple the West Guards and destroy any injured dragon that fell.

Keep the beach, Sanna said to all the dragons. *Don't let the sea dragons come onto it, because we'll have nowhere to land with our wounded between the sea and the cliffs. We may lose dragons if we have to fly them to the top of the cliffs or farther inland. Junis, get atop the closest cliff. Keep an eye on the sea dragons farther out. They may try to flank us.*

Yes, High Dragonmaster.

The rest of you, get in the air. Test how high they'll come out of the water, and let me know. What weaknesses can you find? We want to see what they can do.

A chorus of affirmative replies rang through her mind.

Mountain dragons, approach safely and test your acid on

them. *Elis, go with Metok. Spray fire behind his acid. Pay attention to whether that combination attack gives us an advantage.*

Yes, High Dragonmaster.

The breeze on Sanna's face gave her a moment of calm. Seeing even glimpses of the battle helped her feel more part of it. Despite her inherent *lack* of control, no true chaos had descended yet—only the sounds of battle and the intense, high-pitched shrieks of sea dragons.

Go as high as you can without compromising your view, she said to Luteis. *Tell me what's happening.*

His ascent made the hair on her arms stand up. A *boom* of thunder rattled her teeth. Lightning sizzled nearly every other minute, too close for comfort.

A few desert dragons circle behind us, Luteis said. *They seem to be avoiding the rain and the ocean's surges. The sea dragons are still approaching the beach. Some are dead in the water. Aki has lost many warriors already, and one troll has fallen.*

High Dragonmaster, Metok said in his calm, unfailing way. *We have had the most success spraying the sea dragons in the eyes with acid. They leave, at least, though whether they stay away, we can't tell. There are too many.*

Fire?

Annoys them, Elis said, his voice strained. *Not as effective as the acid.*

How far out of the water will they come?

Several full wingspans.

We have already lost twenty mountain dragons, Metok added.

The melody of fire and the drumbeat of the surf rang below. Sanna felt as if she glowed from the strength of the Dragonian magic.

Tell your dragons to proceed with the acid, Metok.

As you say, High Dragonmaster.

Metok screamed as he dove back into the fracas. Luteis followed, preventing a sea dragon from grabbing Elis's tail. Blood arced over Sanna as the sea dragon tumbled back toward the water. Next to her, a shrieking mountain dragon fell into the waves, wing broken. Flashes of color burst out of the ocean as sea dragons leapt forth, snatching mountain dragons with their fangs.

Our fire, Luteis said, sounding frustrated. *It glances off their scales.*

Sanna gave him her magic. *Test your secundum,* she said.

The hissing of his fire deepened into a low roar. Its heat intensified, but only for a short burst. The targeted sea dragon squealed and plunged back beneath the waves.

Luteis circled in a tight spiral. *That,* he said, *was most effective.*

What happened?

The secundum appeared to attach to its scales.

Do you think the water will douse it?

Eventually, yes, but not right away. Like in the North, when we created the lake for the trolls, the secundum will burn for at least several heartbeats. It should last much longer, though I'm not certain.

Enough to cause damage?

And death.

The forest dragons can't use their secundum all night. They'll tire. We'll have to be strategic about it. Save it for the strongest, perhaps. Use acid on the smaller ones.

Luteis informed the other forest dragons. They chattered in the background of Sanna's mind. She studied the patterns in what they were saying, trying to imagine the battle from what she remembered of the beach.

The forest dragons flew above the waves, engaging with and harassing the sea dragons surging toward the shore.

With every moment, the ocean felt closer, bigger, and stronger. Eight trolls still stood strong, lashing in the waves, throwing heavy fists at the largest sea dragons that approached them.

Rain fell in earnest now, drizzling down her neck. Luteis darted through the battle, snapping commands. He deftly maneuvered away from the pursuing sea dragons and used his talons to injure others.

There are so many, he said. *I cannot see their end.*

Junis, what do you see from the cliff? Sanna asked, wincing at the sound of two bodies colliding nearby. A mountain dragon shrieked, then quieted.

There is little beach left, though the trolls continue to fight for it. The ocean rises.

Tashi and Aki?

I have taken them to safety at the top. The female witch flies above the battle with her dragon, watching.

So Tashi and Tenzin were there—that was something.

Prana's raising the water, and it's almost to the cliffs, Sanna said to Metok. *Are the wounded mountain dragons off the beach?*

Yes, High Dragonmaster.

Luteis dove, bellowing fire. Sanna gave him magic, not paying attention as they swooped through the air, dodging waves and the spray that came with them. She moved with instinct, trusting his body as if they were one. The gentle movements of his wings soothed her, even as he darted around, bellowing fire.

Magic, she thought desperately. *How do I create imbalance in the magic?*

How does one fight the sea? Elis asked, panting. *They are so many.*

The sea dragons sang on, uninterrupted, as if they didn't

stop singing even when they dove beneath the waves. A rumble sounded from the cliffs, followed by a squawk from Junis.

Some rocks gave way, High Dragonmaster, Junis said. *The desert-dragon caves are now getting hit by the massive waves. The sea . . . it's growing higher every second. The trolls are climbing to the top now.*

Distant calls of distress chilled her blood. Hatchlings and young desert dragons lived in those craggy rocks. Most couldn't fly yet. Once the ocean breached the cliffs, it would head toward the desert—and oases. Homes.

This would be the beginning of the end for the West.

Take me to Aki, Luteis. Metok, meet me there. Forest and mountain dragons, give up the beach. Take to the air, and meet me on top of the cliffs.

How long had they been fighting? Likely just under an hour, but it felt like ages had passed. A yank and a sudden flash of yellow made Sanna gasp. Luteis roared fire as they pitched to the side. She clung to him, flames whipping around them in an arc as they fell. A sea dragon had Luteis by the leg.

Release me! Luteis commanded. *You cannot enter the water.*

Sanna shoved away. For half a second, she remained airborne. Her heart seemed to stop. Time stilled. Before she could catch her breath, something hard hit her, snatching her away.

High Dragonmaster, Metok said. *I have you.*

She clung to him, looking back. Fire burst was all she could see in the darkness.

Luteis? she called. *Luteis!*

I am . . . fine. Meet me . . . on the beach.

Flying with Metok wasn't the same. His deft turns meant a choppy flight, and Sanna clung to his neck, her stomach pitching. The unnerving chants of the sea dragons softened as they flew higher, headed for the tops of the cliffs.

Where's Luteis? she demanded. *I can't tell.*

Fighting. Metok's neck moved as he glanced back. *All the sea dragons seem to be trying to grab you. You are their target.*

He's—

Fine. More capable without you on his back.

Rain fell in earnest now, soaking her. Her teeth chattered as forest-dragon voices sang through her head. She tried to pay attention to what they were saying, but couldn't focus.

We can't do this, Metok, she said as he dropped out of the sky, headed toward the beach. *There are too many. Do you agree?*

Yes, High Dragonmaster.

Mountain dragons, get to the rocks, she commanded. *Save as many desert hatchlings as you can. Help those that are struggling. We have only minutes. Junis, take all the witches to the top, including Elliot and Trey.*

Ocean spray kicked up with the wind, buffeting them. The roar of the surf grew louder with each passing moment as Prana unleashed her fury in wave after wave.

As soon as Metok landed, Sanna slid off his back, landing in the thick dirt. She whirled around to find Aki standing twenty paces away, glaring at the sea. The ocean had almost closed in now. Witches scrambled, frantically trying to climb the precarious path to the top. Every now and then, Junis gently scooped two up, one in each claw, flying them higher. Seven remaining trolls stood on the edge of the cliffs, glaring down.

"Aki?"

He turned to her, grim-faced and coated with blood and sand. "We will fight at the top," he said.

Sanna shoved him. "Get out of here while you can.

Command your contingent to leave. There will be no fighting up there, only floods. None of you will survive without a dragon to ride, and it's too late for that."

Aki frowned. "We never leave a fight."

"Your Network will need you if Prana floods the desert."

"Are you giving up?" he asked.

"Never."

He reached out, tapping a finger against her vest. "Good, because only the worthy wear such a thing. My Guardians and I will see you at the top."

Sanna stood there, staring at his back as his powerful legs bore him up the path. The onyx sky boiled overhead. Her thoughts spun out a thousand directions once, then came rushing back to the moment in Letum Wood when Deasylva gave her the vest.

It is not unbreakable, she had said. *If it becomes necessary, you have my permission to destroy it and all it stands for by force and fire.*

Sanna sucked in a sharp breath. *Mori,* but it was that bloody simple.

"Luteis!" she cried. He'd landed on the beach not far away. Despite engaging with several sea dragons in their absence, he looked no worse for wear.

I am here.

"I know how to break the Dragonian magic."

"I HAVE TO BREAK THE TOTEM."

The totem?

Sanna grabbed the whittled bone necklace. She'd ripped it from Pemba right before he died, when she'd uttered the words *I accept* and changed their lives forever.

Her thoughts came so quickly now she couldn't slow them.

"The totems! Avia was wearing a broken piece of glass when I saw him in the West. He never confirmed it was Sarena's totem, but why wouldn't it be? It was broken, inert. And Deasylva sort of alluded to it herself back in Letum Wood."

His steady gaze met hers.

We do not know what this will mean. The magic may be broken instantly, or it may take generations, or change nothing.

"But what choice do we have? If we break the magic for the mountain and forest dragons, we create an imbalance. The magic can then destroy itself, and we win."

It didn't work for Sarena.

"But Sarena wasn't the High Dragonmaster over two races. Maybe that makes the difference."

Can we make this decision on a maybe?

Rain lashed Sanna's face as she studied him. She could already hear the defeat in the dragons' voices chattering in the back of her mind. They were tired. Weary. Below it all, the chanting of the sea dragons continued, like a bizarre hymn to the violent night.

Fatigued mountain dragons attempted to navigate the gale coming off the ocean, some crashing into the beach or clinging to the rocks. The wind tossed them like rag dolls, sending them careening upside down and sideways. Several slammed into the cliffs, saving themselves from the waves only because they knew rocks so well.

"We have to do it."

Slowly, he closed his eyes. *You are correct. We must.*

High Dragonmaster? Elis interjected.

Are you all right, Elis? she asked quietly.

Struggling. The sea dragons—

Then came a violent scream. Sanna spun. Elis's pained cry came from the cliff edge.

A sea dragon has grabbed Elis's tail with its teeth, Luteis hissed, wings unfurling. She leapt onto his tail and scrambled up his back.

"Go after him!" she yelled.

My wing! Elis cried. *They have broken my wing. I feel . . . my blood. It's . . .*

We're on the way, Elis. Hold on!

I cannot.

Where's Jesse?

Silence.

Elis? she called again, a knot in her stomach. Luteis had already taken to the stormy sky, cutting through the squall with terrible speed.

"*Jesse!*" she screamed.

The sea thrashed around them as Luteis dove into the spray, snagging something from the waves. A sea dragon leapt out at them, roaring, white teeth bared. Sanna swung her knife in desperation, slicing the dragon under the jaw. Her knife stuck in the bone as the sea sank back to the water, taking the blade with it.

I have Jesse, Luteis said.

Alive?

I feel . . . something in him. I believe he broke the merging.

Elis?

Despair filled Luteis's voice as he flapped away. *He is already beneath the surface. I cannot reach him.*

Elis? she asked, reaching out. *Elis?*

He didn't respond.

Her heart cracked. The buoyant effect of the magic had started to fade, leaving her feeling like an empty shell. Not Elis. Not now.

Luteis winged toward the top of the cliffs just as the waves crashed into the rock wall. Sea dragons chanted in the background.

As Luteis flew, pitching in the wind, Sanna yanked Selsay's totem off her chest. The smooth, hard planes of the carven dragon were as familiar as her hands. The cries of dragon voices reached a frenzy. Some dragons were lost in the wind, unable to see. Others were injured, seeking help on the desert sand.

Sanna eyed the figurine.

It was now or never.

"Metok," she whispered. "For you."

The mountain dragons stirred in her mind. With a guttural yell, Sanna summoned her strength. Fire ignited in her hand as she tried to bend the stone. It withstood her. She channeled all her magic into it. At first, it resisted, as if defending itself.

Grunting, Sanna wrapped it firmly in her fist, forcing the magic into the totem. The heat built in her hands, so hot she glowed. The waves crashed louder. Higher. The magic swelled in her body until she thought she'd break herself.

Sanna yelled, pouring all her strength into it.

A tiny *crack*. She bent, twisting.

The totem gave way.

It snapped, gleaming bright yellow and smoking where it touched her hands. Sanna jerked. The remnants tumbled away, falling into the darkness below. Her body convulsed as the magic withdrew, draining life from her like the ebbing sea.

"Mountain dragons," she gasped, "I release you."

A distant, startled cry rippled through her head, then fell silent. Pain washed over her. Her teeth ground into each other as she collapsed onto Luteis's back. The chaos in her mind calmed as the magic withdrew all at once, whisking the mountain dragons away.

Sanna lay doubled over, holding back a scream.

Ahead of them, mountain dragons collapsed on the sand. Dragons in flight plummeted, as if suddenly without strength, and crashed into the ground. Sanna struggled to see through the rain.

Little one, Luteis's stark whisper pierced her heart, *what have you done?*

29

T otal silence reigned in Vasily's dining room.

Vasily and Dante stood at the table, glaring at Isadora, who stopped three paces into the room. Maximillion knelt on the ground not far away, bound and gagged and surrounded by South Guards in the exact image of a wisp she'd seen back in the turret. The murderous expression on his face revealed purpling bruises around his left eye.

Serafina and Arayana sat on the floor next to each other, eyes wide, mouths bound. A red slap mark brightened Arayana's right cheek.

"This is between you and me, Dante," Isadora said, advancing. The door closed behind her. "Let them go."

"No."

"I won't let you steer the Networks onto a disastrous path," she said, opting for the relative safety of politics. "A one-ruler solution populates millions of possibilities, none of them good. The evidence is overwhelmingly against it."

"So you did come to influence the outcome."

"I came to support my husband, and I bring you the truth now. I don't believe in trying to predict the future based on possibilities, but there are trends that can be useful."

Dante's nostrils flared. "And you expect me to believe you when you say that isolationism fares so much better?"

Isadora pressed her lips together. No. She didn't expect him to believe that, because she wouldn't, in his place. In truth, neither option showed total peace. Neither offered perfection. But isolationism *did* seem to buy them time.

She could appreciate how frightening this magic must seem to someone who had never been exposed to it. Never known its fickleness, the strange and almost random shifts of fate, time, and choice.

Even the magic didn't seem to know itself some days.

"No. I don't expect you to believe that."

Dante spread his hands. "Until you can prove it to me, we are at an impasse."

Memories of pulling Cecelia into the paths stormed through her mind. The clashing of the magic. The tussle of darkness and light. Such a powerful exchange of power back and forth had unleashed a level of terror Isadora had never experienced before, and Cecelia hadn't equaled her.

Would it be the same for her match—or worse?

To pull her match, an equally powerful opposite, into the paths could mean certain death for her. Cecelia had alluded to as much. But wouldn't it be far worse if Dante won?

Isadora held out an arm. Maximillion shouted from behind his gag, eyes wide. He shook his head back and forth emphatically. She ignored him.

"Let me show you what I see."

Dante hesitated, breath held. He studied her for several moments, then straightened. Vasily muttered something under his breath, but Dante waved it off. He strode toward Isadora with cocky arrogance, closing the distance between them.

Maximillion shouted again, only to be silenced by a punch in the stomach from a South Guard.

The moment Dante's hand slid into hers, Isadora opened the paths.

The dining room disappeared.

IN THE PATHS, Dante looked like death warmed over.

The magic always revealed witches as they truly were. Even Cecelia had appeared haggard here, nothing like the striking beauty that so many coveted and feared.

The only word for Dante was *sinister*. His eyes were dark, set deep in a wrinkled face. Shadows hovered near him.

He stood across from Isadora, hands at his side, and said nothing at first. His head tilted back as he took in the sprawling splendor of Letum Wood. Behind Isadora lay the familiarity of the paths, pulsing, moving, changing. No comfort rushed over her here, not with Dante so close.

With him here, everything felt different.

Isadora braced herself, waiting for the surge of power. For the darkness to rise from him and spread out at his feet, the way it had with Cecelia.

Nothing happened.

Dante turned to her, eyes wide. "This," he whispered, "*this* is what Watchers see?"

"It's what I see. I cannot speak for the others."

She glanced behind him. Where was the past?

If he was her match . . .

A heavy feeling began in her stomach. Dante sucked in a sharp breath, turning in a tight circle. Light sprouted at his feet, and wisps immediately appeared.

Isadora looked around, uneasy. The magic felt different. It was quiet. Subdued. Changed.

"The paths," he murmured, spinning. "These are . . ."

"As you see."

"She saw this?" he asked. His eyes filled with something. Fear. Hope. Love. She couldn't tell in the tangled web.

"Cecelia? Yes. She was here. Sort of."

He let out a long breath. Isadora waited for the clash of darkness against light, but nothing happened. The entire world seemed inert.

Something wasn't right.

"It's so . . . clear. So . . . real." He waved a hand in front of his face, then looked at the wisps. His expression darkened. "And these are the possibilities. There are so many."

"You *are* my match," she said, stepping toward him. A niggling suspicion had grown in her mind. "You *are* the most powerful Defender . . . are you not?"

"No," he said, half-laughing. "Not at all."

Isadora nearly broke.

"What?"

He twisted to face her, almost giddy. "I'm not your match. I'm not even part of that magic, and yet . . ." He grinned. "Yet my plan worked exactly as I desired it. Every single step. You did precisely what I needed."

"Your . . . plan?" she whispered. Her lips could barely form the words.

"To see the paths myself," he said impatiently, already eyeing the wisps that had appeared on his paths. "To figure out exactly what needed to be done to ensure my reign. It was only too easy, Isadora."

Her mind spun, trying to remember everything. The scent of tobacco in the forest. Their discussion in the library. No doubt his extensive work with Defenders had helped him learn how to navigate their world. Had taught him about matches. How to draw her in and get what he wanted. He *had* led her to believe he was her match, and she'd fallen for it.

Even his taunt in the dining room.

Until you can prove it to me, we are at an impasse.

She'd stumbled into his carefully laid trap.

"I have done the impossible!" he cried, exultant. "The most powerful Watcher has pulled me into her magic to show me my future. It has never been done. Oh, I shall change the world and bring true glory to the Aldana name!"

An infernal flash of the depths of his motivation shivered through him. As he spoke, the wisps behind her rearranged themselves into something new.

He stopped, rapt with fascination.

"They move," he whispered. "They change."

"Endlessly," she said, drawing in a deep breath. "But you shall never have a chance to truly see them."

With all the power she possessed, she set her mind to closing the magic. To pull the real world back into this, the way she had with Cecelia. She closed her eyes, expecting a rush of darkness, and then the momentary disorientation of fully returning to her body.

Nothing happened.

Dante looked up at her, still half-dazed, then turned away. "Perhaps," he said, "you are not as powerful as you think."

With that, he darted away.

Frantic, she attempted to pull him out of the magic. To push the magic into the Southern Network. Even to take herself out.

But nothing happened. The magic lay inert. The paths of Letum Wood encompassed her as if this were the only world that existed.

Dante disappeared down a path, laughing gleefully.

Isadora followed with a cry.

FEAR CHASED Isadora deeper into the magic.

Dante rushed from path to path, studying wisps. The intertwining trails that had started in the middle of the circle were complicated, packed with branching alternatives. Isadora quickly became lost in possibilities, surrounded by witches she didn't know.

"It doesn't work like this!" Isadora called. "You can't just see a future and make it happen."

"I beg to differ."

She whipped around, rushing in the direction his response had come from. She found him studying a faint path. The wisps on it showed him in the Central Network, sitting on the throne.

"Is this it? The moment of my takeover?"

Isadora skidded to a stop. Behind the wisps, three trails appeared, showing him in three unknown places. One of them must have been familiar to him, because his eyes widened. "*Chesu*," he breathed. "It *is* possible."

"Dante, you must listen to me. The paths—"

"Show it. They prove that it's possible for me to rule all of Antebellum. Look!"

"Just because it's possible doesn't mean it will happen."

Dante brushed past her, studying every wisp on that trail. He drank them in, murmuring under his breath as if memorizing every detail.

"Close the paths," Isadora commanded the magic.

Nothing happened.

No friendly stir of air or whiff of honeysuckle. None of the usual warmth. Had his presence changed something? Was it all different now that she'd pulled him in?

Would they ever get out?

She turned to find Dante several paces away, stalking down another path.

"I can't believe none of my predecessors ever thought of this," he said. "Their hatred of Watchers blinded them to their true potential. And now I shall step into the place they could have occupied."

The sheer number of wisps growing around her pressed in with a suffocating weight. She'd never felt this kind of terror in the magic before. Sure, it had been uncomfortable. A little scary at first.

But now? Now it had changed. Everything felt stalled. Sluggish. Could they die in the paths?

Isadora tried any number of commands while he paraded around, studying the wisps.

"No," he muttered, "can't go that way. A decision was made somewhere near here that made this happen. What was it? Doesn't matter. Avoid the blond, bearded male in the Central Network."

Isadora watched him helplessly. Eventually, her body's own energy would run out. She wouldn't be able to keep the paths open. Would potentially die there *and* here.

That would, at least, close the paths.

"Close Dante's paths," she commanded.

Her voice rang in the trees, an empty echo. Nothing

happened. Wisps changed here and there, some moving, others vanishing, still others appearing. Regardless, the magic worked. Dante stopped short as a wisp disappeared right in front of him, eliminating the rest of the path he'd been tracking.

He frowned.

"Dante, knowing future possibilities doesn't mean you'll make them happen, or even know how," she said, desperate. "Don't you see how quickly it can change? Please, stop this madness. I don't know what effect this magic may have on you. I . . . I don't even know if I can get us out of here. The magic wasn't supposed to do this. It wasn't made for you to come here."

Dante turned, striding back to the original three-way split, finding only two paths now. His grimace deepened. The light on the first path had grown slightly stronger, and he stared at it.

"I know," he said absently.

"What?"

"I've spoken with enough Defenders who could see into the past to know what could happen if a witch were brought here. They could see that others have tried to pull witches who were neither Defenders nor Watchers into the magic, and failed."

"Failed?"

Dante made a noise in his throat. "Mmm. Yes. But other paths existed that those witches didn't take. They *could* have done it, if only a different witch had attempted to pull the non-Watcher in. We believed, though we couldn't confirm, that the witch in question was the most powerful Watcher."

She swallowed hard. "And?"

He sent her a dark smile. "I was clearly correct."

Isadora hurried after him. He'd headed back toward

their starting point with infuriating confidence. The humiliation of *Dante* knowing more about her own magic burned in her throat.

"How did you know it was me?" she asked.

"The Defenders from La Torra. They told me what happened. They saw the paths differently but knew what you had done. And Cecelia had mentioned you as a *lavanda* maid to me before. You were easy to find."

"If it's true that I cannot work the magic in the same way when you're here, you've ruined your own plan!" she cried, unable to restrain a bit of triumph from her voice. "If we cannot leave, you'll never be able to act. To even *try* to make the future happen the way you want."

"I disagree."

They were back in the circle now. Isadora refused to look at the paths filling the other half of the circle. She'd see Max —hopefully—and it would only distract her. Or maybe she'd see nothing. Nothing but darkness. Or light. Or some strange in-between.

"I'm more than willing to stay here forever if that will prevent you from ruling Antebellum," she said quietly.

The words cost her. The thought of staying here, never seeing Maximillion again, made her physically ache. What of Sanna? Her sister would never truly know what had happened. She'd lose someone yet again. Would Mam recover?

And even if she kept Dante in the paths forever, Vasily might take over Antebellum. The one-ruler plan might be pushed forward, with him at the helm. If not, then how would Dostar, Maximillion, and Vasily ever find peace?

No. This had been their one chance.

Isadora shook those thoughts free. She couldn't focus on that now.

Dante stood at a juncture, tapping his chin. What had once been two paths was now three. He ventured toward the third, which showed him in discussion with Vasily in the Southern Network. The wisp behind it revealed them signing a parchment.

The magic stirred. Isadora thought she felt something—a touch. A gentle pressure on her shoulder. She slammed against the magic in her mind, trying to open it. Close it. Get out. Feel *something*. But only that closed-door sensation remained.

"*You* cannot live forever," Dante said, stopping at a wisp that showed him with Emilia in a carriage. Emilia's paths trailed off to the side, but he ignored them.

A faint smile painted his features as he continued down his own path. "It's my theory that, eventually, your body will die. Your power will move to another witch, and I shall be removed from this place."

"Maybe you shall die with me."

He scoffed. "My Defenders know exactly what I'm doing. We've prepared several spells meant to prolong life, to nourish the body. We have ways of keeping me alive there. In the meantime, I can study every possibility here. See exactly what should and shouldn't be done."

"I have done that, Dante. I've tried! I brought about only pain and misery and almost death. What you want isn't possible. You cannot control fate."

He ignored her, moving on to another wisp.

The magic stirred. Isadora paused, a breathless sensation filling her chest when she looked down. A tendril of darkness slithered through the ground at her feet, crawling toward Dante. The hair on the back of her neck stood up.

"You may think I cannot control it, but I've heard enough of the past through my Defenders to know you're wrong,"

Dante called. "It's a matter of having the right information at the right time."

Isadora backed up when the shadows inched past her.

"I shall win, Mrs. Sinclair," Dante called, oblivious. "Just you wait. I shall win."

"Not," said a voice behind her, "with me here."

30

Metok!

Sanna called for him for the tenth time to no avail. Luteis skidded on a stretch of sand far from the edge of the cliffs. Sanna slid off his back, running past Jesse as fast as she could toward the closest mountain dragon. When she crouched next to its inert body, her heart broke.

"Don't be dead," she murmured. "Please don't be—"

A faint pulse thudded in its chest.

Sanna looked up. Other mountain dragons slammed into the ground. Some of them dropped straight out of the air, their bodies still. Others struggled to slow, weaving back and forth before crashing. All of them were heavy-lidded, as if sleeping.

The withdrawal of the magic, Luteis said. *It's affecting them. I didn't know!*

Sanna darted through the mass of dragons, touching them, tripping over her own feet, the sand, anything in her path that she couldn't see. Most didn't respond. Some opened one eye, only to close it against the rain. Finally, she saw Metok.

"Metok!"

He looked up, eyes bleary, as she collapsed at his side.

Metok, please. Say something to me.

He blinked slowly.

Metok!

The magic is broken, little one, Luteis said quietly. *You will never speak to them again.*

Sobs choked her. She crouched, shoulders trembling.

Metok didn't move. He stared at her as if confused. Did he even remember her? What had this truly taken away from them?

"I didn't know," she cried, putting a hand on his snout. "I'm so sorry. I didn't know!"

The magic, Luteis said, looking back toward the sea. *It doesn't feel different. No more balanced or unbalanced than before. This didn't work. We need another plan. Already, the water is rising. It will breach the cliffs soon. We cannot remove all these dragons in time to save their lives.*

Jesse stood next to Luteis, bleary-eyed and pale with shock. He stared back at the water, his lips moving wordlessly.

Elis. Elis. Elis.

Sanna buried her hands in the sand, pressed her forehead to it, and screamed. Desert dragons soared overhead. West Guards ran, weaving around the broken mountain dragons as they raced away from the growing sea. The ocean would crash above the cliffs within the hour, at the latest. Minutes at the soonest. All these weak mountain dragons would drown.

Summoning all of her strength, she stood.

"We can't leave them here," she said, sniffing. "We have

to . . . we have to move them farther away from the water until they can get their strength back."

But Luteis ignored her, still looking at the ocean. Urgency filled his voice.

Climb on my back, little one. Now.

But—

Now!

With concerted effort, Sanna forced herself away from Metok and onto Luteis's back. The moment her feet touched him, he shoved off from the ground. Swallowing hard, she forced her gaze away from the dazed mountain dragons. Feeling stunned herself, and bitterly hollow, she looked straight ahead through the pouring rain.

What do you see? she asked.

The pause before his response, then the strange pitch of his voice, made her body go cold. *The water is . . . retreating.*

Retreating? she asked.

Yes.

But . . .

Over the crashing waves came a lower tone. A grumbling. As if they had awoken a sea monster, and it wasn't pleased. The forest dragons in the sky spoke with trembling voices.

The sea dragons are disappearing into the water, Junis said.

Junis! Sanna commanded. *Grab Jesse now.*

As you wish, High Dragonmaster.

We cannot be winning, Luteis said. *Prana cannot be leaving us . . .*

No, look. What is that darkness coming? said Gellis.

Dragons, Luteis bellowed, *fly high! A wave comes to crush us all.*

An enormous hiss sounded beneath them. She heard it before she saw the ebony water retreating, sucked back to the ocean. Luteis flew into the rain, buffeted by the winds. A long, sibilant sound came from a gathering wave several times taller than Luteis from head to tail.

Mori, Sanna said. *It will crush us.*

She braced herself as the wave crested. The cliffs jarred in a bone-shaking crash the moment the wall of water slammed into them. The land slid into the sea, crumbling away. Trolls gave way beneath it, swept in the force and sent sprawling into the sand.

Even the air trembled. Sanna had never been so grateful for the stabilizing magic in her life that kept her on Luteis's back. The forest and desert dragons rode above it, oddly silent in her mind.

We are safe up here, Luteis said, panting. *But not for long. The cliffs have been overtaken entirely. The water will flow toward the mountain dragons.*

Her heart nearly stopped. The thrashing bodies of the screeching sea dragons broiled again below. The wave had swept them up with it. Rain sluiced down her skin as Luteis battled the turbulence.

Luteis, what's happening?

I . . . cannot . . . fly.

Junis? A report?

High Dragonmaster, Junis said, *I cannot fight this wind. The spray. I . . . I cannot see.*

Luteis struggled to give commands to the other forest dragons.

Retreat, Junis, Sanna commanded. *Go to a safe place with Jesse and Elliot, and stay there.*

But—

That's a command!

What will you do now? Luteis managed. *There must be another way. What do we not understand?*

Before she could reply, something heavy slammed into Sanna's shoulder. Luteis roared, and then his warmth was gone. A surreal sense of cold wrapped around her as she fell, tumbling head over heels toward a watery grave.

Little one! Luteis cried in anguish.

Flailing, Sanna plunged toward the water. A roar came from above her, followed by the shriek of a sea dragon as she folded into the waves.

Cold water rushed over her, silencing the battle. It filled her ears. Burned in her nostrils. Wrapped her body in a strange embrace. The shock of the icy ocean robbed her of breath. For several moments, she floated there in utter silence.

A chilly womb.

You defy me, witch, came a cold whisper. *Just like your goddess.*

Something tugged on her. Frantic, she paddled, trying to find the surface, but a current yanked her away.

No, Sanna thought. *Not like this.*

Little one? Luteis's voice found her even here. *LITTLE ONE!*

She imagined him overhead, roaring, fighting, thrashing. Killing every sea dragon in his attempt to find her. Her thoughts fragmented. She didn't dare speak back. She'd breathe. She'd sob. She'd only frighten him further with goodbye.

Sanna. The cold voice again. *To fight me is futile. Don't you see? I have total control now.*

Sanna's chest burned.

No, she thought. *None of us control anything, do we?*

A slippery body wound around her torso, wrenching her from the current. She tried to focus. What had her now?

The ocean skimmed past her with unusual speed until it disappeared, replaced by fresh air.

Sanna gasped.

"Daughter of the forest," Yushi hissed. "You fight valiantly, even if you are a fool."

Her response was lost in another surge. Water crashed over her head again. She sputtered, her throat burning as she flailed for the surface. Yushi tightened his hold, pulling her back to the air.

Yushi has me! she said to Luteis. *I don't know where I am. Farther out, I think.*

Another desperate bellow overhead, much farther away.

Waves buffeted her. Disoriented, she fought for the surface, only to be pulled there again and again by Yushi's body. A current tugged her down, its swift force trying to swallow her. Yushi himself seemed to struggle to keep her head above the thick waves.

"Tell your dragon to get down here," Yushi snapped, "if you have any desire to survive. I cannot hold you here forever. She's determined to kill you because you are the only one who can finish this for good."

Luteis, she called frantically. *Luteis. Come for me, please! I cannot find you!*

Another engulfing wave. It slammed into her as if to crush her. Only the tight hold of Yushi's body kept her from the ravenous undertow. She surfaced again, gasping. Her nose and chest burned.

Something cool slipped into her hand. She grasped it.

"You can't destroy a magic you aren't a part of," Yushi hissed in her ear, "and you can't destroy a magic in pieces. Accept your place as High Dragonmaster, and end this for all of us. Destroy it entirely. My fate is already sealed, but Mushi can still be set free. May I see you one day in Halla."

He tossed her into the air.

Sanna barely had a chance to scream before Luteis whisked her away from the grasping waves.

You are well? Luteis's voice was harried. *Little one?*

He hovered far above the ocean, barely holding them in one spot with firm wingbeats against the raging wind. Yushi's words thrummed in the back of her mind.

You are well? Luteis demanded.

She realized he'd asked several times. Her throat and nose burned, leaving her feeling charred from the inside out. Even her chest ached.

Fine, she said, shaking her head. *I . . .*

You fell, and I . . . I was . . .

She reached out, her fingertips finding his snout. *Me too. But I'm not.*

A slimy touch on her hand drew her attention. A piece of seaweed, it felt like. Strung out and tough, but wet. Liquid, almost.

Sanna coughed, shoving the hair out of her eyes.

A plan, Luteis was saying as he attempted to fly back toward land. *We must come up with a plan. The mountain dragons . . .*

Her breathing was fast, broken. Chaos unfolded around them. Sea dragons writhed on the sand now, heading for the weakened, dazed mountain dragons as the surf surged from behind them, spilling onto the sand.

Forest dragons threw their secundum, but the sea dragons dodged it more easily here. The four remaining trolls grabbed the dragons closest to the see and dragged them farther away. Still, it wasn't enough. With them trying to save the mountain dragons, they would all die. The rain had turned to freezing sleet, dancing with the rolling thunder.

Everything had fallen apart.

This was the opposite of control. No matter how hard she worked, or what she did, control eluded her. Is this what Talis had felt like? Had he grasped so desperately he simply lost it all?

If she couldn't guarantee the dragons' fate, what was she leaving them subject to?

Life, Luteis said.

She hadn't realized she'd given him her thought until his voice entered her mind.

I wanted you to be safe, she replied. *I wanted to protect the dragons so that we could build a life together in the forest, without outside interference.*

Like Talis?

Sanna's heart hiccuped. Though she'd never meant for it to happen that way, it *was* just like Talis. He, too, had been put into an impossible situation. Forced to make decisions to keep them all safe.

Life is not about controlling an outcome, Luteis said. *Life is about doing what Talis never could—allowing bad things to happen to good creatures. It's not about control. It's about . . . acceptance. Whatever will be will be. You fight hard and let the rest come. True freedom is sometimes painful and always imperfect.*

Tears filled her eyes. *I don't know how to do that.*

You do, little one.

Deasylva's words whispered back through her mind. *In acceptance, you'll find what you seek.*

Sanna swallowed hard. She had to let the dragons go. She had to do what Talis never could. Train them. Prepare them. Then surrender her ability to protect them. Their future wasn't hers to control. Trying to do so had only brought about the exact fate she'd wanted to avoid.

And, as she knew so clearly because of Talis, continuing to try would only cause far greater evils.

Little one, do you see? Luteis said. *The land has grown.*

What do you mean?

A wall is forming against the approaching ocean.

A wall?

Luteis turned, sailing on a smooth patch of wind. The gusts calmed ever so slightly. Rocks boiled out of the desert, expanding with every passing second. It was as Luteis had said—a wall was forming around the prostrate mountain dragons, blocking the sea.

"Selsay," she whispered.

Trees! a forest dragon called, elation in their voice. *Trees appear from the rocks. Deasylva is here.*

Trees grew from the soil, sprouting roots that raced through the sand and burrowed deep, anchoring the rocks in place. The roots grabbed at the nearby sea dragons, strangling them.

"Deasylva," she murmured.

The timing couldn't be an accident. Sanna fingered the odd object in her hand. The way it hummed, teeming with something. With power. This was no ordinary piece of seaweed.

This was Prana's totem, and it was awaiting the right words.

Accept your place as High Dragonmaster, Yushi had said.

Sanna let out a long sigh. "Not again," she muttered.

Forest dragons, return to the desert with the mountain dragons, she said with renewed confidence. *But first, fly low and draw the sea dragons toward the cliffs. Selsay will send a landslide on them.*

How she knew that, she couldn't tell. But Selsay would

do it. Because *this* had been the plan all along, and Sanna hadn't seen it until this moment.

Now, she knew exactly what to do.

Luteis?

He turned, nudging her.

Yes?

Forgive me.

With trembling hands, she held the totem in front of her and whispered, "I accept."

HER BONES MELTED.

Magic infused her. Her skin burned from the sheer power of it. Whether the world had gone silent or Sanna had started to die and couldn't hear anymore, she didn't know.

The seaweed Yushi had given her grew hot, then froze against her palm. Blistering ice traveled from her fingers into her blood. Dark magic slithered through her like a snake. It turned her muscles into liquid ice, consuming her from the balls of her feet to the top of her head.

She gasped, feeling the caress of every raindrop on her body. The liquid in the air, in her lungs, in her blood. Every sensation of water sharpened as if she could pull it all into herself. The sea called hungrily to her, followed by a deep, watery cold. In the distance, she thought she heard Luteis, but his voice faded away. Lost in the midst of others.

All the others.

An endless cacophony of voices filled her thoughts now. She didn't know them. They were wet. Slippery. Cold. Unknown. The pressure on her mind grew. The only thing keeping the magic from destroying her body *was* the magic.

More whispers. More songs. The sea dragons spoke, but not to her. Did they know that she was their new master? That she'd done the impossible in claiming three races of dragons? She could feel remnants of Selsay's magic still within her.

And now the impossible sought to kill her.

Dragonian magic pressed on her. Instead of swirling through her, it commanded her. Took ownership of her body with its presence. There was so *much* of it she could barely breathe.

Slowly, Sanna became aware of something besides the arctic magic. She felt sand on her fingers. Then grit against her cheek.

"Luteis?" she whispered. Her voice was as deep as the sea. She shivered.

Little one?

Confusion clouded his voice. The sea stirred behind her like a boiling monster—she could sense its movements. *Feel* its impatience and power.

Sanna willed her body to move, but it would go nowhere. Panic infused her from within. She had mere moments before Prana realized what she'd done.

If even that.

Come on, she thought, clenching her eyes shut. *Move.*

The whispers grew louder. Far-off voices. Not Yushi. Not chants. Not goddesses. Something infinitely more . . . hopeful.

Free us.

Free us.

Captivity.

Set us free.

Sanna grimaced through another jolt of pain. The pressure intensified. She gritted her teeth. This plan had been stupid. She couldn't do it. Bear and lose the magic of three races of dragons?

Of *all* Dragonian magic?

She couldn't handle it.

Little one, Luteis said, his voice distant. *I cannot help. What is happening?*

The ground trembled, rattling Sanna's teeth. A sharp tang of earth filled her nostrils. No doubt up on the cliff she would have seen rocks cascading toward the sea. The earth raging toward the ocean.

The sea dragons wailed. She longed for the sea. Craved the water.

Sanna reached for Luteis. "Help me," she croaked.

What do I do?

She lifted the totem Yushi had given her. It crackled, cold as ice. Thunder snapped overhead. Waves surged toward them, not far away. Sanna forced them back with a rush of rage. They retreated.

We have to . . . we have to break it.

Fire?

No. Rocks.

Sanna let out a cry when he moved her onto his back, though his touch was gentle. The magic anchored her, and she had no strength to cling to him. Instead, her body shuddered as they flew farther from the water. A shout stuck in her throat.

Take me back to the water!

Hold on, Luteis said grimly.

Her mind floated in and out of reality as they flew. One moment in a dark circle. Eternal darkness. A current forming an impassable whirlpool that spun forever. Distant whispers pled for her help. The next moment, fire. Flame.

Heat. Depth. Endless, endless darkness and cold. Then back to the water.

Sanna gasped as if the water already surrounded her. The fathoms below the sea beckoned.

Luteis landed, jarring her from the half-dream. She cried out as she rolled off his back and onto the trembling ground.

"A rock!" she shouted, groping blindly in the dirt.

Here, Luteis said amidst the chaos of her mind.

Something rolled into her knee—something sharp and pointed. Dragon voices raged relentlessly in her mind. Their panic. Their fear. Behind that, something bigger. Darker. Infinitely more terrifying. The darkness reached for her—as cold as the ocean's depths.

Prana sensed her now.

She'd found her.

You will never have the strength, you fool!

Sanna let out a cry, wrapped her fingers around the rock, and slammed it into the totem. Pain, bright white and stunning, ripped through her. She flew back, falling on her spine. Her teeth jarred.

Little one, what can I do?

"Secundum," she gasped. "Try it."

The water sought her now. She could feel it closing in, greedily calling her back. She screamed, pushed herself back onto her hands and knees, lifted the rock, and hit the totem again. Luteis's secundum burned her hands, a bright backdrop against the gritty sand.

The chanting stopped. The world seemed to quiet—perhaps she'd simply lost her mind—as she heaved the rock up again and slammed it into the totem.

The sea, Luteis said, frantic. *It approaches. Another wave. I cannot—*

"Don't touch me!" Sanna cried. "Wait!"

Prana reached for her through the darkness. Evil, greedy, devouring. She came for her. Sanna could feel the rising ocean. The current's thirst for her life. Water lapped around her legs.

Little one, Luteis said, *it will consume you—*

"It won't!"

The moment the water touched her, Sanna felt all the light in her body fading, as if Prana could pull her to the depths even while she stood on land. Something warm and coppery trickled down her nose. With a shaking hand, she brought up the rock once more.

Time seemed to pause.

"No master ever again," she cried. "Sea dragons, I release you!"

The magic shattered with her final blow. The depths froze her blood, rendering her paralyzed. Her entire body tightened as the darkness screamed. The ocean itself held still.

What, Prana whispered, *have you done?*

Her voice disappeared.

The pressure faded. Sanna's hearing returned. She gasped all at once. Life rushed through her body.

Heat.

Sound.

Little one, said Luteis, *the sea dragons are . . . they are silent. They are . . . gone.*

"No," she choked. "We're not done. We must . . . finish."

Sanna chucked aside the broken totem. The roar of the sea still pounded in her ears. Screaming. Confusion. Thunder resounded through the clouds as Sanna rolled onto her back.

Rain pounded against her face. She blinked, staring at a

stony blackness for half a breath. Around her, the chaos intensified. Antebellum itself seem to recoil. Her body, nearly destroyed by the magic, could not seem to live without it now.

Another part of her soul shriveled. Her body was an empty structure. Nearly gone.

Nearly.

Sanna didn't think. She couldn't. Couldn't imagine her next task. What it would mean to finish what Sarena couldn't. To force the magic to break itself by breaking *all* the Dragonian magic left in the world.

No matter the cost.

With a sob, she reached down, yanking off the vest.

In the distance, the rumbling of boulders intensified. Stone on stone. A deep, visceral groaning from the depths of the earth, like a goddess filled with sorrow and rage.

A breeze brushed past, carrying a hint of honeysuckle and a distant echo of the voices of the trees. Sanna felt it like an afterthought, distantly.

Vaguely aware of a memory attached to it somewhere . . .

Little one, Luteis demanded, pulling her out of her half-dead stupor. *What are you doing?*

She struggled to her feet. Her body yearned to give up. To close her eyes and wake up in the bright halls of Halla, where Daid would be waiting. By the end of this, she would.

Destroying the magic would destroy her.

Clinging to the ragged edge of life, she leaned against Luteis, her eyes closed. Her face pressed against his scales, which remained comfortingly warm despite all they'd been through. She focused on the vest in her hands and swallowed a sob.

She had to do it.

Stand back, she murmured in her mind, lacking the strength to speak.

Harnessing the flow of magic came easily—surprisingly so, considering her intent. The truth of what it meant to destroy the magic circled her mind like a buzzard. Fear lived within her, wanting to be part of her, consume her.

If she destroyed the vest, she destroyed all of the Dragonian magic.

She would break her connection to Luteis.

But if she didn't, the magic wouldn't be broken irrevocably. It could be repaired. Prana could return again with her dragon army another day. This had been Deasylva's plan all along. Sanna could feel it in her bones.

The vest warmed like a coal in her hands. Like Luteis. Sanna gripped it so tightly her knuckles ached.

I must, she whispered to him. *But I don't think I'll survive.*

Anguish filled his voice. *Is this the only way?*

Yes.

A long silence swelled between them.

I know, he murmured, pressing his snout to her. *It was always meant to come to this, but I have not wanted to see it until now.*

Tears welled up in her eyes as his tail wrapped around her ankle. *I shall be with you every step of the way, in this life and the next.*

She pressed a hand against his scales, and a tear tracked down her cheek.

I wouldn't have it any other way. Help me?

Yes, little one. With my last breath.

Sanna yanked the vest from both sides and Luteis slashed it with his claw, tearing it in half. The tension in the threads of magic broke into four chunks, reverberating all the way into Sanna's bones.

"Forest dragons!" she called with a sob. "I . . . release you."

Heat raced up her arms and coursed through her heart like fire. She screamed. Luteis roared. Flames crackled above them.

The power surged through her body. She let it go, unwilling to restrain it.

Fire and power and light swelled within her all at once. She dropped to her knees, and Luteis fell next to her.

In the distance, she heard a bellow. The magic broke not once but three times over her heart. Power burned there. A roar filled her ears. Her last thought went to her sister with a flash, and a memory, and a feeling of warmth deep, deep inside.

31

Isadora stared at the approaching figure.

A woman strode through the paths, chin held high, walking with a confidence Isadora recognized. A strange, new contrast of darkness and light brightened her features, making her appear powerful.

Lucey.

She stopped a few paces away. Darkness curled at her feet like fog. The vapor hesitated as if awaiting a command.

Glittering shadows trailed behind Lucey in a dazzling black skirt—an untold number of wisps, all solid and unmoving. The shadows of the past, ensconced safely out of reach forever.

The two women stared at each other warily until Lucey reached out to stroke a tree, a half-smile on her face.

"It's the same," she whispered to Isadora. "This is exactly what I see."

Lucey gazed beyond Isadora then, registering the future possibilities. Somewhere out there, Dante shifted around, obsessively studying the wisps.

Lucey licked her lips. "I've long wondered if you see

exactly what I see. So many other Defenders and Watchers spoke of blackness. Of seeing possibilities in a void. But it's never been dark for me. It's always been this."

"My match?" Isadora asked shakily. "You are . . ."

"Your match."

Isadora spun through a thousand memories. Lucey had been there the very first time she was in the paths. She'd been captured at La Torra. She'd been . . . sick.

Overwhelmed, Isadora asked, "But . . . how?"

"I met Maximillion when I left Anguis for the first time," Lucey said. "When, in shame, I disappeared so that my parents wouldn't have to face the fact that I was in love with another woman, didn't want to follow their ways, or ever touch a dragon. I didn't want them to know the madness in my mind. The things I saw about them—about Talis and his history. Isadora, I see it *all*."

A harshness laced her voice, the same desperation Isadora felt about the magic—the sheer enormity of it. Lucey's fear stirred something inside her.

"Lucey—"

"In my innocence, I thought a bigger city would be safe for me to run to. I fled to Chatham City from Anguis, chasing a woman I'd met in the forest several times. But I never did find her. My second day there, I was attacked."

The wisps changed. In the closest one, Lucey lay on the ground, nose bloodied, dress torn open across the front. Mud soaked her skirt. She lay seemingly unconscious in what appeared to be a gutter, rain streaming down her face. Blood stained her legs, her dress, the ground.

"The good gods," Isadora whispered.

Lucey's voice grew distant. "When I ventured into Chatham City, I was completely oblivious to its dangers. A group of men attacked me. After all five of them had their way with me, Maximillion found me. Took me home. Nursed me back to life in a moment when I wanted nothing more than death."

The wisp changed, revealing Maximillion watching over a sleeping Lucey with his usual frown. He cut a strong figure, though his expression was carefully distant. His face seemed younger, less riddled by stress and time. Lucey looked away as if she couldn't bear to see it.

"He let me stay for a while as a guest. I think because I didn't speak much and never asked questions, he didn't mind me. I stayed as small as I felt, cleaned his house, and fixed his meals without really saying a word. He was never inappropriate, and always treated me with utmost respect."

"Did you ever tell him about the paths you saw?"

"Never."

"Did you know he was a Watcher?"

"Yes. I *felt* it. At first, I thought I'd go mad. I wanted to stay, though. Couldn't return home, and didn't know where else to go. Eventually, I learned how to get rid of the urgency that his magic provoked in me. It's possible for a Defender to coexist peacefully with a Watcher, but many do not choose that path."

She let out a long sigh.

"After the attack, I . . . I just wanted to heal those who were sick. Maximillion found me an apothecary school and paid my way. One night, he brought me someone who needed help and swore me to secrecy. I agreed to help without telling anyone about it." She half-shrugged. "That's how it started. Eventually, he let me help more. My thirst for seeing the world was satisfied. Learning more about Watchers allowed me to learn about my own magic, perhaps in ways I never would have understood otherwise."

A wisp behind her dissolved, fading into another that

showed a younger Maximillion carrying a girl in his arms, Lucey standing nearby.

"My time with the Advocacy," Lucey said breathlessly, "gave me a reason to live. My own family shunned me, thought me strange, spoke about me in whispers behind my back, all while still using my services as an apothecary. If they had known what had happened, they would have shunned me totally. Talis would have named me *unclean*. But not the Advocacy."

"Then I came along," Isadora whispered.

The wisp behind Lucey changed, showing the first moment Lucey, Isadora, and Max had all met together, when Isadora's transition had almost killed her.

Lucey stared at the wisp. "Yes. You with your headaches and your massive amount of unpredictable power from the beginning." She offered a smile. "I knew about matches, but I didn't know you were mine. Maximillion had spoken of his now and then, and of an occasional Defender-Watcher pair in the West. But I never thought much of my own. I didn't know I was special in the magic until you came along."

Lucey's visit to the turret rippled through Isadora's mind. She'd sat at the table, trembling. When Isadora had put a hand on her shoulder, she'd drawn away, flinching, saying, *I thought I was ready.* Isadora had assumed Lucey had meant facing the Defenders again.

But she hadn't been ready to face Isadora and her raw power.

"Not until Carcere did I realize we were matched," Lucey said.

"Why there?"

"Until then, I thought you might be matched to Cecelia, whose power was legendary. I saw Cecelia's paths. Her power. Could . . . sense it in her, I guess. She was, arguably, the most powerful known Defender. But I knew I had more than she did. More ability. More power. I saw more, because I could see her and everyone."

"Did Cecelia know about you?" Isadora asked.

"No."

"So, all that time in Carcere, you could have been free. You could have told Cecelia, and she would have let you out."

"If I'd broken trust with the Advocacy," she said, putting a hand on her heart as if she couldn't bear the thought. "And lost the opportunity to observe things from the inside."

"They tortured you," Isadora whispered.

Something filled her eyes. Darkness. Vapor. Shadows. "Yes," she said. "But such had been done before, and neither broke me. My struggle since returning has been with your power. After Carcere, your power seemed so much greater. Although mine has responded equally, it's difficult to endure. Maybe the deaths of Cecelia and her match meant we gained their abilities. Or perhaps we just needed the magic at this level."

Lucey paused, seeming confounded. "There's so much I don't know. I don't know why the Defenders feel our connection so keenly, or why Watchers seem oblivious to it. Or why some Defenders can fight for good, like me, and others cannot—or choose not to. Like Cecelia."

Isadora struggled to catch up with all these revelations. She remembered things so differently now.

Defenders and Watchers *could* work together, clearly. Perhaps they were even meant to. But it hadn't been that way in so long.

One question lingered above the rest.

"Why didn't you tell me?"

Pain crossed Lucey's face. "Fear, I suppose. I've seen in

the past the results of matches that harmed each other. Besides, there has always been so much going on, and I've been known as myself for so long. I didn't want that to change. Max didn't know about me being your match, either. Not until I sent him a message a few hours ago, warning him. I didn't know you suspected Dante, or I would have told you both immediately."

The messenger bird Isadora had seen just before everything fell apart. Maximillion's determination to stop her from pulling Dante into the paths.

Isadora felt sick.

Lucey looked back. The wisps had re-formed into unmoving pictures. "I admit it makes sense. Stunning sense, in fact, for the magic is a thing of balance, isn't it? We're equal, aren't we? Both raised in Letum Wood, without the influence of magic. Forced from our homes to live the life we were meant to have. Struggling with a power we could never hope to understand. And all along, we hold opposite sides of it."

Isadora looked away, hoping to comprehend it all.

Magic is a thing of balance, isn't it?

What Lucey described resonated all the way through Isadora's chest, pulsing like the heartbeat of the magic itself.

Yes, it *was* balanced. Lucey, her match, was the missing piece in the equation. She balanced the magic.

Which meant something now . . .

Lucey looked down at her hands as if they held the answers. "Such a strange magic. It feels so . . . so oddly pulling, as if it wants me and doesn't want me at the same time. As if it, too, is broken. Pulled different ways. I cannot stay away, but I fear coming back. No matter how much time I spend here, I can never make sense of it. I've lived half my life craving the other side of the magic."

"Now you're here," Isadora murmured.

"Yes. Now I'm here."

"Why?"

"Because I've seen it in the paths. Watchers and Defenders working together. Matches uniting. I've never seen exactly what's happened when the most powerful Watcher and Defender are in the paths together, but suffice it to say that we're stronger together than apart."

The magic stirred again. Isadora glanced behind her. In the distance, Dante continued to sort through the possibilities, moving from one to another like a madman. Lucey stepped forward, standing next to her. They watched him together.

"I may see the past," Lucey said, "but you see the future. I'm here now for support, but this battle is yours."

Isadora pulled her shoulders back and drew in a deep breath. This was her moment. *The* moment. The only redemption they'd get would have to happen right now, on a battleground both terrifying and familiar.

Beams of light sprang out from Isadora's feet and crawled into the forest. So many of them, expanding like roots. Lucey's gentle vapor followed, twining with the brilliance.

Isadora's heart thrummed. "I'm ready."

"We have to break him," Isadora said with confidence.

She and Lucey advanced into the magical version of Letum Wood. Dante strode amongst the crowded wisps, muttering. Darkness curled at Lucey's feet, and the magic ventured ahead of Isadora in lines of light.

With Lucey at her side, Isadora's power had unlocked

again. It stirred within her, blooming in the forest. Flowers fell from the treetops. Honeysuckle thickened the air.

Everything felt different. Complete. Whole.

"How do we break such a man?" Lucey asked.

"With what he came here for."

Isadora's heart raced, but not out of fear. The tingle of the magic wrapped around her, both comforting and completing. She knew what to do. At least, she thought she did. If not, the magic would guide them.

"With the future?" Lucey asked.

"*And* the past."

They stopped a few paces from Dante as he studied a wisp. In it, he lay alone on a bed, peering into the distance, his face blanker than Isadora had ever seen it. Beyond him was the sea, outside a balcony door. The room was empty otherwise.

Lucey tensed.

"Let me introduce you to him, then you reveal your powers first," Isadora murmured. "You deserve a chance to get some closure for what he did to you."

Lucey sucked in a sharp breath and reached out, squeezing Isadora's hand.

"Your plan is doomed to fail, Dante," Isadora said, all traces of fear gone from her voice. "Because there is one thing you didn't plan for."

"What's that?" he snapped.

"My match."

Dante looked up, then straightened when he saw Lucey. His eyes flickered, uncertain.

"Recognize me?" she asked lightly, though her jaw hardened. "You should. You helped Cecelia torture me to try to get the truth out of me. To betray the Advocacy that I so deeply loved and would give my life for. In fact, *I* am what you had hoped Cecelia was. The most powerful Defender. The one who could have told you not to try this foolish plan. The one who saw enough to stop you, though you wouldn't have listened."

Isadora could sense wisps appearing. The magic shifting. Dante glanced beyond them. His expression elongated. An expression of horror appeared there briefly before sliding back to his usual indifference.

"I'm sure you have it wrong," he muttered, turning to leave.

"Cecelia didn't see what I see now. She suspected but couldn't confirm the other women you collected, just like her. Her biggest regret was falling in love with you."

Dante froze but didn't turn around. Isadora glanced back to see half a dozen women standing there, frozen in time. Most of them appeared heartbroken. Hands wringing. Eyes luminous. Lips downturned.

His hands shook. "I loved Cecelia."

"Not enough," Lucey hissed, stalking toward him. "Do you know what it feels like to live in the past? It's so much more powerful than you'd ever think."

The vapor floated forward, collecting at Lucey's feet and swirling toward his. Isadora felt her own magic respond. The paths near him brightened. Out of the dark mist came solid wisps from the past, circling him.

Dante whirled around, attempting to escape, but the memories pursued. "Get away from me!"

Lucey regarded the wisps. All of them were witches. Men, women, a few younger teens. Isadora recognized none of them until . . . Alessio. A young pianist she had helped Lucey extract from the East on her first Advocacy mission. Then another. The Watcher who had died at Cecelia's hand —on Dante's order—at La Torra.

These were Watchers.

More damning wisps appeared around Dante. Cecelia in the East, diving off the side of Carcere. Witches screaming. Mothers crying, lunging for children they'd never hold again. Limp, lifeless bodies. So many lifeless bodies.

"They may have been Watchers, Dante," Lucey said, strolling amongst their still forms, "but they're still witches. Witches you killed, or tried to kill, or forced to flee. Witches irrevocably changed because of you."

"Stop!" Dante called, his voice shrill.

"Do they frighten you?"

The wisps crowded him. He backed into a tree, shuddering. Lucey appeared in one of them, blood bubbling beneath her nose and dripping onto her dress, which had been ripped open, exposing bruised, slashed breasts.

"Difficult to face, isn't it?" Lucey asked, staring at him with a dispassionate gaze. "The past doesn't lie. What is even more terrifying is what you don't see here. The possibilities you missed. Here." Lucey touched the wisp of the young Watcher Isadora had seen die at La Torra. "What if you *hadn't* chosen to kill Selena?"

As if by command, paths sprang from Lucey's feet. With a horrified expression, Dante remained transfixed on Selena.

"She could have been a mother," Lucey said, displaying the complicated tapestry of paths denied Selena. "A wife. A leader who would have brought peace to her borough. Do you see all these possibilities? All these that you have broken?"

"No," he whispered. "That—"

"It's true. How could it *not* be?"

More paths sprang off from that one, winding into more

possibilities. These were dimmer wisps, muted gray but still vivid.

Dante shoved his hands into his hair with a scream. Isadora marveled at the intimacy a Defender had with the witch they saw the past for. Every decision taken and not taken. Everything done and left undone, every shameful moment, every emotion.

Which power truly was greater—the future or the past?

Or were they equally powerful?

"Stop," Dante pleaded. "I beg you."

The wisps disappeared in a puff of ashy smoke. Lucey watched him, expression icy.

"You tried to break me but couldn't do it. You've killed countless witches and will never have the power to do that again. And your time here hasn't even begun, my friend," she said softly, turning to Isadora. "For it's Isadora who truly holds your fate in her hands. As terrifying as this is, your future will be far bleaker."

Power bubbled up in Isadora, flowing free. Feeling the full extent of the power—even beyond what she'd experienced before—Isadora met Dante's gaze. The magic stirred, and she released it. Light broke at Dante's feet and raced away from him, away from the wisps of the past. Shadow flowed with light, equal powers working in harmony.

Now she understood the magic.

Understood what it had been for all along.

"The future is what you wanted, Dante," Isadora said. "And the future is what you shall have."

Beyond them, the darkness pooled. Isadora's magic grew in response. Luminescence cut through the shadows. She reached for the magic and pulled. Light crashed into the darkness.

A path started at Isadora's feet and raced away. Shimmering roots spread across the ground, crawling into the forest floor. Everything illuminated overhead, countering the burgeoning darkness swirling from Lucey.

And from Lucey's feet, shadows bolted after the light as if to catch it. In the wake of the darkness, the wisps disappeared. Everything faded as the shadows chased the light, hiding the forest, the trees, the paths . . . save for one single, certain line.

With every path that closed, Isadora's throat thickened. The power whipped through her in a surge now, like a gale. Lucey winced, one hand on her head, one on her heart, and let out a cry. Dante screamed, but Isadora couldn't hear it over the roaring in her ears.

Wisps vanished. More reappeared, lining the heaviest light. The weight of the magic felt like a mountain as it coalesced. The power, equally matched, would destroy them at this rate.

Lucey fell to her knees with a gasp.

Where did this end? Didn't their magic originate from the same source? How could the magic be divided—or would it be? Perhaps it would simply destroy all of them.

Isadora held her ground, ready to die, until a glimmer caught her eye. She thought of Max. Of Sanna. Of the world about to dissolve back in the Southern Network.

She hesitated, looking into Lucey's terrified eyes. Suddenly, everything else felt a lifetime away. Dante. The Networks. War. It all seemed to have occurred in some distant past, with everything else coming into sharp focus.

The magic wasn't about power or control. It wasn't even about the future. It was about trust. Releasing something.

This magic was about surrender. Surrender to what would be, not what they tried to *make* it be. The paths were another opportunity to let go.

To know witches.

So Isadora let it go.

Light exploded.

Isadora flew backward, slamming into a tree. Her physical body ached, feeling every movement, somehow pulled into the paths. She was here, fully present, in her body now. Dark spots and bursts of illumination crowded her vision. When her eyes opened, she stood with Lucey and Dante in the middle of the circle of the Ancients.

Calm darkness covered the forest. She thought she saw a sparkle of diamonds on the ground and a stone wall to her right, but they faded back into the mist. As if the two worlds overlapped. She longed for Max.

The wind whispered by.

Powerful...

Burning white lines started at their feet and bolted through the ground in front of and behind them. The magic surged through her again, flowing like a river.

Isadora spun. The wisps had solidified in living color, looking so real Isadora felt she could step into each scene. Her breath caught. She saw herself in the turret, terrified as she came out of the paths. Dante at the dinner table with his wine glass. Maximillion protecting her. Snow flurries around the Cage.

The entire night laid out exactly as it had occurred. The past as it had actually happened. No other possibilities. No other paths. Lucey's magic meeting her own had brought the past to life, moment by moment. The wisps stretched beyond, into eternity.

Everything was there.

"The good gods," Isadora whispered. That meant...

Lucey let out a little cry as she, too, must have realized the same thing.

Isadora turned.

Eerily lifelike in their appearance, wisps marched in an exact line, one in front of the other, into darkness in the other direction. Isadora glanced at the first wisp.

Sanna.

Blood streaked down Sanna's pale, anguished face. She looked to be moments away from death. Seeing her sister's pain, Isadora's heart nearly stopped. This would be her last view of her, surely. No one could survive whatever Sanna was experiencing. The wisp had taken a solid form now. Isadora touched her sister's cheek.

"I believe in you, Sanna," she whispered. "I love you, *amo*."

The wisp faded, moving behind her and revealing the next.

Maximillion, surrounded by South Guards in the dining room with Vasily. Vasily stood over Dante's limp body with a sword drawn, hovering a breath from Max's neck. Serafina and Arayana huddled in the corner, tears on their cheeks.

The terrible majesty of the magic laid manifest filled her with terror. Together, Isadora and Lucey revealed the true past and the precise future. Everything as it had happened and would happen. No uncertainty.

Only truth.

Isadora took a step toward the future, her heart full of questions. Was Sanna all right? Would the Networks fall apart?

Now she could know everything. Could see whether Maximillion would choose to stay in her life. To watch Sanna, Mam, and Letum Wood run through her future. To be comforted by the certainty of knowing what happened. She stepped toward the path with a jolt of glee, then stopped. Two words whispered through her mind.

Don't look.

The note from Taiza. The cryptic parchment suddenly made sense. It had been a note from Watchers—likely a Watcher who *had* looked. And having seen this, they would have known what to say. May have even known what would happen if she did study the future.

She paused.

Was there power in knowing?

She would never truly live if she knew what was coming. Would never really trust, always wondering over every decision. Could she change this future just by knowing it? Perhaps even break it. Render it null. How absolute could this magic be?

Would she have wanted to know that Daid would die?

That Maximillion would turn away from her?

No.

Freedom didn't come from knowing the future. It came from accepting the present. Surrendering to the uncertainty of what *could* happen against what did. The torture of the past was reliving a decision that could have been different. The torture of the future was knowing what decision to make, then agonizing every moment until it came.

Either way, that was no life.

Slowly, Isadora turned her back to the path. When she looked up, Lucey was watching her, eyes brimming with emotion.

"Are you going to look?" Lucey's quiet singsong reminded Isadora of a little girl. At her side, her hands trembled. Whether it was from the force of the magic or the enormity of this experience, Isadora couldn't tell.

"No."

Behind her came a crumpling sound. She turned.

Dante knelt on the forest floor, expression distant. Half

gone. He had walked several wisps into his future and fallen. Into a future that, from what she saw, didn't extend far.

Isadora glided over and put a hand on his shoulder. "You will get everything you asked for. An intimate knowledge of the future. With that comes a heavy price—the truth. No matter how willing you are to bear it, it is now yours by your own request."

He trembled, then fell.

Isadora met Lucey's gaze. "Together?" she whispered, holding out a hand. "Shall we end this mighty power as one and never institute it again? Remove ourselves from this world, or it from ours?"

Lucey nodded.

"Together."

∼

THE MAGIC CLOSED.

A breath, a heartbeat, and a moment of fading darkness revealed the Southern Network dining room. Isadora sucked in a sharp breath. Letum Wood dissipated, but the magic still crackled in the air. Lucey stood next to her, shaking so hard her teeth chattered.

Dante lay at their feet, tucked into a ball. His arms and legs jerked.

Across the room, Maximillion and Charles stared at her, eyes wide. Each held a knife in one hand, their hair disheveled as if they'd been fighting side by side. Isadora swallowed hard, taking in the dining room.

All the Guardians stood along the edge as if thrown there. She looked more closely at them. Pale faces. Fast breathing. Terrified expressions.

Had she and Lucey brought the magic here as well?

Dante slowly stood. He looked around, locked his gaze on Isadora, and snarled. "I have seen it all!" he cried. "It is mine to know and to conquer!"

He lunged.

Isadora threw her arms up, but a hand on Dante's neck slammed him to the ground. He landed with a *thud.*

Maximillion stood over him, a foot on his neck. "Touch my wife," he growled, "and you die."

Dante stared at him, hissing through his teeth. Then his body slackened. His head lolled to the side as his eyes rolled back in his head.

A pale hand appeared on Max's arm, pulling him back.

"Let me bind him," Charles murmured.

In two steps, Max was at her side. Isadora crumpled, but he caught her, crushing her against his rock-solid chest.

"The good gods, Isa," he whispered. "I thought . . ."

The magic in the room faded like a curling parchment. The vestiges of the trees disappeared, their roots shrinking into tiles. Out of the darkness appeared several faces. Vasily, stricken, followed by a stunned Serafina.

The power settled in Isadora's chest with a breath, then faded. A spell issued by someone released the wives from their bonds.

Isadora trembled. The energy drained her, robbing her of her thoughts. Her breath.

"Hang in there," Max murmured against her temple.

Serafina and Arayana rubbed their wrists, eyes shifting uneasily.

"That path," Arayana whispered. "I saw a path. It . . ."

Serafina stood slowly, a shaking hand pressed against her head. The door burst open, and Emilia rushed inside, darting toward her mere. Serafina grabbed onto her with a sob, and the two sank to the floor.

"We all saw the paths, I think," Maximillion said quietly. "You pulled the magic in, and, if they saw what I did, they know the future of their Networks. As if . . . as if the magic knew exactly what to show to make this happen. To make peace."

Vasily crouched, slack-jawed. His blanched lips and gaunt eyes didn't move from Dante's inert form.

Fatigue clouded Isadora's mind. The withdrawal of the magic left her feeling utterly naked and empty. She'd conjured the future. Not just for herself, but for everyone present.

She turned to Max. "Sanna," she whispered. "Please, take me to Sanna."

32

S anna had imagined Halla to be much brighter than this.

Pain wound lazily through her body—odd, because she shouldn't be able to feel. For a long moment, she didn't move. She just lay there, waiting for the light of Halla. Would she see Daid? Luteis?

For some reason, just then, she thought of Isadora.

Memories from the battle slipped through her mind slowly, then all at once. Remembering it again felt like a punch to the gut. Her heart had been torn apart.

She must not be dead, then.

Luteis?

She reached out with her mind, but only emptiness responded. Quiet. An odd sense of stillness.

Luteis?

Did he die, or somehow survive? Recalling the firm *snap* of the magic breaking in her body sent a horrifying thought jolting through her mind. Something stirred above her. Not sand. Not a storm.

Leaves.

She sat up, bracing herself for a rush of light when her eyes opened, expecting the sun to glare off the desert sand.

Nothing.

Sanna blinked. She waved a hand in front of her face.

Nothing.

Absolutely nothing.

Her nostrils flared in sudden panic, but she forced the fear back. Instead, her thoughts fragmented, skipping everywhere at once.

Darkness.

More raw panic tore through her chest. Where was she? Where was Luteis? She groped around. Something sharp, wet, and goopy filled her hands.

The forest. The tang of the soil in her nostrils meant the forest. But . . .

"Luteis? Luteis, where are you? I can't . . . I can't hear you." Tears clogged her throat as she pushed to her feet. "Where am I? Luteis?"

A familiar snort came from behind her, accompanied by a roll of heat. Relief weakened her. She knew that noise.

You're here! Are you all right?

Silence.

Why didn't he speak to her? She put a hand out.

"Luteis?"

Something scalded her hand. She let out a cry, stumbling back until she collided with a tree. His heat, which had been so comforting before, was overbearing. She sat there for a moment, chest heaving.

"Luteis," she whispered, her fingers touching her ears. "You're gone. I can't . . . I can't hear you. I can't see you. *Mori.* You're gone, Luteis."

Another wave of heat rolled over her. She turned away, grimacing. Then she sank into the ground, weak-kneed, and wrapped her arms around her legs. She was alive, that much was clear.

Somehow, she'd survived breaking an ancient magic.

She'd survived the wrath of a goddess.

She'd survived the moment she severed her connection to Luteis, sealing herself off from him forever.

Now she wished she hadn't.

Snuffling and snorting and a distant bellow confirmed they were back in Letum Wood. Somehow. Other forest dragons were around her—she could feel waves of their heat. But where was everyone else? And what had happened after she broke the magic?

Did it matter?

Sanna tried to control her panic, but she couldn't breathe. She was alive, but blind and without Luteis. Without her soul. He was her eyes. Her heart.

She forced herself through the pain and shock as Isadora flashed into her mind again. They wouldn't even age together as twins now. Not really. Sanna would always picture Isadora the way she did now. Blondish hair cut short. Snapping eyes filled with love and fire. A pert nose.

Sanna was already forgetting Daid. Saw him only in flashes. Would she even remember that? Would color fade from her memory as well?

She'd never see glimpses of Mam in her own aging face, nor in Isadora's. Never know Jesse as an old man, or Luteis as he aged.

She'd never know light from darkness ever again.

In some strange way, she felt no surprise. Losing the final vestiges of her sight had seemed inevitable. A bitter sense of relief filled her. The darkness terrified her, yes, but now it was done. She didn't live in the fear of losing it anymore.

The worst had come.

Her heart still beat. Her brain still formed thoughts. The what-ifs could fade. She just had to deal with the present. Or so she told herself. Just when her despair threatened to overwhelm her, she heard a soft voice.

"Sanna?"

Her head jerked up. "Isa?"

Footsteps in the undergrowth, then a pair of arms wrapped around her. "Oh, Sanna!" came Isadora's broken cry. "I've been so scared for you."

Sobs bubbled out of Sanna. She let Isadora hold her as the pain, the fear, flowed out in long, painful breaths. All of the pressure from the magic, the uncertainty of life and death that had haunted her for so long, disappeared in her sister's arms. Isadora held her tight—so tight it hurt—and Sanna wouldn't let go.

Sanna cried for what felt like hours. When she could finally bear it, she pulled away.

Isadora wiped her tears with a soft thumb. She smelled like earth, and her touch was soft and comforting.

"Sanna!" Isadora said. "I'm so sorry. I know that—"

"No. It's me, Isa. I should apologize."

"No!"

"Listen—"

Isadora clamped a hand over Sanna's mouth. "All is forgiven, and now we can start new. Fresh. Without fear of war, death, or famine. Agreed? Everything is going to be all right now, Sanna. We're back together."

Sanna sucked in a breath, then nodded.

Isadora sat next to Sanna on the ground, intertwining their fingers. For several moments, neither spoke.

Sanna sank into the moment, the darkness, the disorientation of having her mind all to herself. Without the dragons constantly chattering in the background of her thoughts, she felt empty. She must have slept for days, but her body was weary. A husk. She longed to return to sleep. To oblivion.

Mustering up her courage, Sanna croaked, "Where is Luteis?"

"On an overhead branch, staring at you with what appears to be profound concern and . . . despair."

A deep-throated keening sound confirmed Isa's words. The impatient flicking of his tail in the leaves threatened to break Sanna's heart again. He wanted to grab her ankle, but now she had no protection from his heat.

Was he worried? How much had breaking the magic taken away from them? Did he remember her? He must remember. Sanna wanted to reach out, but remembering the scorching pain, curled her fingers into a fist.

"Sanna," Isadora murmured, understanding flooding her voice. "What's happened? How come you didn't know where Luteis was? Are you . . ."

"He's gone," she whispered, pressing a shaking hand to her head. "I can't hear him. Just like I can't see."

"What?"

More tears poured down Sanna's cheeks. "The dragons," she said. "I broke the magic and set them free. But it cut the merging. I . . . Luteis and I are no longer merged. I gave up everything so they could be free, and now . . . I've lost them."

"Sanna!"

Isadora's hand found Sanna's, squeezing. Before Sanna could get a word out, she caught the scent of honeysuckle. She turned her face toward it. The entire forest seemed to have quieted.

"Isa? What's wrong? I can feel something. The hair on the back of my arms is standing up. I—"

"Oh," Isadora whispered. Her hands turned to ice. "The magic. It's . . ."

Sanna of the forest, said a rich voice. *Close your eyes and come with me.*

A prickling sensation began in her fingertips. Rendered speechless, Sanna obeyed. It felt like stepping somewhere, into a different place.

In this new place, she opened her eyes, feeling distinctly . . . apart. Light unfurled around her, and she let out a cry.

She *saw.*

They stood in Letum Wood, in the midst of the circle of the Ancients. Only it wasn't Letum Wood—not really. It was . . . a different version of her beloved forest. Isadora stood next to her, smiling, her eyes filled with tears. Isa, who she'd grown up with. Who had giggled with her in the old attic at Anguis. The Isa who, no matter what happened, would always be her sisterwitch. The other side of her heart.

Isadora seemed drawn, weary, but silently resolute. Something deeper lived within her now.

"Isa," she said. "You're . . ."

"Different."

"Yes." Sanna reached out, touching Isadora's hair. The different colors of her eyes were bolder than ever now. "What happened?"

Isadora tilted her head back and laughed. "That will take a while to explain, and we have plenty of long winter days ahead." Her eyes brightened. "Sanna, this is where I go. Somehow, we're in the paths. This is *my* magic. Or . . . maybe not really mine. I'm not sure if I brought us here, but I don't think so."

Sanna looked down, feeling the pressure of her sister's hand in her own. The forest unfurled around them, empty paths snaking throughout it. In the midst of them lay one, more solid than the rest. Her heart ached.

A voice rang above them. "Both of you have done well."

Sanna and Isadora turned to find a woman standing behind them. Isadora tightened her hold on Sanna.

"I know this feeling," Isadora said, eyes narrowed on the woman. "I . . . I've felt it before. You . . . you *are* the source of my magic."

"Deasylva," Sanna murmured.

Magic infused the goddess Deasylva. Her brown skin, rich as the earth, glowed from within. Umber hair cascaded all the way to her knees, gently curled and swaying like tree roots. She looked on Sanna with warmth.

"You set the dragons free," Deasylva said. "As I had always hoped you would. For what you've done, you have my gratitude, as well as Sarena's."

"The dragons are all right?" Sanna asked. "Do they remember? Are they suffering because of it?"

"Those that survived the battle are home. Yes, they will remember, though they cannot communicate with you. They are now free to roam, although I doubt any forest dragons will leave Letum Wood. Metok sends his admiration and gratitude."

Sanna said nothing. She'd miss them. Their voices, their occasional snark about the way witches lived. But beyond that was a profound sense of relief. Joy.

No . . . *freedom*.

"What happened?" Sanna asked.

"One witch bearing all the magic put it out of balance. By releasing all the dragons, you destroyed the basis of the magic. You would have died, but you released the dragons in time. It was the only way to set them free—something we didn't know the first time Sarena attempted it."

Deasylva paused, then smiled softly. "Sarena sends you her regards, and this."

She extended a familiar water pouch. Sanna stared at it in shock.

"Tashi?" she whispered.

"Yes."

Sanna's mind vaguely reviewed everything she remembered about Tashi, but it all felt like too much. She accepted the water pouch with a numb sense of disbelief, remembering Avia's words about the desert goddess. *The desert. Sarena is a simple goddess with few needs. The land reflects the goddess.*

"Did you know this is how it would happen?" Sanna asked, staring at the water pouch as if it had all the answers.

"I knew how it should and could happen. Revealing to you more than I did would not have been wise. After thousands of years, things came together now only because of you. You, who didn't care for goddesses and had fierce loyalty only to dragons. No other witch would have gone through with it but one who loved their dragons so fiercely."

Sanna swallowed. "And now," she whispered, "I can neither see nor hear them."

"Was it worth it to you?"

"Yes," she said.

"While you wield no power over the dragons anymore, acting as an emissary may be a new path for you."

Deasylva turned to Isadora. She inclined her head for a long pause, then straightened.

"Isadora, you have not only protected the witches of Antebellum but proven that witches can redeem themselves —or at least work out their problems. For your toil, I grant you continued growth in the Watcher magic, which originates in me and in goodness. You will advance in ability and strength, and as I see, will find ways to use it for good. Abuse it, and you shall enjoy my wrath."

Isadora breathed in sharply. "I would never dream of it."

Deasylva's lips twitched. "I trust you. Your power as a Watcher was so great because the magic responds to rising evil. You will feel a surge in your abilities again in the future, when need arises. For now, it will abate. Not all evil can be banished, and more is in store for Antebellum."

Deasylva turned back to Sanna. "Sanna, in giving the dragons the freedom they have always deserved, you have lost everything you held dear, except for your sisterwitch."

Sanna's troubled gaze met Deasylva's again. She still couldn't reconcile the goddess with the writing that had appeared on the tree trunks.

"Luteis," she whispered. "And Daid and Anguis."

Deasylva's expression softened. "Unlike Isadora, you cannot continue in your magic. In recompense, I can grant something in restitution. While I cannot remake Dragonian magic—nor would I wish to—I will restore what is most important to you."

Sanna's heart skipped a beat. "Luteis?"

Deasylva's brow rose. "You do not choose your sight?"

"He will be my sight," she said softly.

"Then you shall remain blind, and your merging with Luteis will be restored, but without the power of the Dragonian magic. You will not be able to communicate through your thoughts with any dragon but him. You will remain protected from his heat and from falling while flying."

Sanna nodded.

Deasylva continued, "I go now to rest within my forest. I shall retire for many years according to the timing of witches, but I trust Letum Wood to your capable hands. When you go to Halla, one shall rise in your place, for my trees know those who belong to them. There is always one who responds to their cries."

Isadora put a firm arm around Sanna.

"Thank you, Deasylva," Sanna murmured, feeling a sense of loss and finality. There would be no interaction with the forest goddess again, and she was startled to realize she'd miss her.

Deasylva faded, her form dwindling into mist. The smell of honeysuckle and a faint breeze stirred up as she closed her eyes, and was gone.

Isadora let out a long exhale. "Well. One can't say that we don't keep things interesting around here."

Sanna studied her, trying to commit this last look at her sister to memory so that she could never forget it. "When we go back, I will never see you again. I'll never *see* again."

"Not until we return to Daid in the halls of Halla," Isadora said, gripping both of Sanna's hands. "But I will be with you forever."

Sanna wrapped Isadora in her arms.

"Forever."

SANNA RETURNED TO DARKNESS.

She stood there for a second, disoriented. Then she drew in a breath. Mentally settled in. Her sight was gone—she'd see no more. But she'd be fine. Isadora still held her hand. Luteis would be with her. The forest dragons still lived, and so would Letum Wood after proper care and attention.

Someone had to take care of all that strickenine moss and the trees that fell to Prana's salt water.

A rustle of leaves accompanied a breathless voice in her head. Sanna turned.

Little one, Luteis whispered, voice stark, *have you returned to me?*

With a cry, Sanna flung herself at his heat, her arms enveloping his snout. His heat didn't scorch her, settling to its usual pleasant warmth. The emptiness that had been haunting her faded as he joined in with her thoughts, where they both belonged. Tears tracked down her cheeks.

"Luteis," she whispered. "I'm so relieved you're back."

His tail wrapped around her ankle.

Deasylva tells me of your sacrifice. My love and relief is great. Only death shall part us now.

She stood there, touching him, until the ache in her chest began to fade. She pressed her forehead to his.

Let's go home again, she said, *and this time, let's stay. For decades. Maybe forever. Long ago, Isadora promised to teach me some spells that have practical purposes.*

Sounds like a worthy investment of time.

She grinned. "Maybe magic isn't so bad. Besides, we have our work cut out for us in Letum Wood."

I am inclined to agree.

"You're already mapping out a plan for cleaning up the fallen trees and strickenine moss, aren't you?" she asked, thinking about the complicated canopy that awaited them.

Patches of strickenine moss would still be everywhere. Fallen trees cluttered the forest floor that would need to be cleaned up. It was difficult to navigate some areas, and many trees weren't handling the close space well. They needed to be thinned out.

His wing twitched next to her.

False. I already have a plan and am looking forward to implementing it. The forest desperately needs us. We may have defeated our enemies, but we are not yet completely healed. It's time for us to focus on Letum Wood and allow Deasylva to rest. The mountain dragons ate enough of the beluas that we need not fear their numbers anymore, but it will take time for the forest to regrow.

It had all been so surreal. She still questioned whether she'd really lived through so much.

"Perhaps," she said. "But at least we have each other for the rest of our lives now."

That, he murmured, *is my ultimate plan.*

"I CAN'T BELIEVE it's still standing," Maximillion said.

Isadora, Lucey, and Maximillion all stared at Lucey's old house, not far outside the perimeter of Anguis, hidden amongst the cracks and crevices of the forest. A perfect circle of black ringed the structure, left by the flames that had consumed the rest of the Dragonmasters' homes.

But not Lucey's, which had clearly been protected by some kind of magic. Quiet birds, no larger than a hand, flittered in and out of the open window. Although winter air poured into the house, Lucey felt no need to close it up.

"I have long protected it," Lucey said. "Several Watchers have used it as a safe house. I didn't want them to lose their escape in all this madness with Talis, so it still stands."

A week had passed since the confrontation with Dante, and three days since the final meeting of the summit. The Mansfeld Pact, named for Serafina's pere who had inspired her love of politics, had been settled after two days of negotiation between the parties. The isolationism plan, with a few addendums, had finally been agreed upon by Dostar, Vasily, Charles, and Serafina.

The gypsies, granted land at Charles's gracious insistence, were on their way to Letum Wood, where they'd live amongst the trees. Serafina, with input from Emilia, had added provisions to change the situation for Watchers in the East. While it would be a while before things became truly safe, great strides had been made across Antebellum.

Through it all, Isadora had remained home in the Central Network. The display of her power had made everyone uneasy—but it had been she who'd made the suggestion that Watchers be addressed in the agreement, allowed useful professions without political power until the individual Networks clarified their own laws.

In the intervening days, when she wasn't repairing Pearl's house or sleeping long hours at Mam's, she'd returned to the refugee camp in Berry. Rumors abounded that the town was being renamed Newberry as a symbol of new beginnings and hope.

She'd seen no sign of Baylee. She wished her well in her new world.

"Dante is settled at home," Maximillion said. "Serafina says none of his mental faculties have returned, but he's stopped screaming. They're able to keep him quiet in a room by himself, with a view of the sea, and a discreet staff. Serafina rules in his place now."

"A fitting end," Lucey murmured. "For he certainly did what no other member of his family had done, didn't he? Instituted a woman at the helm."

A bird appeared at Lucey's ear. She listened, then turned to them with a gentle smile.

"My love calls to me," she said, touching Isadora's arm. "I'll see you later, with your sister."

Lucey, Sanna, and Isadora had made plans to meet to record the history of the massacre as it had really happened. Lucey's power as a Defender ensured they'd get it right.

With one last smile, she disappeared into a transportation spell.

Isadora and Max stood side by side, not touching. The final negotiations of the Mansfeld Pact had kept him away for days. Now that he was back with her, a part of Isadora's soul had settled, like an empty hole had been filled. She breathed easier with the smell of vetiver in her nose.

"Your powers?" he asked gruffly.

"Fading," she said. "I don't think they're needed right now."

"Why not?"

She reached up, pressing a hand to her chest. "The magic is ebbing. It's still with me. The paths are still visible. Everything is working. But . . . there's not so much of it. It's not so restless."

Maximillion paused, then asked, "You think the magic comes and goes as it's needed?"

"I know it does. As if controlled by a goddess who knew what we needed and when, perhaps?"

She hadn't told him about Deasylva. Not yet, but perhaps one day.

"Hmm." He canted his body to more fully face her. His gaze remained as aloof and unreadable as ever. "I have something to tell you."

Her breath caught in her throat. She tilted her head back. "Yes?"

"I spoke with the Advocate."

"Oh?"

"Pearl is alive and well."

Isadora grimaced lightly. "So you know my secret? That I harbored the truth from you to keep you focused?"

A wry smile appeared briefly on his lips. "Indeed, and the irony is extreme. All is forgiven. Pearl will be returning home soon. As soon as Dante's Defenders began their rampage, the Advocate went to save her. The ransacking of her house was deliberate—he did it so any Defender would pass it by and not seek her out."

Relief flooded her. In the chaos, she hadn't dared bring it up. Charles had been with Maximillion in the South, and her quiet inquiries here and there hadn't panned out. Not even a quick visit to Pearl's favorite library.

"Thank you for telling me. You, ah, said *he*. The Advocate is male, then?"

To her surprise, one side of his lips quirked into a half-smile. If he was handsome while brooding, he was down-right gorgeous while smiling.

"Indeed," he said. "He's coming here to speak with both of us."

Her eyes widened. "What?"

"He's here," said a voice from behind her. "And a troublesome fellow he is."

Isadora whirled around, then grabbed a tree to keep from falling.

Charles stood there, a grin on his face. Gone was his usual stammering hesitation and uncertainty. His voice had been as clear as a bell, with no sign of a stutter. He'd controlled his hair and donned a pristine white shirt and brown breeches, looking not only immaculate but quite normal.

"You?" she whispered.

He spread his hands and bowed. "At your service."

"But—"

"I know, it seems so unlikely." He straightened, his expression all business. An alacrity she'd only seen hints of before marked his features, but his bright eyes still twinkled. "It's the unlikely witches you have to watch the closest."

She struggled to find the words for her many questions.

Charles laughed. "Not to worry, Isadora. It's nothing you should have figured out. Maximillion and I have been keeping this secret since we met and first formed our idea, years and years ago. That, however, is a story for another time."

"Then . . . the Advocacy. You being . . . well . . . *you*. It's all been planned?"

Charles nodded. "I started the Advocacy with Max's help, and began my ruse as a weak-willed Council Member to hide our work but give us access. Becoming High Priest was not in our plans." He exchanged a grim look with Maximillion. "Still, we worked through it."

"Max attending the summit?" she asked.

"Intentional. Of course I was capable, but being the idiot High Priest allowed me to stay back, giving me unprecedented access to the Networks without their rulers there. I would investigate, search, continue to deflect the Defenders as we were able."

"Does anyone else know?" she asked, half-laughing. "I-I mean this is . . ."

"No one." He sobered. "Not even Lucey. I am disguised at all times when acting in my role. We'd like it to remain that way, for the Advocacy will continue as long as Watchers and Defenders need it. Maximillion and I mutually agreed that you deserved to know."

Max cleared his throat, glancing at her from the corner of his eye. "You and I spoke of magical matches?"

"Yes."

He nodded toward Charles. "You have found mine.

Charles is a powerful Defender in his own right, and the reason the Advocacy was so successful."

All the blood drained from Isadora's face. She sat down this time, taking several moments to comprehend it.

Charles put a hand on her arm. "Have we made you ill?"

"No." She managed a smile. "No, thank you. I'm . . . startled, that's all."

Charles crouched next to her, concern in his eyes. "It's a lot to absorb."

"You could have told me you had Pearl," she said, a note of bitterness creeping into her voice. "I've been sick with worry."

He winced. "I could not. Max and I decided at the very beginning that secrecy regarding my true abilities and identity was important above all. I created and played a character, and had to remain true to him as best I could. To protect the Advocate, I said nothing."

She stared at Charles, her thoughts whirling in earnest now. "The Defenders helping Watchers in the West," she said. "You were part of that?"

"Guilty."

"And that night on La Torra," she whispered. "There were the *aquila* birds. One of them had a reddish tint to its feathers. That was you?"

He clapped her on the shoulder. "She's something, isn't she, Max? Never seen a witch so canny. Yes, Isadora. I often joined Max or checked on Cecelia as an aquila. Well spotted."

"Did you know about Lucey?"

He shook his head. "I see only for myself. Just like Max. She never appeared in my paths outside Advocacy work."

"And when the two of you met? Does the magic do anything?"

"No. Nothing truly happens, though I feel a special bond with Max." He nudged her in the ribs. "It certainly doesn't show us the future!"

"But you," she said, turning to Max. "You said you knew nothing of Defenders and their magic."

"I meant it." His tone was unyielding. "I don't know much. How can we? The magic is deep and complex. There is little we truly understand. And we *didn't* understand Cecelia and how it worked for her. The magic, as it unfolded, was unknown. Even now, it changes for you."

"An argument for an all-knowing goddess, almost," she said lightly.

He rolled his eyes, scoffing.

Charles clapped Maximillion on the shoulder in his usual jaunty way. "Max, my boy. I must be going. Loads of business to catch up on. My new Assistant has updates on the gangs in Chatham City. She's a wonder, that girl."

"Gangs?" Isadora echoed. "In the city?"

"They're already shoring up the black market," Charles said, rubbing his hands together with great excitement. "Now that the Mansfeld Pact prevents passage across the borders, you can bet your life that witches are going to be smuggling. Baylee has been a real saving grace."

Isadora suppressed a laugh. "Baylee?" she said in disbelief. "The orphan? Red curly hair, attitude bigger than Chatham City?"

Charles lit up. "You know her?"

"We were friends at Miss Sophia's School for Girls."

His nose wrinkled. "Of course! Yes, she's told me all about her life there. Big changes coming soon in our school system. She works for me now—our main contact for all things underworld. She's quite happy and I'm quite impressed."

Isadora laughed again, recalling their discussion over Baylee's new *benefactor*. "I'm sure she is."

"Max, I'll see you tomorrow morning for our usual meeting. Isadora, thank you for everything. We could not have done this without you. I owe you one, dear woman."

Her mind still churning, she nodded. "Thank you, Your Highness."

He strode away, then stopped and spun back around. "Almost forgot. The annulment of your handfasting. I'll put that through tonight. Should be final within a week."

With that, he disappeared. Isadora stared at the spot where he'd been standing, suddenly sick to her stomach. Maximillion had stiffened.

There was a long silence.

Isadora cleared her throat. If there was any time to tell Max how she felt, it was now.

But the words felt bigger than her.

"Well," she said, "I suppose there's a few things we need to discuss."

"Indeed."

Another pause. "Ah, I meant to thank you."

"For?"

"You were a perfect gentleman. You kept me safe and were . . . my friend. I needed that. I-I needed someone on my side after—"

She gestured to the burnt wood around them.

Max frowned and looked away. "What do you want, then?"

"What do I want?"

"What will you do now? What is next for Isadora Sin —Spence?"

She paused. The question had hovered on the edge of her mind for days now, but she hadn't really acknowledged it. So much lay behind it. Things she hadn't wanted to face yet. Like the fact that she felt desperately ill at the thought of not seeing him every day. Of not feeling his firm touch.

The fact that she bloody loved the man.

"The Head of Education reached out to me," she said. "They're thinking that a Watcher who can see personality traits in witches would be a good qualifier for admission. Identify quality students they can start preparing to serve in the Network, instead of the ramshackle way they find Council Members now. Charles wisely wants to start from the ground up in rebuilding the Network, emphasizing competent Council Members."

"Sounds perfectly boring."

"I know." She grinned. "Isn't it wonderful?"

He hesitated, brow furrowed, then nodded. "After all this war? Yes, it is."

"But that's not what you really asked me. You asked me what I wanted. I want a cottage in Letum Wood." She drew in a deep breath, then let her shoulders fall. "Close to Sanna and Mam. I want a job that makes a difference for the Network, and I want a house full of the teacups that Mam and I paint together. Then, maybe, it will feel like our lives haven't totally ended. As if . . . Daid could still be with us."

And I want you in all of it.

"What about you?" she asked instead. "What does the great Ambassador Maximillion Sinclair desire?"

A bird wheeling by interrupted the long silence.

Max's brow furrowed. "Peace."

"You have that now. The new plan is—"

"Are you going to leave?"

"Leave?"

"Are you . . . do you want something else?"

"What do you—"

"The good gods, Isadora!" he cried. "You *know* what I mean. Do you want to remain handfasted or not?" He paused, heartbeat visible in his throat. His voice became husky. "Because if you want to go, I won't stop Charles from granting the annulment. But if ..."

The words trailed away, leaving Isadora stunned. She stared at him, hardly able to comprehend.

"But if?" she whispered.

His nostrils flared. He stepped closer to her, grabbing her arm in a surprisingly gentle grasp for all the passion in his face.

"But if you didn't want to go. If you wanted to stay. With me. Then ... I believe we could build something together. Something ... peaceful and real and ... not empty and cold."

She inhaled, her nostrils thick with the heady scent of vetiver.

Max drew her so close she felt the soft caress of his breath on her face like a piece of velvet.

She swallowed hard. "In the South, when I asked you whether you were afraid of me after Carcere, you said yes, but not for the reason I thought. What was it, then?"

His expression softened. "I thought I had lost you," he whispered. "That I couldn't protect you, and it almost destroyed me. It was then that I realized the depth of my feelings, and that frightened me."

Her breath caught. "Do you really want more, Max? Can you handle me being near you every moment?"

His eyes darkened. His hands tightened around her waist.

"I crave it, Isadora. Like a dying man. I ..." His nostrils flared. "I don't want you to go. Will you stay? Will you endure a man as insufferable, arrogant, and terrified as I am?"

Isadora pressed her palm against his pounding heart.

"Yes," she whispered. "I want you, Max. I believe I've loved you since we first met."

His lips claimed hers, his arms tightening around her. No magic had swept through her so thoroughly, with such ravenous power, as his touch.

Isadora slipped under his power willingly, overwhelmed with the knowledge that she'd never have to leave it again.

THE END

NOTE FROM THE AUTHOR

Ending a trilogy is never a fun matter.

There's all kinds of things to remember, keep aligned, wrap up, and celebrate. Not to mention children to raise, A business to run, and viruses to battle. I also feel like I have to have a moment where I say goodbye to the characters and comprehend those two little words at the end of the book.

With FREEDOM, that was a hard moment.

To all of those who helped and supported me through this intense endeavor, I say *thank you*. I can't say it enough, truly.

First, to my readers.

YOU ARE SERIOUSLY THE BEST, FULL STOP.

You are the reason I write these books and stay in this game, and every single email from all of you makes my heart glow. Thank you for being here with me.

This book would never have happened without the steady patience—and constant availability—of Kelsey Keating. I don't think it would be possible to count the late hours we spent hashing over my magic systems, attempting to make sure it worked at every angle, breaking down goddess history, trying to find every single plot hole, and diabolically trying to make Lucey have a big reveal at the end. (Trust me —it wasn't so kind in the first iterations.)

Kelsey, your support was inspiring and humbling. Thank you.

She wasn't the only one! To my other beta and sensitivity readers who fielded countless questions and thoughts, I owe you so much. Catherine, Stephan, Samantha, Brandy, Darcee, Lianne, Marcia, and Patricia. *Thank you, thank you!*

Of course, a massive thanks to my family, babysitters, and support team at home.

Warrior Princess and Little Man—I could never write a book without the constant stream of magic you bring into my life. I adore you to the end of time. And yes, dragons are *so cool, Mom.*

—KC

33

THE NETWORK SERIES

ey there!

If you want more of the infamous sister witches, you're in for a real treat.

Fast forward in time after the Dragonmaster Trilogy to see what happens next in the world of Antebellum—100 years later.

Sanna and Isadora and the forest dragons are still part of the world, so if you want to see them again, don't wait! Trust me, the world of Antebellum still needs these fearless ladies, because the Central Network is now up against another massive, magical foe.

Miss Mabel's School for Girls is the first book in The Network Series, and you can buy it right now on all the retailers as a paperback book or e-book.

In fact, here's a sneak peek into the first chapter.

~

Miss Mabel's School for Girls
Chapter 1

. . .

I STARED at the lavender flowers on the white china and willed my heart to stop pounding. Papa's advice whispered through my head like the balm of a cool poultice, settling my nerves.

Don't be afraid, Bianca. The old woman will perceive your personality no matter what you do or say. You can't hide information from a Watcher. Let her remain in control of the conversation and things will be easier.

"You said that your family is from Bickers Mill?" The old woman, Isadora, startled me from my thoughts with her question. "That's not very far from here."

"Yes," I said, turning around to face her. "I grew up in a cottage outside the village."

Don't think about how important this is.

That wouldn't be too difficult. She only determined the rest of my life.

Isadora smiled in a distant way, as if she were lost in thought and only keeping up with the conversation to be kind. She was a stringy old woman, with a curved back and foggy, pistachio-colored eyes, although one of them looked more blue than green.

"Your grandmother is sick, isn't she?"

My throat tightened.

"Yes," I said, swallowing past it. She studied me while I continued. "The apothecary said she may not have much longer to live."

"Well, I'm glad you were able to come here today so that I did not have to come to you. Living near the school helps me keep this part of Letum Wood safe for the students. Now that school has started, I don't like to leave."

"I'm sure they appreciate your work as a Watcher," I said,

circling back around to face the tea set. *Confidence,* I told myself. *Even if she can see into your soul and it isn't very organized.*

My hands trembled when I set the fragile cups and saucers on the antique silver tray. Was that right? No, the teacups went on the plates. Or did they? Was I supposed to set out a fork for the little cakes? Or tongs? Or nothing at all? An interview I'd prepared for my entire life, and a tea set flummoxed me. This was a promising beginning. Deciding to leave the cups off the plate, I set them off to the side, lifted the tray and turned to serve the tea.

Isadora moved away from the window with a hobbled step while I approached the little table. Her quaint cottage at the edge of the trees aged with a quiet grace, decorated in an opulence that made me nervous, afraid I'd take one step too far in any direction and break something, like the witches' bottles hanging from one wall by strings of twine. A simple nudge and they'd fall, shattering, the whispers of their bottled incantations rising into the air like a mist.

Despite her reputation as one of the most powerful witches in our world, Isadora lived a discreet life in the midst of her porcelain tea sets, of which she had many, and her white curtains. A buttery loaf of bread gleamed nearby, smelling of warm yeast and flour.

"Is this part of Letum Wood dangerous?" I asked, taking measured steps so I didn't rattle the china. Letum Wood, the weather, my chances of survival at the school, I would have picked any of these topics for conversation. Anything to avoid the silence that meant she searched my soul, hoping to understand the secrets of my mind.

"It can be a frightening place," Isadora said, lowering into a wooden chair. "But not when I'm watching."

For all my precautions in getting there, the tray landed

on the table with an ungracious clunk, and I murmured a nervous apology.

She smiled, surveying the layout of the china with puckered lips that looked suspiciously close to a smile. I'd gotten the tray wrong, of course.

"I was an awkward teenager too, you know," Isadora said. "Big teeth and whatnot. That all changed when I turned sixteen."

"Oh?" I stammered, forcing myself to sit down. "Sixteen?"

"Yes, your age."

She's going to know many things about you. Don't be surprised if she mentions details you haven't told her. She sees.

"It's a wonderful age," she crooned before I could reply, lightly sliding her cup onto her tea plate. "I started learning how to control magic at a Network school, though not Miss Mabel's School for Girls. It changed the course of my life." She paused for a second, then continued as if she'd never stopped. "Miss Mabel's is a grand place. There's so much history in that big old estate, you know, and so much to learn."

"Mmm-hmm," I hummed as I reached for the pot. The tea tumbled in a coral waterfall into the fragile porcelain cups. Steam rolled off the boiling liquid, filling the air. A drop or two slipped out, falling to the white tablecloth when I tipped the spout back. An instant stain spread.

"Miss Mabel's been teaching there many years," I said, quickly setting the teapot on top of the diffused pink circles, hoping she didn't see. My heart pounded. This wasn't the time for mistakes. Perhaps I'd spent too long perfecting the big things and too little on the mundane.

Our eyes met for the first time. Isadora didn't smile, just stared into me with a troubled expression. I waited under the scrutiny of her gaze, my heart pulsing in my throat, making me sick to my stomach. Her worried expression had nothing to do with my inability to properly set out and pour tea.

Isadora doesn't care about trivialities.

"Yes, Mabel has been teaching for a long time." She finally took the offered cup to sip, breaking her intense study. "She's one of the best teachers in the Network."

Her face scrunched a little, and I fought back a frustrated sigh. I had steeped it too long again. Herbal teas always stumped me.

"So I've heard," I said.

"Mabel gears her teaching toward action, not books. Education these days involves too much reading. Learning magic should be about practice, not recitation."

I heartily agreed but remained silent. Bookwork was never my cup of tea, so to speak. Her cup set itself down as I reached for the sugar. I didn't know how to respond, so I remained quiet and stirred the sugar into my tea. *Above all, show confidence,* I reminded myself. *Sometimes silence does it best.*

"Tell me, Bianca, why you are here today."

I looked up in surprise. Part of me hoped that our entire interview consisted of this strangled, awkward small talk. Then she could probe into my mind and personality in silence, discerning what I already knew. *You're determined to attend this school. You've spent years learning magic to prepare. You hope to control fate, but you can't because she's a fickle mistress.* Then she'd tell me I passed and I'd never have to really answer anything.

She lifted her eyebrows, waiting for my response, shattering any hope of an easy escape.

Never lie to a Watcher, Papa's voice returned. *Most of the time they already know how you are going to respond. The test is in your emotions, and you can really only control how you use them.*

Elaborating on all the possible life benefits of attending Miss Mabel's tempted me, but she'd know I didn't really care. Trivialities, I reminded myself. Isadora may already know the answer to her question, but she might not.

A bargain I couldn't ignore.

I finally settled on the one answer I knew would be true.

"I want to work with Miss Mabel."

We sat in silence for several minutes. The snap of the fire filled the background. I stirred my cup. Most girls probably had a ready answer for that one. Perhaps I'd been learning how not to set out tea.

"Yes," Isadora said, taking a sip of her tea with a quiet chuckle that didn't sound humorous. "You certainly don't lack motivation, do you?"

She looked out the window again. I pulled the tiny silver spoon from my tea and set it next to the cup. My hands still shook, so I folded them in my lap instead of taking a drink, braiding them into a ball of icy fingers. I wondered if she'd notice if I didn't take a sip. After her reaction, the taste probably wasn't worth it.

Isadora opened her mouth to say something, then closed it again. I began to wonder if I could stand a silence so loud.

"My job is to interview prospective students to see if they would be a good fit for Miss Mabel's School for Girls," she said, turning away from me. "It's a difficult education to complete, with a demanding schedule, and isn't meant for everyone. That's why the High Priestess of the Network requires you to qualify."

My knuckles tightened until my hands blanched to a

shade of white. This was it. She would turn me down, say I wasn't the right kind of girl. My whole life and future hung in the balance. It would be quick as a guillotine but infinitely more painful.

High stakes are what you get, I reminded myself, when you have a lot to lose.

I wished I'd worn my hair in a bun instead of loose on my shoulders. But I couldn't act myself by pretending to be something I wasn't, so my hair remained down where I liked it.

"I've met a lot of students, but never in my life ..." she faltered. Her fidgeting and blank stares began to unnerve me. Wasn't this a witch of great magical knowledge and power?

She set the china cup down with a resolute clank.

"I'm going to let you in, Bianca, but I do so with one warning."

Her creaky, anxious voice took away any chance to feel relief. I waited, holding my breath, while she stared into my eyes.

"Don't underestimate her."

I didn't need to ask whom she meant. The name hung in the air between us like an anvil on a fraying string.

Miss Mabel.

We stared at each other. I wondered just what she saw about me, what facets of my personality, and what motives she understood that I didn't. Before I drew up the courage to ask, Isadora turned away again, as if she couldn't stand to look at me, and took another sip of her tea.

My right wrist burned. I grabbed it, which gave only a moment of relief.

When I pulled my hand away, a black circle of ancient, minuscule words lay on the inside of my wrist. The circlus.

Without it, the magic surrounding the boundaries of Letum Wood that housed Miss Mabel's School for Girls wouldn't allow me in.

My stomach flipped.

I did it.

My chest sank, heavy with fear and weak with relief. I suppressed the rush of panic, banishing it to the corners of my mind. No panic here, just confidence.

I spent years preparing for this. It won't frighten me now.

I was a terrible liar. Attending Miss Mabel's School for Girls did frighten me, but so did staying home, forfeiting my only chance at freedom.

Isadora seemed to recover her wits with surprising speed. She sat up, set her napkin on the table, and straightened her wobbly legs.

"Have you said goodbye to your mother?"

"Yes," I said, wincing inside. The fear in her eyes haunted me. Mama didn't want me to go, not like this. *There has to be another way,* she whispered to me last night, tears in her eyes that she never shed. *I don't like this, Bianca. What if something happens to you?* I hated leaving her.

But I still did it. Because I had to.

Nothing bad will happen, I had promised her. *I can do this. I know I can.*

Isadora nodded once. "Very well, come. Let's continue your education. I can see that Mabel will be quite ... pleased to have you."

Grateful to get out of the close little parlor, I walked past the window to see a figure moving out from behind a tree. Mama stood amongst the dark woods with her queer gray eyes, her ebony hair restless in the wind.

"Merry part, Mama," I whispered. The memory of Papa's

voice ran through my head as I stared at her, my homesick heart already raw and throbbing.

Mabel is the one of the cleverest witches in the Central Network. She's the only one that can remove your curse. You must remember: Mabel does no favors. Be careful, B.

Your life depends on it.

ISADORA LED me through her house to a rickety back porch where a torch illuminated the ground. A single trail ran from a set of wooden stairs, disappearing into trees and deadfall beyond. The gray and muted brown leaves matched my simple brown dress. Winter robbed Letum Wood of color, leaving it stark and ugly.

"Well, keep to the trail." Isadora cast a look at the sky. "It looks like rain, so you better hurry. It's at least an hour's walk to the school from here."

"Thank you."

I pulled the hood of my cloak over my long black hair and took a few steps forward. Every minute of my life led to this moment. *Fate may be a fickle mistress,* I thought, glancing at the sky, *but she isn't entirely unforgiving.*

Isadora called to me, stopping me in my tracks.

"Did you know they are taking volunteers for the Competition tonight?"

I kept my hood up and my eyes on the ground so she couldn't read my expression.

"Yes," I said. "I heard that rumor."

I left before she could ask more, evaporating in the mist of Letum Wood.

I HOPE you enjoyed this sneak peek. You can purchase this book at Barnes & Noble or Amazon.

Thanks for reading.

I'm so honored you're here.

—Katie

ALSO BY KATIE CROSS

The Network Series

Mildred's Resistance (prequel)

Miss Mabel's School for Girls

Antebellum Awakening

The High Priest's Daughter

War of the Networks

The Network Series Complete Collection

The Isadora Interviews (novella)

Short Stories from Miss Mabel's

Short Stories from the Network Series

The Dragonmaster Trilogy

FLAME

Chronicles of the Dragonmasters (short story collection)

FLIGHT

The Ronan Scrolls (novella)

FREEDOM

The Dragonmaster Trilogy Collection

Coming Soon

The High Priestess

ABOUT THE AUTHOR

Katie Cross is ALL ABOUT strong girls that don't need to be perfect, and certainly don't need anyone to save them. Creating new fantasy worlds is her jam.

When she's not hiking or chasing her two littles through the Colorado mountains, you can find her curled up reading a book or arguing with her husband over the best kind of sushi.

Visit her at www.kcrosswriting.com for free short stories, extra savings on ALL her books (and some you can't buy on the retailers), and so much more.